Finding A Way

The Delamere Files

Book One

Finding a Way

The Delamere Files Book One

First published in Great Britain in 2023

Copyright © Jackson Marsh 2023

The right of Jackson Marsh to be identified as the Author of the Work has been asserted by him in accordance with the Copyright, Designs and Patents Act 1988.

All rights reserved. No part of this publication may be reproduced, stored in a retrieval system, or transmitted, in any form or by any means without the prior written permission of the publisher, nor be otherwise circulated in any form of binding or cover other than that in which it is published and without a similar condition being imposed on the subsequent purchaser.

All characters in this publication are fictitious and any resemblance to real persons, living or dead, is purely coincidental.

Proofread by Ann Attwood

Cover Design by Andjela V

Illustration by DazzlingDezigns

Formatting by Other Worlds Ink

Printed by Amazon.com

ISBN: 9798856631813

Imprint: Independently published

Available from Amazon.com and other retail outlets.

Available on Kindle and other devices.

ALSO BY JACKSON MARSH

Other People's Dreams

The Blake Inheritance

The Stoker Connection

Curious Moonlight

The Mentor of Wildhill Farm

The Mentor of Barrenmoor Ridge

The Students of Barrenmoor Ridge

The Mentor of Lonemarsh House

The Mentor of Lostwood Hall

The Clearwater Mysteries

Banyak & Fecks (A prequel)

Deviant Desire

Twisted Tracks

Unspeakable Acts

Fallen Splendour

Bitter Bloodline

Artful Deception

Home From Nowhere

One Of A Pair

Negative Exposure

The Clearwater Inheritance

The Larkspur Mysteries

Guardians of the Poor

Keepers of the Past

Agents of the Truth

Seeing Through Shadows

Speaking in Silence

Starting with Secrets

The Larkspur Legacy

www.jacksonmarsh.com

www.facebook.com/jacksonmarshauthor

Finding A Way

The Delamere Files

Book One

CONTENTS

ONE	1
TWO	13
THREE	25
FOUR	38
FIVE	52
SIX	63
SEVEN	76
EIGHT	86
NINE	97
TEN	107
ELEVEN	118
TWELVE	128
THIRTEEN	140
FOURTEEN	151
FIFTEEN	162
SIXTEEN	173
SEVENTEEN	185
EIGHTEEN	196
NINETEEN	209
TWENTY	222
TWENTY-ONE	232
TWENTY-TWO	244
TWENTY-THREE	256
TWENTY-FOUR	264
TWENTY-FIVE	278
TWENTY-SIX	293
TWENTY-SEVEN	308
Author Notes	313

Larkin Chase 1892

ONE

June 1892

It began with a man sobbing in the night. An oppressive night, with the stone and brick of drab buildings along Kennington Road still warm after a blistering day. An airless, inescapable darkness where the open spaces of the parks donated nothing to relieve the suffocation of the starless city. It was a time for loneliness, and wishing to be somewhere else. Yet, through the cloying, sickly silence of the gone-midnight hour, a man walked upright with purpose and, as always, with hope.

Larkin Chase wasn't poor, but he wasn't rich. Although he lived in the fashionable area of Kingsland, he had no designs on fashion, other than to be comfortable while being well-dressed, and although he had been well-educated, it was only to a standard, university degree. Any knowledge he had gained above that came from self-study, and any income he made above his allowance, came from his own labours. Thanks to his father, who was well-off and generous, Larkin could work at whatever he pleased, and it pleased him to work on behalf of others. This he did through prose in his own style, bringing to the public's attention the hardships and plights of those less fortunate than himself.

That was what gave Larkin pleasure; to observe, to report, and to make a difference. To make a little money from his words was a bonus, and having a brother as the editor of the Pall Mall Gazette was another. Since beginning his writing career, and thanks to his father's enthusiastic allowance, he had saved enough to purchase a house in a desirable district of Hackney where he lived a quiet life alone save for a housekeeper and her daughter, his maid.

It was his housekeeper to whom he said the prophetic words, 'Don't wait up. Who knows what I might find this night,' as he left the house on the evening of his thirtieth birthday to seek a cab to drive him to Lambeth. For Larkin Chase to spend whole nights away from home was not uncommon, because his love of investigation didn't keep daylight hours. The fact that it was his birthday, and he had spent the day in solitude like any other, was also not unusual, because he liked his own company and, for the most part, kept himself to himself.

As he left his town house, he turned his mind to the task ahead. Not the finding of transport to carry him the five miles to South London, there was a reliable rank at the junction with Dalston Lane, but to his intentions at the Lambeth workhouse.

'An inspection of your casual ward by night,' he had written to the workhouse master a week before. 'For the purpose of bringing to the public's ear and eye the way your good selves manage the facility, and to highlight to those in authority what more is needed to ease the plight of the Lambeth poor.'

'We don't welcome snoopers,' was the curt reply from an alarmingly named Archibald Shithole, pronounced, the housekeeper suggested, *Shitholay*. Larkin duly replied to the letter, reminding Mr Shithole of his readership, and giving his brother's name as a reference, while stating the date and time of his arrival and his purpose.

It did no good. After a cab ride during which he formulated his list of points to note and questions to ask, after showing his card, and explaining his intentions to a porter with more belly than compassion, he was ejected from the workhouse porch with the lyrical direction,

'Gert yerself gone, Guv, or yule 'ave the roz on yer.' A phrase that took no time to translate due it its aggressive delivery.

His mission unsuccessful, there was nothing more to do than retrace his steps in the hope of finding a cab home. While doing so, he concluded the only way he would be able to examine the Lambeth workhouse was in the guise of a pauper, and as he walked, so he contemplated a new mission; to one day, dress in rags, to go unbathed for a few days and join the queue of casuals before the porters closed the register. Larkin Chase would become one of those he sought to assist.

'To become the investigated,' he suggested to himself as his footsteps echoed in the empty street. 'Now there would be a novel approach.'

The potential adventure was taking shape as he came to St Mary's church, and a new sound joined that of his leather soles. Someone was crying in the inky gloom of a guttering streetlamp. It was not the sound of wailing or hysterics, nor of abject despair, but more, a deep, sad moaning, as of someone approaching the threshold of hopelessness. As the sound grew, so did the silhouetted outline of a hansom cab, tall and sturdy on its two large wheels, but driverless. The sound came from beside it, and with no-one else in sight, the person upset could only have been the cabman.

Larkin needed a ride, but was loath to embarrass the man he expected to find in anguish, and so, gave a loud, warning cough as he approached. A dark form arose from where it had been sitting on the step, and sniffing, wiped its face on a handkerchief as if clearing sweat; a viable disguise on such a close and heavy night. To make the driver less disconcerted, Larkin did the same, and used the damp pocket square to attract attention.

'I hope I find you available and willing,' he said as a man's features came into vague view.

'Morning, Sir. Yes, I am,' the driver replied. 'Where to?'

'Four hundred and seventy-one Kingsland Road, a little before the junction. Is that possible?'

'It is, Sir.' The cabman's sadness had been erased by the

handkerchief which he stuffed away as he opened the folding doors. 'Three shillings.'

'A fair price,' Larkin said, and, at the same time, it occurred to him that his late-night outing needn't be in vain. 'I will add more if you agree to an unusual request.'

About to haul himself up to his seat, the cabman turned his face, catching the light for the first time.

'Unusual, Sir?'

Larkin also stepped into the lantern glow, allowing his driver to see he meant no harm and was in no way suspicious, and the two men regarded each other in a pause of mutual examination. It was up to Larkin to answer the question, but the cabman's gaze caught him unawares, and no words came. There was no sign of the man's previous weeping, save for a little red about the eyes, which may have been due to the poor lighting, and his expression was one of interest rather than mistrust. When Larkin failed to answer, the cabman's mouth twitched into an expectant smile, highlighting a slightly protuberant top lip, and he raised his brow in a question which lifted his bowler hat from his smooth forehead.

'Unusual, Sir?' the cabman repeated.

Larkin tore himself away from his intrigue, put aside all thoughts of the Lambeth workhouse, and leapt on his new assignment.

'Apologies,' he said. 'Impertinent might be a better word. I wonder, young Sir, if I might ride on the bench with you. I would welcome the opportunity to ask you about your life as a cabman, if you would not find that contumelious. I am, you see, a writer of articles for various publications, and I seek stories as told by real people. Goodly, hardworking people such as I can see you to be, and as it is a fair distance to my destination, I would like to use the time for you to tell me of the life of a cabbie. I shall, of course, renumerate you well for this, and will only write what you tell me. I expect you would appreciate the extra finance, which might, I hope, enable you to take me as your last fare, and return to your wife and family earlier than usual, there to enjoy a no doubt well-earnt rest. What do you say?'

The cabbie removed his hat, swiped away his fringe, replaced his hat, and opened his mouth to speak. He closed it again, and for the first time since stepping into the light, glanced at the deserted street. Having found his words, he looked back at Larkin with a quizzical expression, and said, 'You want to sit up top with me?' as if Larkin's speech had not been clear enough.

'Indeed.'

'Why?'

'In order that you might tell me of your work. Cabmen are renowned for their stories.'

'So they say, Sir, but why would you be interested in mine?'

Larkin Chase was an expert at processing thoughts, admitting things to himself, and being honest, but he was also adept at filtering what he wanted to say from what was acceptable. Where he was tempted to admit he found the man's features and presence compelling, he was unable to explain why, and where his purpose in talking was to learn why the cabbie had been in distress, he knew that to take such a personal path would require a cautious tread.

His thoughts shuffled in an instant, and he said, 'Primarily, because I believe my readers should know more about the lives of the men who serve them.'

The cabman remained dubious.

'Here, I shall give you my fare now...' Larkin handed over three shillings. 'And more for your story when we reach my destination. Let us say ten shillings in total.'

The eyes widened, but not enough for Larkin to see their colour.

'What stories?'

'Anything you care to tell me. How you came to the job, what it is like to wait in all weathers, how your working conditions might be improved, what events have befallen you that might entertain or shock the readership. This manner of discussion.'

'It ain't possible to sit on the bench, Sir. There ain't the room.'

'Then may I stand in some way? I don't mind.'

'Ain't safe to stand neither, Sir. Even if it were, you'd unbalance the traces. Can't allow it, Sir. Anyways, you'd be warmer inside.'

'My friend, if I were any warmer, I should think I were in a Turkish bath.'

The cabman's smile returned, and with it a glint that could have been a trick of the lantern, or the recognition of a decent fellow who shared a sense of humour. Whatever it was, a bond formed through the lateness of the night, and the cabman, still smiling, said, 'How about you kneel on the seat and poke your head through the hatch?'

'An admirable compromise,' Larkin enthused. 'To travel backwards while kneeling will be a novel experience.'

While the driver readied the vehicle, Larkin reminded himself of the dangers of being so frank with a stranger, and how, once before, his openness had led to disaster.

'A time ago, and completely different.'

Undeterred, he climbed in, and assumed the position, but it wasn't until he had the hatch open, and his head poking through it, that he admitted to himself the reason for his request. It was the face. Not so much the youth, for the driver was only a few years younger than himself, but the look of faraway sadness. With the cab beginning its slow rumble, and the streetlighting improving, he caught flashes of a firm, unshaven jaw, a soft mouth with its intriguing upper lip, and a confidence he'd rarely noticed in a man on first meeting. It was the gaze, however, that betrayed the story, and Larkin felt it to be a sad one. That had to be the conclusion, not only because of the sobbing, but also because of a forlorn quality behind the eyes.

They dropped to him, again questioning.

'What d'you want to...?' The driver's question became a laugh. 'Sorry, Sir, but you don't half look funny. Feel like I'm driving a severed head.'

'It is a most unusual sensation for me also,' Larkin replied with a chuckle. 'And I am not sure how long my knees will hold. If I vanish, at least you will know I have not fallen beneath the wheels.'

'Best ask away, Sir. The roads are clear tonight, there won't be much traffic over the bridge yet, so Shadow will get you to your home quick as you like.'

Kneeling, gripping the back of the seat, and with his shoulders pressed to the ceiling, Larkin was unable to see or even reach for his notebook, so anything he learnt, he would have to remember.

'Perhaps, seeing as how we share unusual views, we should start with names,' he said. 'I am Larkin Chase, your horse is called Shadow, and you are...?'

'Jack Merrit, Sir.'

'I see you have plenty, Mr Merrit.'

'Plenty what, Sir?'

'Merits.'

'Ah, yeah.'

It seemed the cabman had heard the play on words before; he didn't look impressed.

'Not one of my best,' Larkin admitted, and cleared his throat. 'Have you been driving long?'

'A few months, Sir.'

'I meant today. If you will forgive the observation, you appear tired.'

'Sorry about that,' Merrit said, and touched the rim of his bowler. 'Started out at seven this morning.'

'Good Lord. That's nearly a whole day.'

'Needs must, Mr Chase. I took a couple of hours kip at the yard when I changed horses.'

Weeping and long hours. The two had to be related.

'I imagine long days are common in your job.'

'Can be. We all have to make a living.'

Larkin survived a pang of guilt. As someone who didn't need to make a living, he enjoyed late mornings, later evenings, and a few hours of writing when he was in the mood. This man on the other hand...

'You must be exhausted.'

'Never you mind, Sir, I'll be away home when I've delivered you safe.'

'And where is home?'

'Limehouse.'

'Then you are a long way from it. Is it common to end your day south of the river when you live north and east of it?'

'Never know where you'll end up. Two days ago, I started out at Limehouse station as I always do, and ended up at Edgware. That was a long way back with no fare.'

'And you drive day and night?'

'Not usually, no, but... Well, something happened, and I got to put in the hours if I want to...' Merrit sniffed, and when he spoke next, his voice cracked as if tears were imminent. 'Never mind about that. You'd be more comfortable sitting down, Mr Chase. I don't think I've got nothing to interest you.'

Far from it. Larkin was already fascinated by the young man and what he was not saying. Merrit had a story, and it was Larkin's job to know it.

'The music is not in the notes, but in the silence between,' he said, and shifted his weight to ease the growing pain in his right leg.

'What's that, Sir?'

'Mozart.' The name made no impression on his driver. 'Can't say I understand it fully, but it strikes me, Mr Merrit, you are in a predicament.'

'Am I, Sir?'

'I can tell this because of the silence between your words, and I would like to help you. We can begin by taking our acquaintance to the level of vague friendship, if you will allow. I sense you and I could be of assistance to each other, and who better to assist than a friend?'

The darkness between streetlights swallowed Merrit's face, but when it came to light, he was regarding Larkin with confused interest.

'I don't know you, Sir,' he said, and didn't look away as he turned the horse into a different street.

'Then we begin our friendship on level ground. I will ask you three questions, Mr Merrit, and your answers will direct my course of action. As I think you can see, I am neither vagabond nor untrustworthy. I have already paid you the requested fare in advance, and in this ridiculous position, I am unlikely to attempt a robbery, not that I would. May I ask you my three questions?'

'Is that the first one?' the cabbie quipped.

'Ah. No.'

Larkin was sure the man had more humour than sadness about him, more trust than scepticism, and beneath the veneer of his outward attitude, had something he wanted to share. Most men in Merrit's position would have changed the subject, or objected to the questioning, particularly if a stranger had talked about friendship so soon after striking a conversation, but Merrit was open to the offer. Larkin was as sure of that as he was himself confused as to why he felt an affinity with the driver. There was a connection, as Mozart might have said, in the silence between the notes.

'Go on then,' Merrit said, his features one moment shadows, the next, a pale-yellow glow.

'Thank you. Firstly, as I am apparently caught in the stocks before you in a most unusual alignment of limbs, and can look nowhere else but at you, I really think we could attempt first names. Would you call me Larkin? It may only be for the next half an hour, and then I will be no more than another eccentric fare for you to discuss on your rank. What do you say?'

'If that's what the customer wants, Sir, but in return, you must call me Jack.'

That, surely, was a sign the cabman trusted his passenger and was open to assistance.

'It would give me pleasure,' Larkin said, and in the brief flash of a brighter lantern, the two men exchanged smiles. 'As an investigator, I have, so far in this most unforgettable ride, established your name, that of your horse, and your working hours of today. I can tell by where we have passed, that we will soon cross the river. I can also tell you are nearing exhaustion, and I assume you are hungry. May I propose we pause in your journey around the area of Covent Garden, or another place you may know where men can find respectable refreshment at this late hour? I will be more than happy to buy you a decent meal or whatever you require.'

Most men, when offered such a proposition, would assume Larkin had a dubious ulterior motive, but if that was what Jack thought, he didn't let it show. He did, however, present a problem.

'Mightily kind of you... er, Larkin, but as you said, I'm keen to get to bed soon as I've dropped you off.'

'Of course. Then let me up the stakes, as they say. You have not yet told me any story that might inspire a piece for my brother's periodical, and to that end, I would like more time with you. However, I understand your desire for rest, so I will make this proposition. Deliver us to a respectable eatery of your choice, there to take an early breakfast or a very late supper, and after, when you have taken me home, I will increase my payment to cover a day's average earnings. Armed with that, you may return to your home at any hour, and sleep the whole day tomorrow if you wish.'

Sometimes, when Larkin delivered one of his verbose speeches, he received a similarly intellectual and pleasing reply. In this case, however, his new friend stared blankly, and said, 'Eh?'

'How much do you need each day to hire your cab and feed your horse? Or do you own them?'

'I don't own nothing, Sir... er, Larkin. But you can't pay me for doing nothing.'

'I may if I wish, and I do wish.'

As he had done before, Jack scratched his head beneath his bowler, and glanced to the street as if that was where his decision lay.

'This week, the basic's ten shillings a day,' he said. 'And the offer you made before covers me for tomorrow, so you done enough.'

'One can never do enough for a man in need.'

'Who says I'm in need?'

'My instinct, Jack, and I trust it implicitly. Now, let us assume you have agreed to a meal and a day off with pay. You will want to know what you must give me in return.'

'Er... Yeah.' Suspicion clouded Jack's face for the first time, but was soon swallowed by the night.

'Then my third question will explain,' Larkin said. 'Before I ask it, I apologise for my directness and lack of tact. My working life as an investigator demands both, and I am hardened to self-inflicted embarrassment. Therefore, before I ask, I would like to know if there is anything you would ask of me.'

Jack smiled at that and took a moment to hold their shared gaze; more signs he was enjoying Larkin's company as much as Larkin was enjoying his. During the contemplative pause, he shook his head as if trying to resist temptation while knowing he couldn't, and finally said, 'A couple of things.'

'Fire away, old chap.'

'Old?'

'A turn of phrase, I mean no offence.'

'You strike me as a man who wouldn't care even if he did.'

'That's true.'

Jack laughed. 'And that's better,' he said. 'Me first request was to ask you to turn down the gas on your words—no offence.'

'None is taken, because I don't grasp your meaning.'

'I ain't an educated man, and I ain't used to long sentences like you've been spouting. To be honest, I'm a bit fuddled by what you've been saying, and it's taken me time to work out your meaning.'

Larkin had been accused of verbosity on many occasions, and usually took it as a compliment. This time, Jack's request plucked at a string, and wanting to know the man more, he agreed.

'I shall see what I can do,' he said. 'Anything else?'

'Yeah. Why are you interested in me? Why you being so generous?'

Larkin had been asking himself the same question, and had not yet found an answer other than the one he gave.

'It feels right to be so,' he said, and when Jack shrugged, added, 'The best I can do. Anything more?'

His humour still apparent, Jack said, 'No. Go on then, what d'you want to know?'

Larkin saw his curiosity as a kettle on a stove that had been coming to the boil over the past mile. Now, the lid was rattling as ardently as his nerves, and the whistle was ready to blow. What he was about to say would either seal their trust or bring the cab to a halt, and his journey and the atmosphere of unexplained possibility would come to an end.

Faced with an all-or-nothing situation, he said, 'I would like to know why you were so distressed when I found you, and I would like to know what I can do about it.'

Jack looked away, pulled on his reins, and the cab came to a stop.

Larkin's heart stopped with it. Half a mile ago, he had been sure of an instant bond, that Jack wasn't just chatting out of politeness, and that he had met someone whose company and presence were irresistible. He had been certain Jack felt the same way. The confidence that their meeting was meant-to-be had been built on sand, however, and he prepared himself for a rebuke.

'I have offended you,' he said. 'I apologise, and will leave you now, but I will give you the shillings I promised.'

'Hold your horses while I hold mine,' Jack said, and tied his reins. 'I ain't stopped to throw you out for your nosiness. We're at a cabman's rest, and as there's not many hansoms here, I thought we'd have a cuppa and something to eat while I satisfy your curiosity. I need to talk to someone, Larkin Chase, and I got this notion it's meant to be you. Now then,' he chuckled, 'can you get out of there, or have you got your head stuck?'

TWO

After some investigation of the cabmen's shelter, Jack returned to the hansom to announce that Speckle Sam was frying them each a grunting peck, and two mugs of prattle broth were waiting for them on the bench, because the night was so warm, and the hut was so ard, he could barely catch his breath. 'Besides,' he added, 'there's a couple of trumpeters inside who's set in for a right old jabbering.'

'That sounds most... unintelligible,' Larkin said, following Jack to a bench lit by one of London's more successful streetlights. 'Let's start with Speckle Sam. What or who is that?'

'Little Speck, some call him. Happy young chap works mainly as a night waterman and loves horses. He'll be out to look after Shadow once he's done his frying.'

'I see, but Speckle?'

'On account he was blind as a bat until the rank put in to buy him a pair of spectacles.'

'That was kind of them.'

'Not really. He kept trying to water the customers instead of the horses, so something had to be done. Sam's like a pet at this rest. Just about lives here 'cos he ain't got nowhere else, and he fries up a decent grunting peck.'

'Which is...?'

'Piece of meat. Might be pork if we're lucky. Light's no good in there.'

'There being that hut, which is... Ard, was it? Or hard?'

'Ard. Hot, you from north of Shoreditch would say. Another of your Turkish baths. We'll sit here, and Speck'll bring it. There's your prattle broth.'

Tea, Larkin translated, as he investigated a tin mug. There was no need to ask about trumpeters and jabbering, because the hut door opened, and the sound of an argument poured forth as a man stormed out and made for his cab.

Jack took a seat and invited Larkin to do the same. Now under better lighting, the dark rings around Jack's eyes were obvious, as were the shadows beneath his drawn-in cheeks, and Larkin wondered if he shouldn't send the man on his way and find another ride across the river. When he offered this option, he expected the driver to accept and vanish, but Jack, who had already surprised him with his affability, surprised him again.

'Good of you,' he said, 'but you're alright, and I got this idea I can trust you. Can't explain why. A fare's a fare to me, but there's something I like about you, Larkin Chase, and what I got on my mind, I got to get off it, if you don't object.'

'Not one bit,' Larkin said, thrilled the man enjoyed his company. 'But you must promise you will accept my offer and take tomorrow to rest. Were I at one of Mr Maskelyne's mysterious entertainments, I might mistake you for an apparition.'

'And you call me unillegible,' Jack scoffed.

'Unintelligible,' Larkin corrected, enjoying his companion's tenacity. 'Which you are not. Not when you refrain from cant.'

'Can't help the cant, mate, not when you're brought up in Limehouse.'

'I'm sure, but promise me you will take tomorrow to rest.'

Jack settled into the corner of the bench, eyeing Larkin over the rim of his mug, and forcing Larkin to adopt the same pose to see his new friend more clearly.

'I got to ask again, why've you taken to me so quick?' Jack said, but there was no hint of mistrust. If anything, his words were coloured by delight.

'One of the great mysteries of the universe.' Larkin smiled. 'Unexplainable, I am afraid. All I can tell you is that I am a man who takes pleasure in assisting others, and when I heard your distress, I wanted to do what I could to help.'

'You ain't some vicar, are you? Only, I don't have much time for them.'

'I am as likely a clergyman as a politician is honest.' Larkin sipped his tea, strong and sweet. 'But enough of this fore-chat. I am here to listen to whatever it is you require unburdening from your chest, and, if I can, I will help in return for you allowing me to write your experience for my periodical.'

Jack became dubious. 'I ain't sure I want everyone knowing my business,' he said. 'What you going to say about me?'

'Perhaps I shan't write a thing. So far, all I can tell my readers is that I have, by chance, made the acquaintance of a fascinating cabman who was kind enough to find me prattle broth and a grunting peck, served by a myopic waterboy somewhere near the Thames on a sultry June night. On thought, perhaps I should make my piece about the language and cant of the cabbie. Language fascinates me.'

'Yeah, well, you use enough of it.'

Larkin laughed. 'And that's another reason I am entertained by your company; your direct and humorous ripostes. We have known each other barely thirty minutes and we are, as they say in common parlance, *getting along nicely*. Now, with all that said, and with our meal approaching, will you tell me what is on your mind?'

'Soon as I've had a mouthful.'

When Jack had called Speckle Sam young, he had not been making a joke. In Larkin's estimation, the lad who delivered two pieces of hot pork and onions wrapped in bread rolls was no older than twelve. His name was well-earnt, for his eyes were magnified to massive proportions by two pieces of glass that might have come from the bottom of a milk bottle.

Larkin paid what the young boy asked.

'The least I can do for your story,' he said, when Jack objected, and they were left alone.

Again, Larkin was unable to use his notebook, because his hands were full of bread that bled so much grease, he had to lean forward so the drips fell harmlessly between his knees. Apart from the occasional roll of carriage wheels and spasmodic laughter from within the hut, the night around them was still and silent. There was no breeze, so no danger of being enveloped by fumes and smog from the tireless factories to the east, and, being so late at night, few carts or pedestrians passed. Larkin imagined the time was well after three of the morning, and yet, as he waited, he didn't feel tired, because Jack Merrit's company was invigorating.

Once he'd had his mouthful and washed it down with a gulp of tea, Jack gave a sigh and began his tale.

'I'll be honest with you,' he said. 'Things ain't been that good since I started cabbing. Not the work, that's been alright, and I like it no matter the hours, but we lost our grandma just after I started, see? She'd lost her husband, Reggie, last year, which is why I took up the driving. Will can't do much, that's another problem, and Ida's eyes went along with her health, so she had to give up the washing and stitching she were good at. Leaves just me and Will, 'cos our dad's... another story. With me out most of the day and half the night, I worry about Will.'

Family members, Larkin assumed, and tried to picture the scene of their lodging in Limehouse as questions began to queue in his mind. Unwilling to interrupt, he kept them there for later.

'Them's my problems, not yours,' Jack went on after another mouthful. 'But Will's always on me mind because he's special, and Grandad Reggie made me promise to look after him. That was on his deathbed, but there were no need for me to promise, because Will's me brother and I'd do anything for him. It's for him I'm putting in eighteen-hour days, more some nights, and getting in what money I can.'

'You are a noble man, Jack.'

Jack's reply was garbled through his chewing, but when he'd swallowed, he said, 'Ain't a case of being noble. If I don't come up with the rent, we're out. If I don't get Will fed, he starves. If I don't get Reggie's debts paid off, I'm in court. Trouble is, all them things are due, and I ain't got two brass farthings to knock together.'

It was in Larkin's instinct to offer to pay the man's debts, but it was in his experience that to offer generosity to a stranger often led to accusations and trouble. If he deemed Jack open to a gift or a loan, he would know when the time was right to offer it, but that time was not now. Now was the time to listen, and by doing so, he hoped, allow Jack to release some of his anxiety.

'Anyways, tonight, I thought I had a way out, see?' Jack continued. 'I have to make me shillings to get the cab each day, and as the one I'm driving was Reggie's favourite Fordham, and as Shadow's me favourite horse, I give the yard an extra sixpence to keep them back for me. Tonight, I was nowhere near what I needed on account of having to pay double. Night rate and day rate, see? Two horses, because not even Shadow can do a full eighteen or twenty hours, and that means two feeds and an extra for holding me cab while I took me nap. I work out of Harris' yard, see...'

The more the cabman talked, the closer to him Larkin was drawn, and not just as a fellow city-dweller, or a social investigator keen to know more. Beyond those things was something less tangible, and the attraction to his company and instant liking increased. It was reciprocated in Jack's easy affability and his honesty, as if the pair had always been the best of friends.

'Today was a slow one, and though I weren't in profit, I had some coins in me fare purse. Just needed a few more...'

He was talking to the grass, now and then glancing up to address his hansom some feet away, and watch as Speckle Sam offered the horse water. It was as if he was unaware of Larkin on the bench, and instead, told his woes to the gloom.

'Time to jack it in, I thought as I waited on the rank up Tottenham Court Road. This was around midnight, just after, and there was few people about. I'd made me rents for the day, and another fare would get me a bit extra. You can always do with more. So... Anyways, I'd been there ten minutes when this gent comes along and offers me ten shillings to take him down to Kennington. That's more than a fair price, and the strange thing was, he made the offer instead of asking me the fare. Ten shillings would have squared me well enough, and I'd have money to feed Will and get me best boots out of pawn. Of course, I went for it. Who wouldn't? But then I didn't know what he had in mind, did I?'

A sigh and he sat back, still not looking at Larkin as he flicked crumbs into the darkness, and wiped his mouth.

'Then it got strange. This other bloke comes up, greets the first, who tells him he has the ride. Then they both look at me, have a chat, then one of them says I look like a man keen to make money by staying silent. They was a bit odd-looking, these two, but they had money, and I've met worse. "Just here to drive you, Sirs," I said, and asked them where in Kennington. They said they'd tell me when we got close, but first, I was to take three of the shillings on good faith, and share a swig from their flask. Some cabmen drink on the rank, but not me. I told them that, but I took the three shillings.'

Jack faced him for the first time since he began his story, and leant back into the corner as before.

'A couple of times I've had a fare dive on me. You know, you get near where they want to go, and they throw themselves out and scarper without paying. Other times, they simply ain't there when you pull up. Can't always keep an eye on your horse, the traffic, and what's happening below. So, I took their shillings up front, and opened the gates, but they wanted to talk more. I reckon they was a bit on the ale, because they was slurring. "You might wonder what we are about," said the one with a bit of an eyebrow missing. "When we arrive, we need you to wait while we see to some business. Then, you will take us north." I told them there'd be an extra charge for coming back, and he upped the three in advance to five, saying he would award another five when we left Kennington, and give me the same again when I dropped them at their final destination. It's a fair bit of driving they wanted, it was late, and I had Will on me mind, but money's money when you ain't got none, so I said alright. There was one pound three shillings to be made, and no-one's going to snub at that.

"'You see, my friend is in trouble,' said the one with a scar so close to his eye it made me uncomfortable. Couldn't take me eyes off it. "Unable to access his funds for another two weeks, his landlord has barred him from his premises until the rent arrears are paid. My friend is a decent man and needs his equipment. He cannot earn without it, thus, cannot pay his arrears until he has it and can work again." Or some blah-di-blah like that. Then he said, "Therefore, we are to access the property with a spare key and rescue his tools, so at least he can continue to work until his funds are free."

'He was all a bit posh-spoken, but I reckon he was putting that on. Didn't sound right, but... Well, I didn't care what they was about. They seemed decent enough, and they'd already given me five bob and promised ten more, so I told them their business was their business, but would they like to hurry along, because Shadow needed to get home.'

On mentioning the horse's name, he looked back to her and smiled, but the expression soon vanished, and he returned his troubled eyes to Larkin.

'On the way to Kennington, they're below, larking about and sharing their flask. Rum, it were, and they kept offering it through the hatch, and I kept saying no. "I say, cabbie," one of them calls up. "I have no light for our cigars. Would you assist?"

'This hand comes through with a bit of paper, and he tells me to light it like I was his servant. Well, me matchbox was empty, so I leant over the roof, opened the lantern glass, caught the corner of the card, and passed it down. Bit dangerous when you're driving, but for fifteen shillings... Anyways, we got south, and they told me to pull up in this street off Kennington Road. So, I did.'

'"Now," the scar says, "you drive around a little and come back in fifteen minutes. If there is a chalk mark on the wall, wait. If not, drive another five minutes and return. Here is another shilling to secure your service." He said he'd give me the rest when they'd done what they had to do, so I set off one way and them the other. Drove around, kept an eye on the time, got back, no mark on the wall.'

Jack closed his eyes and shook his head as if berating himself, and when he opened them, he frowned.

'So, I drive some more and come back, and there they are, none too happy to have waited, but I was only following orders. They got the man's luggage with them, a suitcase and stuff rattling inside a big bit of rolled carpet. It had a great big bird on it and looked fancy, and when they picked it up, it sounded like the contents of the sink drawer. It ain't a cabman's place to be nosey, and though I wondered what business this bloke was in, I didn't say nothing, but when I went to take the luggage to store it up on the roof, they whipped it away. When they did that, this big silver cup falls out. Looks like one of them things from a church, you know, expensive. It had red and green jewels, and there was other silver that scattered on the pavement. Didn't look like no workman's tools, but what's all that to me? The bloke collects stuff, I thought. Maybe he's selling it to pay his rent. I know what that's like, not that I've had anything worth near what he had. Anyways, they didn't half make a clatter as they bundled everything in, put it in their laps, and told me to drive quick.

'I did. We passed the Lambeth spike, and a bit further on, they wanted to stop at a pub. They was still all matey and stuff, said they'd buy me a beer. "My good man, we insist, for you have saved my friend from destitution." Blah-blether-blah.

'Then, when I got down, he dropped another four shillings in me pocket as promised, arm around the shoulder and all that, as matey as you like. I was getting a bit fed up with this lark by now, but fifteen shillings...' Jack stared, pinning Larkin to the bench with intensity. 'Yeah, I know, I'm stupid and greedy, and you'll say I deserved what I got.'

Larkin shivered under the glare, and waited for more, but that appeared to be the end of the story.

'I think you are neither stupid nor greedy,' he said. 'I assume these men ran away before paying?'

'They did. They went inside to fill up their flask, so I went for a... to, er, relieve meself in the pub yard, and when I come back... Gone. At first, I weren't bothered. I'd pick up a fare on me way home, I thought. They'd given me ten shillings... I thought.' He sniffed, and the mug trembled in his hands. 'Then it all fell on me. Somehow, at some point, they'd stuck me for me purse. All of it, even what they'd given me not two minutes before. Dippers and thieves, both. Left me with nothing for Will's dinner, the yard, the debts, and after Ida dying, and... I reckon... Ah, I had enough...'

His eyes welled up at the memory, and his head dropped. Emitting the same sound as before, he covered his face with his hands.

Even if he'd agreed that Jack had been naïve, Larkin had nothing but sympathy for the man. He didn't know his home life, but it was clear he cared for his afflicted brother. His grandparents had recently died, and there had been only a passing mention of a father, so it was safe to assume the parents were also absent or a burden. Jack was working all hours just to afford to work all hours more, so it was no wonder all those things combined to bring him to tears. The sobbing was a release of the tension caused by worry, and as there were no other witnesses, Larkin didn't intervene, but let him pour out his pain, until, driven by a man's natural instinct, Jack took a mighty breath, and sat up straight.

'Sorry,' he said. 'I embarrassed you.'

'Not at all, and not yourself either, before you think it. Did you call for a policeman?'

'Ah, no point.'

'Would you recognise them again?'

'For sure, but I ain't got time for a summons, not even to find a rozzer. Just got to put up with it and get back on the streets.'

'Your determination moves me, and makes me determined to replace what they stole.'

Jack blew his nose, and shook his head.

'I can't take money from a stranger without giving something in return.'

'But you have. You have given me your trust and companionship.'

'I'll drive you home.'

'Wait...'

The cabman had stood, and his change from anguished victim to business-like driver came so fast, Larkin was unnerved. It wasn't that he didn't want to get home, it was because he was fearful of losing the man's company.

'It's very late, Sir, and I should get Shadow to rest.'

'I agree, it is late, but why am I suddenly Sir once more?'

'Because you were wrong,' Jack said, collecting the mugs. 'I've embarrassed myself in front of a fare. I've been too free with me stories and cheek, and the sooner I get to be alone, the better. Please, don't write nothing about me.'

It was as if their meeting, their earlier exchange of humour and mild insults that insulted neither, had not happened, and Larkin was, in the instant, nothing more than a customer.

This would not do, not after the pleasure Jack's company had given, and as he followed him to the cab, he tried to think of a way he could further help the man, or at least, stay in his presence a little longer.

'I'll drop back the mugs,' the cabman mumbled, and strode over to the hut with his shoulders slumped.

The inside of the hansom was barely lit when Larkin climbed in. His legs were still complaining from his earlier position, and they wouldn't see proper respite until he reached home, because the cab's gates, when closed, allowed him no room to stretch. Waiting, and thinking how he might help Jack further, he adopted the sideways-sit he had employed on the bench, and while placing a hand against the back cushion to drag himself to the corner, his fingers fell upon a piece of litter left on the ridge of soft leather.

Although unable to see what it was, it had clearly been discarded because it was crumpled, and he thought it would make a souvenir of his first backwards ride. More importantly, it would remind him of Jack Merrit.

Why he should feel sad knowing the cab driver would soon only be a memory was no mystery, but nor was it a cause for contemplation, and he slipped the paper into his pocket beside his notebook. When the time was right, he would place it on his desk as a reminder of the ease with which the two had talked. Perhaps it would make it easier to recall the man's handsome features, his vulnerability, his manly stature and strong hands, the dark eyes, and the soft upper lip that Larkin was keen to investigate...

'In safe, Sir?'

Jack's face came into the lantern spill, causing Larkin's heart to jolt. With it came an idea, and he leant out to stop the cabman climbing to the driving seat.

'A final proposition, Mr Merrit,' he said. 'One to which I shall take no refusal.'

'What?'

'As soon as we spy a vacant hansom, I will pay you, and change cabs. Thus, you can be abed more promptly.' The offer only served to cloud Jack's already dark expression. 'I will still pay you our agreed fare to my home, and I will pay you that now.'

'There's no need...'

'Here... No, your passenger insists.'

'You're a gent, Sir,' Jack said, slipping the coins into his pocket.

'Ah, not a complete gent yet.' Larkin took out two sovereigns. 'This, is so you may have a free day tomorrow and give yourself and your very tired horse a rest.'

'Honestly, Sir, no...'

'Insistently, Sir, yes. Take it.'

'It's two bloody quid.'

'No, it's quite clean, I assure you. Here, accept, or must I take your hand and thrust my insistence into it?'

Jack's brow rose, and his eyes flashed from the money to Larkin's face, he sucked in his lips and gave an expression that was, at first, hard to understand. When the cabman twisted his lip into a smile, however, it was easy to read it as salacious, as if the two were speaking in a mutual code, and 'thrust my insistence' had been entendre.

Larkin's pulse raced.

'I mean...' he stammered. 'Would you force me to put the money in your palm?'

'But what for?'

'Must there always be something for something? Cannot there never be a gift in the life of Jack Merrit? Hang it...'

Larkin took Jack's wrist, placed the money in his palm, and wrapped his fingers around it. They were long, calloused fingers, yet somehow tender, and neither they, nor their owner complained at his touch, not even when their hands remained unnecessarily clasped.

Flustered by the effect of the touch, Larkin said, 'Think of it as an advance on a story you have yet to tell me, and use it for your brother.' Letting him go before Jack could protest further, he backed away. 'I spy a carriage approaching. I shall say goodnight, Mr Merrit, and I shall say good luck. My last piece of advice is this; give no more rides to alleged gentlemen this night, but drive directly to your yard and thence, to your home. Perhaps I will be lucky enough to find you available and willing another time when you can treat me to more of your story. Until then, farewell.'

With that, Larkin ran across the road waving his hat to attract the oncoming cab. As soon as it stopped, he threw himself in and ordered the driver northwards. The cab turned and came close by where Jack stood alone with his horse, and Larkin viewed him through the window until the distance robbed him of the sorrowful sight. Sorrowful yet intriguing, because as Larkin held Jack's stare for as long as he could, so the cabman held his.

Jack might have been pondering the abrupt departure, but Larkin wasn't. If he had stayed any longer with the man, he would undoubtedly have said something inappropriate and given himself away.

THREE

There was money to be made on the way home, but Jack ignored the potential fares as he passed through Borough, and turned down the drunks and those leaving the all-night coffee houses. Hopeful men waiting at an empty rank shook their fists as Shadow cantered past the railway station and onto London Bridge, where, even in the early hours, she knew to be alert for the carts, and private carriages. City bankers hurrying north flagged the hansom with rolled newspapers as it dodged sweeping-boys and turned towards the dawn clawing its way from behind the smoking stacks in the east. Newspaper carts slowed with no warning, discharged their piles to waiting sellers and clattered on, while drays pulled out from side streets at will. Shadow skirted them in her dogged fashion, as Jack lolled on his seat fighting sleep, until the streets narrowed, the smell of factories and refineries intensified, and the way ahead changed from black and white dimness to the first silver of the day.

His mind was less on the road ahead, and more on the unusual encounter with Larkin Chase. While wondering why he had found it so easy to tell his story, he also wondered about their parting and their final handshake. Something had happened during it to remind him of a training drive with one of the younger cabbies, Charlie Flex.

Along with other cabmen from Grandad Reggie's rank, Charlie had been helping him learn the streets, the 'knowledge' as the drivers called it, and it had happened just after he'd shown Jack how to listen to the road.

'Street names ain't no good to no-one when the fog's in, you can't see a dog's dick's length ahead, and you're travelling blind,' Charlie told him on their fourth night out. 'It's then you need to know how the roads sound.'

'Sound?'

'Yer. Listen to the wheels and the nag's hooves. We're on Kingsland Road. You can tell from the pits, knocks, gravel here and there, get it?'

'Yeah.'

'Now, turn next left by the Dodgy George, and we'll be in Harman Street, and how do I know that?'

"Cos Pearson Street's on the right when going north.'

'Good man. Listen how the sound changes. Getting towards poorer parts here, see? Dreadful road. Not flat. What's next?'

'Straight on and we'll cross Hoxton Road.'

'Good. So, what if I want Ivy?'

'Street or Lane, Sir?'

Charlie had told Jack to treat him as a customer, and to be polite no matter how drunk, obnoxious or hostile his fares were, and had worked with him on previous nights to better his language.

'I want the Lane, but wait a minute. Close your eyes. It's alright, the horse knows what she's about. Go on, and you'll hear when you're in Ivy Lane.'

Jack did as he was told, and with the ribbons slack in his hands, allowed the horse to lead. When he felt a jolt, he thought his companion had unbalanced the hansom, but it was the cab dipping, twice.

'Double drain beside the Turkish bathhouse,' Charlie said, as Jack looked behind. 'A good marker on a dark and foggy night, and there's loads more to get to know. Now, let's say I want to get to De Beauvoir.'

'Square, Crescent or Road, Sir?'

'Square. How will you get me there?'

'Easy, Sir. Quickest is back to Kingsland, north, over the canal...' A while later, Jack continued his commentary. 'Next right's Hertford, but it's a dead end, and I ain't leaving my fare to walk, not if he's rich enough to live in De Beauvoir. Two right turns on is De Beauvoir Road, but before that, there's Mortimer, and that leads straight into the square where I'll ask him which side.'

'Well done,' Charlie said, and gave him a matey hug before letting go to tighten his coat against the night.

It was only a touch, but it meant much. The pair were snuggled in close on the bench. Built only for one, the space was cramped, but it wasn't uncomfortable. In fact, there was something reassuring about being forced close to Charlie, a married man in his thirties, a supporter of the temperance movement and a nonconformist churchgoer. However, it wasn't the thought of Charlie's abstinence or piety that thrilled Jack and made his heart skip, nor was it the praise he gave when Jack made the turns with accuracy. Nor was it the friendship shown to him by Uncle Bob and his colleagues, and particularly by Charlie, who had encouraged and praised him the most. There was something else; something undefinable caused by the brief hug. It was only a show of manly support, and as affectionate as anyone had been with him, but because it came from a man and not doting old Ida nor daft young Will, it brought a sensation that chilled as much as it thrilled. If Charlie knew what reaction his gesture had caused, he'd likely throw Jack from the bench and drive the hansom over him, churchgoing or not, because that was how men were taught to react to the abnormal interest of other men, an interest that had been stirring within Jack for some years. Always denied, never expressed, but impossible to ignore, the thought he was different to normal men plagued his mind when he allowed it to, and although he kept the thought as deeply covered as he could, it rose to the surface in moments such as the one that had just passed.

To send it back to the depths, he remained silent, and listened to the wheels and hooves.

The same wheels and hooves that joined the confusion of noise and activity as he pulled into the yard, where he extinguished the images of

Charlie Flex and Larkin Chase along with his carriage lanterns, as the stableboy ran to take his horse. The yard resounded with the noise of its early morning madness. Other drivers were whistling and calling, the farrier was already at his hammering, and the din was intensified by tiredness. Jack's head ached so much his eyes hurt.

Only able to bid Shadow a vague farewell, he left her in good hands, found the keeper and mumbled he wouldn't be needing the hansom that day, and told him Shadow should also rest. Harris complained about having a cab off the streets, but Jack insisted, paid the horse hire, and lightheaded, left the yard.

The walk from there to home happened as though he were someone else, and the warmth of the rising sun only increased his drowsiness and longing for his bed, but he kept enough about him to stop on Milligan Street to buy matches for his pipe and milk and sausages for Will's breakfast. From there to his ground-floor rooms was a blur, but his focus returned to sore eyes on entering the kitchen.

Will was pacing from sink to sill dressed only in his underclothes. His straw-coloured hair was dishevelled and his face red, as if he had just woken from a bad dream. The sight was not unusual.

'Elsie Clarke wants the three shillings and eightpence Grandma Ida borrowed this time last year,' he said, as if he and Jack were already halfway through a conversation. 'I told her it was only two shillings, but she said there had to be interest. I said, in that case, it should be two shillings and ninepence-ha'penny, but she told me I belonged in the Bedlam. You have been a long time.'

'Will, I am done in,' Jack said, throwing the provisions onto the table. 'I'm going straight to bed, and I don't want to be woken for nothing.'

'I have been well, thank you.' Will turned at the window. 'I cleaned the room, as you can see, and in the afternoon, I aired the bedding and put those buttons back on your shirt. Charlie Flex called by to see I was well, and I told him I was, because I am. Last evening, Johnny limped in from next door to show me how he'd crushed two fingers beneath a box of earth, and seemed quite proud of his missing fingernails, which I said looked disgusting. Elsie called again about her shillings, but I told her you were working to get them, and no-one calls it the Bedlam anymore. Sausages.'

'Have what you want.' Jack's boots were off, and as soon as his feet were free of his socks, he planted them on the cold flagstones to bring them numbing relief. 'I got to sleep, Will. Sorry you've been alone all day.'

'And all night. I am accustomed to it. I have been reading.'

'You been out walking?'

'Shunter's Yard to West India, south, followed the old wall where the windmills used to be, on to Blackwall, and home. Six thousand and fifty-six paces. Twice. Money?'

His body aching, his head thumping, Jack regarded his brother with a mixture of affection and shame. It hurt to leave him to his own devices for so long, but he had no other choice, and Will had enough about him to ensure he was never bored. For anyone else, arranging the furniture and cleaning the house repeatedly during the day would have been a burden; to Will, it was not only a compulsion but an enjoyment. Jack's brother prided himself on keeping the cleanest step on the street, the cleanest windows and neatest curtains, and when he was in the mood, he knocked on the neighbours' doors and offered to clean their parlours and sculleries. It would have been more useful if he charged them for his service, but there were worse things he could be doing while Jack was working.

'Money?' Will repeated, his hand outstretched.

'Yeah, yeah.' Jack pulled himself to his feet, and dug in his pockets. 'Picked up a strange fare early morning,' he said, counting shillings and dropping them into his brother's palm one at a time. 'This for a chat, that for a short ride, and that for no bloody reason other than he was nosey.'

'This is all you made all day and all night?'

'I got robbed.'

'You don't look hurt.'

'I wasn't hurt. Take it, put it in your jars, then leave me be until Christmas.'

'You're not being serious.'

'No, Will, I ain't. I just need to sleep.'

Will dropped the shillings into various jars he kept in a straight line on the mantlepiece, one marked 'Rent', another 'Food', and one that displayed a question mark Jack never asked about.

'I made your bed, washed your drawers, and put a stitch in your sock,' Will said, counting. 'There's not enough here for Shadwick, and he will be here at noon.'

'How much do we owe him?'

'Ten shillings.'

'Then give him this, and tell him two are against the next rent. Make sure he writes that in is bloody book, yeah?'

'A sovereign?'

'So I can have a day off.'

Will scratched his scalp, and examined his fingernails. 'You need it, brother. Will you eat first?'

'No.' Jack was already at the curtain.

'Shall I keep you a sausage?'

'Do what you bloody like.'

'John Anthony Merrit, there is no need for rudeness.'

Sometimes, Will sounded like his grandmother, and his tone brought Jack up short. It happened then, and he stopped with one hand on the doorless jamb.

'Sorry,' he yawned. 'I'm done in. Good night, mate. Love you.'

'That's better,' Will chirped. 'And because I love you too, I shall tell the people upstairs they are not to shout, row or throw things until you wake.'

'Yeah, well, good luck with that.'

* * *

Larkin received no such welcome when he let himself into his house early that morning. Mrs Grose was not yet up and about, and the basement door was closed. The stairs creaked in their accustomed fashion as, once he had removed his shoes, he climbed to the first floor, dropped his jacket on the back of the study chair, and placed the contents of his pockets on the desk. From there, he took the next flight to his bedroom, and changed into his nightclothes. It was a routine to which he was so accustomed, he did it without thinking, but, as he turned the bedside clock to face the wall, he noticed it was well past the usual time he took to bed.

The evening had started with anticipation, and thanks to the guard dog at the Lambeth workhouse, developed through annoyance and frustration into something far less tangible.

'Far less tangible?' he questioned as he lay on his back listening to the first street-rustles of the day; the grinding of wheels, jangling bottles, and whistles from newsboys. 'What was intangible about it?'

Hands behind his head, he would be unable to sleep until he had fully examined the facts.

It had begun with a man sobbing in the night.

'Sounds like the start of a novel,' he mused. 'A little intrigue leading to an opportunity.'

An opportunity to expose the hardships of working men by learning from a cabman what it was like to work through the night. That had been the intention, a way to fill the time as he rode home, but without the opportunity to sit beside the driver and make notes.

'You wanted to sit with him, why?'

So he could more easily talk and listen. Kneeling backwards had been a novel experience that soon turned to a painful one, but that pain had been eased by the sight of the man's face.

'Ah, so this is where it starts.'

Where what starts? The intangible thing?

'Yes. Be honest with yourself, Chase. You asked him little about his work. You were keener to know more about his plight.'

Why not? When he got around to it, the fellow was affable and open with his tale, and its telling was only delayed because Larkin wanted to eke out their time together.

'Closer.'

Closer to the intangible. He already knew what it was, but examining the night's events was a way of putting off the self-confession he didn't want to declare.

'Poor chap, being duped and robbed,' he muttered, and turned onto his side.

Jack Merrit didn't seem like a man who would allow himself to be either, though he was clearly poor, why else would he put in such long hours? A man built as he was, with wide shoulders, a firm jaw, large hands, and the whole of him sturdy, would have no trouble working manually for more reliable money and fewer hours. There had been something about his grandfather's hansom, so perhaps his Jack Merrit had the desire to keep a family business running.

His Jack Merrit? That was an interestIng way to look upon a stranger.

'No stranger.' Larkin stifled a yawn, and wished his mind would turn down its gas and draw him into the longed-for darkness of sleep.

It refused, and continued to churn as he sought comfort on his other side, reliving the way Jack had told his story.

A couple of crooks playing the part of gents, duping a lone cabman who might not have had the full shillings to the pound...

'That's unfair. The man seemed quite erudite in certain matters. He spoke as one would expect a man from that area, and was exceedingly honest.'

As far as Larkin knew, Jack was certainly willing to chat and happy to be in Larkin's company. Maybe because he wanted a break; that was the more likely scenario, and not because he was as attracted to Larkin as Larkin was to...

'We shall not take that route,' he whispered to the room as the first hint of dawn appeared at the edge of the curtains. 'We shall not use words such as attraction.'

Even though there was no denying its existence?

It was in the sadness of the cabman's face, the hopelessness in his red-ringed eyes, and in the resonance of his sobs. That sound in the darkness was Larkin's first call to action. Someone was in need, in trouble, unhappy... Soon followed by the sight of a robust man hiding his sorrow and becoming a professional on the instant. That showed an appealing manliness.

'We shan't use manliness, either.'

Something else then. Something in his presence...

'We have considered this before. Sleep.'

The touch of the man's skin and the thrill it brought. That was the answer that must remain unspoken, that was the reason Larkin had to flee. There had been a mutual attraction in the spaces between their words.

'Highly unlikely, highly illegal, and nothing more can happen, just as your rest will not happen until you stop talking to yourself and go to...'

Another yawn interrupted, but it didn't bring him any closer to the respite he craved. His skin was still tacky with the residue of the balmy night, dust and sweat, and he hadn't washed. The water would be cold, it would wake him up.

'Oh, hell.'

He'd not left a note for Mrs Grose, so she would barge in at the usual time, and that was in only a few hours. That wouldn't do, but neither would rising to write a note and leave it on the stairs, as that would also cause further wakefulness.

'Perhaps I should just work,' he considered, lifting one eyelid to examine the lightening room.

To work on what? The night's adventure? The recounting of Jack's story? To jot in his journal how he came by the man, what they discussed, how they spoke as old friends after only a few minutes, and how he had to run from him else pull him close and kiss him?

'Kiss?'

It might as well be admitted. That was what Larkin had wanted to do, and he blamed Jack's salacious smile for sparking the urge.

'You cannot blame anyone else when it's your fault you are as you are,' he said, and shifted onto his back. 'This will not do.'

None of it would do. Not the way he was unable to sleep because he couldn't remove a cabman's predicament from his mind, and not the way he pictured Jack even when he thought of numbingly mundane matters.

The lamp on the desk; Did Jack use candles or oil lamps? That time when Larkin walked through Hyde Park, met a soldier in uniform and struck up a conversation; he'd not had the same appeal as Jack, and had been a mistake. He tried picturing Mrs Grose in the glory of full complaint, but could only compare the colour of her dress to the dark shadows beneath his cabman's eyes.

'This is intolerable.'

There was only one way oblivion would come and that was if he gave in, not to sleep, but to the desire to remember every feature of Jack's face, fingers, smile, the way he held his tin mug, his language, that soft, slightly large top lip, his hair, brown-blond in the lamplight, the jaunty tilt of his bowler hat, the way he cared for his horse, his loneliness, the touch of his hand...

As predicted, Mrs Grose woke him at the usual hour, welcoming him to the day with a complaint about the weather.

'Sweltering,' she declared, throwing back the curtains in a blast of anger and light. 'Milk's churning, cold shelf's warm, and I opened the windows to let in some air, only to breathe dust. Tea's stewing. Newspaper on your chair. Second edition.'

She was gone in the swish of a floor-length skirt, leaving Larkin stunned.

'Good morning,' he called after her, only to receive the threatening reply, 'We'll see about that.'

His eyes were heavy, but his drowsiness was not unpleasant, as if he had taken just enough narcotic to put his body into a state of gentle relaxation, but leave his mind unaffected. The dream he'd had might have been one reason for his mild euphoria. There had been large wheels turning like the merry-go-round on which he was sitting backwards, facing a cabman who...

The dream evaporated leaving behind only a longing for its return.

'Let's not start that again,' he muttered, climbing from his bed to find his slippers.

Discovered and slipped into, they carried him to the washstand where the water was not as cold as he anticipated, and from where he could squint into the street below. Nothing out of the ordinary; carters, pedestrians, wandering newsboys and hansom cabs.

'No.'

He pictured Jack's cab and Shadow in a yard, and the cabman sleeping long hours with no shirt, his wide chest rising and falling, his eyelashes flickering, his mouth slightly open, dreaming of his unusual passenger...

'I said, no.'

The soap smelt of lemons, a new brand by the looks, and he tried to remember what Jack smelt of, but could only recall fried onions. That didn't seem right.

Saying, 'Sweat, probably,' didn't dull his enthusiasm to recall the previous night, but the thought of Mrs Grose complaining about his tardiness did.

The threatening yap of, 'Tea!' from one floor below sent the image of Jack scuttling for cover, and Larkin hurrying to his study.

As was her unmovable desire, Mrs Grose had set the tea tray beside the wingback chair, laid the folded newspaper over the arm, and left the toast and its accompaniments on the far side of the room. It was her way of ensuring Larkin took exercise, and at least made the trek between toast and tea before he spent the rest of the morning at his desk.

The newspaper brought more hideous news of politics and murder, and one article tempted him to read of a cannibal, but its heading was misleading, so he gave it little heed. The advertisements were of no interest, and there were pages of them, it was always the other, more philanthropic reports that appealed. A discussion about the state of the slums, developments planned in Shoreditch around the 'Old Nicol', the widening of various roads in the West End leading to the clearance of poor housing, which was fine, as long as they found somewhere else for those wretches to live, and didn't just throw them further east, as had happened at Covent Garden.

It was the usual mundane round of word-chewing, printed in tiny lettering which, in places, required a magnifier to read, and he was about to throw the paper aside and make another expedition to the toast, when a line in larger print caught his eye.

"A Theft Last Night in Kennington", the bold line screamed as if crime was an unusual occurrence. It wasn't, but the details leapt from the page with such lucidity he almost offered them tea.

Last night, or in the early hours of this morning, Clarington's pawnbroker shop in Kennington was burgled. The thieves made off with extensive amounts of silver, jewellery and other valuables including a rare and valuable carpet. Clarington's, known for their service to the more genteel class, are, along with the police, offering a reward of twenty pounds (£20) for the apprehension of the criminals, or information leading to capture. Information may be given to the station at Kennington Road or any policeman.

The newspaper continued to laud the pawnbroker and police for the reward and their alacrity at offering it, and itself for reporting the theft in time for its second edition. What it didn't explain was the need to state the reward in words and numbers, as if the editor thought its readership was ignorant.

That was an aside, while the obvious took centre stage; that the men who hired Jack and robbed him had also robbed Clarington's. Once that probability had made its entrance, a chorus of supporting cast quickly followed, being both comedy and tragedy, or at least, presenting either side of an argument.

Jack had seen the crooks and could identify them; but doing so might bring reprisals. Jack was a witness; but the police might think he was involved. There was a reward, and Jack needed money; but would he be willing to come forward? There was a mystery, the solving of which would assist a man in need; Jack Merrit, who had driven Larkin to a park, while also driving him to distraction.

'There must be a denouement to this tantalising scene.'

'Are you talking to me?'

Mrs Grose had crept up on him, and was inspecting his teacup over his shoulder.

'No, Housekeeper. I am talking to myself.'

'You'll go mad.'

'I already am. Thank you for the tea, I shall be here in my study all day. Do I have callers?'

'You never have callers.'

'Just as I like it. Is Emily still intact?'

'Much as the local football team would like her not to be, yes. I'm going out.'

'What a comforting thought. A light lunch at one, if you will.'

'Don't I always?'

With that, the housekeeper abandoned the room, leaving Larkin to reread the article and wonder what it was that nagged at the back of his mind.

'It had something to do with cigars,' he said, and began another trek to the toast rack.

FOUR

The weight of sleep was hard to lift, but Jack stirred himself from beneath it with the unusual feeling of being late for work. There should have been dawn light at the backyard window, but if it was dawn, the sun was rising elsewhere. Besides, hadn't he already seen a sunrise? His watch, hanging on the bedpost, read just after seven, but it was too dark for morning, and why was he wearing his work trousers?

Realisation dawned as the sun set; he'd slept for over twelve hours. That meant another day with Will left to fend for himself. Had he paid the rent man, or was that him in the kitchen now? It didn't sound like Shadwick's voice, and Will was offering tea. Did they have any tea?

His legs were as heavy as his eyes as he dragged himself from his bed and stood at the wash bowl. Will had only recently put it there because there was no dust floating on the surface, and he could read the maker's mark through the water. Eyes closed, he plunged his face, flinched at the cold sting, and surfaced with a gasp that expelled drowsiness. An ewer of the same over his head, a ruffle with a towel, a splash beneath the arms, one between the legs to dampen his need-to-piss ardour so that he could relieve himself in the guzunder, and he was ready to face the day. Or the night, as the room was darker.

'A little quieter if you would, Sir, and please, the spoon must be the other way up in the saucer and perpendicular to the handle. No, like this.'

If a saucer was involved, Will was serving tea to someone important, but as he changed his shirt, and adjusted his belt, Jack couldn't think who. A glance in the mirror showed unkempt stubble. Will was using the china, the guest was *very* important, and Jack needed a shave before making an appearance. Listening as he lathered and scraped, he heard only his brother's voice, and by the time he'd finished, the kitchen had fallen silent. In fact, when he pulled back the curtain, had it not been for the teacup, he'd have imagined Will had been talking to himself. The candles flickered, the oil lamp glowed from its hook, and Will was alone.

'Who was that?' Jack asked, slipping into a chair at the table and testing the pot.

'Good evening,' Will beamed, whipping away the china cup and passing down Jack's tin mug. 'I know you slept well. Her upstairs came down to complain about your snores. Of course, I told her they were nothing compared to when she sits on the floor and breaks wind. The number of times I've gone to answer the door when it was her answering a call of flatulence...'

'Who was that?' Jack repeated. When Will started on a tale, he could ramble for hours, and Jack wasn't yet awake enough to cope with that.

'A gentleman in a state of excitement,' Will said, removing excess sugar from the teaspoon. 'I made him tea in the hope you would wake, but when it became apparent you wouldn't, he left. You just missed him.'

'What gentleman? Not Harris from the yard, I hope, 'cos I paid him.'

'No. He's not a gentleman.'

'Not Shadwick.'

'Neither is he, and he called at noon. I gave him the pound, and watched him write the two shillings advance in his book. I insisted we both sign it, so he didn't diddle next time.'

'Then who?'

'He didn't leave a card, but he will be back.'

'When?'

'As soon as he has bought a lantern.'

This was becoming stranger by the second.

'A lantern?'

'Yes. As it grew darker, and I lit ours, he said one would not do, and left to buy us another.'

Jack shook his head, but it did little to make the conversation clearer.

Will stirred his tea. 'Nice man. Said it had taken him most of the day to detect you. He knew you started your day at the Limehouse station rank, so it might have been Uncle Bob who told him our address. He wouldn't tell me what it was about. I saved you two sausages, but there is also cake.'

'Cake? When did you buy a cake?'

'I didn't. It's a good one, and there are strawberries.'

'What?'

'A gift.'

'Who from?'

'Your visitor.'

'Whose name you don't know, and who didn't state his business.'

'Oh, I know his name.' Will placed a tin on the table. 'Want to look?'

'At what?'

'The cake.'

'What was the name?'

'Strawberry sponge. See.'

It was a very fine cake in a very fine tin, and topped with slices of something Jack had only eaten a few times in his life, but it brought no answers, and Will's games were beginning to irk.

'Will,' he sighed, 'it's a fine-looking treat, but can't you just tell me who came calling?'

'Yes, I can, but asked me not to.'

'Why?'

'Now, how would I know a gentleman's intentions? I'll cut you a slice. Your caller won't be long because I sent him to Albert's chandlery on the corner.'

Jack gave in and accepted the slice, savouring each bite as his teeth sank into it, and swilled it down with warm tea. Will fussed at the sink, rearranged the crockery on the shelf, wrapped the best teacup in its cloth and stowed it away at the back of the dresser before returning to the sink to wipe it, dry it, and admire his handiwork. Finally, he retook his seat.

'You look more awake,' he said, and Jack agreed he was.

'But still in the dark about this bloke. How old?'

'I didn't ask.'

'Guess.'

'Thirty.'

'Anything more?'

'Possibly thirty-one.'

'I meant anything more about him. A description.'

'Moustache nicely trimmed. Fine features, you might call them handsome depending on your taste. No pockmarks. Hair oiled and parted at the side, very dark brown and groomed. Not from nearby, because he was clean, wore a suit, and didn't smell like fish. Perfume, but not unacceptably feminine. Well-spoken. A bit odd. Comic would be a better word.' Will regarded the wall clock, closed his eyes as he thought, and held up a finger. 'You will meet him in... Three, two, one...' A knock at the door brought a smile to his lips. 'Your caller also walks at a standard pace.'

Jack ruffled his brother's hair, knowing that putting it right would give Will a distraction for a full minute, and answered the knock to find a vaguely familiar face in the hall. Behind it was Elsie Clarke nosing from her front door, and the woman upstairs leaning over the rail to stare, because well-dressed strangers were an uncommon sight in their tenement.

'I found you!' last night's fare announced, and lifted a lantern by its handle. 'You might say I travel light. May I come in?'

Not only was it confusing to wake in the evening having missed a full day's work, and to have someone bring cake, but it was also baffling to wonder why a fare would come calling. Unable to process the events, Jack waved the man inside.

'It's me stockbroker, ain't it,' he snarled at the spectators, and slammed the door on their curiosity.

'Would that I had the acumen to hold such a position,' the fare said. 'Hello again, William, and thank you for the tip. Albert's certainly does have a chattel for every occasion. I hope you don't mind the forwardness, but I also bought a can of oil as a donation.'

'Very kind of you, Sir.' Will grinned at his brother. 'Told you he was a nice man.'

Will and the stranger took the lantern and set about filling and lighting it as though they had known each other for years.

Jack stared, trying to remember the man's name. Yesterday had been such a long day, by the time night came, he had existed in a dream, and only fragments of it remained. A head on the cab roof, an entertaining chat, a sense of humour and a lot of clever words... Generosity, too, which was why he didn't need to work... A pork sandwich and the telling of the story...

The memory of being robbed returned, but the pang of anger it caused vanished when the reality of what was taking place landed along with the man's name.

'Mr Chase?'

His name, and the way he had touched Jack's hand, and Jack hadn't pulled away.

'At your service, Mr Merrit. Once again, I apologise for arriving unannounced.'

'More tea, Sir?'

'No, no, thank you, but no. A seat in your parlour and a conversation with your brother is all I require, William. If you will allow me the honour of a visit.'

'This is our parlour, Sir, and the honour is ours. We've never had a gent call before.'

'How flattering you are.' Chase gave Will a quick bow, and addressed Jack. 'Would you mind if we chatted?'

'About what?'

'All will come to light. By the looks, you were enjoying my gift. I am happy. Many men would not accept such a thing from a person they hardly knew and who called without a prearrangement.'

'He likes to talk.' Will said, checking the lie of his hair in the mirror as he hung the new lamp beside it.

'What can I do for you, Mr Chase?' Jack asked, and deciding there was nothing to be done but offer him a seat, did so.

The man's arrival, at first a shock, was now a mystery, and Jack could think of no reason a casual fare should track down a cabman, bring cake, and buy a much-needed lantern for his home. The increased lighting reduced the shadows and highlighted the mould patches not even Will could remove, and he suffered a shiver of embarrassment.

If Chase had noticed their poor conditions, he made no comment, and kept his eyes firmly fixed as a broad grin grew beneath his moustache.

'Last night you were good enough to tell me a story,' he said. 'Tonight, I have one to tell you. I assume you reached home without incident?'

'I did, Sir, thank you, and thank you again for your gifts. Shadow will be well rested when I hook her up tomorrow and start earning to repay your two sovereigns.'

'Oh, there is no need for that. I thought I made that clear, but then again, some recollections of last night are rather vague. It was very late.'

'If you let me know where to send the money, I will get it you in good time, Sir.'

Chase tutted. 'Last night we were Jack and Larkin. I should like to be so again, because we have a task ahead, Mr Merrit, and it is one on which we can embark together. It could be a most exciting journey.'

'You need a ride? There's plenty of cabs at the...'

'No, not a ride. Perhaps I should start at the beginning. Would you rather we spoke elsewhere?' Chase nodded towards Will, now cross-legged beneath the lamp reading one of his books.

'No. Whatever you want to talk about, I don't mind if Will is listening.'

'I'm not,' Will said, proving the opposite. 'Take no notice of me. I'm in conversation with Wilkie Collins.'

'Oh, which one?'

'The Moonstone, but shush, Sir. I am absorbing his use of language.'

'He does that,' Jack whispered. 'It's how come he's so toffy spoken.' Louder, he said, 'He's not being rude, it's just how he is. You was saying?'

Chase threw inquisitive eyes to Will, but returned serious ones to Jack.

'Did you read today's newspaper?' he asked.

'Newspapers is luxuries, and I only got out of bed just back a bit.'

'Oh yes, well...' Chase produced a cutting from inside his tailored jacket, and lay it on the table. 'Read the headline... That's the bold type there.'

'I ain't ignorant, Mr Chase, I keep up with today's newfangled words. Will makes sure of... Blow me!'

'Exactly. Now read that line there...'

Jack did, and held back a swear word. 'Twenty quid?'

'Quite. Twenty quid for a quid quo pro.'

'What?' Jack said with a sneer, thinking Chase was taking the rise.

'Possibly yours in return for an investigation.'

'Into what?'

Chase delved into a pocket for a second time, and produced a scrap of paper.

'Last night, after you told me of your unfortunate incident with these villains...' He tapped the newspaper. 'I waited for you to return the tea mugs. Do you remember?'

'Yeah, sort of.'

'I sat inside the cab where those two men had not long before ridden. While waiting, my hand fell upon this.' Chase slid over the scrap. 'Cast your glance, and tell me what you hypothesise.'

'He means have a gander and see what you think.'

'I ain't dumb, Will.' Jack wasn't, but he wasn't as well read as his brother, and was grateful for the translation as he flattened the crumpled paper. 'It's half gone.'

'Most of it has been burnt away, yes. By you.'

'Me?' A memory stirred. 'Oh yeah, they asked me to set light to it so they could spark their cigars.'

'Thus, it came from them. I would say it is a common, printed invitation as one might arrange for a public event such as a raffle. It's not an expensive print, nor is it from a business. I believe it is, or was, a handbill. An advertisement as one might put in a shop window, or on the ledge in a public house.'

'So?'

'The other side.' Chase pointed. 'Read what survived the inferno.'

Jack did as instructed, and read aloud what remained of the printed information.

...and Road, was the first line, followed lower down by, *...une eighteenth*. The last line stated, ... *Arty will take the chair.*

'What does that mean?'

'What does it mean to you, Mr Merrit?'

'Sod all, pardoning me rough speak.'

Chase waved it away. 'I shall tell you what I think,' he said, taking back the paper and placing it beside the newspaper clipping. 'The men who hired you last night were out and out crooks intent on robbing Clarington's as well as yourself, and used you as their driver. This, we can assume to be the case because of circumstantial evidence, very compelling circumstance, I'd say. This handbill, I believe to be an invitation to a gathering. The meeting might be for anything, but for them to have this invitation about their person surely indicates they have an interest in attending. If they do, and if we can discover the where and when, and if you recognise them there, you can, with alacrity, fly to the nearest police station, alert the authorities, and have the men run in. You, Jack, are the closest witness to this crime. You saw them, and you can identify them. The police will know how to gain a confession, thus, the outcome will be...'

'Twenty pounds.' Jack was there ahead of him.

In fact, he had been beside him as he spoke, imagining spying the villains, reporting them, and pocketing the money. With it, he could keep a long-ago made promise to Will and search for better lodgings. Or, the reward would cover most of his cab costs for a couple of months, so anything he made would be his to save. Or, he could clear Reggie's debts, and maybe put down a part-payment on a cab of his own. Or...

There was no point running ahead of himself. Cabs didn't go before horses.

'You appear dubious, Jack. May I return to using your familiar name? I feel we are partners in this venture.'

'Partners? You'd want a cut of this twenty?'

'No.'

'You got something to do with the pawnbrokers what was robbed?'

'No'

'Then why are you so interested?'

Chase sat back in his chair, glanced at Will, whose head was well into his book, looked at Jack, and twitched the corner of his mouth. His trim moustache rose with it in an unusual gesture Jack was unable to decode. The man also raised his eyebrows, and nodded once, as if imparting, 'You know', while shaking hands with himself.

'Are you ill, Mr Chase?'

The man gave a hopeless sigh, and his features straightened.

'As you may remember from last night, I am keen to help those who need help.'

'Me?' Jack bristled. 'I don't need your help.'

'I thought last night you and I came to know each other a little. We enjoyed each other's company, did we not? We bantered somewhat, and...' His voice dropped to a whisper. *'Got along.'*

'As well as I might with any other fare.'

'You told me your story. There was trust.'

'Until you forced a handout on me like I was some pauper, and scarpered.'

'There was a...' Chase flustered, and his cheeks reddened. 'A reason for my hurried departure, perhaps a necessity... I didn't want you to reject my offer.'

'Because you think I'm a pauper?' Jack scorned. 'I know we don't have much, but what we got's ours.'

'You misunderstand me.'

'Do I? Coming over here with cake for me brother, buying a lamp.

What you saying? I can't afford to look after me kin? What you getting pleasure from, Mr Chase? Doing some Christian charity to make yourself feel better about the money you got?' Anger replaced annoyance. 'I bet you go on slumming trips so's you can see how the likes of us live in squalor, then write about it from up on your high horse, but do nothing more. You can take your scraps of paper, mate, and your grand ideas, and stick them...'

'Jack Merrit,' Will snapped.

With blood pounding in his temples, Jack thumped the table. 'Get out me home and take the rest of the cake with you. And the flipping lantern. We don't need no charity.'

'John Anthony Merrit!' Will slammed shut his book, and Jack froze. 'We count.'

'Leave it out, Will.'

'Ten, nine, eight...'

'Will, I'm warning you...'

'The reverse is true, brother. Along with me, now. Ten, nine...

Aware he was the one now blushing, Jack took a deep breath through his nose, and knowing his brother was right, counted down with him through long breaths. The trembling subsided until the counting was over, and Will said, 'He apologises, Mr Chase. Except, he doesn't, so I do it for him.'

Jack said nothing because it was true. There had been times he'd lost his temper when Will wasn't around to calm him, and none of them had ended well, and whether Jack's fault or not, none had involved an apology.

Shamefaced, he returned his gaze to his visitor in silence, and expected him to leave in disgust.

'Now, you will ask me how we find these men,' Chase continued as if nothing had passed. 'That is where we need your expertise. Your knowledge, I believe cabmen call it.'

The difference between expectation and actual happening was too great to fathom, and Jack said, 'What?'

'I return to the handbill. There we have an incomplete address, "... and Road." I say it is an address because of the capital letter, R. Can you identify which road it might be?'

'Not from three letters.'

'Three letters that are the end of the road's name,' Chase said, his moustache bouncing with enthusiasm. 'How many London streets end with something-and Road?'

'I'd need time to think on that.'

'Band is unlikely,' Will piped up, once again with his nose in his book. 'Sand is possible as are strand and hand, but I would start with the obvious and put an L at the front,'

'Land?'

'It's an example. How many road names end with land?' Will turned a page.

Chase shrugged, and opened his palms across the table. 'I know of one, but you are the expert, Mr Merrit.'

Jack thought, pictured his maps, his routes and previous journeys, and said, 'I can think of three.'

'Which are?'

'Portland Road, Queensland Road, and...'

'Kingsland Road,' Chase enthused. 'I know that, because I live at one end of it. Only three?'

'Within a cabbie's usual driving distance from the centre of town, yeah. But why's that important?'

'It doesn't take much imagination to suppose our villains will attempt to sell off their goods at some public, or more likely semi-private, meeting to be held somewhere on one of those roads. This invitation is of the type unscrupulous men put about to others in the same nefarious trade. A legitimate public auction known only to a choice few, where stolen items may be sold, usually so money can be raised to engage a... what's the word? Oh, a mouthpiece.'

'A defence barrister in a court of law.'

'Yeah, Will. You think I don't know that?'

'This meeting will take place soon,' Chase continued. 'In fact, I will state that it will happen on the eighteenth of June, probably in the evening, and in a public house or other social setting on one of the three roads you just mentioned.'

'You sound very certain, Mr Chase.'

'Jack, please, can you call me Larkin? We shared an experience last night, and I would like us to share this one.'

Chase wasn't going to give up or leave until Jack agreed to something, and assuming he'd never see him again, he said, 'Yeah, alright.'

The strange facial twitch came again, and Jack wondered if the man had always had it. Whatever it was, he thought he should ignore it out of politeness.

'June the eighteenth,' Will said. 'We can assume this from the letters, and the year from the existence of the burnt paper. It's doubtful such an advertisement would have survived since last year, and highly unlikely it has been printed in advance of next.'

'You must be proud of your brother. He is quite the scholar.'

'Yeah, I am, and he's sitting right there, so you can talk to him not about him. He might be odd, but he's not thick.'

'I am not odd, I am precise.'

'So, what do you say, Jack? Will you join me in this enterprise?'

'What? To find one pub out of hundreds on three long roads, where dodgy characters may or may not turn up to sell what they nicked, and to do it in three days?'

'A fair summary, but we may add the granting of a substantial reward if successful.'

Jack was already working day and night to pay the rent and debts. Where would he find the time to trawl the streets, and how would he know when he'd found the right place? What if Chase was right, and the men were there? They'd run when they saw him, or, more likely, beat him up and leave him for dead.

Then, there was Will, daily devouring more pages than hot meals, in need of clothes that didn't have holes, and with nothing to do except walk and read. If Will could drive, he'd have been happy to examine every public house on every street of London and write them in alphabetical order in his notebook, but Jack would worry about him being alone in places he didn't know.

No. This wasn't something Will could do, and nor was it something Jack had time for.

There was, however, the reward of twenty pounds.

'What do you say, Jack?' Chase enthused. 'Does it sound like fun?'

'Fun? No. Some of us have to work for a living. This sounds like a jolly jaunt for the likes of you, and a waste of my time. Talking of which, we've taken too much of each other's, and I got things to do before I go back to bed.'

Chase's eagerness faded to disappointment. 'Then perhaps, you will think about my proposition and let me leave you my card,' he said, placing one on the table. 'I will begin my investigation in the morning, and find another way to bring the criminals to justice. If I am successful, I will return to you with the reward. This, I am happy to do. Not because I believe you live in squalor, Mr Merrit, but because I believe you deserve the reward for the wrong that was done to you last night. There is my address, call on me if you change your mind. I will leave the lantern and what's left of the cake because they are gifts, if not for you, then for William.'

'Very kind of you, Sir,' Will said, and stood by the door ready to see the guest on his way.

'Not at all. Before I leave, though, Jack, may I shake your hand.'

'If you don't thrust no insistence into it,' Jack grumbled, and hoping it would hurry the man along, held out his palm.

When they shook, it wasn't just their hands that met, it was also their eyes. Something passed between them, and Chase gave a fluttering smile of recognition. It was only once the man had left, that Jack realised he had inadvertently done the same.

'What do you make of all that?' Will said, turning down the new lantern to save the oil.

'The man's as cracked as an old pot.'

'You're not being fair on him.'

'Oh, am I not? I tell you what's not fair. Him coming here and saying I can get meself twenty quid by catching rough'uns, when I don't even have time in the day to piss.'

'I'll help him,' Will offered. 'I can use my saved coins for a cab, and find his house.'

'No, you won't. I ain't having you roaming over town on your own.'

'I am twenty-one, and I'd be with Mr Chase.'

'Even worse.'

'Why do you say that?'

'There's something about him unnerves me, that's why.'

It wasn't so much something about Chase, it was what he made Jack feel when he took his hand, and it wasn't an unpleasant or untrustworthy feeling as he'd made out, but something exciting, as if the touch held a promise. Of what, was a matter he was too out of sorts to consider.

'Anyways,' he added, 'I've got work. I'm going back to bed.'

'You won't sleep,' Will predicted. 'We'll talk about this again tomorrow. It's an opportunity.'

'Whatever you say. Don't stay reading too late. Goodnight, mate. Love you.'

Will was right, Jack didn't sleep, not at first. Unable to settle, he lay pondering the strange Mr Chase, what he had already given, and what he had offered in spoken word, evidence, and in the spaces between the words. They troubled Jack the most because they were without definition and thus, open to interpretation. Although there was an opportunity to have revenge on the men who'd robbed him, it might lead to dangerous reprisals and another spell of trouble like before, and he'd promised Will; never again.

The concerns and possibilities battled within his head until the church rang twelve, by which time, his brother was safely abed across the room, and he was no longer able to resist sleep.

FIVE

Jack leant on the gatepost to finish his pipe, and watched waterboys as old as eighty slopping and lumbering from butt to stall, while others, some as young as ten, heaved the hansoms by their traces and fitted them to weary animals. Above, the morning sun battled through a haze of fumes, throwing random beams onto bales of straw, feed buckets, and the dung heap, where two men were loading manure into a cart, and through it all came the seven chimes of the station clock.

Harris' yard not only hired out hansoms to drivers with their own licence, but also held cab licences of its own, and the proprietor favoured his indentured men, and gave them better hire rates for his vehicles. Although he held his own license, Jack didn't own a vehicle, and was obligated to the miserly master and his cab-rental charges, suffering his weekly increases through the summer, while having to pay for his horses' feed and care on top. It had long been Grandfather Reggie's ambition to purchase his own trap and horses, and take the rent on a mews, from where he could run his own affairs free of an employer, but the years he'd put in to achieve his ambition had killed him. Unperturbed, Jack had decided to do the same, and he eyed the traps and carriages as they came and went, not with envy, but with interest as he assessed them, and imagined what he would buy should he ever make the money.

A vehicle bought second-hand from a grand house would be a start. A gentleman's brougham, with its crest removed and the woodwork painted black, a take-down cover for good weather, but well-fitted windows for bad. If he couldn't come by one, a reworked growler would do, a once-fine Hackney made smart again with new wheels and fresh leather upholstery. It would be pulled by two level-headed horses like Shadow and Treader, or, when they retired to a field on the marshes, a pair of Cleveland bays, young and gracious.

His business would be called Merrit and Son, or maybe just Merrit's, because he had no inclination to look for a wife and have a child.

It would happen one day—the business, not the children—and when it did, he could employ Will, and call the private company Merrit Bro's. The thought of Will stacking bales in exact order, and keeping a stable meticulously clean wasn't an unpleasant one, yet it didn't seem a fair one either. Then again, it wasn't fair that Will had nothing to do except keep house and read books.

'You working or dreaming?' Bob Hart called down as he drove out, bringing Jack's mind back to the day ahead.

His pipe knocked out, he entered the yard with his hands in his overcoat pocket, his bowler pulled down, and in no mood to talk to anyone or share morning pleasantries. The night had consisted of more waking than sleeping, as thoughts of thieves, justice, possibilities, and Larkin Chase plagued his mind. The cure was to forget about it all, and concentrate on earning a living, and he'd left home promising that, thanks to the second sovereign, he would only work one shift, and bring back something decent for dinner.

Shadow was already in her traces and feeding when he arrived at her stall, and her boy was brushing her with care and pride. The cab was newly washed and cleaned to Jack's satisfaction, and the axle had been greased.

'All done inside and out, Mr Merrit, Sir. The master be looking for you,' the lad said, as Jack greeted the horse by stroking her nose.

'When ain't he?'

The stableboy doffed his cap, and widened his eyes in expectation of the sixpence Jack tossed him, and having caught it and hidden in it one well-practised move, shot off to his next job.

'Days off and throwing money about? Both promising signs to a creditor, Merrit.'

Harris appeared from the next stall with his ever-present ledger under his arm. Moving like a fox about to ravage a chicken, he slunk towards Jack and gazed at the cab.

'Fine cabman was Reggie Merrit,' he said, but praise from the master always sounded like an accusation.

'He was, Mr Harris. Is there a problem?'

There was always a problem. Harris lived for them.

'We might say there is a dilemma,' the master drawled, and made a great show of sliding his book from under his arm and holding it open in his palms as if about to read a lesson in church. 'The dilemma is this...'

Licking a finger, he peered through his half-spectacles in the way a rich lady might examine a servant who had failed to please, and flipped over a page. Another slow scan followed while Jack waited, aware the other cabmen were setting off to take their pick of the morning fares. Shadow twitched her tail, annoyed at the delay.

'Ah.' Harris grimaced at an entry, and Jack knew what was coming. 'Six pounds, ten shillings and sixpence ha'penny.' It was an allegation not a statement.

'I know.'

'I know you know. What I don't know is whether I should continue to wait for said amount, or select another option.'

'I'd appreciate it if you could wait, Sir.'

'Waiting for the payment of debt is not something to which I am accustomed, Mr Merrit.'

'Understood, Sir. I hoped to have an amount for you yesterday, but I was robbed...'

'Nor is the acceptance of excuses one of my many strengths. If it were, none of this would exist.'

To illustrate the vague declaration, he offered his ledger to the activity in the yard.

'Honestly, Sir. A fare dipped me pockets.'

'And yet, following this alleged event, you must have made enough to allow yourself a day with no work. Do you know how many men I have waiting to take over this hansom?'

The number would be in the book, no doubt, but it wasn't a question Jack was expected to answer.

'I'll have some for you by the end of the day,' he said.

Harris ran his hand over Shadow's shoulder and along her flank, and the horse shook her mane and shuffled in protest.

'She's an old lady, your favourite,' Harris drawled. 'One can't help wondering what income she would make if she were glue.'

'I'll fetch you one pound by tonight,' Jack said, thinking of the second sovereign Will had hidden between two bricks beside the kitchen fireplace.

'You will,' Harris replied, and knocked the cab's traces. 'Your grandfather favoured this rig above all others, and you pay extra to retain it. This, Merrit, speaks to me of more money than you claim to make. I don't begrudge a man making a decent living from my stock, in fact, I am in favour of it, as any benevolent proprietor would be. What I object to is an old man running up rental debts to the sum of six pounds, ten shillings and sixpence ha'penny, and then dying, leaving no provision for his responsibilities in his will.'

'Reggie didn't have a will.'

'My point entirely. I, on the other hand, do, and it is my will to sue for the full amount, damages and costs, if it is not forthcoming within the week.' Harris faced him, with the ledger clutched between them like a shield against Jack's greater height and strength. 'A final warning, Merrit, and no more excuses. If a man can afford to take a day in bed, he can afford to pay his debts.'

'My grandfather's debt, not mine.'

'Ah!' Harris' eyes lit up as if Jack had said exactly the right thing. 'Then by the same reasoning, you might claim this old nag was your grandfather's horse, when it is actually mine. Can I make it plainer? If I am to recoup what your family owes, and you are unable to pay it within seven days, your favourite horse will be sold to Castor's, and I will issue a summons against you.'

'But...'

'There, Merrit, the story ends. One week. I suggest you make a start.'

Harris skirted him sideways and crept away in the manner of a yellow fog creeping upriver, leaving Jack silently swearing a reprisal, not that he would have lashed out at him, it wasn't worth the aggravation. Such threats had been due for some time, and when Harris laid them down, he always, at some point, picked them up and carried them out.

It wasn't impossible to make six spare pounds over a few months, and since taking the licence, he already had. The problem was saving. Cab rent, horse rent and stable costs, his lodgings, decent clothes to attract better fares, the basic cost of food... If it wasn't for Will's ability to share out pennies for here, farthings for there, and keep in order what little income they had, they would have starved long ago.

'No point brooding on it, mate.'

Charlie Flex slapped him on the shoulder as he passed. 'You coming out today, Mr Dreamer, or you standing there looking like the bottom just dropped out of your world?'

If Jack didn't do something to improve his income soon, that was exactly what would happen, and he set about giving Shadow and the cab a final check before taking his bench and leaving the yard.

'Some nob came looking for you yesterday,' Charlie said, when Jack joined the rank behind him, and the two stood waiting. 'Did he find you?'

'Yeah, thanks.'

'Reeked of money. What was that about, then?'

'Was nothing.'

'You know who he was, don't you?'

'Who?'

'The nob.'

'I know his name.'

'Yeah, and so do I, and that's because I read.'

Jack wasn't interested in what Charlie did in his spare time. Attend church and drink at temperance coffee houses, he assumed, and neither was of much interest.

Nor was Charlie until he leant close and whispered, 'Stay clear of that sort, or it'll be trouble for you.'

'Stay clear of fares with cash? You gone barmy, Charlie?' Jack joked, enjoying his colleague's closeness more than he should have.

'It's them with cash that rises the highest and falls the furthest.' Charlie winked and stepped away, leaving a void.

'Don't know what you're getting at.'

The line wasn't moving, and Jack wondered if he shouldn't set off and trawl, maybe try Shadwell, or closer to the City.

'It were a couple of years ago now,' Charlie said. 'All over the Herald. It were a nasty business.'

Jack couldn't picture Larkin Chase being involved in any business, let alone a nasty one, and, trying to sound as if he was just making conversation, asked Charlie what he meant.

'Don't want to talk about it in the street, but seeing as you're not married, got some looks about you, and your brother's not quite the full ticket, you'd better know.'

'Oi, mind your mouth about Will.'

'You know what I mean. A lad like that's easy to take advantage of.'

'Will's not a lad. I know he's special, but he can take care of himself.'

'And what with your history, an' all.'

Jack was tiring of insinuations and veiled words, and was growing more frustrated by the second. There were no fares, there were five cabs ahead of him, and Charlie was being an arse.

'I'm going west,' he said, and was about to pull himself up to his seat when Charlie took his arm.

'Caught with a soldier in Hyde Park.'

'What? Get off me.'

'Caught doing an abomination. Got away with it because he had money, and his brother works for the Gazette. They tried to keep it quiet, but when you're in the public eye, there ain't no such thing as a private ear, if you get me.'

'I don't, and I won't get no fare standing here listing to you prattle, neither.'

'I'll make it plain. Your nob, right, he got caught grappling with a private's privates. The other bloke was doing the same to him, mind, and he got put away for it, but these nobs with the *poney*, they can buy themselves out of the nick. Just saying, if he's come looking for you, it'll be because of your looks, or he'll be after taking advantage of Will because he's dumb.'

Jack heard his brother's voice counting down from ten, and inhaled until his lungs could take no more. Letting the breath out in a gush, he said, 'You call Will dumb once more and I'll swing for you, Charlie Flex. Stick to your bible bashing, and fuck off.'

With that, he hauled himself up with such force, the cab rocked, and Shadow had to scuttle to keep her footing.

Jack pulled into the slow-moving flow of delivery wagons and private traps, and waved to Bob Hart as he passed. Turning left to join the wider road, he glanced back to see a flood of passengers pouring from the station, and claiming their rides.

'Bloody typical,' he muttered, and watched the way ahead.

Commercial Road was wide, and its surface decently covered, in most places, at least. It served as a main route from the outer parts of East London, bringing traffic directly to the heart of Whitechapel, and was popular with omnibuses, delivery men and carriages heading both into and out of town. The shops and houses that lined it, and the narrower streets and alleys that led from it, became more and more shabby as he approached the heart of the East End, where the inhabitants lived their days on steps and picking through gutters for market waste, and the walls were obliterated by bill posters, torn and hanging, or new and still dripping their glue.

'Turn Shadow to the knacker's yard? Bastard.'

Sitting high behind the cab brought a sense of security, despite the dangers of the vehicle toppling if he cornered too fast, or someone siding him while reversing from a blind alley. Shadow knew the roads as well as he did, and she knew he was soft with the whip, which he used more for show than direction. A quick tug on one of the ribbons signalled his intention to turn, and the horse understood. Always on the lookout for a waved handkerchief or parasol, always aware that a cart on the other side might veer in front of him without warning, and knowing pedestrians thought they had the right to cross whenever they pleased, he progressed westwards, half his mind on the road, and the other half swinging between Harris' threats and Charlie's insinuations.

Survival depended on money, and the day, when it finally started, started well with a fare from Whitechapel to Highbury Fields. Even better, it was a well-presented and quiet man, who, when Jack peered through the trap to hear the precise address, was more intent on his papers than a conversation. Sometimes, a fare would want to talk, as Chase had done the other night, while at other times, the customer would take his time to prepare for a meeting, or to read a newspaper. On three occasions, Jack had looked down to find a couple engaged in a kiss and fumble, despite the front of the cab being open to the world, and once, on a late-night run home, he had seen one man stroke the leg of another. The companion pushed it away twice before allowing it to stray higher, at which point, one of them had thrown a coat over their laps, and Jack, knowing what was taking place, stared ahead, trying not to imagine the scene he inexplicably wanted to witness.

A cabman saw a little, heard a lot more, but never mentioned a thing, not unless a man was assaulting a woman, or his passenger was so drunk as to threaten to vomit. So far, Jack hadn't had to resort to fisticuffs with a fare, but Reggie had often spoken of it, and had once been put in hospital as his reward for trying to save a young lady's honour.

There was no danger of that with his first fare, and knowing the distance to be nearly four miles, and counting the shillings he would gain, he watched the road, and enjoyed the sunshine as much as he could with his mind a jumble of thoughts.

Larkin Chase had been caught and arrested for fondling another man, but Chase didn't strike him as a man who would take such a risk. Why would a respectable and published writer dare fumble with a guard in a public space? Had it been at night? By the sound of it, the two were mutually agreeable to what they were doing, but had money changed hands? What did it feel like?

Why did he want to know that? He knew what it felt like to grapple with another man's lobcock, he'd done it himself.

'Yeah, but seven years ago and I had no choice.'

It happened in the warehouse in autumn. The ships were in, he was unloading and delivering, and on one trip, arrived with his sacks to find the warehouse empty save for one man. Jack was eighteen then, the other, not much older but in a better position; one of the clerks from the office come to count the stock. The two fell into a discussion while Jack was hauling, and the clerk stayed close, trailing him back and forth. At one point, the clerk knocked into him, causing Jack to drop his sack, sending the senior man into a rage and threatening dismissal. Jack pleaded, the clerk bargained, and in the end, Jack had to agree to a demand; to bring the clerk to fulfilment behind the stack of crates, and quickly too, before the others returned.

Jack did it to save his job, but also because he wanted to. What he wanted more, at the end of the short affair, was for the clerk to give him the same service, and perhaps more, but he was left wiping his hands, and with a painful swelling between his legs that didn't abate for some time.

No-one knew of this, of course. Ida would have thrown him out, Reggie would have disowned him, and Will... There was no telling what Will would have done. Been devastated probably, because he doted on his older brother. Since then, Jack had kept his secret while suppressing a longing to relive the occasion, not with the clerk, but with someone he could trust.

It had never happened, and he'd mostly been successful in keeping the incident, the thrill and urge far from his thoughts. They'd returned in a shot the other night, when Chase shook his hand and sent his pulse thumping. It was the moment they met and held each other's gaze as if they had met before. That was ridiculous, of course. There was no way one man could make another dizzy just with a look, or just by being there, but on seeing Chase, Jack's first thought was of the clerk in the warehouse, as if he knew Chase was the kind to engage with another man and keep it secret.

A cab on its side at Holloway interrupted his musing, and he stopped to ask if the cabman needed help. He didn't, he was quite capable of punching the drayman who'd backed into him, and his horse was uninjured. Jack continued, dropping his fare a little later, and

FINDING A WAY

receiving a healthy tip. Not enough to pay for the day, and nowhere near what he needed for Harris, but it was a start.

The fare complete, he was about to return south when another man hailed him.

'A quick ride if you will, Cabbie,' the fare chirped. 'How much to Benwell Road?'

Jack thought for a second. Highbury Fields, Holloway Road, right into Drayton Park, left into Benwell. Jack gave his price, the customer accepted and climbed in. Apron doors closed, and he pulled the cab into traffic.

It was later, while accepting the fare's change and thanking him with a touch to his bowler, that Jack realised where he was. Benwell Road ran north into Hornsey Road, and two streets along was Queensland. Jack pictured it with terraced houses on either side, and a square at the end. At least, that's what he'd seen on maps. Any of the shaded blocks of grey might have been a pub.

Larkin Chase was doing it again, but from a distance this time. He was in Jack's head, not as a man caught in an illegality with a soldier, nor as a man who'd cast some weird trickery over him, but as someone who had opened the way to twenty pounds.

What harm could it do to drive up the street and see what public places it might contain?

The only harm he could think of, as he moved on, was that it suggested he was considering Chase's offer. An offer from a man who had been arrested for indecency, and who, Charlie suggested, had intentions towards Will.

'I doubt that,' Jack said. 'What do you say, Shadow?'

The horse gave no reaction. Head down, walking in a steady rhythm, she was probably thinking of her next watering. In any case, Jack didn't care what Charlie Flex had to say about anything, and Shadow probably cared less.

Queensland Road proved to be a welcome distraction, but if it was to be the meeting place for crooks auctioning stollen goods, the event would have to take place either in a private house or on wasteland. Dead-end lanes ran off on one side, behind which viaducts waded across an empty space. The area was open to view from two towering railway lines, and judging by the number of locomotives screeching and puffing, they were the busiest lines in and out of Kings Cross.

'Far too public.'

The rest of the street was nothing remarkable, though it wasn't shabby like Limehouse, there were no churches or halls, and no pubs, and it ended in a respectable square. Retracting his path, he took the trouble to look for nearby pubs on Benwell Road, but the closest was too far from Queensland to warrant that street as its address.

'That's one off the list,' he thought, as he headed back to Highbury Fields in the hope of gaining another fare.

It was nearing lunchtime, the sun was burning his nose, and he considered stopping for some shade and a drink from his can. A rest wasn't to be, however, because he was hailed before he reached a cabmen's shelter, and was ordered further west to Regent's Park, 'Always a good place for wealthy punters,' Reggie had once told him, but not that day. After an hour of waiting near the Zoological Gardens, he tried going up west, where he found a fare. It was only to Kensington Gardens, another playground for the wealthy, who, it seemed, preferred their own carriages to hansom cabs.

A shilling fare to Clarendon Place took him by Hyde Park where he couldn't help looking out for soldiers, and picturing Larkin Chase being thrown in a paddy wagon protesting his innocence.

'Poor man,' he whispered, as a cold shiver of memory engulfed him. 'Getting done is bad enough, but getting done for that...'

Another interruption, this time from a policeman asking to see his license, examining his badge and hansom, and wishing him a good day.

So it progressed. A few fares, fewer tips, and by the time he was due to finish his shift, not enough to pay the day's charges let alone give Harris the promised pound. The only thing he could do was drive home and use the sovereign hidden between the bricks.

Except, when he arrived there, the money was gone. So was the change in the jars, and where there was no sign of Will's mystery savings, there was also no sign of Will.

SIX

'How the hell would I know?' Elsie Clarke protested when Jack knocked. 'I ain't your brother's keeper, you is.'

'When did you last see him?'

'I don't know. Last night?'

'You didn't see him leave today?'

'I got better things to do than watch your bleedin' home, what with me own falling about me ears. Ask her at twenty-seven, she's the one what knows others' business.'

The gossip at twenty-seven couldn't help, nor the German family upstairs, not even Old Clarence who did nothing all day except sit on his step smoking his pipe and throwing stones at the children playing in the narrow street. His aim was always off because he was blind, but he heard everything.

'Probably gone on one of his walks,' Mary the knocker-upper suggested when Jack found her heading home. 'He'll come back when he's hungry.'

Will only walked in the mornings, he was always home by the time Jack came in, and he wouldn't have taken the money to walk his required number of paces around the Isle of Dogs.

Back towards the yard, he parked Shadow out of sight of the gates, and waited for someone he trusted to come by, all the time trying to think where his brother might be. As he'd said that morning, Will wasn't stupid, and he could take care of himself, but as Charlie had also said, someone might have taken advantage and lead him on; but to where? Or to what?

The station clock had chimed the second seven of the day when Uncle Bob turned the corner heading for the yard. Jack attracted his attention, and beckoned him to the kerb.

'Seen our Will?'

'Ain't he back yet?'

'Back from where?'

'Didn't you plan it?' Bob said, controlling a horse that was keen to be in its stall.

'Plan what?'

'He came by not long after ten. "Hello, Will," I said. Waiting up on Gill Street, I was. "Where you off to?" He was in his Sunday coat. Looked smart. "Up West," he said, so I had to ask why, 'cos it wasn't his usual walk...'

'He was walking?'

'Well, he weren't swimming, was he? "Can you take me?" he asks, and I said, no, 'cos I had a fare in the shop, and I were on waiting time. "What you doing up West?" I asked, and you know what he said?' Bob laughed at a memory. '"Catching criminals," he said, and buggered off to collar Paddy Mick down the road.'

'Mick took him?'

'I suppose. Me fare came back, and I was off east.'

'Is Mick back in?'

Bob pulled on his reins, and gave his horse a, 'Whoa!' before laughing down at Jack, and saying, 'I ain't no spiritualist medium. How do I know who's back and who ain't? I ain't been in yet.'

It took Jack a couple of minutes to persuade him, but Bob agreed to send Mick out if he was at the yard, and to do it without letting the master know Jack was nearby. Harris would demand his money. While he waited, there was nothing to do but pace, question Shadow on her opinion of what Will was doing, and hear her tell him he would be safe.

Even if the horse had been able to talk, it would have told him what Jack already knew; that he was anything but safe. Will had been keen on Larkin bloody Chase and his hairbrained scheme, and was probably wandering up and down Kingsland Road, or beyond Highbury Fields, or right out at Portland Road in Shepherd's Bush. While he was there, he was spending the coins Jack needed to keep Harris off his back and food on the table. That was, if he hadn't already been set upon and robbed.

'He knows better than that,' Jack said to calm himself, but it was a vain attempt.

Will didn't wander off to unknown places, he had his route and stuck to it. Neither did he take money for frivolities, he was too pennywise for that. He had, though, been easy in Chase's company. The man had suggested twenty pounds, brought them gifts, and left his card.

'Somewhere in Hackney...'

Jack couldn't recall the address, he'd not looked, but Chase had given it the night they met, and mentioned it again.

'Just before Dalston Junction...'

Since then, he'd had several fares giving him addresses, and there were plenty of roads south of the junction.

'Kingsland Road.' The same as one of the possible locations on the burnt paper. 'Number?'

How many house numbers had he heard since starting out two days ago? It was impossible to recall, but it would be on the calling card, which had been on the mantlepiece. Or had it? Jack had no recollection, and had just decided to return home to look, when Paddy Mick waddled towards him wrapped in a dusty overcoat, his ample stomach arriving before he did. Jack had always felt sorry for his horse.

'You've not come in,' Mick announced unnecessarily. 'Bob says you be wanting...'

'Mick, sorry, mate. You gave me brother a ride this morning?'

'Well I might have done, but I'd need a jug a stout for me old memory to be sure.'

'No time for bribes, Mick. This is important. Will's wandered off, and you know how he is.'

'Ach, don't we all know how the lad goes about?'

'Where did you take him?'

'I'm not sure I did.'

'Mick, I'll lay you out...' Jack's tone carried such a threat, the red-nosed Irishman squared his shoulders ready to defend himself, but he must have seen the concern in Jack's expression, because he relented.

'Alright, lad, calm yourself. Aye, he came to me for a ride, and I gave him a fair price, seeing as how he's Reggie's boy.'

'Where to?'

'Now there's the thing,' Mick said, fishing out a cigarette and leaning on the wall, ready to settle in to one of his cabman's tales. 'He's a fine lad, your...'

'Just the address, and quick. Me patience is running thin.'

'Wasn't I just about to tell you? "Mick," he says, "I need to go to Shoreditch High Street. We'll take Commercial Road to Whitechapel where we'll turn northwest through Spitalfields..." And on he jaws, giving me every crossroads, street and turning until we're there. Your brother's a fair head on him for cabbing, Jack. I'll give him that.'

'Shoreditch High Street?'

'Aye, and there, I set him down, he paid me the fare, I told him to keep the tip, and off I trots.'

'Did you see which way he went?'

'Why would I be watching a customer's business after they've left me waggon? Can't help you there, but me information's worth a jar, wouldn't you say?'

'No. You going back to the yard?'

'I wasn't, why?'

Jack didn't want to give away all his business, but he didn't want Harris carrying out his threats either. 'Nip back and tell Harris I'm working a double and I'll settle in the morning, will you?'

'Well, I might.'

'And I'll stand you two pints next time I'm flush.'

'Then, I will, and I'll be wishing you a good evening. I hope you find your wee man.'

Mick waddled back the way he had come, leaving Jack to contemplate Kingsland Road as he retook his bench.

From Shoreditch High Street to the junction was roughly one and a half miles. Assuming Will had taken it upon himself to search all pubs and possible locations for the robber's auction, it would have taken him several hours to walk up one side and down the other, writing details in the notebook he always carried. That was one thing. The other was that by doing so, he would have passed Chase's house, and if he had taken the calling card, the likelihood was, he would have called in. If what Charlie had said was true... That didn't bear thinking about, and no matter what Jack thought of Chase, he couldn't deny the man had had an effect on him. Not only when they first met, but also ever since. If he'd worked the same trickery on Will, there was no telling what his brother might have fallen into. Whether he was still pounding the streets, paying for a cab home, or being entertained by Larkin Chase, Jack had to find him, and he needed the calling card.

It wasn't there.

Nor were Will's best walking boots or his notebook. When Jack searched their bedroom, he also found Will's pocket watch was missing, and as that was the only valuable thing in the house, wondered if they'd been burgled.

'What? And Will taken as a captive? Don't be daft.'

The front door locked, just in case, he knocked up Johnny Clarke, topless and wet because he'd been washing after work, and asked him for a favour.

'Listen out for him, and tell him I'll be back later, yeah?'

'Will do, mate,' Johnny said, taking Jack's key, and limping back into his room.

The sun was setting when Jack steered Shadow westwards, choosing not to drive near the yard, but taking a longer route through Stepney, skirting the worst of Whitechapel, and cutting through Bethnal Green. It took longer, and he apologised to Shadow who should have been in her stall by then, and began a slow drive from where Shoreditch High Street met Kingsland Road. Ignoring potential fares, or shouting he wasn't available, he looked left and right, pausing outside every pub in case Will was either going in or coming out. He also read the house numbers hoping one of them sparked his memory. None did as he plodded on. His heart fluttered harder as the light failed, and a thousand unthinkable scenarios grew in his mind, each one worse than the one it was built on, until his eyes were in danger of dropping tears for what might have happened to his brother.

***

Larkin had been reading a galling piece about crime in the East End when Mrs Grose entered the room without knocking, and proclaimed, 'Caller.'

'Call whom?'

'At the door. Caller.'

'Ah.' Larkin folded the newspaper. 'That narrows it down to one of fifteen options. Study door, bedroom, bathroom? Any further clues?'

'Don't be clever. Front. What do you want me to do about it?'

'How about you glean a snippet more information? A name? The caller's business, perhaps?'

'Merrit. Wants to see you.'

Jack Merrit had been on Larkin's mind ever since he'd been ejected from his home the previous evening. That the man should come calling suggested he'd come to apologise, or had seen the light, and was now amenable to the idea of locating the criminals.

'Well?'

'Show the man in, Mrs Grose, and prepare tea.'

'Tea's at five.'

'Let's abandon caution to the wind, shall we? Off you go, quickly, please.'

The housekeeper left, muttering about being given orders as though she was a servant, and once free of her, Larkin rushed to the mirror to check the lie of his hair, the straightness of his tie, and to perfect the tips of his moustache. He was about to enjoy more time in Jack's company, and there was the possibility the acquaintanceship might develop into a stronger friendship, perhaps more.

Should he be discovered at the window, wistfully watching the traffic?

'No. I'd look like the Lady of Shalott.'

At the fireplace with a cigar, nonchalant, in the pose of a great thinker?

'He'll take me for an idiot.'

At the desk, then, deep in study among his books and papers?

'A headmaster.'

The armchair it was and with the newspaper; a gentleman at leisure, legs crossed, debonaire, and concerned at the plight of those who made the news.

'Mr Merrit.'

Even coming from the narrow mouth of his housekeeper, the name stirred Larkin's heart, but he feigned indifference as he said, 'Oh? Show him in.'

It wasn't Jack, it was his brother, his face red and glistening from the afternoon heat.

'William?' Larkin said, throwing aside his hopes and newspaper as he rose. 'This is unexpected.'

'Well, it shouldn't be,' William replied, hovering by the door, unsure what he was meant to do next, but certain of his words. 'It was you who suggested we do it, and you gave me the necessary tools to accomplish at least part of the quest, which is what I have been doing.'

The words ended, and he stood stock still, unwittingly blocking Mrs Grose's path.

'Come in, dear chap, come in.' Larkin invited him with a smile, and William took one step forward. 'You have been walking, I surmise, for you perspire. Mrs Grose, do we have a towel?'

'Of course we do, what kind of housekeeper do you think I am?'

'Sometimes, dear lady, I wonder.'

'What?'

'A towel, please, so Mr Merrit can be comfortable. And take his coat.'

'Where are you taking it to?' William held it closed. 'I ain't got another.'

That the young man was nervous was apparent from his defensive stance and the way his speech altered. His language of books forgotten, he spoke like his brother.

'Mrs Grose will hang it for you,' Larkin said. 'It's quite alright, it will be safe.'

'On a hanger?'

'If that is your wish.'

'Level with the wall on a hook no less than two inches in depth.'

'How about a coat stand? Bentwood. Very secure.'

'May I inspect it once it's hung?'

'If you would like.'

'I might.'

'What's the matter with him?' Mrs Grose sneered. 'Is he touched?'

'I ain't touched, Madam, I'm precise,' William replied having taken no insult. 'You can take me coat and hang it careful. Thank you for your service.'

'Bleedin' hell,' the housekeeper muttered.

William slipped it off, and presented it to her by the shoulders. 'Hang it in this direction, please.'

Mrs Grose rolled her eyes, and skulked from the room. Larkin had no doubt she would throw it over the banister rather than follow the caller's instructions, but as long as William didn't see, she'd get away with the crime.

'In, in,' he enthused. 'Have a seat. Loosen your collar if you are hot. Would you like lemonade, or some water? I've asked for tea.'

The young man blinked several times, and after some thought, said, 'I am, I will, I won't though I am. No, no, very well.'

'I'm sorry?'

'I am in. I will take a seat, thank you, and I prefer my collar as it is, even though I am warm. No lemonade or water, but if you have ordered tea, there is nothing I can say to that, because it's already done, so, very well.'

'I... see.'

Larkin didn't, but he did wonder how *precise* the man was. When he examined the opposite armchair as though he'd never used one before, Larkin sat first, to show him the form, and William copied, taking up Larkin's mirror image.

'What brings you to my door?' Larkin asked, when his guest was settled.

'My feet.'

'Ah. And for what purpose?' A stab of panic. 'Oh, is it about your brother? Is he unwell?'

'Why would you think that? Do you think he is?' William's face also registered alarm, and Larkin learnt to be careful with his words.

'Not at all, no. I was only wondering the purpose of your visit.'

'I've got information for you, but now you've mentioned Jack, I realise I didn't leave him a note.' His alarm became more apparent. 'I should have done. He'll be worried, he might turn angry with me. He ain't usually, but if he is, and I'm not there... I should hurry back. I've been stupid.'

'William.' Larkin delivered the name sharply, and his guest stopped shuffling in his seat to fix him with large eyes that, now Larkin saw him in better light, were a gentle shade of green. 'I am sure your brother is not angry with you, but if you are concerned, perhaps you should tell me why you have come, and then we can get you home so you can allay your fear.'

'He'll be working until seven. Yes. Working. Good,' William said, and calmness returned in another few blinks. 'Now, the reason why I've come...'

The arrival of the housekeeper interrupted his explanation. She entered bearing a towel which she handed to the guest, saying, 'Towel,' as if she thought he wouldn't know, before spinning on her heels and striding out.

'She's very observant,' Larkin quipped, but William missed his humour, and wiped his face.

That done, he folded the towel, matching the corners, and smoothing the folds, before placing it in his lap and resting his hands on it.

'I'll launder it later,' he said, and when Larkin said that wouldn't be necessary, countered with, 'Then I'll pay the penny for its laundering. I've got me mystery money with me, and Jack's sovereign, which I've not had to spend.'

'Not had to spend in your journey to my home?'

'Yes. Irish Mick drove me badly to Shoreditch, and I walked from there.'

'That is some distance. Will you tell me why?'

William's face scrunched into thought, and his eyes pierced like the flames of burning copper as he shook his head.

'I take you for an educated man, Mr Chase, yet you ask me why Shoreditch is some distance from your home. I can only say, because that was the way things worked out for its town planning, and as I am not the one who invented distance, I really cannot say why it is one and a half miles. I am unable to tell you how many steps, because I didn't count them. My mind was on other matters. So, I'm sorry, I cannot tell you why it is some distance.'

Larkin swallowed, and offered a weak smile as he rearranged his question, and reminded himself the young man was prone to take things literally.

'I apologise if I have confused you, William. I was trying to establish why you have walked so far from your cab to my house.'

'To carry out an examination, Sir, and I would prefer it if you called me Will. Only my grandparents called me William, and hearing my full name reminds me they are dead.'

'Then again, I apologise, I had no idea.'

Will nodded as if to himself, and although he faced Larkin, his gaze moved to something a little to his right. To turn and see what he was looking at would have been rude, and Larkin assumed he was unused to being in someone's study, and wasn't sure how to behave. Either that, or the wallpaper was of particular fascination.

'An examination?' Larkin queried, trying not to lean into Will's line of sight. 'Of what?'

'The Kingsland Road.'

'Because...?'

'Because you said we should.' Will examined the ceiling. 'Although, I think you only suggested it, to me, it seemed like a good idea. This morning, I waited a suitable time after Jack left for work, so I didn't run into him, and took a cab. I also took my notebook and pencil, and I went to Shoreditch. That, as you will know, is where the High Street meets Kingsland Road, one of the three streets Jack suggested might be the location of the auction you think the criminals will stage. From there, outside J D Cooper's Boot and Shoe Emporium, Wholesalers and Importers of Fine Italian Footwear, I progressed northwards, one block of houses, shops and establishments at a time. Once I had covered and examined a suitable distance, I returned to the starting place of each stage, crossed the road, and made an investigation of the opposite side. This, I did, until I came to the bridge over the Regent's Canal. I had...'

Mrs Grose interrupted again, and as soon as she appeared, Will sat upright in his chair, and protected the towel.

'Tea.' The housekeeper gave another of her pointless declarations as she set the tray on the desk. 'Towel?'

'I will launder it and have it returned.'

'No you won't.' Mrs Grose held out her hand.

'Go on, Will. She'll do it. It's her job.'

'It certainly is not,' Grose protested. 'Emily will do it. I don't get my hands dirty with...' Much to Will's surprise, she whipped it from his lap. '... Soap suds and water. That's for an all-work maid, and that, I am not.' She continued to blabber as she left.

Will took a deep breath, shuddered, and stared at the wall, this time, to Larkin's left.

'I had, by then, inspected seventeen public houses, four coffee shops, twenty-six other shops, and Saint Leonard's Shoreditch Workhouse, though only from the outside. I stopped for a sandwich at a public house on Canal Road, because it offered a view of the water—the public house, not the sandwich. The barges were at work, and I enjoy watching boats. After, I continued my journey.'

Will fell silent as Larkin attended to the tea tray. Thinking it might be wiser to let him take care of his own, because he would no doubt need it to be done in a particular matter, he made the offer before he poured.

'You are a kind man, Mr Chase,' Will said, joining him. 'And an observant one. You have realised that I can't but help have things done in a correct way. Why I am like this is as much as mystery to me as it is to Jack, and all the medical men Grandma Ida called whenever she had the shillings. There is nothing physically wrong with me, I simply have a way of doing things.'

'And does that include absorbing knowledge?' Larkin asked,

watching as Will levelled off a teaspoon of sugar with his finger, and stirred it into his cup in four rotations.

'In a way, I think it does,' he replied, adding two drops of milk. 'I assume you are referring to my use of language which, when I am worried or not concentrating, slips back to where it was before I began using words and phrases from books. I do this with care, however, because once, while talking to my grandmother, I quoted directly from Edgar Allan Poe, and she took a nasty turn.'

The tea poured, they returned to their seats, and Larkin dared ask, 'How do you come by such books? I don't mean to demean, but...'

'There is no need to be embarrassed by your question. I know we are poor, Mr Chase. I sometimes find books that have been abandoned, but Uncle Bob, who is not our uncle, and Grandfather Reggie's other friends from the rank also donate them to me. I read one at a time, and store those waiting to be read separately from those I have finished. When I have ten of these, I return them to my friends, and if they don't want them back, I leave them where they might be found by others, as long as they are in good condition. The books, not the others. Do you want to know what I did after lunch?'

Larkin did, but he also wanted to know more about Will's life at home. The man was fascinating, and animated when he spoke, which was something he clearly liked to do.

'I could listen to you all afternoon,' he said. 'Chat away, dear boy, and yes, by all means tell me what you did once you were past the canal. Also, if you wouldn't mind, perhaps you can tell me more about your brother. I fear I might have upset him yesterday evening, and I should like to know the best way to mend that bridge.'

'Why?'

The question was as casual as it was direct, and caught Larkin off guard.

'Um... Because I fear I upset him with my interference.' It wasn't the best way to put it, but it would have to do.

'And you interfered, why?'

Another to-the-point thrust of enquiry, and Larkin's teacup rattled in its saucer.

'Well...'

Will began his question to the wall, but turned his eyes to meet Larkin's as he finished it. 'Is it because you have a fancy for him such as some men secretly have for each other?'

Larkin felt his face flush and his skin tighten.

Will's mouth grew into a wide smile of triumph, and he said, 'I knew it.'

SEVEN

Larkin adopted outrage as a cover for fear, but it came too late. Will had seen through him, and as he flustered to find words of denial, the younger man became serious.

'This is not my business,' he said. 'Although it is, and it is not my place to mention anything about my brother, except to say, when he is not worrying about me or money, he can be quite a pleasant man. However, it might be better if I said no more on this subject, and tell you what I did after lunch.'

Larkin's blood was still running cold, his cheeks still burnt, and all he could manage to say was, 'Yes. That would be best.'

'I continued my inspection of each section of the highway, first the left, and then the right, and I called into every pub I found on the pretext of looking for someone, while, of course, searching for information on the auction. These places became less attractive to me with each visit. Some offered polished tables and seating, and the proprietors were pleasant. If they asked who I had lost, I described one of the Limehouse cabmen, but called him a different name, and some of the landlords said they would tell this imaginary man I was looking for him, which was kind. Others, however, told me to get lost. I found no advertising leaflets with the same details...'

Larkin listened patiently as Will continued to describe each building, who he had met, and what he had witnessed. The descriptions became more detailed, and the story didn't seem to be leading anywhere, but by allowing the man to talk, he also allowed himself time to prepare a statement should Will again mention Jack.

'You use your words well,' he said, when Will paused to sip his tea, by then quite cold.

'Thank you, but they are not mine. Words belong to all of us, and all I do is borrow from people who write books. Here.'

Will produced a piece of paper from his jacket pocket, and thrust it across the divide.

'What's this?'

'Read it. While you do, would you mind if I examined your bookcase? I shan't touch anything, unless you want me to put your collection in a more pleasant and sensible order.'

The bookcase in question was behind Larkin, and he turned to it, realising it was what had held Will's fascination. The books were in a mess, some were sideways on top of those that were upright, some piles had documents wedged between volumes, while ornaments hid others. Larkin was not known for his neatness, and Mrs Grose was not allowed to interfere in the study, except to inspect Emily's work after she had cleaned. Cleaned, but never tidied.

'They are rather disorganised,' he said. 'Please, feel free.'

As Will set about his work, Larkin returned to the paper to find an advertisement, and not any advertisement, but a complete copy of the handbill he had found in Jack's cab.

A Benefit is To Be Held

An auction will be held for the sale of unwanted, yet worthy goods collected by friends. All money raised to be for the purpose of attaining a mouthpiece for Mr H A's son.

In the bottom right corner were the lines:

The Dog and Duck, Kingsland Road
Eight of the evening of June eighteenth.

Mr Hoxton Arty will take the chair.

'Good Lord, Will. You found it.'

'Clearly. The pub is half a mile to the south of here. I didn't need to go inside, because there were several of those in the window, and two on the ground outside. That one was the least fouled by footprints.'

Larkin reread the text. 'I like the way they write *goods collected*,' he scoffed. 'Collected from at least one unfortunate pawnbrokery, and who knows where else. We should take our suspicions directly to the police. Will you come?'

'No, and you shouldn't. Do you prefer alphabetically by author or title, or would you rather like to see these arranged by height as I would?'

'As you wish, but why should I not inform the authorities?'

'The answer is simple, Mr Chase. You have only a suspicion, and no way of knowing that the thieves will attend. Mr H A, I assume, is Hoxton Arty, the chairman, and may be a quite respectable gentleman. This auction, on behalf of his son, might be a proper charitable event. The arrival of the police on your information could well place an upstanding citizen in an embarrassing position, and yourself in jeopardy of wasting police time. Although that is not a crime, as such, they would not take kindly, and your reputation would be put at risk. In order of height, and then alphabetically by author.'

'Yes, yes...' Larkin mused, standing at the window to think. 'You are correct, Mr Merrit. We must proceed with caution.'

'We, Sir? We can't go further with this without Jack. Once these shelves are as they should be, I will make my way home.'

'Will you not stay for more tea? An early supper, perhaps?'

Will didn't answer, and Larkin turned away from the sight of omnibuses and cabs to see why. The sensible, well-spoken man had started to rearrange one of the shelves, leaving spaces for books he'd piled on the corner of the desk, and already, the bookcase, looked less like a physical representation of Larkin's cluttered mind and more like a gentleman's library.

'A fine job, Sir, but will you not stay?'

'I must be home for when Jack returns. I always am.'

'I have another set of books that could do with your attention.'

As Will turned to consider the second bookcase, a shaft of reflected sunlight hit his face and highlighted features not dissimilar to Jack's. Smooth-shaven, no sign of pockmarks or scars, and eyebrows darker than his hair. Will's jade eyes were more studious than his brother's, but his top lip was almost as full as Jack's, his hair the same shade, and his ears protruded slightly. He'd removed his jacket, and stood with his hands on his hips, emphasising his slim waist, and Larkin noticed for the first time, his threadbare trousers were too tight.

Instincts he had tried to hide for years, came to the surface with a fluttering in his chest and a stirring beneath, and he looked away, drawing a breath he hoped would blow the sudden, salacious thought from his mind. Will was as attractive as his brother, and his conversation and his fastidiousness added to his attraction, yet, he was not Jack.

'That's not fair of you,' Will said.

For a moment, Larkin wasn't sure if he was telling him he shouldn't be thinking such thoughts, which was true, or saying that to compare one brother to the other was wrong, which was also true. When he dared look, Will was studying the second bookcase with pursed lips, and his fingers were drumming on his belt. Now he'd seen the mess, the man would be unable to leave until the books were aligned, and as the second case was twice the size of the unfinished first, it would take time. Larkin had given him a challenge he could not refuse.

'I am sorry,' he said, unsure how he could mend the situation. 'I didn't mean to cause you agitation.'

'You haven't. I agitate myself, and I can't help doing so. I would be happy to order your books, but I would be unhappy if Jack came home from work to find the house empty. It is already nearing six, giving me an hour to put things right and get to Limehouse. I cannot do both.'

Will became more uneasy, as Larkin thought of a solution. 'I could send a telegram,' he said. 'Emily will run to the post office.'

'Only to find it closed, unless it is one that remains open all evening.'

'Ah, it is not. The nearest of those is in Islington. I could dispatch a note by cab.'

'A cabman might pocket the money and either demand a second payment from Jack should he find him, or continue with his day as though you had not just wasted three shillings. I will continue.'

Crouching to attend to the bottom shelf, Will's shirt lifted from his trousers revealing a patch of pale skin, and the smooth flesh at the top of his backside. Larkin looked away, and to distract himself, said, 'I will help,' and began rearranging books at the opposite wall. It was hard not to turn in the hope of catching another glimpse of Will's smile, so similar to Jack's, but he resisted and, instead, thought of how little Will had reacted when Larkin gave himself away. He'd not fought or fled, he'd not protested or accused, he'd not, as some might, flown to the nearest policeman and raised a charge of lewdness.

It was possible he was happy another man had taken that kind of interest in his brother. Possible, but at the same time, highly unlikely.

'What will you do?' Will asked, breaking the underscore of shuffling books.

A good question. He would think no more of Jack Merrit, available and willing or not, and concentrate on a task that had lain in wait for many months.

'I shall do as you are doing, and put them in height order first, and then by author.'

'I meant tomorrow. Will you go to the auction?'

'Ah.' The sensible thing would be to do nothing and end his involvement with the cabman and his brother, but Jack needed twenty pounds. 'There would be no point in my going alone,' he said. 'Jack is the only one who could identify them. For that, he would need to be there.'

'Jack,' Will said, and said no more.

'We will have this done in time for you to make it home.'

'I don't want to go home.'

'Oh?'

'I like it here.'

'But your brother...?'

'No!'

The cry was so loud and unexpected, Larkin spun on his heels.

'What is it? Have you cut yourself?'

'No,' Will repeated, striding towards him, his face taut with concentration. 'The larger ones must be towards the bottom where the shelves are stronger, else they will bend.'

Larkin stepped aside to let Will do as he wished, and not wanting to be a hinderance, watched the street, berating himself for causing his new friend distress.

'Oh dear.'

Larkin was thinking the same words, but it wasn't he who had spoken. Nor was it Will, on his knees tutting and mumbling. It was Mrs Grose in the doorway with one hand over her heart.

'I thought something interesting had happened,' she said, gawping. 'At least an accident.'

'Sorry to disappoint you, Mrs Grose. Merely my, er, assistant correcting an indiscretion of my making.'

Indiscretion was the wrong word to use, and Larkin regretted it on the instant. His housekeeper narrowed her eyes, and said, 'Another one?'

'Not of that kind,' Larkin hissed. 'Books. In the wrong place.'

Mrs Grose gave him warning look, and Larkin shook his head.

'All is as it should be,' he said, brushing her away. 'Thank you for your concern.'

The housekeeper, clearly unconvinced, left the two men to continue with their work, but also left the door open as a reminder to Larkin of what had happened before, and how he had promised her and himself it would not happen again. For all her faults, Mrs Grose was loyal and discreet; two more reasons he kept her on. In addition to that, with her in the house, he was less likely to forget himself and be led by his inner desire. She was more than his housekeeper, she was also the keeper of his secret, and the custodian of his morals.

With Will's instructions at the forefront of his mind, and the young man's presence as far towards the back of it as he could manage, he returned to his task. However, as he worked, he couldn't deny Mrs Grose's assumption had put into timely focus the difficulty of the situation. Although he had just told himself to think no more on the subject, Will reminded him of Jack, and Jack had caused such a stirring, Larkin couldn't put him from his thoughts. The longer Will stayed, the more Larkin would be tortured, but he couldn't throw the young man out, it wouldn't be fair.

Books. Largest on the bottom shelf... A glance behind to copy how Will had ordered his, and he found him reading a newspaper.

'We mustn't let distractions delay us,' Larkin said. 'Your brother will be worried.'

'Yes, yes,' Will tutted and folded away the paper.

Back to work.

Larkin arranged the lower shelves. Everything in height order, largest lowest, working upwards, alphabetically, straight and no piles, until, with the top two shelves left to see to, Will joined him.

'You must think I am quite mad,' he said, taking on the other end of the bookcase.

'Not at all, dear chap. I am grateful. I should have done this before.'

'Then I am glad to have been of use. What is it you see in Jack?'

It wasn't so much the suddenness of the question that caused Larkin to baulk, it was the change from one subject to another, and he spluttered in shock before managing to say, 'I beg your pardon?'

'This is a nice collection.' Will placed five volumes together. 'But not a subject that interests me. Your interest in my brother, however, is. What is it that attracts you to him?'

Mrs Grose loomed large in Larkin's thoughts, and picturing her just outside the door, arms folded, and listening, he remained guarded.

'His plight,' he said, because it was part of the truth. 'He told me he had been robbed, he needed money, and he has the chance of a reward which would both bring him justice and finance.'

'I see. Anything else?'

'I fail to see where you are heading with this interrogation, Mr Merrit.'

'The purpose of questioning is to discover the truth, Sir, and that is all I am doing.'

'And the truth is, I like to help others. This, I do through my pieces in the journals and in more practical ways, such as attending meetings. I usually stop short of simply handing out money to charities and individuals, because I believe that would only be scratching at the surface. In giving your brother the opportunity to find and report these criminals, I am giving him the wherewithal to help himself.'

'But you said if he didn't, you would, and you would give him the reward, not keep it for yourself. Although, that was not exactly how you said it. Yet, you can't do this, because you did not see the men in question, and, as far as we know, he is the only witness. Therefore, I have to conclude that you are willing to go further than scratching the surface, and I am only interested to know why.'

Larkin wondered if he had met his match. Of all the men and women he had interviewed, whether young or old, from the East End or the West End or anywhere, Will Merrit was the most exceptional, not only in speech, but also in reasoning. Perhaps, also in honesty.

'Mr Merrit... Will, I believe I can trust you, and I know for certain I appreciate your directness of discussion, but before I consider answering your question, may I ask you one of my own?'

'Yes, of course. It's your house. Have you read this Thackeray? Is it any good?'

'What? Yes, and yes. Take it if you wish.'

'Kind of you, but no. I shall look for it, though. A question?'

'Eh? Oh, yes.'

'About Jack, I assume. Ah, Robinson Crusoe. Would you like that over there with the Defoe collection? It's not the same edition and would rise above the spines of his others.'

Holding a conversation with Will Merrit was like catching a cat.

'Will, may I ask you a personal question about your brother?'

'You can, of course, but there is no need. I know what you want to ask, and I am unwilling to provide the answer because it is not my place to do so. The person you should ask is Jack himself. Jonathan Swift? You have a wide taste in reading.'

Larkin's concern grew, and the book trembled in his hand. 'And what is it I want to ask?' he said, and put it down.

'If your interest in him is the same as his interest in you.'

'He has an interest in me?' Larkin's heart bounded.

'No, Sir. If anything, I would say he finds you infuriating, and he doesn't appreciate what he sees as meddling.'

Larkin's heart crashed.

'However, this, I believe is a natural reaction to a dilemma, and you shouldn't read too much into it. You already have enough to read here. Jane Austen?' Will shuddered as he placed another volume. 'It's just a lot of unsatisfied people paying visits and remaining unhappy. I can't get on with all that.'

'No, me neither, and to be frank, I can't get on with this conversation.'

'I'm sorry, Sir, it's just my way. All I can do is tell you my observations, because they are mine to share.'

Larkin's confusion became concern, but his curiosity quashed both. 'What observations?'

Will had neared the end of his shelf, and spoke to the spines, fluently and without emotion.

'That you took the trouble to find our house, and were keen to be seen as helpful and acting in Jack's interest. That you gave an expression of sad fondness last night when you shook hands to depart, and that Jack, having shared that expression, went to bed angry. This, I suspect, was anger aimed not at you, but at himself, because he is often unable to say what he wants to say. Then, when I asked you about your interest in him, describing it as Miss Austen might, as a fancy, you blushed, and gave all outwards signs of being flustered. When I, as is my manner, exclaimed at the way you were arranging these books, and your housekeeper came running, her reaction hinted at a past event which had caused you some trouble. Forgive my impertinence, but you are as easy to read as Herman Melville, though not quite as entertaining. I can add two and two and make a correct result. Therefore, if you want to know if Jack's intentions towards you are the same as yours towards him, you will have to ask him. As for your intentions towards me, having noted your looks of admiration, I will say, thank you, but no thank you. Now, if you will finish that shelf, our job is done, my ridiculous need to see your reading matter in correct order will be put right, and I can hurry home before Jack arrives and finds me missing, although I fear I am already too late.'

Will popped the last of his pile onto the shelf, stood back and admired his work as if he hadn't just thrown Larkin to the floor, trampled all over him, and left him as stunned as if he'd been beaten about the head and face by a policeman's truncheon. Larkin had suffered that before, and although this time was metaphorical, the resulting shock was the same. He had to use both trembling hands to insert the last of his books, and it was only when he had done so and recovered somewhat, that he was able to speak.

'If any of what you have said were true, Will...'

'I believe it is, Sir, all of it.'

'Then, I can only ask, are you not outraged?'

'No.'

'Why?'

'Why am I not outraged?' Will collected his jacket with a shrug. 'I suppose because Jack is my brother, and I only want him to be happy. Jack's happiness comes first, and he won't achieve it until he can set right certain things within himself. There, Mr Chase, I must leave it. Thank you for the entertainment and the conversation. I must get back now. Once home, I will tell Jack about this villainous auction tomorrow evening, and see what I can do to persuade him to attend. By the by, I cannot be upset with you, because you are your own business and not mine.'

'But still, my suggestion must surely have caused you some outrage. For a man to...'

'Caller.'

Larkin spun to the doorway to find Mrs Grose standing with a dark shadow looming behind.

'How long have you been lurking, Mrs Grose?'

'Long enough,' a man growled, and Jack Merrit barged into the room.

EIGHT

'Will. Home.'

Jack's pulse was racing, his skin flamed, and his fists were balled.

'Calm, Jack. Ten, nine...'

'What are you playing at? Coming here, no note...'

'Mr Merrit, I can explain...'

'You ain't explaining nothing.' Jack stood between the two of them, fuming at his brother for putting himself in danger, and furious at Chase for what he'd been saying.

'Jack, don't be angry, we were only...'

'Will. Out, now, and you, Chase...'

'We were arranging books.'

'I should report you.'

'He came because...'

'Mouth shut before I fill it.' One more word and he'd do just that, arrest or not. Another court hearing? Jack didn't care. 'What's he done to you?'

Will stopped buttoning his jacket, and held Jack with a glare of disbelief.

'Done? He has allowed me to tidy his shelves.'

'Why was your jacket off?'

'Why are you sweating? Same reason.'

Jack was sweating because he'd spent the last hours in a panic, terrified of what he'd find when he remembered the house number. What he'd found was Chase talking about something that should have outraged Will. Leading him on, no doubt. Soldiers in the park. Hands in trousers. Will was dressing.

'Jack, Will has found the location of the...'

'No more, Chase. You say no more, or I'll not be responsible.'

'I assure you, Sir, this has been an innocent and entertaining...'

'Entertaining?'

'Jack Merrit, stop where you are!'

He was two paces closer to a cowering Chase when Will yanked him back by the arm, and blocked his path, his face distorted with concern.

'Jack, please. Remember before? I can't suffer that again.'

When Will looked like that, there was no need to count backwards from ten. All Jack had to do was think of a gaol cell, helplessness and shame. The memory brought back the thought of his brother alone, Reggie shunned and Ida in tears. Although blood pounded in his ears, and his throat was dry, anger was bringing tears, and he wasn't about to cry in front of his brother, let alone Larkin bloody Chase.

'It'll be tea for three then, will it?' a female voice said, and Jack realised the housekeeper was still there.

'Maybe something stronger?'

That was Chase, shuffling behind a desk, probably for protection.

'Will you be calm, Jack?'

Will's round eyes, his look of hope, his vulnerability... Jack sniffed in a deep breath, and let it go, dispelling the pressure in his head.

'What you doing here?' he said, as his knees weakened.

'I found the advertisement, and brought it to Mr Chase. You are so unwilling to help yourself, I took on the responsibility.'

Jack pulled his arm free and faced the man behind the desk.

'It's true,' Chase said. 'All perfectly innocent I assure you.'

'Perfectly,' Will agreed. 'Mr Chase was asking about you because he is keen to develop your friendship.'

'Friendship?'

'Oh dear. I'll boil the kettle.' The housekeeper rustled away.

'He only wants to help us, Jack.'

'We don't need help.'

'We do.'

'Not here. We're going home.'

'We've a chance for twenty pounds, and you're the only one who can get it for us.'

'Forget all that.'

'I can't, and neither can you, because, like me, you can't forget Reggie's debts, and you can't forget the promise you made to me, that we would find a better place to live.'

Jack groaned. It was unusual for Will to use the promise as blackmail, yet he had to forgive him because it was true. All of it was true; he'd made a vow, he had debts to pay, and because of Chase's insistence, they had a chance. What was also true was that he had no idea how to admit he saw the sense, nor what to say next.

There was no need to say anything, because Will spoke for him.

'I'm sorry I forgot to leave a note,' he said. 'I thought I'd be back by the time you came home, but it took me longer than expected. Then, when I found the pub, I saw it wasn't far from Mr Chase's house, so I called to show him my discovery. Then, I noticed how terribly he kept his shelves, and I had to do something about them. Why the housekeeper doesn't do it is another mystery, the first being, who is Mr Hoxton Arty, and what's his son done to need a solicitor? That's two mysteries in one, I suppose, and both can be solved tomorrow evening if you will only agree to attend the auction and identify the villains to the police. Assuming the men who robbed you will be there, and are, in fact, villains.'

Watching his brother as he spoke, and listening to his naïve reasoning was as calming for Jack as a walk through a park in summer, and he could have done it all evening. There was a boy minding his cab, however, it had been a long day followed by a troublesome evening, and he needed to be elsewhere. During that day, though, hadn't he gone looking for Queensland Road, considered Chase's proposition, and been tempted to investigate? More, hadn't he been driven by the thought of twenty pounds and justice?

'Are you yourself, Jack?'

Jack nodded.

'Good, then I will apologise to Mr Chase on your behalf, and we will go home.'

'You have no need to apologise,' Chase said. 'And you have no need to leave, not on my account. I would be delighted if you would stay for supper.'

'That is the act of a gentleman,' Will said, and to Jack, it sounded like a telling off.

'Can't,' he grunted. 'Cab's outside. Shadow needs her stall.'

'She is welcome to use mine.'

'You what?'

'My stable,' Chase said. 'It's not been used for a long while, but I am sure the colonel next door will donate some feed and their lad for an hour. It's in good repair and your horse will be looked after.'

'That is kind of you, Sir,' Will said, and smiling, blinked at Jack asking for him to agree.

'The next thing you know, he'll want us to stay the night,' Jack grumbled, wondering why the offer and the thought held the same appeal. 'No, we should go home. Harris'll be after me blood if I don't get his cab back.'

'Come now, Jack. You know that's not the case,' Will said, and when Jack grunted, 'Eh?' went on to explain. 'I assume, when your shift ended, and you found I was not at home, you told him you would be working late, and came looking for me. It is how you are. I also assume... No, I will say with certainty, that you told him through a message delivered by someone else. I say this, because you have Shadow with you, and had you been working a genuine double shift, you would have changed horses. Am I right?'

For the first time since that morning, Jack grinned, and his anger was doused by relief. Will was safe, he had discovered the way for them to earn twenty pounds, and he was behaving like a gentleman in a gentleman's home—if he could think of Larkin Chase as such. Even

Charlie's gossip about the soldier in the park was no longer a thing of concern. If anything, it was a thing of interest. Or was it temptation?

Jack lifted his weary eyes to the man on the other side of the desk. Striking, confident, well-spoken and educated, not someone Jack would ever associate with, but, if he was to be reasonable, also not a threat. Not to Will, at any rate. If Chase threatened anything, it was to stir in Jack memories of the junior clerk in the warehouse, and if he was to present anything other than hospitality, it was the chance to allow Jack to come closer to what he knew he wanted.

'A light supper, your horse stabled, and the opportunity for you to learn what your brother has discovered, thus ensuring you can make an informed decision about tomorrow evening, and whether you want to pursue the matter,' Chase said, and opened his palms. 'Entirely up to you, Mr Merrit. I should be glad of your company. It will cause Mrs Grose apoplexy, of course, but that's always entertaining to witness. Afterwards, you can trot on home full of belly and full of hope that tomorrow, you may apprehend a pair of villains.'

'Yeah, but...'

'And if your yardman... Harris, was it? If he should he be in anyway obtuse, I will be happy to assuage him with a free mention or two in the Gazette, throwing the glorious light of publicity onto Harris Hansoms of Horseshoe Highway, or wherever he operates.'

'Gill Street Yard.'

'Not as alliterative, but just as acceptable. What do you say, Mr Merrit?'

Will pleading, Jack a fool for his outburst, thoughts of the money, spending more time with Chase, and maybe finding out what Will had meant about him not being happy until he set right certain matters within himself... Supper in a townhouse in Kingsland, waited on by a housekeeper, even a crabby one who had barked at him for ringing the bell...

'Jack?'

'Hm?'

'It would be rude not to accept.'

Will's green eyes blinked above a smile Jack had never been able to deny, and he knew he had to give in. Larkin's hopeful expression also drew him closer to his decision, but there was something else that made him want to know more. By saying yes, he would be stepping onto the running board, and from there, it would only be a case of taking a seat and closing the apron gates, and he'd be off on a new and intriguing ride into the unknown. A passenger in a handsome man's hansom on a journey to who knew where.

'Well, Jack? Will you accept Mr Chase's offer?'

* * *

A large room with curtained windows, a sideboard bearing glasses and decanters on a tray that might have been silver, candles in sticks of the same metal, and a gallery of paintings overlooking a long table set for three with silk flowers in the centre. A housekeeper tutting as she came and went, and a maid whose attention was more on two brothers than her duties. Fluttering eyelashes, hopeful looks, both ignored.

Dishes with lids, plates without cracks, hot food, wine and fresh water. Soft chairs, clean cutlery and a lot of it, three glasses, always filled, warm bread, salted butter, and conversation. Will's discovery, what it could lead to, what it could mean, and how the end might be achieved. A kind man's tales, long and wordy, but spoken with humour and passion as time passed and the past was forgotten, forgiven, and understood.

A stranger no longer a stranger but a host, delighting in the company of two men, previously guests, now more than acquaintances, but not quite the best of friends. Two brothers in an unusual circumstance, willing to say yes to the unexpected, willing to listen, agree, disagree, and talk without embarrassment. Accepted by a higher class.

Time passing, plans drawn, and the maid taking away plates to carry them down the back stairs to the scullery, to place them in the stone sink and pour on hot water from the pot, while dreaming of the younger blond guest with the green eyes and manly jaw. From scullery to the back area with a steaming mug, up the steps to the garden, and down the path to the stable, where the lantern burnt and the next-door lad brushed, more enamoured by the horse than the maid's attentions, even more by Mr Chase's payment which went over the garden wall with him as soon as he'd finished his tea.

Beyond the gate, a diminutive boy, no more than sixteen and too short for his age, stood guard over a hansom cab for a sixpence. In the expectation of sixpence more, he polished the number, the leather and the brass, waited, accepted a bucket from the maid, washed the wheels until they gleamed under the oily lantern flames, and waited some more.

A church bell; ten chimes. The sixpence boy roused himself from near slumber at the opening of the back gate, and voices nearing. Brushed himself down, stood to attention, as a powerful, wide man led a fine horse to the traces, where she waited while he singlehandedly lifted the wood and held it as he encouraged the horse backwards. She knew what she was doing and made no complaint.

Voices in the near darkness, not the boy's to listen to, but unavoidable to miss as he waited for his sixpence.

'A letter for Harris, explaining all. Any trouble and I will descend on him with all the outrage of a disgruntled customer. Remember what we have to do, Jack, and we will meet again tomorrow.'

Thanks for kindness, apologies for a misunderstanding, promises to meet, a time, a place, and a younger man clambering into the back of the cab, leaving two in the twisted spill of the lantern. Just enough light to see a handshake. A hand clasp, more like, and held too long to be usual. A whispered word, the sense of something half-said but completely understood, followed by, 'Without a word to anyone,' 'Of course,' and 'I think we know each other well enough now,' whatever that might mean.

Not a sixpence for his trouble, but a whole shilling and many thanks. It was what he always earnt for guarding a cab, because he took such good care, and it was how he'd earnt his nickname, Shilling. The praise was a bonus, and was followed by freedom as the cab disappeared into the night under the masterful direction of the imposing man who had spoken so softly.

Free from duty, the sixpence lad, now a shilling lad, hurried away with a hand in his pocket guarding the coin. Passing back gates, the count of the church clock still ringing in his memory, down the alley, south, and onwards, past mews, in and out of the flickering lamps, the glow of the city vague above the dark shapes of roofs and chimneys, through the clammy balm of the night to a destination more than familiar.

Reward in fist, the shilling boy entered a back yard where writhing bundles grunted and whispered among the barrels and baskets, where horses snorted impatiently, and the straw was sparce underfoot. To a lopsided door, low for most but not for him, and into a tight passage that reeked of stale beer and pipe smoke, and vibrated with the sounds of laughter, a piano, and a fight about to erupt. Through another door into an etched-glass wonder of discord and harmony, to dart among the dusty suits, the bloodied aprons of butchers and market sellers, the grimy skirts of alley whores, and over the sleeping, vomit-marred drunks of all ages on the sawdust-sprinkled flagstones.

His destination reached, his nose level with the copper-covered bar, he stood on the footrail to appear taller, with his shilling still closely guarded, and licked his lips at the bottles of London, Plymouth, and Old Tom on glass shelves. Or, perhaps, tonight, the wine kegs or the beer for a change. A shilling went a long way at the Dog and Duck, where he was guaranteed service from the maid with two teeth because she was his sister, or from the barrel of a landlord who rarely made it sober past eight, and never asked questions, because he was shilling boy's father.

Old Tom it was, and a healthy glass of it with plenty left over from his payment for more, but it came with the instruction to take the corner bench behind the screen and, 'Be ready to scarper if it kicks off. Hoxton's in tonight.'

Hoxton Arty wasn't just in, Shilling discovered, but he was on the other side of the screen, show-offy as always, but louder than usual because he was celebrating.

As the Old Tom went down, each sip savoured and made to last a full minute marked by the lethargic second hand of a clock with no others, so the volume went up, and Shilling's ears opened. If a boy was willing to listen, there was a trade to be learnt at the Dog, and Arty was the finest teacher along the Kingsland Road. Better, if a lad was to do him a favour, he could expect a good reward, more or less anything he wanted from any shop or house in the city. Hoxton had fingers in every pie, and, being a man who liked to get his hands dirty, did most of his jobs himself. The protection, mugging and violent stuff he left for Badger to organise. Shilling didn't like Badger. Hoxton though... He was a hero.

'Badger played it well,' Hoxton Arty was saying. 'Complete dupe of a driver. No questions, all promises accepted. We dipped him for his fare purse, and that's what we're downing now.'

Laughter.

'Then here's to the dimwit cabbie.' It was a voice Shilling couldn't quite place because it had a foreign accent.

The clank of tankards.

'Heard it was a mighty haul.'

'That it was,' Hoxton said. 'Finest in years. Badger played the inebriate down on his luck, and I, the faithful friend. Best voice and all that. Started up Tottenham Court, so less suspicion, over the river to Kennington. It was a good tipoff.'

'He was a good driver, mind,' Badger said. 'Thick as pig shit.'

Shilling recognised Badger's voice because he had a permanent slur brought about, Dad said, by a fit of the brain when he was hit by an advertising board dislodged by high wind. The painted wood had been advertising 'Dr Scott's Genuine Quick Cures.' At the time, they did nothing for Badger who lay immobile for three months, and nearly withered away. Oddly, he recovered after taking some of the quick cure that had nearly killed him.

Shilling had a sharp memory for voices, faces, and facts; the more he knew, the more money he could make among the regulars of the Dog, and the more his dad paid him for information. It was the only way for a landlord to survive.

'And it's all set and safe?' the third voice asked. 'Only, we don't want no rozzer bozzer.'

The owner of the uneducated growl fell into place, or at least the name did; only Snout used that expression, because only Snout thought it was funny. It wasn't, and Snout wasn't his real name. In that business, no-one used real names.

"Course it is,' Badger said. 'Tomorrow at eight, all legit, all advertised...'

'To only the right punters,' Hoxton chipped in. 'They've got a reward out already, but we was careful.'

'The cabman?' Snout said, and there was a pause during which Shilling assumed the other two were looking at each other as if they'd not thought of that.

'Doubt he could read,' Badger said.

'It was dark,' Hoxton added. 'Anyhow, it'll be done and dusted by tomorrow night. Money made, debts paid, all three of us in the clear. We'll do another on Sunday night where we can keep what we reap. All of it.'

'About bloody time. Where?'

'Found a good one in Chelsea.'

'Ain't we done all the Chelsea pawns?'

'No, Snout. There's this new one. Only been opened two weeks, and already crammed with chattels them as thought they could afford have had to hock. It'll be better than Kennington.'

Shilling shouldn't have been listening, but that was what he did. Where one gang made its plans, so another wanted to know them, and being small, and innocent of looks, no-one suspected him when he sat swinging his legs on a bench staring off into the mayhem of drunken gaiety. They assumed the landlord's boy was a simpleton grinning at bulging bodices and ugly women in pretty hats, but Shilling was much more than that.

However, if Hoxton Arty had something going down, it was safest not to know too much, and dangerous to get involved. Besides, the Old Tom needed refreshing and he had plenty of pennies to see him through to a good night's sleep.

Back through the legs and skirts, and up onto the footrail, glass slammed on bar. Ignored.

'Dad!'

Still ignored. Dad was away around the horseshoe dealing with the fight.

'Ma!'

She was draped over the piano, tankard in one hand, fan in the other, screeching out a music hall mess like a cat caught in a hurdy-gurdy.

His sister was busy with her endless, pointless flirting down the other end, so there was only one thing for it.

Shilling grabbed the dark ale pump and pulled himself up, scrambled over the copper, spun on his backside, and slid to the sticky floor behind the bar. Old Tom bottle, glass filled and put on the back shelf for safety, and he dragged out the stool to stand on.

'Yes, mate,' he said to the first waiting customer. 'What's your poison?'

NINE

Despite the letter, money for the day's hire, the night fee and the promised pound, Harris was still not happy the following morning when Jack arrived at seven to start his day. The Harris yard wasn't a business where any cabman could come and go as he pleased, the master bellyached, as Jack inspected the hansom, and put Treader in the chases because he wanted Shadow that evening. Someone else could have used the wagon while he was hobnobbing with the hoi polloi. What would become of the yard if drivers did what they pleased? Maybe it was time Jack looked for another master.

Master? The man came by the yard through someone else's gambling debt, and although everyone agreed he was good at cards, he was useless with men, didn't understand horses, and thought only of his profit, not his people.

Jack ignored the rants and raves, hooked up the cab, and took no notice when Harris bleated about wanting another pound towards the six-pound debt. Jack reminded him it was now only five pounds, and drove off.

'And ten shillings and sixpence ha'penny,' Harris trilled after him. 'Might as well call it six pounds.'

'Might as well call it as good as paid,' Jack grinned, turning out of the gates.

The line at Limehouse station was moving one cab at a time, and being slow, Jack would usually have gone trawling. Today, though, under a warm sun, he was content to let Treader rest, while he took a pipe and considered the unexpected events of the previous day.

Last night, after Will had calmed him, and he'd accepted Chase's rational reasoning and invitation, the evening brought surprises and hope. During the drive home, and before he fell asleep, he'd mulled over what the three of them discussed, and no matter which way he thought about it, the only thing he could do was accept. Will's persuasion started his change of heart, Chase's promises helped it along, and the more Jack remembered, the more he agreed. There was nothing to lose, and there might be much to gain.

The memories extended beyond agreeing to attend the auction in the hope of making an identification. When he considered the way Chase behaved towards him, and accepted that he behaved the same way in return, he realised that what started out as a fare had become a friend. At least, he acted as one towards Jack, and more importantly, towards Will. There was something about the way Chase spoke, how he behaved and how he entertained, that made Jack counter Charlie's gossip and concern. So what if he'd once been caught in an illegal act? Jack had also once been arrested. They were both guilty of previous crimes, and that went some way to levelling the... The what?

'The road surface,' he said, as the hansom dipped into a pothole when he moved one space forward.

It hadn't been Jack who'd asked about Chase's previous problem, but the man himself who had brought it up, albeit, to start with, in veiled terms.

'I mean not to pry, and please, take no offence, but William hinted that you might have had, in your distant past, an issue with the authorities,' Larkin had said.

They were discussing the criminals who'd robbed the pawnbrokers, and Jack had already agreed to attend the auction.

'I ask this not to cast aspersions,' Chased added, 'but as a way into mentioning my own run-in with the law two years ago. If we are to collaborate on the catching of ne'er-do-wells, I think it only sensible we reveal our hands, and I am quite prepared to reveal mine. Not that I expect any trouble from my previous mistake, because I was acquitted, but it strikes me, if you do have something of a past, you should be prepared for its revelation should the authorities question your reliability as a witness when you identify the perpetrators.'

Jack should have found the suggestion offensive, but he didn't, mainly because Chase spoke with such flowery words, it was hard to keep up. Besides, it was true, and also a worrying thought that his past might be dredged up and his twenty pounds taken from him because of what had happened. He was trying to find Chase's question among the barrage of words, when Will spoke for him.

'Jack won't mind me telling you...'

Jack nodded agreement. They were an hour into their dinner, he had warmed to Chase to the point of thinking of him as Larkin, and he had Will's assurance the man had shown him only kindness and nothing else.

'Yes,' Will said, placing his knife and fork as though he was used to fine dining. 'Jack has had a run-in with the law, but like yourself, was acquitted.'

'Then that is all we need to know,' Larkin said. 'They cannot question your reliability if and when you report the burglars.'

'Ah, Mr Chase, but if you want your cards to be exposed, then both sides should expose the details. Jack first.' Will wouldn't let the subject drop.

Jack didn't mind. The more he knew about Larkin Chase, the better. His previous mistrust had withered, and as they started on the third course, he enjoyed the return of easiness; the same ease as he'd enjoyed when telling Larkin, then a stranger, about the theft of his fare purse.

'I was done for hitting a bloke,' Jack said. 'Yeah, I did it, and I'd do it again.'

'Oh?'

'I've got a temper in me.'

'We all have, I am sure.'

'But it's alright, because I am able to temper Jack's temper, and it rarely shows these days.'

'Well, I will drink to that and to your play on words, Will. I must say, you really are both delightful company.'

'Mr Chase, sometimes you border on the patronising,' Will said.

Jack wasn't sure he understood what his brother meant, but Chase clearly did.

'I do apologise,' he said. 'I don't mean to be.'

'That's alright,' Will continued. 'Jack only gets angry when it's about me.'

'Oh?'

'Specifically, when people are mean to me, and he feels he needs to protect me. He, you see, has the muscle while I, with no offence to my older brother, have the mind. When others insult me, he steps in to put them right with fists, whereas I do it with words. Only, sometimes, I am not quick enough, and would you mind if I moved the salt cellar? You left it not quite beside the pepper shaker.'

Larkin waved his hands across the table, his deep eyes boring into Jack.

'It's true,' Jack said. 'Someone shot their mouth off at the Waterman's one night, putting disrespect over me brother, and I took a swing. The bloke went down alright, but raised up a complaint, and I got done. Our grandma was in hysterics, our granddad nearly lost his job because Harris is a bast… is a bad word I won't repeat in this fine room, and I got slung inside waiting for a trial. Came up, told the beak what and why, and… Well, the neighbours who was at the pub, and Uncle Bob and others, they came as witnesses and spoke up for me. Stood up for Will, more like, and the beak took my side. That's what happens round Limehouse. We stick together, and if a magistrate hears honesty, he'll go with it. Anyways, it was the first time I knew me neighbours had taken proper to little Will, and after that, he became something of a name. Popular lad now, ain't you?'

'I wouldn't say popular. Accepted, yes, though I also wouldn't say I was a lad. I am beyond twenty-one years, but I can overlook your choice of words, because I know they are born from a desire to protect me. From what, is another of those mysteries I have yet to solve.'

Larkin was smiling. 'I do admire the way you brothers are together,' he said. 'And thank you for the story, Jack. Be assured I admire a man who stands up for what is right, and stands against what was wrong. I knew I was right to like you.'

Jack knew he was safe to like Larkin, but said nothing. The man's expression seemed to be saying too much already.

'And you, Mr Chase?'

'Larkin, please, Will.'

'I feel Mr Chase is more appropriate while I am in your house.'

'If we are to be formal, I may be compelled to call you William,' Larkin replied, and Jack grimaced.

Will laughed. 'You drive a bargain, Sir,' he said. 'You thrust your rapier, and I counter with a riposte. I have been reading a translation of Alexandre Dumas, so excuse the analogy... Larkin.'

'Bravo.' Their host clapped his hands in delight, and as if by magic, the housekeeper appeared.

'What?'

'Apologies, Mrs Grose, a false alarm.'

The woman rolled her eyes and slid from the room.

'Your turn,' Will said. 'What was your misdemeanour?'

Larkin cleared his throat, and for some reason, whispered to his wineglass, 'Where is Emily?'

'Downstairs,' the housekeeper's bodiless voice came through the doorjamb.

'Then I may continue...'

'She already knows,' Mrs Grose called, and Larkin blushed.

'Everyone knows, it seems,' he said, and straightened the wings of his already straight moustache. 'I suffered a misunderstanding in a park.'

That's not what Jack would have called it, not if Charlie Flex's tale was correct.

'A misunderstanding?' he queried to test the waters. 'I heard you were found with another...'

'Brother,' Will interrupted, nodding towards the door. 'Mind your words.' Addressing Larkin, he said, 'I believe I read about this earlier in a yellowing newspaper that was incorrectly filed by Dickens. I mean, beside his novels, not by the author himself. If I am correct, your *misunderstanding* was mutual, and although you were found not guilty, the other party didn't fare so well. If I say Hyde Park, Light Infantry and rhododendron, would I be correct?'

'Never heard it put like that.' The housekeeper might as well have been in the room.

'Another bottle of red from the cellar, Mrs Grose, and now,' Larkin barked, and the order was followed by the sound of admonished feet descending the stairs. 'Yes,' he continued. 'You are correct, and there is nothing more to know.' To Jack, he said, 'But now you know exactly who I am.'

Jack met his stare, unable to explain that he was thrilled at hearing the truth, and how he understood the message, but although he tried to keep a straight face, his smile twitched of its own accord, and the action was met by the same from his host.

'Well, there we are. Now, shall we remind ourselves of what we shall do tomorrow evening?' Will said, and picked up his cutlery. 'Or shall we imagine how we are to spend twenty pounds?'

The memory of the evening was pleasant, but Jack still had to work, and his first fare was a regular; Limehouse Station to Fenchurch Street, two miles, a couple of shillings, and an unnecessary journey because the man could have caught the train all the way there. The customer, however, preferred to arrive at work in a cab because he was the owner, and wanted his staff to see he had money. Jack didn't complain, because the night watchman was always waiting to take the same cab, and he lived in the Walworth Road. Another three miles, a couple more shillings, and from there, it was a morning spent crossing the river south to north, north to south, before calling in on Speckle Sam for a prattle broth, and a bucket of water for Treader.

The afternoon passed in much the same routine, apart from a decent fare all the way across to Hammersmith in the west, eight miles from where he'd just dropped off in Lambeth, and it came with a healthy tip. Reggie always used to say, in the cabbing world, one good piece of luck lead to another, and that day he was proved right. Jack didn't have to wait more than five minutes between fares, and with the sun shining on him as brightly as his luck, the tips were generous, the routes not arduous, and Treader behaved like royalty.

By the time he'd stabled the horse, paid his dues, taken Reggie's debt down to four pounds ten shillings and sixpence ha'penny, and paid for Shadow and the cab for a night shift, he was left with only coppers in his purse, but enough of them to provide himself and Will with a reasonable supper.

'I have to admit I am concerned,' Will said, pacing between sink and sill while Jack changed his shirt. 'Are you sure these men will not recognise you and cause trouble?'

'Can't be sure of anything. They might not be there, or it might be legit. We'll have to wait and see.'

'That also concerns me.'

'What?'

Jack straightened his collar in the mirror, and reached for his jacket.

'The waiting,' Will said, dusting Jack's bowler hat as he paced. 'I am to wait outside with the cab, correct?'

'Yeah.'

'And how long should I wait?'

'Until I come out. We went over this.'

'And Mr Chase?'

'Playing the part of the customer, in case any old rozzer asks what you're doing.'

'But what if the horse does something.'

'Like what?' Jack laughed, slipping into his jacket.

'For example, runs away.'

'She won't, don't worry about it.'

Jack was doing enough worrying for the pair of them, but made sure they spoke about other things as they walked back to the yard, where he put Shadow to the cab, and signed himself out.

The clock was chiming seven as they set off. It was three miles to the Dog and Duck, but an hour was plenty of time, and Jack took a route where he knew the traffic would be light. It wasn't the first time he'd driven his brother as his only passenger, but it still felt odd, as if Will was a toff or a businessman, and Jack, his groom. It was easy to imagine Will as a man of business because of the way he had taught himself to speak, but what business was another matter.

The first stop was Larkin's house, where Will waited with Shadow, and Jack rang the bell to be met by the maid who had fawned over Will the previous evening.

'Mr Chase asks that you come up. He has clothes for you,' she said, making it sound like an invitation to a lewd act.

Clothes had not been part of the plan, but Jack followed her to the first floor, where he expected Larkin to be waiting in his study, but she continued up another flight of stairs, and asked him to wait, because 'The master is changing himself.'

Had Jack been Will, he would have asked her to clarify if she meant Mr Chase was changing into someone else, or if she meant he usually had someone change his clothes for him, but time was moving on, and he left the questions unasked. The maid knocked on a partially opened door, announced, 'Mr Merrit's here, Sir,' and descended.

'Shan't be a moment,' Larkin called from inside, and Jack checked the time.

When he looked up from his watch, a movement on the other side of the door caught his eye, and it took a moment to realise what he was seeing. Larkin was looking at his reflection in a full-length mirror, and he wore only his undershorts. Jack had a second to admire a physically fit and trim frame from behind, and when Larkin turned sideways, his profile from head to toe. The underwear was snug, leaving nothing to the imagination, except it left everything to the imagination, and when the man moved out of sight, the impression of his slim hips, manly bulge, and well-shaped backside remained.

The vision, which had stirred something he didn't want to be stirred at that time, remained until the door opened fully, and Larkin appeared, his legs now covered by trousers which he was buttoning beneath an open shirt.

'Come in.'

There were rugs on the floor, a quilt on the bed with four pillows, a dressing table cluttered with bottles, brass lamps, and wallpaper. Where Jack and Will's room had hooks for clothes, Larkin had a wooden wardrobe, and where they had a cracked mirror over a washstand, Larkin had a full-length glass, a marble-topped table, and, through an open door, an indoor bathroom.

Larkin was more intent on dressing than looking at Jack's astonished face. 'I found some things in a second-hand shop I thought might fit you. It occurred to me, that should you arrive at the public house as a cabman, there would be more chance of the villains recognising you. Thus, you may want to look over there...'

A light-coloured jacket, a collarless shirt and a tatty waistcoat hung from the back of an armchair.

'Really?'

'Yes, and I located a top hat destined for the midden. It's downstairs. The area we are soon to visit is on the edge of Haggerston, and my enquiries resulted in the news that the Dog and Duck is rougher than a cat's tongue. It is a favourite haunt for local gangs and criminals whom the police are reticent to deal with. There was a shooting there only two years ago. A double murder. You will blend in more if you look less handsome and more local.'

Handsome? Jack shook his head, collected the clothes, and took the place before the mirror. With his shirt off to reveal his tight vest, and having had a shave before leaving home, he almost agreed. There was nothing wrong with thinking of himself as such, and if that was what a well-bred, good-looking man like Larkin Chase had to say about the matter, who was he to argue?

'You look like a ruffian,' was Will's verdict when they met him at the cab.

'A semi-disguise,' Larkin explained. 'Good evening, Will. Shall we?'

Jack turned the hansom in the road to drive south, and as he did so, the enormity of what he was about to do began to occur. A pub where criminals and gangs met, and where the police were too scared to enter. A shooting. A double murder...

Handsome?

Had Larkin said that as a throwaway comment, or had he said it to signal his admiration? Should Jack have admitted to seeing him in his underclothes and finding the sight... Thrilling? Tempting? He hadn't averted his eyes; he hadn't wanted to. A soldier in a park. A mutual, but unlawful act... What park had it been, and where exactly in it would Jack find the same experience?

The experience of being collared, gaoled, tried and shamed. No thank you, and not necessary now Larkin Chase had made his admiration clear.

Had he? So what?

Jack knew very well so what, but what he didn't know, was how to respond.

'Oi!' Will's head popped up through the trap. 'You just drove past it.'

'Eh?' It was true, and Jack pulled up. 'Less obvious,' he said to cover his mistake.

It was the first excuse that came to mind, but it was a good one. They were close, but not close enough to be obvious. Larkin was to sit in the cab while, if anyone asked, he waited for a friend, and Will was to hold the horse. If the men they sought to catch were in the pub, Jack was to race to the police station, while Will remained to count the people coming and going. Jack would give him a brief description, and if the wanted men came out, Will could at least tell the police which way they went. It was a simple plan worthy of one of Will's short stories, but as it had come from Larkin, Jack was satisfied it would work out to his advantage.

All the same, he approached the Dog and Duck with trepidation, the top hat uneven on his head, his waistcoat too tight, and nervous sweat already trickling on his back. The smell of the place hit him along with the noise. A mix of stale ale and smoke seeped under the door as if escaping the out-of-tune piano, caterwauling and raucous shouts from inside.

The window displayed the same paper advertisement Larkin had shown him over dinner. It was tucked into a corner, almost hidden, and only noticeable by those who knew where to look, or someone as observant as Will. This was the place, and there was no changing his mind.

Twenty pounds.

His heart in his throat, Jack put his hand on the fingerplate, and stepped over the threshold.

TEN

Jack was no stranger to public houses. The gin palaces of Commercial Road with their windows etched with fancy lettering, the docker's pubs of Millwall with ladders down to the shore, even the dark and filthy trestle-shops in Whitechapel, he'd experienced them all over the years, but none compared to the Dog and Duck.

It wasn't just the smell of the place that stopped him in his tracks, the air thick with tobacco smoke and men's sweat. That was standard for a popular ale house, as was the yellow lamp glass that might once have been clean. Nor was it the piano thumping out tunes his father might once have sung on the music hall stage, every other note a dull thud where some part of the instrument didn't work. What gave him pause for thought was the atmosphere.

The blue fog just beneath the low ceiling hung thick with mistrust, as if planning to descend and suffocate the roughly-dressed men slumped at the tables who turned weary heads to examine him with expressionless faces, their eyes cloudy with drunkenness. Despite the revelry taking place somewhere out of sight, the lively piano, and the underscore of conversation, walking to the bar was like walking through mud. His feet squelched on the wet sawdust, and strangers scrutinised every step before discussing him in whispers. Convinced that if he looked at anyone he would be lynched at best, stabbed at worst, he kept his sight fixed on the counter, and did his best to saunter, as if he entered a den of thieves every day. By the time he reached the bar, he'd collected a handbill from a shelf to aid his cover, squared his shoulders, and put a snarl on his face to appear as much of a threat as those watching him.

The auction was due to start at eight, but he wasn't about to take out his pocket watch to check the time. It had been a present from Reggie on his twenty-first birthday, and he cherished it too much to lose it to a mugging. The clock behind the bar was of no use, because it only had a second hand, but he had the impression time didn't matter in this place. You came in when you wanted a drink, and were thrown out when you'd had too much.

How to fit in, and how to discover the location of the auction? There was no sign of it in the public bar. What to drink? Without making eye contact, a scan of the room showed him a line of beer glasses thick with stout. What voice? Those around him spoke with the dropped letters and rough tongues of the East End in accents not unlike his own. His voice wasn't a problem, but what attitude? These were all things Larkin said he paid attention to when seeking an interview in a place he didn't know and where he didn't want to draw too much attention. Jack adopted an air of dissatisfied boredom, and leant an elbow on the tacky copper.

'Yeah?' The barmaid had only a few teeth and even less charm.

'Half a stout.'

Drag, pull, slam, a demand for money, and Jack slapped some coins on the counter.

'Has it started?'

'Has what started?'

'Auction.'

The fewer words the better.

'What auction?'

Larkin had said they would be cagey about strangers, and he'd not been wrong. Jack waved the advertisement.

'I'm here for Hoxton Arty.'

'Oh?' That put a temporary smile on her face, and she bared her gums in a snarl to equal Jack's as she pointed to the ceiling, then to the door at the end of the bar.

Jack nodded to show he understood, swigged half of his half pint, drew his sleeve across his mouth and planted his glass with a gasp. Throwing another coin beside it, he said, 'Cheers,' and, hoping he didn't look as foolish as he felt, swaggered away, ignoring the glares.

The door led to a narrow staircase that turned to bring him onto a landing, and across the way, a room the size of the bar below, filled with more smoke, more chatter, and more men, although these wore better suits and respectable hats. The trick, Larkin had said, was to slip in without being noticed, and not to make an impression. These people would likely know each other. They would have connections in the dark underbelly of the world of the thief and fence, and they wouldn't take kindly to interlopers. When Will translated, Jack understood the warning, and asked Larkin if he was trying to put him off.

'Just try and blend in,' had been his new friend's advice, and that's exactly what Jack tried to do as he slipped in at the back, his sagging top hat as low over his forehead as it would go without looking ridiculous.

The auction had yet to start. Men milled and met in groups, speaking quietly, and huddled with their arms across the backs of mismatched chairs, and at the front of the room, a table held nothing but a hammer. To an unknowing visitor like Jack, it looked respectable, but if Larkin was right, these men were involved in crimes at one level or other, from pickpockets and drop coves to assassins for hire. On the face of it, it looked like a gathering of concerned well-wishers, but underneath, who knew what they had done or what they were capable of doing? Somewhere among them were the two men who'd robbed Jack and made off with the more valuable items from a pawn shop, but so far, Jack hadn't seen them. More importantly, no-one had noticed him. At least, if they had, he'd not been challenged.

'Try to be casual, but don't let your guard down,' Larkin had advised over supper. 'Keep sharp and observe.'

Observe was what Jack did but no faces jogged his memory. One, however, held his attention longer than the others. A blond man kept catching his eye and looking away, and Jack thought he, too, was out of place. The man, who he couldn't help but think of as attractive, was around his own age, had a neatly trimmed moustache, and was wearing a newsboy cap. Nothing remarkable in that, but whoever he was, he was watching the room as though looking for someone, and remained alone and silent, while everyone else met and talked like old friends.

After catching his eye for a third time, Jack concentrated on not looking, and to distract himself from his nervousness, tried to recall what he could of the thieves. It had been dark, he had been tired beyond belief, and it had been a few days ago. Well dressed, a little older than himself, neither fat nor thin, neither tanned nor pale, they had been nondescript. Hadn't one of them had a moustache, and the other had sideburns? Didn't all the men in the room have the same? They had been well spoken, or at least one of them had, but accents were easy to adopt. No names had been used.

The minutes ticked away and still nothing happened.

A missing eyebrow.

The memory returned from nowhere, and yet it was such an unusual feature, Jack wondered how he'd forgotten. The man who had, at first, sounded drunk, had half an eyebrow missing. Instead, there was a scar. That was the one who reached through the trap with the handbill asking for Jack to light it; he had seen his face clearly when he handed back the flaming paper. The other man, the one who gave him a too-familiar hug while dipping his pockets, he was the one with the moustache, and it was blond... No, it was yellowed by cigar smoking, and didn't he too have a scar?

Every man in the room probably had several from brawls and battles, but he doubted many were missing half an eyebrow.

A few more joined the gathering, and some stood with Jack along the back wall, but he recognised none, and was wondering if the auction was to happen at all, when the chattering petered out and men took seats. Someone had appeared from the next room, and the sound of clattering metal drew everyone's attention.

'Nice turnout,' the newcomer said, and emptied the contents of a rolled carpet onto the table.

This man wasn't just anyone, he was the man with the missing eyebrow, and it wasn't any old carpet, but the same one Jack had seen that night. As if he needed further proof, from it came a pile of silver candlesticks, knives, forks, jewellery, and the large cup that looked like it belonged on a church altar.

'Gents,' the man said. 'It's sad when a fellow has to empty the contents of his plate safe to raise funds for a child...'

The company laughed, and to fit in, Jack did the same.

'We're here for Hoxton's boy. Wrongly accused of grievous bodily harm against a neighbour, and a few other minor things...'

More laughter, as if every man in the room knew the full story.

'As you know the boy is soon to be up before the old beak thanks to the long nose of Hackney's finest...'

That remark caused a round of jeers and boos.

'Yeah, yeah, alright. We're here for your money, not your opinions.'

More laughter.

'So, gents, like always, we're looking for as much as we can get from you old lags, so be generous with your purse, and Arty's lad won't have no need to cause any more grievous on any of yer.'

Not so much laughter that time; the threat was real.

'We got to be quick, so get to bidding fast, and we'll be out of here in half an hour. Right. I'll shut me hole and bring out the man himself. The one what's got most of you where you are today, and the one you've got to be thankful for, and don't you forget it. Gents, hands together and wallets open, it's all for the lad, and here's the dad, Hoxton Arty.'

The second thief appeared to much cheering, and collected the hammer. Jack had seen enough. It was him. It was them, and that was the haul. They had mentioned only half an hour, but not wanting to draw attention, he waited until the first of the bidding was underway before inching towards the door, where, as a row broke out over who'd won the carpet, he slunk from the room, and pounded down the stairs only to crash into a small boy coming the other way.

'Oi, watch what you're doing!' the lad complained, stumbling backwards. Their eyes met, and he said, 'Say, don't I know you, mister?'

'No, son.' The boy was unharmed, and Jack hurried on.

Through the bar, head down, hands in pockets, as ordinary as he could make himself, and out into the comparatively clean air of the evening. Will was waiting by the horse, and Larkin was peeking from around the side of the cab. Jack raised his hat, to signal the crooks were there, and ran to the hansom.

'One's blond, moustache, checked suit, about forty, same kind of build as Mr Chase. The other's dark, missing an eyebrow, er... Red tie...' Jack was up on his seat. 'A bit heavier, black jacket. Got it?'

'Of course,' Will said. 'Be quick.'

Jack didn't intend to be anything else, and encouraged Shadow to a canter. The last he saw of his brother, he was crossing the street to stand opposite the pub as if waiting for an omnibus.

The quickest way to Dalson Lane would have been to U-turn and head north, but there was no let-up in the line of cabs and carts, carriages and omnibuses, so he took a left into Laburnum Street and another into Queens Road, nearly as wide as Kingsland but freer of traffic. It was under a mile, but he allowed Shadow no time to amble, taking the corners fast enough for Larkin to cry out from below. Jack had almost forgotten he was there; all he could think about was Will left on his own to observe. Only, being Will, he wouldn't just observe. If the auction finished promptly and the men came out, he would be compelled to follow them, note down every detail of their clothing, mannerisms, conversation and probably get himself noticed and set upon. That was if they came out from the front of the pub. What if they used a back door? Wouldn't criminals do just that? Jack berated himself for not thinking the plan through enough, and encouraged Shadow to race, all the while looking out for a policeman.

'Quick to stop you for your papers, but never one around when you want one.'

The traffic on Dalston Lane was thicker. Pedestrians had no thought for vehicles, and vehicles had no thought for which side of the road they intended to use, cutting across on a whim, and parking two abreast when they felt like it.

'Merrit!' a passing cabbie called, and doffed his cap, but Jack only gave a cursory wave. The blue lamp of the police station was alight, and he pulled up, called to Larkin, and clambered from his seat.

'Hold Shadow,' he instructed, and left the man fussing.

The door was open, and an officer sat behind his bars on a raised platform. Jack glanced at the walls, but saw nothing about the wanted men. How was he going to explain this, and why wasn't that woman getting out of his way? She was chatting to the officer about a missing dog, and the man was writing down every detail about how the animal was always slipping its lead, but came when called, and liked its dinner promptly at six, yet hadn't returned, 'Not even for mutton.'

'And the colour of this creature?' the policeman asked, licking the end of his pencil, and turning a page.

'Golden yellow, I always say, but Mrs Skittering across the road describes him as dark red. Now, I don't think one can have a dark red male, and I know my husband agrees, because he is very fond of...'

This was ridiculous.

'The men you're after are fencing the goods right now at the Dog and Duck,' Jack panted, pushing in front of the surprised dog owner.

'Well, really!'

'Someone's always fencing something down there. Wait your turn.'

'The Kennington job, Sergeant. It was in the newspaper. Twenty-pound reward.'

The officer's head shot up as Jack hit a nerve, but the man's face showed no interest.

'And how many times a day do you think we get someone in here claiming a reward?' he said, taking in Jack's dishevelled appearance.

'No idea, Sir, but if you want to catch the thieves and find Hoxton Arty in the act of selling stolen goods...'

'Who?'

'Hoxton Arty.' Jack slammed the handbill onto the counter.

'Bloody Christ!'

'Well, really...'

A sharp whistle set the woman covering her ears and complaining further, and the sergeant shot to his feet. Two more policeman appeared, chin-strapping their helmets.

'Sarge?'

'Dog and Duck. Now. Where's Smith?'

'Directing traffic at the junction.'

'Pick him up on your way, and anyone else you see.' To Jack he said, 'You're sure about this?'

'I was just there. I can identify them because I drove them to the robbery.'

The sergeant's attitude changed on the instant, and the other two skidded to a halt.

'You're their driver?'

'Yes... No!' Jack realised his mistake. 'I'm a cabman. I didn't know they were thieves, but I do know they are upstairs at the pub, now, and there's a whole room full of men bidding on the loot from the Kennington pawn shop. Silver and everything.'

'Hoxton Arty,' the sergeant said, and waved his men towards the door. 'Be careful.'

'My brother is there, keeping watch. My cab is outside...'

Another blast of the whistle brought another officer from behind the scenes, this one was tucking in his shirt.

'What?'

'Take the desk,' the sergeant ordered. 'Take her statement and good luck.'

'Where you going?'

'I'm going to earn myself another stripe, and cabbie, you're coming with me.'

To say Larkin Chase was surprised would have been an understatement, and to say the sergeant was not happy about sharing the hansom would have been too, but they bundled in, as Jack took his seat, and pulled into traffic. He estimated he'd been away from the pub fifteen minutes, and by the looks of the road, it would be at least another fifteen to work his way through the junction and south down Kingsland. The sergeant had other ideas, and blew his whistle, bringing jeers from draymen and shrieks from ladies with parasols, but most vehicles moved out of the way, and Jack wondered if he might invest in a policeman's whistle to help him in his day-to-day. Not a good idea, he reasoned. The officer was already suspicious he might have been involved in the robbery, and he was fairly sure impersonating a policeman was a crime.

They arrived at the same time as three other officers, and

everything that followed happened so fast, Jack could hardly believe it was happening at all.

The sergeant ordered two of his men to the back yard, and told Jack to wait outside.

'If you're right, you'll have to make a statement after you identified them, right?'

'Yeah, of course.'

'And the reward?' Larkin had stumbled from the cab and was straightening his jacket.

'Got to catch them first.'

'No-one of the description has come from the building.'

'Who's this?'

'My brother, Sir. The one I said was keeping watch.'

'Another witness?'

'No. There's only me.'

Their arrival had caused a crowd to gather, and someone inside the pub must have seen the uniforms. Men began leaving, their collars pulled high, their hats tugged low, and, Jack thought, it was highly probable word had reached the first floor.

'Like cockroaches,' the sergeant said, and watching every one of them, drew his stick. 'Right, Smith, with me. Hoxton Arty. You remember his looks?'

'Aye, Sergeant.' The younger officer also drew a truncheon, and grimaced as he followed.

'Wait here,' were the sergeant's last words, and on Larkin's suggestion, the three retired to the cab.

'You appear worried, Jack,' Will said as he stroked Shadow's nose.

'I am, mate. What if they've already scarpered? What if I was wrong? Worse, what if the police think I was in on it. I told him I was their driver, for pity's sake.'

'Ah, now, there I can reassure you,' Larkin said. 'I was somewhat quizzed during our adventurous ride, and having explained who I was and why I was sharing the carriage, I was asked about my involvement. I was able to describe quite honestly our meeting and your distress, and I gave him my absolute assurance of your innocence. The man currently beating villains about the head and shoulders was satisfied you are not part of the Hoxton gang.'

'That's a relief.'

'Gang?'

'Yes, Will. Our ride was brief, but the officer of the law was forthcoming. Apparently, they have been trying to catch this man in the act for some time. His name, of course, isn't Hoxton Arty, it is Arthur... Gray, was it? Or Spay, Flay... Whoever. As second in command, he leads one of the more enthusiastic criminal gangs of the borough. Has done for some time, apparently, and is so feared, he thinks he can get away with anything. Hence, I assume, the public auction under the noses of the police. I was going to suggest, having heard these facts, that twenty pounds was not nearly enough, but there was no time. Maybe I will write a piece about it...'

'Move!'

Jack plucked Will to safety as a chair came crashing through an upstairs window and smashed on the pavement. The crowd gasped and stood back, Shadow shuffled with the shock, and Larkin said, 'Not a Chippendale, at least.'

The chair was followed by several beer glasses that arced into the road, narrowly missing those on the upper deck of a slow-moving omnibus. The front door burst open, and a hoard of swearing, fleeing men poured out. The policemen's description of cockroaches was even more apt as they scattered into the traffic and around the corner. The flood was followed by a moment of peace, as if everyone assembled was awaiting the arrival of royalty, and then the officer called Smith appeared with one of the crooks. Behind him, with more of a look of triumph, came the sergeant, his hands on Hoxton Arty's collar. Both criminals were in cuffs, and neither of them appeared at all bothered.

'Well, wouldn't you know it,' Hoxton said when he noticed Jack. 'Sorry about your purse, mate, but I reckon you've got your own back.'

'Enough from you.' The sergeant turned him to face the window, as if he wanted anyone remaining inside to see him caught, and when the other two policemen appeared from the back, ordered one to fetch the wagon.

The landlord complained about the damage, but Hoxton said one of his men would see him right, and apologised for the fuss, as if being arrested was nothing new. In fact, apart from the broken window and what came through it, the whole affair was carried out in a cordial manner, as though the criminals, having been caught, accepted they had lost this round, and looked forward to a return match at a later date. When the wagon appeared, the sergeant told Jack to return to the station to give his statement, and bundled the criminals into the back.

Stunned by the speed and efficiency of the event, Jack was watching them being driven away when he felt a tug on his arm, and looking down, discovered the boy he'd met on the stairs.

'Oh,' he said. 'Yeah, sorry about that.'

'You gents was at the back of four seven one, weren't you?'

'Sorry?'

'Last night. I held your cab. Recognise the number. You the one what's dropped them in it?'

'He, young sir, is the one who has indeed set the wheels of justice in motion,' Larkin beamed.

The lad drew a breath between his teeth. 'I can tell you ain't got no clue, gents. You've right got it coming now, you have.'

'What does that mean?' Jack asked with the uneasy feeling that he already knew.

The lad accused him with chilling narrow eyes. 'You'll find out soon enough,' he said, and walked away shaking his head.

ELEVEN

'I think a celebration is called for,' Larkin declared. 'Would the two of you care for a sherry once you have made your statement?'

Jack wasn't listening; his mind was on what the lad had said, more, what he had implied. The reality of what he'd done landed on him, his skin chilled, and he held the cab for stability.

'Jack? You are pale.'

'What d'you suppose he meant?'

'Oh, I shouldn't worry about that,' Larkin said. 'If it hadn't been you it would have been someone else. Mention it to the sergeant at the station, though. Just in case.'

It was a helpful yet unhelpful suggestion because it was the sensible thing to do, yet the fact he had to do it reinforced the fear that he'd been responsible for the catching of a hardened criminal, and one with contacts throughout Larkin's "dark underbelly of the world of the thief and fence."

'Just watch your back for a while,' was the sergeant's advice after Jack had given his statement. 'You've put your address as Limehouse, and that's not on Hoxton's patch, so it's unlikely he'll send someone after you. Not there.'

That also did nothing for Jack's state of mind.

FINDING A WAY

'Thank you for your cooperation, Mr Merrit. We will let the people at Clarington's know their goods have been recovered, and will write to you when it's time for you to collect the reward and appear in court. I expect the local newspaper would like a word.'

'No!' That was the last thing Jack wanted. 'I'll wait to hear from you, and that's all. How long will it take?'

The officer estimated only a few days, and said they would write in due course. Jack read his statement, signed it, and wished the sergeant well. As he left the police station, the woman was still missing her dog, and the last words he heard were from one of the younger officers at the desk, who said, 'Likely it's dead, madam.'

A wail of grief followed Jack into the street, but he was suffering enough of his own to feel sympathy. He could only imagine himself as dead as a dog in a gutter as he returned to the cab, where even Will's cheery face failed to lift his mood. Will was keen to return to Larkin's house, but Jack was not.

'But sherry, Jack. When was the last time you tasted a fine wine?'

'Last night. Get in.'

'Can we go? I would like to, and I think you secretly want to see more of Mr Chase.'

Will's eyes were flashing in the cab's lantern light, and he was offering a knowing grin.

'What you on about? Get in.'

'Yes. Maybe the street isn't the place for this conversation. Four seven one Kingsland Road, please, cabbie.'

With shops and businesses closing for the night, Dalston Lane had settled into a quieter place. There were few vehicles on the road, and fewer pedestrians making their way home. The lamps had been lit, but they left shadows where anyone could be hiding, watching, and waiting for the right moment to exact revenge on behalf of their criminal bosses.

'Jack? Can we?'

A deep breath, and a reminder he was more than capable of defending himself, and Jack relented.

'Just one, so we can say thank you for dinner last night,' he said, as

Will took his seat and closed the apron. 'Then, I got to get Shadow back, and us to bed.'

When they arrived at the house, it looked like Larkin was expecting the Anti-Temperance League the way he'd set out bottles and decanters, fine glasses, and a tray of dead things on crackers. Wearing a gentleman's smoking jacket, even though he wasn't smoking, he presented the sideboard as though it was his first-born son, and said, 'Anything you like, gentlemen. We are celebrating.'

'It's not you who has to clear it all away, is it?' The housekeeper was in attendance, bringing what Jack had come to think of as her uncharming charm.

Larkin ignored her, as Jack imagined he did all the time. 'Take, sit, and we will chat,' he said, leading Will to the display. 'I feel we have had quite an adventure.'

That's not what Jack would have called it.

'We can't stay long,' Will said, straightening the line of bottles. 'Jack needs to return the cab, and have a good night's sleep. It's back to the ordinary tomorrow, twenty pounds or not.'

It was true, and it made Jack think. Maybe the past few days *had* been an adventure, the events had certainly been unexpected, and the most unexpected thing about them had been the man now pouring Will a large glass of sherry. It wasn't the way he spoke; Jack had driven all manner of men from all classes, including the nobility. Nor was it his desire to help; Jack had been patronised by more than a few men and women during his months behind the reins. Older ladies would sometimes offer him a decent tip, and ask if he would like to step inside for a rest, 'Because you cabmen work such long hours in all weathers, and you must be exhausted. Besides, my husband is away on business.' The unsubtle proposition was always met with a polite no thanks, itself countered by a, 'I will offer a better tip,' followed by another polite refusal, and on one occasion, when the woman reached up to hold his knee, a quick flick of the whip to set Shadow galloping.

It wasn't always women either. Some men gave good tips because they liked to show off, or because he'd driven fast, and some because they were genuinely charitable, while others made veiled but intriguing offers as they handed over an extra shilling. 'I mean nothing by it, cabbie, but you are welcome to step inside if you need respite from the streets.' A wave towards a house with closed curtains, usually at night, and the fare smelling of alcohol. 'A fine driver, Sir, and a finer looking man to boot. I dare say you would welcome some gentleman's relish before you continue on your way?' The relish up for discussion wasn't anchovy paste, Jack could tell that from the other men sidling into half-open doorways as telegraph boys slipped out.

Unsure why his thoughts had strayed to those occasions, he took a glass and the offered armchair, and checked the time. It was only when he looked up again and straight into a pair of round, enthusiastic eyes, did the reason become clear. Larkin smiled at him from across the room, and his look seemed to be saying, 'Gentlemen's Relish, Sir?'

The past days had been an adventure, but one that had caused Jack as much upset as hope, and it was thanks to Larkin Chase and his assured manner, his soft smile, and even the way his hair was immaculately parted and combed.

'Jack? Mr Chase is making you an offer.'

'Eh?'

The housekeeper had stuck a plate under his nose, on which were small pieces of bread spread with an unappetising brown sludge.

'Oh, no thanks, Miss,' he said, and sipped his wine.

Will and Larkin dived into a conversation about their part in the recent event, discussing the world of the East London criminal, and comparing such characters to those they had read in books, and not wanting to spoil Will's enjoyment, Jack let them ramble on.

Although he'd said he needed to return the cab, he didn't. The hansom was booked out for a night shift, Shadow was stabled and being brushed by the boy next door, and there was nothing to prevent him from staying longer and enjoying Larkin's hospitality.

It wasn't just his kindness that tempted him to stay. It was the way he treated Will like an equal, the way he glanced across now and then, throwing a pleasing look, and then, a little time later, repeating it and embellishing it with a twitch of his eyebrow. Mannerisms Jack had noticed when they said goodbye that first time, and when he'd left Jack's house. He might also have done it earlier, when he had been changing, but Jack might have invented that image; Larkin catching sight of him as he stood in his underwear at the mirror, and giving a flash of delight and invitation through the glass.

Was that what he was doing now? Inviting Jack to... To what? To make the same signals in return? What if he did? Where would they lead, and did he want them to lead anywhere?

'Yes,' Will said.

The timing of the answer drew Jack from his musings.

'Then we shall. Mrs Grose, would you?'

'If I must.'

'You must, dear lady, for it is your lot in life to be at the beck and call of your employer, me, and to serve his guest, Will, and to enquire of his other guest...'

'Yes, alright,' the housekeeper grumbled, and whipped Jack's glass from his hand.

'Not for me, Miss. I don't drink when I'm working.'

'Quite right,' she said, and downed what was left in Jack's glass before clattering at the sideboard.

'You know, you don't have to drive,' Larkin said. 'You are both more than welcome to stay.'

Will's jaw dropped with delight, but Jack shook his head before his brother took hold of any wild ideas.

'Can't do that,' he said.

'Of course you can.' Larkin was again holding him with a look that said everything and yet gave nothing away. 'I have two spare rooms. One on this floor that Will could use, and one upstairs opposite mine.'

A hint if ever Jack had heard one.

'Very kind, but no.'

'It would be a treat,' Will said.

It would be a temptation. Too much of one.

'The yard will need the cab, Shadow prefers her usual stall, and our neighbours think Will's gone missing. In fact, brother, we should go before they start a search.'

'Don't be dramatic,' Will said. 'It's none of their business.'

'But working is my business, and I've already paid out for the night and made no money from it.'

'You have made twenty pounds. Or, you will have before long.'

'No, Will. Thank Mr Chase, and we'll go.'

'I am Mr Chase again, am I?' Larkin didn't look pleased, but he didn't seem annoyed either, just disappointed.

'As soon as I have it, I shall return your two pounds, and we'll be square,' Jack said, standing. 'Will?'

'Am I pouring this or not?' the housekeeper demanded, a decanter held at an angle over Will's glass.

Pleading eyes from both Will and Larkin, but Jack remained firm.

'No. Thank you for your advice and hospitality, Mr Chase,' he said. 'I will call when I have the money.'

'No need for that, but you are welcome at any time. Both of you. I love having callers.'

'Except you don't.'

'Thank you, Mrs Grose. The men's hats, and Mr Merrit's own clothes if you will.'

She would, but not without a great deal of protest.

'Take no notice,' Larkin said. 'She is more of an entertainment than a servant, and better at sarcasm than servitude, but we go back a long way.'

Will took his offered hand, promising to call again, but when Jack shook it, all he said was, 'Thanks,' and he said it without catching Larkin's eye. It was rude, but necessary, because he didn't want to give away his own disappointment.

One upstairs opposite mine.

The hint floated around Jack's mind as he led Shadow from the mews and onto the main road. The chance to stay in a house with rugs was one thing, but the finery didn't impress him. There was nothing wrong with two rooms and shared a privy. They only had one sink, one tap and one table, but they had two beds, a clean floor, and a door with a lock. The Merrits were already better off than some in Limehouse, and very much better off than most in the East End. Comfortable furniture was alien, and thus meant nothing. Expensive wine was all very well, but who did they have to share it with? And having a servant or two was only good because it gave someone else employment.

A bedroom next to his.

Sheets and blankets; Jack had them at home. A pillow. Had that.

Warm water at the washstand in the morning. Jack preferred cold because it shocked him awake. A hearty breakfast no doubt. There was bread on the shelf, and he'd pick up something on the way home.

No, Jack didn't need the soft comforts of a gentleman's house. What he wanted was the gentleman himself, and through the plotting and planning of the adventure, and the polite conversation that followed, Larkin had somehow made it clear than he wanted a gentleman too. Only Jack wasn't one; he was a Limehouse cabbie with little education and a bright brother who needed to be cared for and fed. It was all he could expect from life, but he was happy with that, and the conversation with himself was over.

Despite the late hour, the Kingsland Road was still popular with cabs and carts, forcing Jack to drive slowly past the Dog and Duck. Someone had put a board at the upstairs window, while outside, groups of men swayed and laughed, but Jack could only see them as plotting against him, and he turned his head away. Spitalfields was awash with revelry in the balmy night. Whores in their straws, as Reggie used to say, referring to their hats as much as the stable floors they frolicked on. Drunks out of their bunks, was another of his sayings, referring to sailors on shore leave. Costers who'd cost you, curates with no cure but gin, and motherless babies at two a penny. Jack had never understood that last one, which, when he was a child, had left a frightening image of children being sold to the unscrupulous.

Whitechapel was its usual bawdy self when he cut through from Commercial Road, ignoring the whistles and shouts from drunks and the desperate.

'Giss a ride, mate.'

'I'll give him a ride, and it won't cost him a pretty penny,' one whore cackled when he was forced to stop where two men were fighting. 'Want me to sit on your bench, love? You can use your whip.'

'Oi! Ain't yer goin' a stop fur an old gent?'

Jack wasn't going to stop until he'd reached the yard, which he did near midnight. It was nearer one when he and Will returned home to find next door and her upstairs on the tenement step discussing whether they should send their men out to look for Will. It was touching, and yet meant everyone knew Jack's business. He told them he'd forgotten Will was going up West, and thanked them for their concern.

'I'll buy you both a bun when I next get a good tip,' he said, bundling Will inside and locking the door.

It was a precaution, as was a check of the window locks.

As was the way he kept to main roads on his walk to work the next morning, and the one after that. As was his instruction to Will to stick to his routine of reading and walking, and always on the same route where he was known and looked out for, but as the days passed, so did the fear of retribution from anyone concerned with the Dog and Duck. Particularly, the little oik he'd bumped into on the stairs.

* * *

The only reminder came a week later after a good day for tips and fares, when, having reduced Reggie's debt by a further pound, he came home to find Will pacing with an envelope which he thrust into Jack's hand.

'What's it say, Jack?'

'From Dalston Lane nicking shop,' Jack said, waving it over his head, unable to hold back his grin. 'Any time I like, me twenty quid is waiting for me, and there's a thank you note from the pawn shop too. We'll have this framed, Will.'

Will wasn't as light as he was when Jack used to hold his arms and swing him around in the street, both boys laughing with delight, but Jack still managed to pick him up, hug him, and mess up his hair, before Will fought back.

'Stop it,' he protested, meaning the opposite, and when Jack put him down, said, 'Can I come with you?'

'You can, and we'll ride in style.'

'You mean we'll get Charlie Flex to drive us?'

'No, Will. We'll take the omnibus.'

'And after, we must go to Mr Chase and give him his two pounds.'

'Aye, we can do that.'

Larkin Chase. He'd been on Jack's mind whether he wanted him there or not, and most days, Jack had expected him to visit on the pretence of delivering a book Will might like to read, but there had been no sight nor sound of him over the past week, and the memory of a bedroom opposite his had all but faded.

All but—but not all. The thought that both he and Larkin wanted the same thing had remained, and with it, in part, the knowledge that what they both wanted was available without question or danger, and from both sides. It was now a distant but lingering case of an opportunity missed, but one which would always be there waiting for a time when Jack didn't have Will, Shadow, a cab, a job and keeping a home as excuses to say no.

A time like now, he thought as he and Will boarded an omnibus, with Will insisting they sit up top even though the sky had darkened and was threatening rain. A time when, in an hour or so, he would have twenty pounds and could visit Larkin and square his debt. He could afford a day off work and take Will to the marshes or Epping Forrest, could get his best boots out of hock, buy a decent supper, and use whatever was left over as he pleased.

Books for Will, a new whip, and some put by to start saving for a better home. Somewhere nearer the yard to save the walk, and a place with its own privy in a private back yard. Not a basement, for fear of burglary, but a place with an upstairs. A house. One of the small, respectable ones along Hind Street or Gough where the landlords cared about their tenants' comfort, or at least, that's what Charlie said, and he would know, because he lived there.

The omnibus rattled and clanged, and Jack looked down on the roads, enjoying being driven, now and then catching the joy and wonder on Will's face. Two changes later, and they approached the police station as the last of the sun faded behind the clouds.

'We'll have supper at Cooke's,' he said, as they mounted the steps. 'Pie, mash and liquor.'

'And jellied eels?'

'You're gross, but if that's what you want. Oh, good, it's the same bloke.'

The sergeant recognised Jack on the instant.

'Ah, Mr Merrit,' he said, leaving his desk and stepping down. 'You've saved me a job.'

'The letter said for me to come to you,' Jack replied, and took it from his jacket.

Offering it to the officer, he expected the man to take it, but instead, the sergeant flicked a cuff, and snapped shut the lock.

Before Jack could protest, the other iron was on his other wrist, and the policeman said, 'John Anthony Merrit, I am arresting you for committing grievous bodily harm against a minor.'

TWELVE

Where some people turned to God and preachers, and others found escape in a bottle of Old Tom or Nicholson's Gin, Larkin's salvation was work, and his put himself to the task of writing with gusto. At least, he did the afternoon after the cabman's adventure, because the previous night, he had been unable to sleep for thinking of what might have happened had Jack agreed to stay. His dreams involved images of burnt paper and flying chairs, cabs, dancing police whistles, and crooks cowering in nooks until a strong man dragged them into the light. The man was Jack Merrit, and Larkin was the cowering crook.

The morning brought a new day and a clean sheet of paper, but he'd been unable to put words on it, because Jack continued to occupy his mind. Not only occupy it, but move in with all his chattels, his innocently handsome features, and though it seemed crude to think it, his strapping physique.

Not crude at all, not if Jack remained clothed in his imagination, which, once Mrs Grose left Larkin alone, he didn't. There was more to Jack than his looks, the way he cared for his brother, and the adorable way he held his bowler like a polite and well-bred youth, turning it by the brim, his eyes down until spoken to, and his soft voice when he replied. There was also what remained unseen; his broad chest, possibly smooth and most likely defined, his thick arm muscles, big hands, and long fingers with well-kept nails. Then there were his large feet that supported sturdy legs, and, when Larkin dared to imagine more, he saw them covered with fine light-brown hair which clustered above the magical, untouchable manhood responsible for what seemed an unmovable mound of trouser material. Although he'd only glanced there once or twice by accident, he was sure the way it extruded at the front was the reason the material was so tight at the back.

It had taken Larkin all his strength to remove those thoughts from his mind and stare at his blank paper, but a hearty walk along the canal to Islington and back helped, and after lunch, he sat down and wrote...

Rubbish.

The first draft of something was always terrible, and undeterred, he rewrote the article about the ways of the Hackney criminal, being careful not to name names or places, but using his collection of old newspapers and the Police Illustrated for material. The following day, and for several after, he honed the piece and had Emily dispatch it. Locked away in his study, he wrote more on various other subjects, all the while not daring to let thoughts of the cabman return, in case Mrs Grose barged in when he was in a state of arousal, which he was every time he rewarded himself for a piece of writing by taking five minutes to imagine Jack Merrit naked.

The nights were worse, because as he lay fitfully abed listening to the house settling, the rumble of carriage wheels, and the housekeeper moving around above, he came to accept he was unable to think of anything other than Jack, clothed or otherwise. His life had not been so disrupted by yearning since he was a boarder at Sinford's School for Boys.

'Jacques Verdier,' he whispered to the darkness. Even now, the name held the promise of romance, and the fact that everybody's schoolboy infatuation shared the same name as his current one was not lost on him.

It had been a tragic case of silent longing and hopeful glancing by other boys, and, ultimately, suicide. Not Larkin's, clearly, but Jacques' who, they said, had fallen from the tower by accident. There had been no note, no apparent distress, and no motive to suggest suicide, he'd simply gone up in the middle of the last night of school to smoke a pipe, and had somehow fallen over the battlements. The memory was too painful to recall too often, but now older, Larkin was able to think back on the man with much fondness, and a lot of regret. Not regret for himself, for he had no desires towards his study-mate, but regret for his friends who did. Perhaps, had they been able to express their feelings for Jacques, the man might have been able to reciprocate, and might have found in them a release for the shame, guilt, or loneliness that drove him over the edge.

The tragedy at Sinfords brought to an end not only the forbidden and secret love between three close friends, but also their school years. Like the others of his house, Larkin carried his grief for many years until the numbing tedium of university wore it away, helped by the availability of men like himself who were willing to speak openly, though very much in private, and those among their number who were more than willing to put words into clandestine, thrilling action.

By remembering Jacques, and shedding a tear for him and those who had loved the boy in vain, Larkin hoped to expel his need to see Jack Merrit, but it only made his state of mind clearer. No longer eighteen, and adultly aware of himself, it was impossible to deny what was happening. This wasn't a schoolboy infatuation, it was an adult one, and that could only mean one inexplicable thing. Like his school friends, Diggs and Ceasar, Larkin Chase was falling in love.

Or had fallen in love, for it wasn't possible to say exactly when the moment happened. It—the feeling of being in love—had grown, as the poets would have it, from a seed to a shoot to a stem to a bud, and there it now rested, waiting to flower. But flowers only bloomed in sunlight, and without Jack Merrit, there could be none.

Nonsense.

The sun had continued to shine after Jacques Verdier hit the ground at terminal velocity, and it would continue to throw down its rays as a cabman went about his journeys, the writer went about his social investigations, and the world continued to grind its way around the sun.

On the seventh day after the cabman's adventure, and having put that phrase in his book of potential titles for interesting articles, Larkin decided he would be more able to concentrate once he had accepted he had fallen in love with the possibilities Jack Merrit offered. That was, if Jack was ever interested in offering them, and if, by some fluke, he felt the same way and was able to say so. Or, if he wasn't able to voice the words, called unexpectedly with a bunch of flowers blooming poetically, and keen to know Larkin in the biblical sense. Once Larkin accepted he had more than an infatuation with the cabman, and once he accepted there was nothing he could do about it, he was able to turn his mind to decent writing, and began researching the running of the Hackney workhouse since the previous master was gaoled for embezzlement, preparing for a piece he hoped to sell to The Quarterly Review.

It was while he was reading back copies of the Review to gauge its style, that Mrs Grose arrived in the study to make the first of what would be three surprise announcements of the evening.

'Caller,' she said. 'What do you want me to do with it?'

'Define its gender, perhaps?'

'Male.'

Larkin's mind leapt to Jack, and he swivelled in his chair to face his housekeeper's ambiguity head on.

'More detail?'

'Young. Been here before. Distressed.'

'Really?'

Jack Merrit needed him. He'd raced heroically through the congestion of the Shoreditch High Street to deliver a plea for Larkin's aid, both emotional and physical. Another adventure was in the offing.

'Put your tongue back in your mouth. It's the one with the coat who has to have his bread in triangles. The fussy one.'

'Not fussy, Mrs Grose, meticulous. Show him up.'

It could be none other than Will Merrit. Not the accolade of his brother, but come to Larkin for help. Fear mingled with joy as he waited, glancing from the window to the night outside, and seeing no cab and no Jack, his mind invented all manner of obscure scenarios, until Mrs Grose reappeared, and said, 'I suppose you'll be wanting tea.'

Will was bobbing behind her, trying to pass, his face taut with anxiety.

'Out of the way woman. Will, come in. Mrs Grose, exit upstage right with immediacy.'

Once the scuffle in the doorway reached a natural conclusion, Will strode into the room, and announced, 'I didn't know what else to do, Mr Chase.'

'Take a seat, dear boy. Why so distraught? What on earth has happened?'

Will's eyes flicked around the room, and came to a fluttering halt on Larkin.

'I am not a boy, but I am, I suppose, distraught, and much.'

'You'll have to elucidate. Please, sit.'

'Yes, I should.' Will sat, wringing his cap in his hands, and staring at the rug.

'Tell me, what has brought you here?'

'My feet. I ran.'

'And for what reason?' Larkin drew his chair close, leaning forward awash with concern and hideous possibilities. 'Tell me.'

'Jack got the letter from the police, and we went to collect his reward. The policeman put him in irons and took him away.'

Two weeks previously, Larkin had bought himself a typewriter, and, being unused to the contraption, had hit too many keys so quickly, their levers had become jammed. His thoughts were the keys, and the resulting entanglement the same.

'Police... Irons? Why?'

'Arrested.'

'I assumed. For what?'

'Causing grievous harm to a minor.'

'A minor?'

'It's ridiculous, Mr Chase. We don't know anyone who works down a pit.'

'I imagine they are referring to someone under a certain age, Will. Who, and when?'

'No-one and never.'

'So...?'

'I don't know, Mr Chase. I was there, Jack was there, we was going for jellied eels after, and then the bloody gavver collared him up and pulled him in.'

'This was just now?'

'Not fifteen minutes back. I tried to ask what was happening, but none of them would say nothing. I had to imagine Jack telling me to count down from ten, else I'd have lost myself and spouted off on one, but as they dragged him off, he shouted your name, so I knew to come here. Else, I'd have gone to Uncle Bob, but I ain't the money to get there, but I'm not here for your money, Mr Chase. I need to know what to do.'

'You have already done the right thing.' Larkin hurried to the door and yelled, 'Grose!' only to find himself face to face with the woman.

'You're thinking Fudler?'

'I am, Mrs Grose.'

The housekeeper took her turn at bellowing, and yelled, 'Emily,' at the staircase. Back to Larkin, she said, 'The poor lad needs tea. I insist,' and nearly floored him with her compassion.

'Tea, then, and dispatch Emily to the nearest telegraph station to hail Mr Fudler on a matter of urgency. His fee will be paid immediately in paper money.'

The housekeeper met the maid on her way up, and both vanished below stairs.

'I have sent for my man,' Larkin said. 'There will be tea, but perhaps you might like something stronger to settle your nerves.'

'I want to know what's happening,' Will said. 'Will he be put away? He's been up before the beak before, and got off with a warning, but if he did it again, they said he'd go down for years.'

'I expect it is a mistake.'

'Can you be sure?'

'Well, no, but, I expect it's nothing to worry about. A mix up of identity perhaps. Mr Fudler will sort it out. Sherry?'

'Without Jack, I won't have no income, apart from some mending, but that won't be enough for the rest, though I don't mind going hungry. Maybe Uncle Bob will help me, but Jack'll lose his card and his cab. Who's going to look after Shadow? No-one treats that horse better than Jack. Then...'

'William!'

The man froze, put his hands in his lap, and became rigid.

'Will,' Larkin said more kindly. 'Please, try not to distress yourself. For now, there is nothing we can do except wait to hear from Mr Fudler. I grant you, it is not the most inspiring name for a man of the law, but he is a good solicitor, and will act in Jack's best interest. If, for any reason, he is unable to attend this evening, I will go to the police station to discover the state of play. You, meanwhile, will have a large glass of sherry, some of Mrs Grose's tea, supper if you wish, and I will either give you the fare to see you home, or you may stay here, nearer to where your brother is being held. Now, does that sound like a reasonable proposition?'

Will was breathing through his nose with short, rapid puffs, but they slowed as he glanced from the rug to Larkin, and from him to the sideboard, and when Larkin handed him a glass of sherry, he took it, and became less agitated. He must have been processing Larkin's words as he sipped, nodding to himself one moment, and then becoming quizzical the next, until, with the glass half emptied, he said, 'Very well, and thank you,' and his manner changed.

'Good. I think it is for the best.'

'You are correct, Sir, there is nothing to be done until we know more, and I am grateful to you for offering to investigate.'

'It's what I like to do,' Larkin smiled. 'There is no point in conjecture until the facts are known.'

'I agree.'

'So, all we can do is wait for our tea and a message from my man. Then, once we know what's what, we can plan our next step.'

'Thank you. You are very kind to think as I do.'

'Logic, Will. It's all one needs.'

Logic, tea and a message from Mr Fudler. Beneath the surface, however, Larkin needed to know as much as Will, and was, without showing it, just as agitated.

It was an hour later, with the tea tray cleared, and as he poured Will another drink, that Larkin received his second announcement.

Not as surprising as the first, this one came in the form of a telegram delivered to Emily, thence to Mrs Grose, and from there, to Larkin. Taking his turn, he read it to Will.

'From Mr Fulder,' he said. 'It reads, "Calling at DLPS on way to dogs. Unable to visit after but will dispatch news and act on instruction tomorrow. Regards."'

'Dogs?'

'He breeds hounds on the Hackney marshes. It seems we caught him in time, and he will let me know what he discovers. We can then decide what is best to do next. DLPS would be Dalston Lane Police Station.'

'I assumed.'

'Tell me, Will, does this news make you less anxious?'

'It does, but I can't help thinking of Jack chained in a cell. Will they feed him?'

'I imagine so. It is not a pleasant thought, but your brother is a strong man, and I think shackles are currently out of fashion.'

'He is also an innocent man. If he'd been in another altercation, he would have told me. I can't think when he would have fallen from the rails and hit someone, particularly not a minor. What age is a minor?'

'I am not exactly sure, but I assume the alleged victim in question was young.'

'Like many things about my brother, it makes no sense.'

Unable to resist investigating the statement, and without feeling he was prying, Larkin asked Will to explain.

'Only that Jack does things without explanation,' he said, and when Larkin shrugged, shuffled in his chair, and sipped his drink before continuing. 'I don't mean when his temper flares, because there is always a good reason for that, and I have trained him to count as a way of calming his anger. He is not a violent man by nature, but he does carry a burden, and now and then, he needs to play the kettle and release his steam. We lost our grandparents these past couple of years, and before them, our father. He died on the stage of the Shoreditch Music Hall singing a duet with Marie Lloyd, but I expect she was more upset than we were. I never really knew him, but Jack did. All that, and trying to keep us out of debtors' prison... Well, sometimes, he angers for no apparent reason, but I suspect the reason is me.'

'Why should it be you?'

'Because I am the burden he must carry. Believe me, Sir, I want to work and be normal like other young men, but there are so few people who understand my ways, and I am unable to change them. If I try, and I have on many occasions, I become the kettle, but one whose lid is welded shut. People say there is something wrong with me, and maybe there is, but despite an array of treatments, no-one has been able to tell me what.'

'Treatments? I can't imagine what would be the treatment for meticulousness.'

'They have called it many things, but never that.' Will gazed towards the curtains. 'I have an engrossment, one doctor said, while another accused me of being delusional. Grandma Ida was always careful who she took me to, for fear of me being sent to an institution, because some doctors, quacks, I'd call them, said I suffer from a disorganised mind which can only be treated with ice baths and restraints.'

Larkin gasped at the thought. Will was too gentle and too erudite to be suffering a condition of the mind; he was, as he had said, simply precise, and there was nothing wrong with wanting to put books in a neat order, or have bread cut into triangles.

'That would be terrible,' he said. 'And quite unjustified. You have a lively, healthy mind.'

'And a compulsion for things to be just so,' Will said, and moved the coaster on the table beside his chair so it was in line with the edge. 'Case in point.'

'As I said, nothing wrong with that.'

'Except it means I am unable to work unless it is something which satisfies my need for precision and detail, accuracy and straight lines, neatness, and whatever else might be in there. Jack tried getting me a job at the docks, but I failed at that. I clean my neighbour's houses, but can't ask them for money, because it is not right, though I do make a few pennies from sewing for those along the street. So, Jack is now our only breadwinner, and the hours he puts in he puts in for me. The least I can do is repay his kindness.' In a move that took Larkin completely by surprise, Will put down his glass, rested forward with his forearms on his knees and said, 'He thinks very highly of you, Mr Chase. One might even think he was infatuated.'

Larkin spluttered on his sherry, and tried to think of a way to dismiss the statement which had left a question begging to be asked.

'Good Lord,' he said, finding it hard to swallow. 'What a thing.'

'I only say this because he won't,' Will went on as though the subject of a man's infatuation with another was acceptable. 'It's the same as when I apologise for him because he's too proud to do so. He's also too shy, you see, but I know him better than he thinks, and care more for him than I show, and knowing what he holds inside, I feel no compunction about telling you.'

Larkin's glass shook as he placed it, doing his best to mirror the way Will had placed his, so as to cause the young man no upset.

'Telling me what?'

Will's mouth dropped open, and he glanced at the ceiling, then at the door. 'Of course,' he said, and nodded vigorously. 'You.'

'Me?'

'If my brother did lash out at someone, it would have been for a reason, though I repeat, he would never have hit a child. That reason can only be you.'

Larkin's imaginary typewriter keys had been clacking away in harmony with the conversation, but now, they struck the roller all at once, as tangled as a game of Jack straws.

'I don't understand,' he said.

'Mr Chase, you have been on Jack's mind since he met you. I believe I insinuated as much the other day. I did my best to have us stay the night when you invited us, with the intention of retiring to my room so the two of you could be alone. There is much to be said between you, even your housekeeper can tell that, and, for my part, I wish the pair of you had got on and said it. If you had, Jack would not have been so distracted since the incident at the Dog and Duck, and would, I believe, have found the kind of happiness he craves, as much as I crave to put your desk chair at a correct angle. May I?'

Stunned, Larkin waved towards it and watched as Will not only straightened the chair, but also every item on the desk. That done, he removed a kink from the curtains before returning to his seat.

'I assume your silence comes from knowing that what I am suggesting is illegal,' Will said, as if there had been no break in his speech. 'Or, you may find it immoral, but I think not. Had you, you would have already sent me home. Now...' Leaning forward again, he took on the air of a friendly schoolmaster. 'You may say this is not my business, and from your side, you would be correct. However, Jack is my business. I notice things, Mr Chase, it is part of my preciseness, and can't be helped. You, I notice, have words you want to say to my brother, and the same in reverse. Once this current mess is shown up for the sham it is, I suggest the two of you have a good old, honest chat. Believe me, you have nothing to fear. Oh, was that the door? Perhaps it is news.'

Will was on his feet and helping himself to the window view before Larkin could stumble upon any words. He was still processing Will's very welcome insinuation when Mrs Grose discourteously delivered a letter, 'By the courtesy of hand.'

Larkin dismissed her, and for added security, closed the door. Not even Mrs Grose could hear through walls.

'Yes, Mr Chase? What does he say?'

Larkin took a deep breath as his heart sank. Not only did it founder, but it also bled for the fate of both brothers.

'Mr Fudler reports that Jack has indeed been arrested for assault, and will be before the magistrate on Monday. Until then, there is nothing to be done, and he will be held at the gaol. My man can only have a few minutes with him before the hearing, and, from what he could glean, the prospects do not look good. I am sorry, Will, but at least, he says, he has paid for Jack to be fed and as comfortable as a few shillings will allow.'

Will was crying silent tears, and staring at nothing. Larkin stood useless, wanting to comfort him, but not brave enough to do so, and for all his verbosity, no words came.

It was only when there was a knock on the door, did Will sniff himself back to attention, and Larkin was able to speak.

'Admire the far bookcase,' he whispered. 'If you want to keep your distress from my dragon.'

Will gave a mild laugh, and did as Larkin suggested.

'Come in.'

Mrs Grose already had. 'I don't know what you're up to,' she said, studying a card, 'but you got another bloody caller. That's the second tonight.'

What with Will, a telegraph boy, and the hand-delivered note from Fudler, it was actually the fourth, but it was never wise to correct the dragon.

'And do we have a gender, purpose... anything of use?'

'Ask him yourself. He followed me up.'

Intrigued and concerned, Larkin told her to show the caller in, and with no time to pose himself, stayed between the door and Will in case it was a policeman.

If it was, he wasn't in uniform. The housekeeper admitted a well-dressed man no older than Larkin, and the first thing he noticed was his moustache. The observation was followed by the newsboy cap he held, and a battered knapsack slung from one shoulder. Larkin thought he recognised him, but Will definitely did.

'I've seen you before,' he said, facing the room with his eyes now dry. 'You were outside the Dog and Duck the other night watching the fracas.'

'I was,' the stranger said. 'And now I am here, and I am here because you need my help, and I need yours.'

Larkin bristled at the intrusion and the stranger's forwardness, although he couldn't help but admire his features and confidence.

'Help, Sir? First, your purpose and your name.'

'My purpose, Mr Chase, is to save Jack Merrit from being wrongly convicted. As for my credentials...' He snatched the calling card from Mrs Grose, thereby proving he had pluck, and handed it to Larkin.

It was white, embossed, and expensive, and above an address were the words, *James Joseph Wright, Private Investigator*.

THIRTEEN

'Ten, nine, eight...'

There had been no assault. Who'd brought the charge?

'Seven, six...'

Stairs to a badly lit passage smelling of mould. An iron door, a narrow slit with bars.

'Five, four...' It wasn't working, but he mustn't lash out.

What would happen to Will?

'Three, two...'

The countdown concluded with the slam of metal that echoed until only the hiss of a solitary gas lamp and Jack's deep breathing remained.

The high window let in no light, leaving the bench and a bucket as murky forms, and much as he wanted to destroy something, he'd need both of them. At least he was alone in the cell. Alone with no idea how he came to be there, and no information other than he'd be up before the magistrate on Monday, whenever Monday was. Time, the world, everything around him stopped the moment the irons went on his wrists. It happened too fast, he'd not been told who'd accused him, and been given no chance to ask before they dragged him into the charge room. There was time only to shout a name to Will, left behind and panicking.

It was the first name that came to mind, but it made sense. Larkin lived nearby, he would know someone who might help, and he would look after Will.

As for Jack...

There was no point wondering about the time, or thinking about his hunger, what Harris would say, how he'd lose his job... There was no point wondering what Will was doing, how Larkin would have reacted, or what was happening beyond the cell doors. The world turned, and time passed, but they were turning and passing without him. Jack Merrit was no longer a part of existence; he was a suspected criminal kept below ground in near-darkness, and facing years inside, so what did it matter what happened beyond the four, grimy walls? The world was no longer his business.

Pacing, he remembered from before, was a way of passing the time. As was counting the bricks or stones, the bars at the window and in the door, though that wouldn't take long. It would take longer to read the tatty bible chained to the wall, except it had pages missing, no doubt used in the bucket which, he noticed, had no lid. Measuring the floor with one foot before the other in neat rows back and forth? That could take half an hour, especially if he recounted until he reached the same total three times in a row. Anything to keep boredom away; anything to keep his mind occupied so he didn't worry about Will.

Impossible.

The gas flickered, his eyes adjusted to the gloom, and he lay, staring at the ceiling. Waiting.

Revenge from the crooks he'd identified? It was the only explanation. How had they engineered it? Who had they set up to set him up? How could they get away with it? How could *he* get away with it?

There was nothing to get away with; he'd done nothing wrong.

'Ten, nine, eight...'

Waiting.

They'd send him down for two years. Hard labour. The crippling treadmill, oakum, sacks. Will made homeless. Will starving.

'Seven, six...'

Waiting.

Was it time to sleep? Did they put the lamp out or did it stay hissing and stinking all night? Where was his brother now? Had Larkin come to offer bail? Could he do that at this time of night? What time was it?

Waiting.

'Five, four...'

Resigned and fearful, but less angry. What was the point?

At least he'd not heard a rat. Yet.

In fact, Jack heard nothing until he was roused from the bench by the sound of approaching footsteps and jangling keys, and knowing the form, stood with his face to the wall furthest from the door. The panel slid open, then closed, and the keys rattled.

'Turn.'

Someone stood silhouetted in the doorway, a policeman for sure, but which one? That didn't matter either, what mattered was he was there to tell Jack he'd been let out on bail.

'You've got friends,' the silhouette said, and Jack's hopes rose. 'Someone's paid for a blanket and supper.'

Which meant he was not to be freed until at least the morning. It could only have been Larkin, which meant Will had been to him, and that meant Will would be safe, for now. That was something.

The blanket was his only comfort, and he used it to lie on because the cell was already stifling, and the bench was made of stone. The supper, when it came, was passable; his benefactor had money.

Was Larkin Chase now his benefactor? Was Jack now indebted to him for trying to help? How had he come to rely on a man he'd met only a few days ago? There were too many questions hovering in the shadows of the arched brickwork, each one jostling for a place in the queue, and none of them came with answers. Instead of torturing himself by looking for solutions that didn't exist, he turned his mind to happier times. Picnics on the marshes with Reggie and Ida, Will fishing for eels, watching the cattle herders drive their animals towards market, the fresh air away from the city. Tall ships gliding on the Thames where wherries weaved among the tugs and barges, the creak of ropes, the rumble of dockside carts. Maybe they'd have him back at West India once this was over. That was as unlikely as Larkin wanting to see him again.

Why should that matter?

That was a question he could answer only by being honest with himself, and with no-one else to hear his thoughts, he could be. The man was attractive, he was kind, and he was the same as Jack, of that, he was certain. As soon as Larkin appeared out of the darkness on a Kennington street and said, 'I am hoping I find you available and willing,' Jack knew his words had two meanings, and he was a... What did they call it? A kindred spirit?

A spare room opposite his, welcome to stay for the night, Will upstairs in comfort, Jack and Larkin alone. What could have been.

Sleep waded through the disjointed thoughts, but it took a while to arrive. When it did, it had to fight with the unforgiving bench, the clammy heat, and occasional shouts from somewhere else, but it came.

It also stayed, and only left when keys rattled at the door, and an officer delivered bread and water. There was no ceremony, and he slammed the ironwork, leaving Jack in a stream of murky daylight that squeezed through the high window.

Time passed. More waiting, not knowing, imagining only the worst, and counting down from ten when he thought of the injustice, but, just when he was considering beating the wall, the keys clanked again, and the same officer reappeared.

'Visitor,' he said. 'Hands.'

Jack held out his arms, received the irons, and followed instructions.

'Walk ahead. Up the stairs. Door on the right. No nasty business.'

The room was no bigger than the cell he'd left, but it had a more successful window. A cap lay on a table beside a knapsack, and standing behind it was a face he thought he knew. A blond man with a moustache. The out-of-place observer from the Dog and Duck.

'You can take those off,' the stranger said, and it wasn't until the officer removed the cuffs that Jack understood what he meant. 'My colleague will be here before long. Show him straight in.'

'I can only give you ten minutes with the prisoner, Sir.'

'Rubbish. You will give me as long as we need to free this innocent man.'

'That's not the way we do it...'

'Officer,' the man barked, and leaning over the table, scrutinised the policeman's collar and made a note in a book. 'Officer one seven two, there is no need to tell me how you do things. What's more important is that you know how I do them. For a start, I report any breaches in protocol and law, and in the few minutes I have been here, I have noticed three. When my colleague arrives, bring him in, and provide us with tea. You may go.'

The policeman's mouth opened and closed a few times, but he backed away, making a point of showing his annoyance by slamming the door.

'Bloody hell, he thinks he's worth more than his ruddy job,' the blond man said, rummaging in his knapsack. When he'd taken out some papers and placed them on the desk, he looked at Jack as if he'd forgotten he was there, blinked a few times, and said, 'You, Mr Merrit, are both a pain in the arse and a godsend. Have a seat.'

Jack had no idea who this man was, but he wasn't going to mess with him. He sat and waited in silence while the stranger hung his jacket, rolled his sleeves, and glanced over his papers. That done, he leant back in his chair, folded his arms and fixed Jack with a thoughtful stare.

'You go first,' he said.

'What?'

'You have questions, Jack. May I call you Jack?'

'Yeah.' The man was right, Jack had so many questions, he didn't know what to ask first, so he started with the most obvious. 'Who are you?'

'James Wright, private investigator, detective, sometimes an assistant barrister at law—but that's not strictly legal—keen sportsman, and, in your case, a stroke of luck. My card.'

Jack read the words, 'Clearwater Detective Agency, Delamere House,' and pushed the card away.

'I didn't do what they pulled me in for, so you're wasting your time.'

'Yeah, well, we'll see. Before we start, I need you to make me a promise.'

'Before we start what?'

'Getting you freed and back to your brother, who, by the way, is fine.'

'How d'you know?'

'I'll explain as we go.'

'Go where? Where's Will? Is he here?'

'As we go along, and no, he's with Mr Chase.'

'Did he send you? Was it you what brought the blanket? Or are you on the side of whoever's got me put here, 'cos I'm telling you, Mr Wright, I didn't do it. I'm a hard-working cabman who's got done by those two scags you saw at that auction, and now they're getting back at me, 'cos they got run in. What were you doing there anyhow? And what you doing here if you ain't a lawyer?'

'I can tell you've been in a cell by yourself. Blimey. Slow down, Jack, listen, and everything will come clear. First though, a promise.'

Jack wasn't going to learn anything if he didn't do what this man asked, so he shrugged and said, 'What promise?'

'Honesty. That's all. No matter what it is, whether you want to say it or not, you must be honest with me.'

'I already told you I didn't do nothing.'

'Promise?'

'If you're here to get me out, Sir, then yeah, of course.'

'You don't have to call me Sir. Oh!' The detective rummaged in his bag again and produced two flasks. 'Water,' he said, placing one and holding aloft the other. 'Or beer?' he added with a mischievous wink.

They shared the beer.

'Here's what's going to happen, Jack,' Wright said, and became business-like. 'Shortly, a colleague of mine is going to arrive, but there's no need for you to be alarmed by who he is, what he says, or how he says it.'

That sounded ominous, but Jack remained silent.

'Before then, I want to talk about the other night, and how come you were at the Dog and Duck.'

'Oh well, that were Mr Chase's idea really, and Will persuaded me to go along with it...'

Jack told the detective his story, from meeting the two men and being robbed, to how Will found the pub, and how he went to identify the thieves. Wright smiled all the way through its telling as if he was impressed.

'Clever man,' he said, when Jack had finished.

'It were Larkin's idea, and it was him who found the remains of the advertisement. I'd have chucked it out.'

'He's a nice man. I only met him last night, but he is one of us.'

'Hang on, didn't he send you?'

'No. He knows I'm here, but he'd sent his own lawyer. It was him who brought the money for some comforts, but Mr Chase has told him to stand down, because you have me.'

'But you ain't a lawyer.'

'No need to worry about that. What's more important is that Mr Chase, like you and me, is one of us.'

If this man had come to help, he wasn't doing a very good job. Jack was more confused than ever.

Mr Wright must have seen it, because he said, 'I have a message from your brother. Now, there's a man I wouldn't mind having on the team. Is he really self-taught?'

'Yeah, why?'

'Anyone would think he'd been to Oxford the way he talks. I was impressed with him. As I am with you, but... His message. He whispered it to me when Mr Chase was battling with his housekeeper. I am to tell you that Larkin feels, and is, the same as you, and will welcome you to his house at any time, which, he hopes will be in the near future.'

Bloody Will, discussing Jack's personal business with a stranger.

'You have nothing to fear, Jack, and I have no fear in reassuring you that it's alright to be the same.'

'The same as what?'

The detective sighed and said, 'Must I speak plain?'

'I wish you bloody would, mate. I ain't got a clue what you're talking about.' It was a lie, because Jack had an inclining that made him uncomfortable, but it was also what any man would say to cover the truth, especially a man under arrest in a police station.

'Your reticence is understandable, but you have promised honesty,' Mr Wright said, and continued to hold his stare.

Jack suffered the creeping skin of the guilty, and his only defence was to say, 'What?'

The detective broke the stare to glance at his watch, but his eyes, hazel and wily, were soon back.

'We must move on,' he said. 'So, for expediency, let me tell you this. You are not the only one who would not say no to an invitation from Mr Chase. He's a fine figure of a man, and clearly quite enamoured with you. If I were Jack Merrit, I'd leap at the chance to chase Chase, although catching him wouldn't present you with much of a challenge. The man's desperate to see you again and to see more of you after that. Now, before your expression of horror turns to one of fury, know that you are talking to a friend. My agency specialises in dealing with *friends*, and each case is treated with discretion, equality and without judgement. Its founder owns an establishment that specialises in helping talented young men of a similar heart, and the Cheap Street Mission for boys who used to be renters. You may have heard of it.'

Jack had driven by it on many occasions, but what did any of that have to do with him?

The answer came when Mr Wright said, 'And by *similar heart*, he means of the same inclination.'

Jack's similar heart had started to pound as soon as he heard Will's message, but he'd forced himself not to show his delight. When he realised Will, Larkin, and now this Mr Wright, knew what he was, delight turned to confusion, and he was left with a frustrating mix of both.

Delightfully confused, but more importantly, feeling safe enough to ask, he said, 'How can you be so sure about me.'

'Because I'm a detective.'

'You only just met me.'

'I didn't detect it in *you*. My God, I've not seen such a display of over-manliness since I was last in Greece. No, Jack, I detected it from Mr Chase. The way he was concerned about you, wanted to help, and wouldn't stop talking about your virtues and innocence. If that wasn't enough, your brother made it pretty clear. Anyway, I only brought that up to put you at your ease, and to reassure you, you have friends on your side. Now, that's that, and we need to move on, otherwise, we shan't be ready when my colleague comes to get you off the hook. May we continue?'

Jack threw up his hands. What choice did he have?

'Good. Then the next thing is for me to thank you.' Mr Wright smiled. His moustache stretched, and had Jack not still been thinking fondly about Larkin, he would have found the detective attractive.

Would have? There was no question. Attractive, honest, and not at all bothered that Jack was how he was.

'Thank me for what?'

'Doing my job for me,' Wright said. 'For catching Hoxton Arty in the act of fencing stolen goods.'

'Was that your job?' Jack's confusion crashed head-on into a nasty thought. 'Did I mess something up?'

The detective's smile grew. 'Kind of you to think that way,' he said. 'No, you didn't. Some weeks back, I was asked by a friendly adversary of mine, Inspector Adelaide of Scotland Yard, to do what I could to bring evidence against Arthur Flay—Hoxton Arty, as he's known—and his nest of criminals. I'd been watching him for some time, and with my staffing problems, that wasn't easy. One of my contacts told me about the auction, and I was there to learn where the goods had come from, because without hearing them admit they came from a robbery, there was nothing I could do. You, I have now learnt, not only saw the men with the stolen goods, but drove them away from the scene of the crime.'

'I didn't know...'

'Of course. The police know you had nothing to do with it. Anyway, by being in the wrong place at the right time, you did my job for me.'

'It was Will who found the pub.'

'Then I owe him my thanks too.'

'But... Hang on...' Jack took a sip of water as he put his thoughts in order, and the detective waited, still smiling, still at ease. 'How did you know I got pulled in last night?'

'As I said, because I'm a detective.'

'That's not fair. You got to tell me how. You went to Larkin's house, you said. How did you know to go there?'

Wright laughed, but it wasn't a mocking laugh, it was more of a chuckle made by a man who was satisfied with himself.

'After the arrest at the auction, I followed you hoping to ask if you had any other evidence. I waited until after you'd made your statement, but you took off in your cab before I could approach. Not being one to leave a loose end untied, I made a few enquiries about your cab number, and called in here. Sergeant Culver told me you'd be called in to collect your reward, and he'd let me know when. When, was last evening when I saw you go in, but only your brother came out, and in such a state, I had to follow him to see what was amiss. He went to Chase's house, I went back to Culver for an explanation, and a few more enquiries later, learnt what had happened. So, off to meet Mr Chase and your brother, both of whom I'd noticed with you at the Dog and Duck, and a quick telegram to my colleague, and here I am to get you freed, but we'll wait to see what the expert says about that. Have some more water, you look pale.'

There was so much to take in, it was like trying to remember the route from Saxon Drive in the west to Plaistow Park in the east via the rookeries of Whitechapel without going through Canning Town because of roadworks.

Before Jack could come up with a question that would explain his unexpected situation, Wright stood, and his chair dragged on the tiles.

'Speaking of my colleague,' he said. 'I hear him coming. Remember what I said. Don't be alarmed, we are here for you, and we are on your side, although he's not... Well, you know. He plays for the other team.'

Jack stood because Wright had, and faced the door, on the other side of which an altercation was taking place.

'Ridiculous,' a well-spoken voice boomed. 'We will take as much time as I see fit.'

There came a deep mumbling, followed by the booming voice demanding, 'Darjeeling, on the instant,' and the door flew open to reveal a tall, imposing man in a cloak and top hat wielding a cane. He was followed by a fawning young policeman, saying, 'Sir, we don't serve tea to just anyone.'

'We are not just anyone,' the newcomer said. Having glanced around the room and turned up his nose, he addressed the policeman. 'By the way, did you know you are in violation of the County and Borough Police Act of eighteen fifty-six? Section twelve subsection three-A. Your buttons, Sir, must be kept clean, yet they are a disgrace. I'd tidy yourself before you're up before the inspector. Sugar, lemon and...' Whoever he was, he broke off to look Jack up and down. 'Biscuits. You have been starving my client.'

'We have not, Sir. We gave him...'

'Out. And take the pot to the kettle.' With that, he shut the door in the policeman's face, turned to Mr Wright, and said, 'Right, Wright, let's get on with it. I'm lunching at White's. This him?'

'Who else would it be?'

'I assume you are drawn to his plight by his features, physicality and form.'

'No, to his unjust circumstance.'

'Oh, really? Bloody hell, Wright. I am missing a perfectly good game of croquet for this.'

'Jack?' Wright said. 'You're now in very safe hands, one of which you should shake. Jack Merrit... Sir Easterby Creswell, barrister at law.'

FOURTEEN

Jack was in deeper trouble than he'd thought. A barrister? Not any barrister either, not by the sound of the man, nor by his looks. A cloak of the finest wool which he threw like a rag over a vacant chair, a brushed topper that landed on it upside down so he could drop kid gloves into it, and the cane had a silver wolf's head. His suit was of the sort only wealthy gentlemen wore, and his fob was gold. More than all that, however, was his size and the way he'd dominated the room from the moment he entered. Once again, Jack's legs weakened, and when the barrister ordered him to, 'Sit, speak only the truth, and otherwise stay silent,' he did as he was told without question.

Mr Wright must have known his colleague well, because he didn't seem at all intimidated, and told him to 'Stop blustering, Creswell, I'm sure we've all got better things to do on a Sunday, and as far as I remember, you are useless at croquet. You'd only have lost.'

The barrister said, 'Bugger off,' and the pair embarked on a conversation Jack had no hope of following.

'How's Clearwater?' the barrister asked as he read Mr Wright's notes.

'Thriving.'

'Enjoying Lady Marshall's inheritance?'

'You mean bequeathment.'

'Don't get smart.'

Mr Wright laughed. 'Yes and no. Stoneridge is now the academy, and Baron Kubinsky has Academy House.'

'The Russian renter?'

'Ukrainian horse master.'

'Tell Archer I'll make a visit in hunting season.'

'He doesn't hunt.'

'The man's too good for his own good. How's Tom?'

Mr Wright threw Jack a quick glance before he replied. 'Busy at Larkspur. We only see each other now and then.'

'Fine fellow, fine fellow... What a load of rubbish.'

'The police report?'

'If you can call it that. Who is this Master Shilling? Is that his real name?'

'I very much doubt it.'

'Good. That's their first error. Age?'

'Sixteen, looks and acts twelve from the little I've managed to glean.'

'Gleaned from?'

'Informants around the Dog and Duck.'

The barrister threw aside a piece of paper, and studied another. 'Bugger it. That's all in order,' he said, and glared at Jack, taking him so much by surprise he shot back in his chair. 'Well? Did you?'

'Did I what, Sir?' Jack stammered, appealing for support from Mr Wright.

'Did you beat up this miscreant?'

'I've not beaten up anyone, Sir.'

'Liar.'

Affronted, and yet suffering guilt for no reason, Jack protested. 'I didn't, Sir. Honest.'

'You did. Here's the charge sheet. You work fast, Wright, I'll give you that.'

'How kind.' Mr Wright addressed Jack. 'He's talking about your previous arrest.'

'Oh. Yeah. Well, they were saying bad things about my brother.'

'Not an excuse... Ah, good,' The barrister put down the papers, but continued to glare. 'You were acquitted, but that only means someone either felt sorry for you, or couldn't be bothered. Still, it means it can't be used against you. As for... Whatever date this attack is alleged to have happened... Different matter. Witnesses?'

'To what?'

'Is he an idiot, Wright? He looks like he should be playing rugby. Do you?'

Again, Jack had to look to Mr Wright for help, and the detective didn't let him down.

'No, Creswell, Mr Merrit is not an idiot,' he said. 'Far from it. He and his brother located the criminals, and Jack was present at the auction, during which, he ran for the police, and confirmed the gang were selling stolen goods. He'd seen them...'

'Because he had driven them to and from the crime, loot and all.'

'I was only doing me job, Sir.'

'So am I,' the barrister barked back. 'Prove you were not involved in the robbery.'

'Eh? How?'

'Exactly. Listen...' The barrister touched the tips of his moustache, and ran his eyes up and down Jack's face. Turning to Mr Wright, he said, 'You boys are incorrigible,' and it sounded like a secret message, because Mr Wright only twitched his eyebrows above a slight smile. Back to Jack, and in a kinder voice, the man called Creswell said, 'You will be a witness in the trial against one of the biggest criminal gangs in the east of London. You will have to do better than *Only doing me job, Sir*, but Wright will work with you on that when the time comes, assuming he is still interested in you, and with your countenance I am sure he will be. Meanwhile, you are being hobbled.'

It was the first time Jack had heard someone say he would be a witness at a trial, and it turned his insides.

Pushing the thought from his mind, he said, 'Hobbled?'

'Yes,' Creswell said. 'From the Middle English meaning to restrict a person's activity. In your case, a perfectly reasonable slang word for being interfered with. Case open and shut, Wright, yes?'

'No. I mean, yes, from where we stand. It's obvious to me that the Flay family are trying to tamper with the witness, and are prepared to go to any lengths to stop Jack testifying. Their first move is to get him put away.'

'Hence the assault accusation, yes, yes. Open and shut.'

'But no, because what do we do about it?'

'Call me away from my croquet, apparently,' Creswell said, and attended to the papers again.

While reading them, he asked Jack to describe his movements on the night of the auction. Jack explained how he had met with Chase, taken his advice, changed his clothes, and attended the event. He was explaining how he'd watched from the back of the room when Creswell interrupted.

'Distance?'

'About twenty feet.'

'You can identify items rolled in a carpet from that distance, can you? You only saw them once and at night.'

'I could, Sir, yes. One of them was one of them silver cups like posh churches have...'

'A chalice?'

Jack shrugged.

'Like a hundred and one other chalices from a hundred and one churches?'

'Maybe, but with red and green jewels I'd recognise again. The stuff was rolled in a patterned carpet, and clanked around with forks and knives, and everything made the same sound.'

'Sound?'

'Yes, Sir. A cabbie uses his ears, see, especially in fog. When they tipped the stuff onto the table, it made the exact same sound as when they loaded it in my cab. A cabman uses his eyes, too, and that carpet had a whacking great bird on it, all blue and gold with big feathers. Never seen none like it.'

'A list of items.' Mr Wright passed the barrister another paper. 'Peacock carpet, very rare, chalice hocked by the vicar of St Mary's, who is now being investigated for its theft. There are other things Jack is positive he saw.'

Creswell grunted as if he was still not satisfied.

'But, Sirs...' Jack waited until both were looking at him. 'As the policeman brought the crooks out of the pub, one of them recognised me. He said, "Sorry about your purse, mate, but I reckon you've got your own back."'

'Meaning?'

'They'd not only robbed Clarington's, but they'd also taken Jack's fares.'

'Dipped you?'

'Yes, Sir.'

'Good. Another motive for your wanting to see justice done, thus another reason they'd want to interfere with you, and I don't mean it in the pleasurable sense, Wright. All well and good, Mr Merrit, but when did you attack this boy called Shilling?'

How many times did he have to say it? 'I didn't hit no-one, Sir.'

'According to this lad, you battered him on the stairs to such an extent, he was unable to speak for several days.'

'That's a lie.'

'Prove it. Witnesses?'

'To something that didn't happen?'

Jack's temper was rising, and not even the sound of Will's voice in his head could hold it at bay. Mr Wright, however, was more successful.

'We know it's lies, Jack,' he said kindly. 'The point is, the magistrate will need to be convinced of that, and if there were no witnesses, and if you can't prove you were elsewhere, it's a case of word against word.'

'The word of a sixteen-year-old against a professional cabman?'

'Makes no difference. The lad's a minor, and you are, as Sir Easterby says, built for the rugby field.'

'So, you're saying I got no chance?'

'No. You have every chance.' Mr Wright pointed to his colleague. 'But we need to know the facts. Did you, at any time that night, come into contact with this boy?'

'I don't even know what... Oh, shit.'

Both men snapped to attention, and Jack's heart froze.

'The lad on the stairs. It was only a bump, and it weren't on purpose.'

'A bump?' Creswell derided. 'Explain.'

'As I was hurrying down from the auction to go for the police. I came around the turn, and this boy was coming up. We bumped into each other as I passed, that's all.'

'Are you sure?'

'Yes, Sir. I mean, he stumbled back a bit, but he didn't fall.'

'Were words exchanged?'

'Yes...' Jack pictured the scene, and tried to remember. 'He said something like, watch where you're going, or doing... Then he said he thought he knew me.'

'Did he?'

The barrister was staring intently with his moustache twitching from side to side as if it had a life of its own, and despite it all, Jack fought hard not to laugh.

'Did he know me? No, I... Wait. I think he were the same one who minded my cab round the back of Mr Chase's house... Yeah. When Will and I were leaving... This was another night... The boy had cleaned it up right proper, so we gave him a shilling. It was dark, but it was the same lad.'

'Interesting, but probably not useful,' Creswell said, reading one of the pages. 'Who is this Mr Chase?'

'Larkin Chase,' Jack explained. 'He was with me.'

'The Larkin Chase who writes that column in the Gazette?'

'Yes, Sir.'

'Interesting chap. He'll make for an entertaining witness,' Creswell said, and Jack was about to ask him what he meant by that, when the barrister returned to the incident. 'On the night in question, did the boy say anything else to you, other than the altercation on the stairs?'

'It wasn't an altercation, Creswell,' Mr Wright said. 'It was a bump.'

'You do your job, Wright, and I'll do mine.' To Jack, he said, 'Would you say this lad was intoxicated?'

'I reckon everyone in the pub was, Sir.'

'Good, good. And was there any other exchange between you?'

'Yes, Sir.' This one was easy to remember because it had played on Jack's mind for the first few days following the auction. 'We was outside as the men got taken away...'

'I can attest to that,' Mr Wright said. 'I was there.'

'You get everywhere, Wright. Continue, Mr Merrit.'

'The lad came up to me, and I apologised for the thing on the stairs. He didn't say anything about that, but he said he recognised my cab plate from the other night. Then, Sirs, he went on to say I had it coming.'

The moustache stopped twitching. 'Had what coming?'

'It, Sir. He said, "You've right got it coming now."'

'Terrible English,' Creswell muttered.

'But English nevertheless,' Mr Wright said, and the barrister nodded thoughtfully.

'Anything after that?'

'Yeah. I asked him what he meant, and he said something about me finding out soon enough, and walked off. Mr Chase and Will were there, and others. Everyone would have heard it.'

'Right!' Creswell slapped the table. 'Then that is that, and this is poppycock. Jimmy, I have a rather important case tomorrow morning and would rather be at that than wasting the time of a Shoreditch magistrate. Therefore, let us have this innocent man released, and the charges dropped without delay, shall we? Mr Merrit, follow me and say nothing.'

With that, and with Jack none the wiser about what was happening, the barrister stood, swiped up his cloak and hat, and marched from the room.

'He moves fast,' Mr Wright said, gathering his things. 'Go, don't lose him.'

Jack obeyed, and found the barrister heading towards the front of the station where he spun backwards through a pair of doors. Running after him, Jack stumbled into the charge room as surprised as the sergeant who shot to his feet to protest.

'Mr Merrit's release papers,' Creswell demanded, calmly putting on his gloves.

'I beg your pardon.'

'No need to beg, Sergeant. Not yet. You were the arresting officer in this case?'

'Yes, Sir, but...'

'Then, you are the one who doesn't know how to read a medical report.'

'Excuse me?'

'I cannot.' Creswell slammed down a sheet of paper. 'The medical report stating that the alleged victim was beaten to the extent he was unable to report the alleged attack for some days. Am I correct?'

The officer glanced at the paper and agreed.

'And this charge sheet. Date, place, charge all correct?'

'Yes, Sir. Wilful and grievous assault on a minor.'

'And this. What is this?'

'The statement the prisoner made a few days' earlier following the arrest of named criminals at the Dog and Duck...'

'Your ability to read is astounding, Sergeant, and yet it is not. Finally, this...'

Mr Wright had joined them, and just in time to hand Creswell yet another piece of paper, which the barrister shoved under the sergeant's nose.

'This is my officer's report of the same arrest.'

'Quite. Now then...' Creswell put on his cloak with a swirl. 'Please read me the penultimate line of Mr Merrit's witness statement.'

'Er... "The boy left me with a threat that suggested I would be in trouble." So? That's not an offence. In fact, considering the prisoner had shopped a criminal like Hoxton Arty, I'd say it was good advice.'

'Good, sound, spoken advice?'

'Yes.'

'Spoken?'

'According to my officer, yes.'

'Spoken by whom?'

'Er...' The sergeant looked again. 'By the lad known locally as Shilling.'

Creswell switched the papers.

'And this complaint, the one that led to Mr Merrit's arrest last evening? This allegation was made by?'

'The same boy.'

'Master Shilling?'

'Yes, Sir, but I don't see...'

'Clearly you do not, Sergeant, but we do. Let me save the magistrate's court some time, and save you from demotion or dismissal, by, as my colleague Mr Wright would say, stating the bleedin' obvious. Master Shilling has shortchanged you, Sir. This boy was unable to report a crime for several days due to his injuries, agreed?'

'Yes.'

'Then how the hell could he have given Mr Merrit spoken advice less than half an hour after the spurious altercation that allegedly caused those injuries?'

'Well, maybe...'

'Maybe the injuries incurred by being beaten speechless only appeared long after the event?'

'I don't know.'

'I do, and the word you need is impossible.'

'Then, perhaps...?'

'Perhaps it was a different boy?'

'Yes, I mean... Let me see...' The sergeant was shuffling papers back and forth as though he'd lost a five-pound note, his face had reddened, and although his mouth was moving, there were no words.

'According to your officers, and countersigned by yourself, it was the same boy. Apparently, a miracle boy who manifests grievous injuries long after an alleged assault. This medical report reads as though he were run down by the Oxford Street omnibus, not, as was actually the case, bumped into on a staircase by a man in a hurry to help the police. Honestly, Sir. One wonders what the force is coming to. In fact, and I say this without prejudice, I can't help but wonder if someone in this establishment is not in close cahoots with Mr Arthur Flay and his family. Unless the lad *was* run down by the number sixteen, the medical examiner of this report has been intimidated or bribed by criminals, themselves aided and abetted by someone at this station. The point being, Sergeant, you have arrested and held an innocent man.'

'But...'

'You have either made a simple mistake, or done this as a favour to one of the East End's most hardened criminal gangs. If that is the case, the Commissioner will want an inquiry. I shall ask him over lunch at White's.'

'No, no, Sir... It was a simple mistake, I'm sure,' the sergeant muttered, reaching for a ledger. 'One I will rectify directly.'

'Good idea. As for the matter of compensation...'

'A huge apology, Mr Merrit.'

'No apology will make up for a day's missing wage,' Mr Wright said. 'Nor the stigma, and not to mention the emotional distress. You are emotionally distressed, Mr Merrit, are you not?'

Jack didn't know what he was, but he said, 'Yes, Sir,' because it sounded like the right thing to say.

'Compensation?' The sergeant broke off from his scribbling.

'You have detained this man with no lawful authority to justify detention,' Creswell said, brushing his top hat. 'I'll have Mr Wright complete the necessary action and file it. Offences Against the Person Act, eighteen sixty-one should cover it, Wright. Your name sergeant?'

'Adams, Sir, but it was a simple mistake,' the officer bleated.

'Good of you to confess before witnesses,' Mr Wright said. 'That'll make my job a lot easier.'

'Do you have any personal effects here, Merrit?' the barrister asked while checking the time.

'They took a few off me, Sir.'

'Then if the sergeant will return them, I might have time for a shortened game.' Creswell pocketed his watch. 'Now, you sign that... I'll take that...' He whipped the papers from the sergeant's trembling hand, tore up the charge sheet, and gave the rest to Mr Wright. 'By the way, Sergeant Adams, I understand Master Shilling, like everyone else at the Dog and Duck was inebriated.'

'I dare say, Sir, but aren't most men in pubs there for the purpose of getting drunk?'

'That's as maybe, and it really isn't my job to teach you yours, but I refer you to the Licensing Act of eighteen seventy-two. To wit: It is an offence for anyone to be drunk on licensed premises, just as it is an offence for a person to be drunk when in charge of a carriage, firearm, sheep, pig or cow. I know. Odd, but there it is. You may want to keep a closer eye on the Dog and Duck, and Master Shilling in particular, for

I suggest he is a few pennies short of his own name. In fact, a fine for being drunk might teach him not to waste your time.' To Mr Wright, he said, 'Thank you, Jimmy. It has been entertaining as always. I'll think of you when I am pegging out.'

Creswell swished from the room and out through reception, where several other officers stood gawping through the grille.

'You're free to go, Mr Merrit,' the sergeant said, mopping his brow, and handing over a paper bag containing Jack's handkerchief, pipe and a book of matches.

Jack was too stunned to take them, and didn't move until Mr Wright put them in his hands.

'I assume they didn't give you the reward?' he said.

'The what?'

'Twenty pounds?'

The words took Jack from one state of shock to another. 'Er, no.'

'It's here, Mr Merrit,' the sergeant said, hurrying to offer an envelope. 'With the kind regards of Clarington's.'

Mr Wright snatched it from him, placed it in Jack's top pocket, and said, 'Let's go and tell your brother.'

Taking his arm, he led Jack through the gathering of whispering constables and outside to freedom.

FIFTEEN

Larkin sat by the drawing room window watching the road. The book in his lap had gone unread since he'd opened it, because his mind was occupied by what Mr Wright might be doing, and whether he would be able to have Jack released. Now and then, his thoughts wandered to where Will might be, but having given him free rein of the house, the chap was probably reading, or also watching the street and hoping for his brother's safe return.

'I am here because you need my help, and I need yours.'

The detective's words rang in Larkin's ears, and the reason for his appearance still rankled him as an unexplained mystery. Mr Wright said he was working to bring the Flay family to justice, and they were the largest and most feared criminal organisation working out of Hoxton, just over a mile from where Larkin lived. He gave no reason for his investigation, but explained why he was present at the auction, where Jack had succeeded where he had failed. By the time he explained what he could do to help, Larkin had warmed to him, and agreed to call off Fudler in favour of Sir Easterby Creswell. The mention of the man's name was impressive enough, and when Mr Wright offered to call him in, and promised that if anyone could have Jack freed it was his personal friend the famed barrister, first Will, and then Larkin, begged him to send a message. Later, they agreed the young detective was something of a saviour.

There followed a strange night. Mr Wright left, saying he would be back in the morning with news, and preferably with Jack, leaving Larkin with a choice; to pay for Will's cab home, or invite the young man to stay. Jack's situation agitated Will as much as Larkin, but neither were as disturbed as Mrs Grose when Will accepted the invitation, and Larkin ordered dinner for two. With nothing else to be done except fret, and with reassurance in short supply, because there was no way of knowing what was happening to Jack, all Larkin could offer was conversation and, after dinner, a game of chess. Rather, several games, because after Will announced he didn't know how to play, and after Larkin showed him the basics and won the first game, Jack Merrit's younger and most unusual brother went on to win the rest.

The man was now somewhere in the house, having made himself quite at home. That morning, he'd appeared for breakfast as well-spokenly chatty as he'd been the night before, but admitted to a restless sleep because he was worried, unused to a soft bed, and troubled by the 'Not exactly exact hanging of the wardrobe door.'

Larkin said he would have it seen to, and asked if he would like to attend church with Mrs Grose.

'Certainly not,' Will said as if he had been insulted. 'No offence to your housekeeper, but I will not allow myself to be told how to behave, what to say, when to sit and stand, and what to think, not by anyone, least of all a prattle-box prattler in a dress. With your permission, Mr Chase, I would like to wait quietly for news of my brother.'

Which was what they had both done, while Mrs Grose fiddled with her straw hat, and bustled from the house with her prayer book tucked under one arm and a flouncy parasol under the other, and while Emily pottered around the place doing this and that ahead of her half day.

The morning passed as if the time between breakfast and noon was actually a week, and Larkin, unable to concentrate on his book, gazed from the window, hoping that every passing cab would stop and regurgitate Jack, cheery and exonerated.

It still hadn't happened by half-past ten when a knock at the drawing room door heralded the arrival of Emily, red-faced and flustered.

'What on earth's the matter?' Larkin put aside his book. 'Have you finally caught one that has agreed to wait until after marriage?'

'What? I mean...' A half-hearted courtesy. 'Sorry, Sir, no. It's that boy.'

'What is which boy?'

'Him, Sir. Your guest, he's...' She emitted a sound which rather resembled the air being let from a Benz pneumatic tyre. 'Getting in the way.'

'Oh? How?'

'Take a look. Sir.' The 'Sir' came as an afterthought.

Thinking it would make a distracting pastime, Larkin followed her to the dining room at the back of the house. There, he discovered Will scrutinising a plate with his sleeves rolled, his jacket off and a cloth over one arm. When he moved the plate away from his face and noticed he had company, he put it down, flicked the cloth over it and smiled.

'It's the pattern, Mr Chase,' he said, and pointed to the dresser.

As far as Larkin could see there was nothing amiss, and all Will was doing was helping Emily with her dusting.

'There is an error in the printing,' Will continued. 'As you can see, there is no scene, only the ring of flowers at the rim at one quarter of an inch in on the dining plates, one eighth on the others. Very pretty. However, one of the flowers is missing a petal, this one here...' Larkin couldn't see from that distance, but nodded. 'And, to my mind, the set should be placed on the dresser, so the holding bar covers the mistake. I have nearly finished.'

Emily glared at her master as if her life was his fault, and Larkin found it hard to suppress his mirth.

'Come now, Emily,' he said. 'Mr Merrit is doing you a favour, and he is no way criticising the way you keep the crockery.'

'Well, I was, actually,' Will said, placing the recently dusted plate. 'But now it is all as it should be. Shall I do the cutlery canteen?'

'No!' The maid appealed to Larkin. 'Sir...?'

'Will, why don't you sit with me in the drawing room? I am watching for Jack, and I think we will soon have news.'

'Do you?'

'I do.'

An altercation averted, Larkin left Emily to either rearrange the dresser or accept it was easier to leave it be, and escorted Will to the drawing room. It was there, only ten minutes later, when they saw Mr Wright appear from behind next door's shrubbery, with Jack at his side.

Will was in the hall with the front door open before they reached the step, and in his brother's arms before Larkin could invite the pair inside, but when they entered, it was as conquering heroes. Jack's face was grubby and unshaven, and his clothes were crumpled, but otherwise, he was the perfect picture of a man Larkin had pined for through the night, filth and all, and he was momentarily jealous that Will got to hold him while he couldn't. Mr Wright was keen to have tea, because although they had asked for it at the station, none had been forthcoming, and he was, 'As dry as a witch's tit,' an expression which betrayed his South Riverside roots, and one which made Emily gasp and scurry to the scullery to boil the kettle.

Jack admitted to being in shock, and said he didn't know how he came to be free, who Mr Wright was, nor what the man in the cloak had said, but he'd bashed the police about the head with lots of words, and now, there he was.

There he was indeed. Recovering from his ordeal and babbling like a child, his eyes dancing, his lips fixed in a permanent smile, and although describing his hideous hours to Will, passing Larkin glances as if to reassure him he knew he was there.

That was probably Larkin's imagination, but it brought him joy each time their eyes met. Once, just after it had happened, Mr Wright noticed and passed a similar look of recognition as if to say he was happy the pair were reunited.

Again, that was quite possibly only Larkin acting like a bad journalist and making up what he wanted to believe, because there was no evidence they were a pair.

There were, however, facts. Jack was free and with no blemish on his character, he had his twenty pounds, and was keen to be home. The other fact was Larkin wanted him to stay, and it took a good twenty minutes to persuade him that Emily would have no trouble extending the lunch to accommodate all four men. Mrs Grose would be more biting than usual when she found out, but Larkin would remind her she'd just been to church, and to forgive was divine.

It was settled, and Larkin was overjoyed. Emily delivered the tea, and once Will had rearranged the tray and poured, the men talked about what Jack would do with his reward as if the four of them were old classmates at an alumni reunion. The only thing that caused Larkin disquiet was the way Mr Wright continued to study Jack. It was hard to read his expression, and harder still to imagine what he might be thinking, but he questioned both brothers in depth, asking about their situation, their past, and the way they had caught the criminals. Such questions were understandable from a detective, but there was another reason for them which Larkin couldn't fathom, and the way Mr Wright appeared to be admiring Jack, became troublesome. The detective was stealing the guest from under Larkin's nose, and it could only be for the same reason; he wanted Jack to himself.

Something had to be done.

'Jack,' he said when they'd finished their tea. 'Why don't you pop upstairs to the room opposite mine and refresh yourself? There is spare shaving equipment on the stand, and Emily will bring hot water and towels.'

Although he said he might be up there a while, Jack took the offer with gratitude, and left Larkin free to learn more about Mr Wright, and make polite conversation until Mrs Grose returned. Even then, her ominous appearance couldn't dull the happiness within the house.

Will and Mr Wright fell into a discussion about, of all things, filing, and how Will had to have his books arranged in a particular way, and how the detective was terrible at keeping records in a sensible order. Aware that Jack was alone upstairs while he was suffering inanities, Larkin lost the battle against temptation, and excused himself.

'I just want to make sure Mr Merrit has all he needs,' he said, and ignoring Will's raised eyebrows, left them to discuss the Dewey decimal system of classification.

What had actually tempted him to check on his guests was the possibility of seeing Jack without his shirt, and having knocked, called, and been invited in, he wasn't disappointed.

Jack was standing on a towel at the bowl before the mirror with his face lathered, and his head tilted. Seeing Larkin in the reflection, he paused with the razor to his cheek and said, 'This is kind of you. Thanks.'

Larkin wanted to thank him for offering him the sight of his broad shoulders and naked back that narrowed to the top of his underwear showing above his unbuttoned trousers. Although he only had a side view, the mirror revealed a defined, smooth chest, unblemished and with dark brown nipples. Jack had washed, because, like his back, his chest glistened, and drips fell from where the muscles overhung his flat stomach, rippled as if it were a summer pond recently kissed by a passing breeze.

Having taken it all in within a second, and lightheaded at the sight, Larkin said, 'Do you need anything else?'

'You've done enough for us both already, Mr Chase. Thank you again for looking after Will. I didn't know what else to do.'

'And again, I say it was, and remains, my pleasure, but please, Jack, call me Larkin.'

Jack nodded, and resumed his shave. There was no need for Larkin to remain, but unwilling to go, he searched for an excuse to stay, and found one on the bed.

'If you don't mind me saying so, your shirt looks far from happy. Would you like Emily to launder it?'

'Don't worry, it'll do until I get home.'

Home. A reminder that the vision was not to be permanent.

'I may have something that will fit,' Larkin offered, knowing all his shirts would be too small, but wondering how Jack would look in one with his muscles bulging through, and the collar open to reveal a neck he longed to caress.

'Honestly, I'll be fine,' Jack said, delivering disappointment as he rinsed the blade in the bowl. 'But you could do us a favour while you're here.'

'Of course, what?'

Take the razor and draw it gently over his fair skin while supporting his head, his lips a breath away, their bodies pressed together...

'Pass us that towel, would you? I don't want to risk dropping foam on your rug.'

He could drop more than foam; his trousers, for a start, and maybe he would, if only Larkin could drop his inhibitions and ask. It wasn't about seeing the statue of a man naked, however, and it was about more than his physicality. Whatever *it* was, it was noble, and meant, natural and out of Larkin's grasp.

'Here,' he said, and pushing his luck, gave a short laugh. 'I thought you were going to ask me to dry your back.'

'Can if you want.'

Good Lord.

As he positioned himself to scrape his other cheek, Jack raised his muscled arms, revealing tufts of downy, dark-blond hair beneath, and the expression he passed to Larkin through the mirror became questioning.

'I will if it wouldn't make you uncomfortable,' Larkin said.

'No. I don't mind.'

Larkin stood behind him on unsteady legs, and held the towel to his shoulders with one hand on each solid curve. Applying a gentle pressure, and hardly believing what he was being allowed to do, he began. First one side, and then the other, patting and drawing a little lower each time, and relishing the firmness through the cotton, until he reached the dip of Jack's spine, and could go no further.

'Are you prone to ticklishness?' he asked. 'I don't want to give you any shocks if I dry your sides.'

'Carry on,' Jack said, and changed his stance.

In doing so, he released the masculine scent of a man returned from hard work, a potent mix of sweet and sour, that caused Larkin's head to lighten more with each hard-to-control breath.

'Here I go,' he said, and wrapped his fingers beneath Jack's arms, the thin towel the only thing preventing him from touching his skin.

There was less to dry at the sides, and he expected Jack to say that was enough, but when he began again at his armpits, Jack was gazing from the mirror, his lips in a crooked grin.

'Would you do me chest?' he whispered. 'I'm feeling lazy.'

Good heavens.

'Er... If you are sure this is not making you...' Larkin's voice cracked, and he swallowed. 'Uncomfortable.'

'No, you're alright. If you don't mind.'

'I will have to stand closer.'

'I know.'

Larkin shuffled forward, reached around, and placed the towel over the chest. Jack remained motionless, the razor away from his face where islands of white decorated on his smooth chin, and an iceberg of foam remained on his upper lip. A little more pressure and Larkin circled the towel over sturdy muscles, where a finger brushed each nipple as the chest rose and fell with calm, controlled breathing. Larkin lingered there, and Jack made no complaint. Down and over each ridge of his stomach, gently into the dip of his navel, and to the place beneath where once more, the waist of the underwear prevented him from exploring further. Eyes locked in the reflection, tentative smiles remained immobile, and two Adam's apples rose and fell in unison.

'That's as far as I should go,' Larkin whispered, the pressing of his manhood surely noticeable against Jack's buttocks. 'Else I really will make you uncomfortable.'

'Only because there is a detective in the house,' Jack said, and broke the stare with a blink.

'Perhaps you might like to stay a night to recover from your ordeal.'

'Perhaps I would, but I can't.'

Larkin dared to remain as he was, and tightened the pressure both in front and from behind.

'It would be my pleasure to accommodate you.'

'You have been accommodating enough, Larkin. I have to see to my business.'

'I understand.'

Trembling, Larkin began to withdraw the towel, but Jack trapped him with his elbows, and pushed back with his buttocks.

'In a moment,' he said, and placed the razor on the stand.

A large hand gripped Larkin's and lifted it from the towel. For a moment, Larkin though he was going to kiss it, but instead, he took the towel, and with Larkin clamped to his tight, warm body, wiped every blemish from his face.

'You look like a new man,' Larkin said.

'Only 'cos you've uncovered one,' was Jack's ambiguous reply.

'I should let you go.'

'I don't mind.'

'No, I must. I hear the sinister creak of my housekeeper mounting the stairs.'

Larkin leapt away, Jack said, 'Shit,' and both wrestled with the front of their trousers, spinning their backs to the door when Mrs Grose knocked. Larkin threw open the wardrobe, ushered Jack behind its door, and posed himself so when he called, 'Come in,' he was found handing Jack his shirt with no hint of impropriety.

'Yes, Mrs Grose?' he asked, attending to the washstand.

'Just to confirm it's four for lunch at half past one,' the housekeeper said, averting her eyes.

'It's quite alright, Mr Merrit is decent,' Larkin said, trying not to let his regret show. 'And yes, about lunch. I'll come down with you.'

From then on, the late morning and the late lunch rolled on as any household would expect. However, beneath the dining table, one man's foot occasionally touched against another's, and each time it did, the silent signal was reciprocated.

* * *

The room was draped in a perfumed grey cloud of cigar smoke, but only one person was smoking. There were enough chairs at the table for everyone, but only one person was allowed to sit, and although the boy had brought a new bottle of the best gin, there was only one glass. An anniversary clock ticked from its place on the mantlepiece, its pendulum rotating back and forth, and politely chimed four of the afternoon. It was the only politeness in the room, and the only thing that dared make a sound as six men waited to hear the commands of one woman. She was the one smoking, drinking, and contemplating the clock, and she was the one planning a man's demise.

About her wide neck hung a gold and diamond chain that was once owned by the wife of a Canonbury solicitor, and it glittered beneath a fur collar which had once been the favourite cat of an enemy's daughter. The head was still attached, its eyes replaced by sapphires from a dressing table in De Beauvoir Square. Her fat fingers drummed the table beneath the weight of someone else's rings, one platinum, the rest gold, and when she moved her hand to raise her gin glass, the charm bracelet that had once belonged to the daughter of a member of parliament, jangled as if ten shop doors had opened at once.

The clock finished its announcement, and she sipped with her carmine-caked lips, which were little more than a narrow slit in a billowing bloat of broken-veined cheeks. Above the folds, her yellowing eyes were magnified through spectacles that rested on ears adorned with another woman's prized earrings that hung alongside her silver hair arranged in spaniel loops and long, elegant twists, once the height of fashion for the meek and proper.

'We'll fuck the bastard over.'

There was nothing meek and proper about Violet Flay as she uttered her first words for several minutes. Although some of the men jolted at the rasp, none disagreed.

'My Arty and Badger pulled in? Well, Snout?'

Called to attention, Snout took a step forward. 'Aye, both, Mother. It will be an Old Bailey trial, they think, in a few days. It's going to be up quick.'

'Get 'em out meantime?'

Snout looked at his brother-in-law for support, because no-one liked to say no to Mother, but Crank looked the other way.

'Well?'

'No, Mother. Nothing we can do. They're going down.'

Talons for nails dragged across the table as a hand clawed.

'We'll do the bastard over,' the woman repeated. 'Chancer, you'll do it tonight.'

'Will do, Mrs Flay.'

'What about Harris?' The woman scowled. 'He done yet?'

'Sent Abott over a while back,' Snout reported. 'He'll tell Harris his cabman got put away for bashing up Shilling. Merrit won't have no job to go back to.'

'Merrit?' Her mouth contorted at the name as though she had something stuck in her teeth. 'Any chance related to that one on the stage?'

'We think so, Ma,' the youngest son said. 'Still looking into that.'

Violet Flay considered the name, her sons and her daughters' husbands, as behind the layer of Blanc de Perle face whitener, her mind churned the milk of possibilities into a thickening paste of determined action.

It was, though, action for later.

'And how's Shilling?' she grunted, returning to the present.

'Nothing wrong with him, Mrs Flay,' Lucker said. 'Not now he's got the greasepaint off.'

'But they let the cabman out?'

'Aye, Mother. This morning. Adams had no choice.'

'What a fucking disgrace.' The gin glass shot across the room, narrowly missing one of her children. 'Right...' She swigged from the bottle and slammed it down. 'Do it, boys, and do it soon. No-one gets my Arthur put away and lives to read about in the fucking newspaper.'

SIXTEEN

Jack had made it as clear as he could, and Larkin had done the same. The touch of his foot beneath the table caused thrills, and Jack only felt nervous the first time he reciprocated. From then on, they played a game, with both players knowing what the other was saying, and, for Jack at least, knowing he wanted it to lead somewhere. Where, however, was unknown, but without being alone with Larkin, he had no way of asking. As much as Jack wanted to stay and find out what came next, the immediate future was more important.

After lunch, and before he left, Mr Wright said it was unlikely Jack's arrest would have made anything but the local newspapers, so he could return to work and say nothing. If, though, word reached Harris, Mr Wright would vouch for him and explain it was a false arrest. The offer went some way to appeasing Jack's concern, but he knew Harris, and he'd not take kindly to any suggestion Jack had been in trouble, even if he'd been innocent. His priority was to call at the yard and book his hansom and Shadow for the next day, and, if necessary, say he'd missed work because he'd been unwell.

After that, it was back to normal, except now there were other considerations, namely, being a witness in court, twenty pounds, and what to do about Larkin Chase.

His watch read five when he and Will left, and standing on the step, shaking hands, he tried to pass looks without Will noticing.

'You are welcome here any time, gentlemen,' Larkin said. 'In fact, I hope to see more of you soon.'

His meaning was obvious. 'More of you.' In other words, not only Jack's top half. How long he stood at that mirror lathered and waiting for Larkin to knock, he was unable to say. As he trembled with anticipation, there came a point when he thought he'd misread the sign, 'The room opposite mine.'

Patience led to reward in the end, though, and although it had not been as much as he'd hoped, it was a beginning.

'Now we can put all this behind us,' Will said once they had given a last wave from the gate. 'Those horrible men, your terrible ordeal, even Mr Chase need no longer be part of our lives if we don't want it.'

'I thought you liked it there,' Jack said, determined not to turn back for one last look.

'I do, and I like him, but I wondered if you did. The two of you said very little during lunch.'

'My mind was on everything that's happened.' It had actually been on everything that was taking place beneath the table. 'We'll get a cab at the junction, unless you want to ride the omnibus again.'

'Whatever is cheapest,' Will said. 'Your twenty pounds is for you. What are you to do with it?'

'Bugger me, I forgot.' Jack came to a standstill. 'I said I'd pay him back that two quid.'

'I don't think he's worried. Besides, you don't have the notes changed yet.'

'That's true.' The four five-pound notes were safely inside his jacket with the pocket buttoned. Repaying the two sovereigns would give him an excuse to call back one day without Will, and without a detective snooping about.

They started walking again, heading north, away from the Dog and Duck, dodging those on their way to evensong, and navvies weaving from post to post after a Sunday in the pub.

'What will you do with it?' Will asked.

'First thing is to pay off Reggie's debt. That's all but five pounds taken care of. After that...? What d'you reckon?'

They discussed possibilities, from putting it away to save for better lodgings, to using it for the rent, and from rescuing boots from the pawn shop to new books for Will, an offer he turned down because he could find books for free, and Mr Chase had offered him use of his collection. The name came up again when they found a cab, and began the journey home, and it was Will who mentioned it.

'I rather like that man,' he said. 'I admit, when I first met Mr Chase, I thought he was untidy, and I wasn't sure I could stay in his study room for very long. I was on edge, but it wasn't him, it was the state of his books. Then, after being with him a while, I thought, well, he's alright. Talks a lot, doesn't he?'

'So do you.'

'You like him, don't you?'

'You also ask too many questions, brother.'

Jack pulled Will close by his shoulder and drilled his knuckles into his head.

'Get off me, you loon.' Will struggled away and straightened his hair. 'Oh, there's your hotel.'

They were passing the police station on Dalston Lane, and Jack wasn't pleased by the reminder.

'Very funny.'

'I can see it, Jack.'

'So can I, mate. It's right there.'

'No. I can see how much you like Mr Chase.'

'Yeah, alright.'

'He likes you, too.'

'I said, alright, Will. Just shut up and watch the scenery.'

'Ha! Scenery?'

Rows of shop fronts selling groceries, cloth, and flowers, matching windows set in yellow brick for three storeys above. Identical streets offering a line of identical houses either side, children in Sunday dresses and sailor-boy suits driving hoops with sticks, and spinning tops on the pavement where men and women dodged and tripped.

Passing hansoms, their drivers high at the back, some not sparing the whip, and having no thought for their horses, and grander carriages, broughams, Hackneys, and private vehicles of the kind Jack might one day own if he could save his money. Junctions where crossing vehicles danced around each other amid shouts and swearing, newsboys getting in the way and hollering, costermongers returning trays and barrows, manure sweepers with their carts and spades, brushing-boys attending to the wealthy towards Bethnal Green, clearing the shit from their paths, and holding out caps for pennies.

Wider roads led to narrower ones, and grander buildings became things of another borough as their cab took them east and then to the south, where the children wore rags and dug deep in the middens and gutters for food, not toys. Where frumpy women in wilting bonnets slouched against pub walls in the gathering dusk, swinging their skirts at weathered men who either spouted God at the whores, or dragged them into the alleys; sometimes both. The shops sold less, the pavements became more congested, and the smell of the air changed from manure to sewage mixed with the sweet, throat-clawing stink of burnt sugar, and the nostril-burning tang of industry.

From one world to another, Jack thought. From a well-appointed house with a garden, a stable and servants, to a place where he was a servant to anonymous fares, and where Will didn't know what rugs felt like beneath bare feet, or what oil paintings looked like hanging against wallpaper.

The twenty pounds would help with that. The fifteen pounds, once Reggie's debt was paid. When that was done, he had no need to put aside his tips and earnings for Harris, but could use them for his family; him and Will.

'What about Mr Wright?' Will said out of nowhere as they passed into Stepney.

'What about him?'

'Stroke of luck, wasn't it? Him happening to be at that pub for the same reason as you.'

'I suppose.'

'Did you find him...' Will sought the word among the crowds and stink. 'Dashing?'

'Dashing?'

'Yeah. Smart, flashy, knows his stuff, and certainly knows the right people. What was the barrister like?'

'Scary.'

'Mr Wright said he was the most brilliant law man in London, and never as grumpy as he makes out, whatever that means. Imagine being friends with a barrister.'

'Imagine being quiet.'

'Oh, come now, Jack, I know you're keen to talk about Mr Wright.'

The man had been on Jack's mind, it was true, but only because of the way he'd passed looks similar to those Larkin gave, and because of the strange words he'd used in the interview room. *One of us*, or something. Jack had been too addled to understand whatever coded message the detective had imparted, but thinking of it reminded him of something Wright had told him.

'That's a point,' he said. 'What did you mean by your message?'

'What message?'

'When Mr Wright got me on me own, he brought word from you, and said he was to tell me... Hang on.' Jack thought hard, pushing aside the cramped cell, the running sweat, stinking bucket and clanks, shouts and the drunken screams of the night, and fought his way into the interview room where the dashing—it was a good word for him—Mr Wright had told him he was a pain in the arse and a godsend. A pain, Jack assumed, because he'd somehow put the detective out, and a godsend, because Jack had caused the arrest of people he'd been chasing.

That wasn't it.

'What message?' Will repeated, and Jack told him he was still trying to remember.

Wright had made Jack promise to speak honestly, and that wasn't a problem. There had been beer, welcome, though warm, and then... Talk of Will, self-taught...

'Yeah,' Jack remembered. 'It was something about how Mr Chase feels and is the same as me. What was that all about?'

Will grinned as if he'd planned to get Jack on the subject. 'Simply that,' he said. 'Mr Wright observes and detects, he told me so, and when Mr Chase was otherwise occupied, he also told me that Mr Chase likes you. Then he said such a thing was not a problem for him. You see, I also observe and detect, and I detected both are men who have a preference for other men like themselves. I didn't say anything of course.'

'I don't know what you're saying now. You're talking all posh again.'

'What I am saying, Jack...' Will stuck his head around the side of the cab. They were crawling past Saint Dunstan's and All Saints, and the congregation was crowding close by the road. 'What I am saying, brother,' he whispered, 'is that I think Mr Wright and Mr Chase are of the same inclination.'

Words the detective had used, and Jack knew exactly what they meant.

'Not our business,' he said.

'Not mine, I agree, but it is yours.'

'What?'

'Observe and detect, Jack. I am happy you have stumbled on two men of your disposition. I only wonder which you will choose.'

For someone who'd been called an imbecile, dumb, deranged, afflicted and affected, Will was bloody... What? Annoying? Right?

Both of those things. This was the first time he'd seen through Jack so clearly, but then, it was the first time there was anything to see, and no question that Jack could deny it. In fact, knowing his brother knew, and seemed, if anything, happy about it, was an unexpected relief.

'You've gone quiet,' Will said. 'No need to say more, and I shall say nothing to anyone. Of course, I won't. You've already been in enough trouble. Besides, you are my brother.'

Was that to be the end of the matter?

'I'd be done for if you did say anything,' Jack said, not denying Will's observation, but not admitting it either.

'Even though you have done nothing about it?'

As far as Will knew, Jack hadn't, and apart from a clerk in a warehouse, and a moment at a mirror, he was correct.

'Yeah. Say nothing, and we'll not mention this again.'

'We will, I am sure,' Will countered. 'But only if and when you want to. Oh, now look at that! There's a brawl at The Old Ship.'

The horse panicked, and the driver slowed to avoid the men spilling into the street. Jack would never have taken Shadow or Treader so close to a commotion, he wouldn't even have taken that road, but his anonymous colleague above had his preferred route as all cabmen did, and who was Jack to question a fellow cabbie?

'I'm going to drop you off and then get to the yard,' he said, once they'd left the fracas behind. 'I'll find something special for our supper on the way home. You'll be alright, yeah?'

'Of course.'

'I won't be long, just want to book for tomorrow.'

'And finally pay off grandad's debt. You're a good man, Jack Merrit.'

'And you're a good brother. The best.'

Will's green eyes widened like a puppy needing love, as he put his hand on Jack's wrist, and with a wink, said, 'I know.'

With Will safely at home, Jack had the cab drop him near the yard, paid his fare, and took the last part of the journey on foot. As he expected, the yard was quiet. Waterboys went about their tasks at a steady pace, but were mainly waiting for returning vehicles, the blacksmith wasn't at his forge because it was Sunday evening, and as the farrier was dozing among his shoes and irons, there was no rasping or tapping.

Charlie had just come in, and was brushing the dust from his bowler while chatting to Stan, and behind them, the stable boy tended his horse, and another washed the cab's wheels. Seeing Jack approach, Stan doffed his cap and made for the gates with his head down, passing Jack without even a hello.

'What's up with him?' Jack said, as Charlie replaced his bowler.

'Got to get my shillings up to Harris,' he said, and set off towards the office, counting coins. 'After that, church.'

Jack trotted to catch up.

'Had a good day?' The standard enquiry was met by silence as they mounted the outside stairs to Harris' upstairs office. 'Charlie?'

'Look, Jack, I'm sorry to hear it, but there's nothing I can do, alright?'

'Sorry to hear what?'

The wooden steps were suddenly less steady than usual.

'Merrit!'

Harris was at his door, glaring down, and Charlie muttered, 'Oh dear.'

'Charlie, what is it?'

Again, silence as they turned onto the walkway, Harris ahead, his hands on his hips.

'Inside,' he barked, and was gone.

Jack took Charlie's arm. 'Charlie...?' but his colleague pulled away.

'I'll not be long,' he said, and followed the owner inside.

Harris was annoyed that Jack hadn't told him he'd not be working that day, that was all. There was no way he could have heard about the arrest, the *false* arrest, and what was it to do with him if he had? Jack would explain, and for all his miserly ways, distrust and faults, Harris was a businessman, and Jack a loyal and hard-working driver.

Apart from not caring about horses, another of Harris' faults was discussing one man's business in front of another, and he started on Jack with Charlie in the office counting his shillings.

'Disgrace,' was Harris' first word, and it came with an accusing finger. 'Well? What have you to say for yourself?'

'I've got no idea what you're talking about,' Jack said, looking to Charlie for a clue, but finding none.

'You just cannot keep your fists to yourself can you, Merrit?'

'Oh, that. Yeah, well it were...'

'A child. You attacked a child.' Harris roared so loud a horse in the stable bellow whinnied.

'No such thing. I dunno who told you, but that's a lie, and it were proved so by a barrister.'

'Oh? Been to court as well have you, and all on a Sunday?'

'It's a long story, Mr Harris, and an untrue one. I didn't hit nobody. I got pulled in for something I didn't do, and soon as they found out, they let me go.'

'Exactly. Let you go from gaol.'

'I had to have today off because of it, but I'm booking in for tomorrow.'

'Here you are, Sir.' Charlie tried to hand Harris some shillings, but the owner wasn't interested.

'Tomorrow?' he said. 'Booking in? You don't think I am accepting the license of a criminal, do you?'

Jack's world stood still, Charlie gawped, and Harris glared.

'I ain't no criminal,' Jack protested through gritted teeth. 'What you saying?'

'I thought that would be obvious even to a rogue like you. Your card, Mr Merrit, is no longer acceptable at my yard.'

'You can't do that... Why?'

'Why? Striking children, being arrested...?'

'I didn't hit no-one. Who's been telling you this?'

By his expression it wasn't Charlie, as stunned and confused as Jack.

'Happen I had a caller today,' Harris said, standing behind his chair, perhaps because he feared Jack's fists. 'Someone from Hoxton way who told me one of my cabmen was engaged in a robbery, and was seen driving a pair of criminals to and from a burglary.'

'Yeah, but that was...'

'Then...' Harris would stand no interruption. 'Discovered at an illegal gathering where the stolen goods were to be fenced, and there, attacked an innocent boy who works for the Flay family no less, before fleeing the scene, only to be dragged screaming into a police cell.'

'That's a load of...'

'I learnt other things too, Merrit, and none of them savoury. You are no longer welcome at my stables, nor will you be welcome at any others in the district. I have been putting this news around.'

'This is...'

'Stay calm, Jack.' That was Charlie, but his warning was unnecessary.

Jack wasn't angry, he was frightened.

'You got it all wrong, Sir. None of that...'

'There only remains the matter of the four pounds ten shillings and sixpence ha'penny, and you are dismissed.'

'Dismissed?'

'Yes, Merrit. I will have your debt before you leave. Ah, but then I expect you spent it in the Dog and Duck, or on one of the whores that frequent that lair. More likely lost it to gambling with the Flay brothers of Hoxton, for I hear you have made quite a home there.'

None of this made sense. Jack had never gambled, never even been to Hoxton apart from to drive through it, and would never go with a prostitute, nor even a woman.

'If it were in my power, I would rip up your card, but as I cannot, your debt, Sir, and your departure.'

'Come now, Mr Harris, this has got to be a mistake.'

'I'd stay silent, Flex, else I might think you are in cahoots with the criminal.'

Jack was more moved by Charlie's words, than he was outraged at Harris', and it might have been that which caused him to stop and take stock. It was a fleeting moment, but in it, he heard Larkin's voice, felt Mr Wright's reassurance, and imagined what Will would say.

'Mr Harris,' he said, taking a step towards the desk and reaching into his inside pocket. The action caused Harris to stand back. 'I don't know where you got these lies, but that's all they are. Yes, I was pulled in, but it was a mistake, a set-up, and all because I helped the police catch two thieves. This, I did in my own time, and without the use of your vehicle or horse. Now, you suggest I'm a man what can't make good on his debt. Charlie?'

Charlie was still gawping at the scene, but on hearing his name spoken so calmly, his head jerked. 'Yes?'

'Witness this.' Jack took a five-pound note from his pocket, and slammed it on the desk. 'Your ledger, Mr Harris.'

'Ill-gotten gains?'

'Your ledger, Sir.' It was Larkin's voice, and it came with barrister Creswell's authority. 'Four pounds ten shillings and sixpence ha'penny.'

Harris wasn't moving, so Jack helped himself to the book, found the page, and slammed it open before the owner. Once the record was made, his time with the Harris yard would be over, and as there was nothing he could do about that, he resigned himself to starting again elsewhere.

'Write, sign, and I'll be gone. Charlie, will you witness?'

'I see the repayment of Reggie Merrit's debt, Mr Harris, and I can swear it's been made honest and fair. You'd best take it, else lose it.'

Determined not to show he was quivering, Jack handed the owner a pen.

'You can keep the change,' he growled, not because he was losing his temper, but to make Harris think he was.

The ploy worked. Harris made the entry with a shaky hand, and signed. Jack also signed, and Charlie Flex put his name.

'Right,' Jack said, and the word had such an air of finality his legs nearly gave way. That was it, the end of the Merrit family's connection with the Harris yard, but not with the business of cabbing. Despite what the owner said, Jack would find somewhere else. There was, however, one last thing to see to.

'I'll say my goodbyes to Treader and Shadow and be gone,' he said. 'I know Charlie will look out for them, because I know you don't give a fig about your animals, Harris. You talk about spreading bad words about me? You wait and see what I spread about you.'

'Jack...' That was Charlie, his face a picture of concern, but he was interrupted by Harris.

'Treader, by all means,' he said, shoving the fiver into his wallet. 'But Shadow? No.'

'Why? Is she out?'

'I believe our agreement was one week, Mr Merrit, and that week was up this morning.'

Agreement? A week?

Jack's stomach churned.

'What have you done?'

'Exactly as I promised,' the owner gloated. 'I got a good price too. Eight pounds for the beast.'

'You sold my horse?'

'Don't get angry, Jack,' Charlie warned. 'That was the arrangement.'

'I sold *my* horse, Merrit, as is my right.'

Sold for eight to pay a debt of less than five, which Jack had now settled.

'Be calm, Jack.'

'Where d'you sell her to?'

'It doesn't matter, it'll be strung up and stripped by now.'

'Castor's,' Charlie said, and nodded to the wall clock. 'She went around noon, Stan said, but they shut the gates at seven.'

SEVENTEEN

It was a quarter-to, and Castor's was two miles away by the banks of the Lea on Bromley Marsh. On a Sunday, traffic would be unpredictable, and by the time he'd hooked a horse to the traces, and backed out a cab... Even by the time he'd hailed one at the station, if he could find one...

Jack planned his route as he sprinted from the yard. Two miles wasn't so far to run. East India Dock Road was a direct route, but the pavements would be crowded around Saint Anne's and the other churches, and he'd have to drop down south at some point anyway, so better to take the side streets. A cab could drive faster, but there were works on the Brunswick Road junction, and they meant delays. There was a short-cut from Poplar High Street wide enough for a hansom, but blocked by bollards at the warehouse end. No problem for someone on foot.

Past the inner basin with its barges, barques and warehouses, avoiding the trolleys and carthorses, the sellers and their stalls, running in the gutter to avoid the congested pavement, and leaping out of the way of oncoming traffic. Counting off the landmarks, The White Horse, Hale Street, the coroner's court, Cottage Street, under the arches, and past the barber where Reggie once got his hair cut and hated it, he came to the Chinese grocery shop. An omnibus clanked past with a free run ahead, and its conductor on the upper deck. Jack leapt onto the bottom step and hung from the back until polished shoes and uniform trousers appeared above, when he jumped down, narrowly avoiding a brewer's dray, and ran on. The chalk kilns, tea sellers, opium dens he'd never visited, and finally, Brunswick Road. He'd been right about the roadworks, but he squeezed between tailboards and ducked under horses' necks, sidestepped bicycles, and skirted newsstands.

Coming to the East India north quay with his chest burning as fiercely as his legs, he rested, panting, his hands gripping his knees, and his mind a jumble.

Three streets left to go. She was probably already dead. Under the next railway arch. A dead end, or had they opened it to pedestrians? Who was Harris to sell Shadow? Who'd told him about the arrest? No, it was still open for the dockers, it was only carts that couldn't get through. Five minutes. Aberfeldy Street.

If they'd slaughtered Shadow, he was already too late, but if they hadn't, she'd be stabled, waiting for the morning. He could come back then, so why run? Because there was a chance. She might be the last of the day. The axe might be falling while he dithered.

There was a law. It went back to the days of mad King George. No horse that entered a slaughter yard came out alive or as a horse. Had the law changed? Garratt Lane in Wandsworth, the largest slaughter yard in the city... It had been in one of Will's newspapers, and to Jack's disgust, he'd read the process aloud. First, they were disfigured by cutting off the mane and put in a pound to be kept there for no more than three days. There was still a chance.

Two streets, two minutes.

After that, a swift axe—at least it was swift—but the indignity that followed... Shadow didn't deserve to be strung up, to have her hide stripped from her muscles as easily as a cloth from a table, and have her hooves cut away and boiled.

Was the sickness in his stomach caused by the thought, or by his exertions? Neither, it was the thickening smell of boiling flesh and singed hooves.

The yard was at the end of the street, and one of the gates was already closed. Two men gripped the other, preparing to heave it into place, and Jack had no breath to shout. Limping and staggering the last few yards, he fell forwards against the gate, and meeting it at speed, slammed his hands onto it, rolled and fell into the yard.

'What the blazes...?'

Two dumbfounded workmen stared as he wheezed and grunted when he wobbled to his feet, and held up a hand begging for their patience.

'What you playing at?'

'Please...' Breathless, sweating, dizzy. 'Please...'

'What d'you want?'

A swallow, a gasp, another, and he gathered his determination.

'Please. I must see the master.'

'What's your business?'

'A horse.'

One of the men laughed as he bolted the gate. 'It's not likely to be nothing else,' he said. 'Who are you?'

'Jack Merrit. Please. May I see your boss?'

'Welcome to try,' the other shrugged, filling his pipe. 'If he's still 'ere. Round the side, far from the vats. Best be quick.'

Jack limped away before they changed their minds. An austere, stone building came into focus when he wiped the sweat from his eyes, and on it, a sign directing him to 'The Office of Mr Castor'. The place was ominously silent, as if the stench of death subdued all sound except his uneven footsteps as he followed a narrow lane bordered by the windowless building on one side and a high brick wall on the other. Dusk was settling, and as no lamps had been lit, the lane drew him into near darkness, until it ended in a junction. Nothing to his right but a closed gate, but to his left, the back of the offices, with lamplight in windows and an open door where a man stood rummaging in a briefcase beneath a lantern.

Another brush of his jacket, and some deep breaths to steady his heaving lungs, he approached and managed to adopt something akin to a smile.

'Sir, good evening,' he waved. 'Hello?'

The man, respectably dressed, moustached and youthful of face, looked up from his business, and registered surprise.

'Hello, sorry,' Jack said as he arrived. 'Are you the one in charge?'

'So they tell me.'

The man seemed intrigued at the approach rather than annoyed, and that gave Jack courage.

'Thank God,' he said, and Charlie in church flashed through his mind. 'Sorry to appear like this, Mr Castor, Sir, but I need to ask about a horse.'

'Then I shall direct you to a livery stable.'

'A horse that was brought for slaughter today.'

'Ah. And you are?'

'The name's Jack Merrit, Sir. I was her driver, and I want to buy her back.'

'I am not in the business of selling ingredients until they have been made into a complete product. There is a perfectly good dealership on...'

'You don't understand, Sir. She's been wrongly sold.'

'I doubt it. We only take animals that have fallen in the street, or are so unwell as to be useless. I am unable to help you, Mr Merish. I am away home.'

'It's Merrit, Sir.' Jack was not going to give up, nor was he going to lose his temper. Even though the man walked away, he followed at his side. 'Mr Harris had someone bring in a mahogany bay with a white snip. She's called Shadow...'

'We don't use their names, Mr Merrit. The men would be in danger of attachment.'

'I understand, Sir, but I am very fond of this animal. Served me and my grandfather well for these past four years. She's strong, and has a steady temperament with a hansom.'

'A cab horse? Four years? I'm surprised she lasted this long. Look, Sir, I can no more help you than I can recall buying your animal.'

'She means much to me, Sir.'

The truth must have shown through, because Castor stopped walking, and regarded Jack, first with mild annoyance, and then with sympathy.

'When an animal comes in, it never goes out,' he said. 'When did you say yours was brought?'

'Around noon today. From the Harris cab yard, and she hadn't fallen in the street, and she wasn't sick. Please, Mr Castor, I only need to know if there's a chance.'

'And if there is?'

'Then I'll do what it takes to get her back.'

'Back behind a cab?'

Jack hadn't thought that far ahead, he hadn't even thought where he'd put her. There was a house at the end of his street where Joey Shovelpick kept a horse in the parlour, but it was a working animal, and he was a lunatic. A horse, in Jack's two rooms, with Will?

'Not behind a cab, no, Sir. Not yet. Not until I get the money to buy me own vehicle. Until then... I'll find her a field. Please, Mr Castor, I'll do anything.'

The man held up a finger for patience, and placed it on his lip, thinking. As he did so, his eyes travelled from Jack's face to his boots, and back up to a central point where they lingered too long, before he glanced behind, and said, 'Assuming she is still in the pound, what price are you prepared to pay for this animal?'

It wasn't only the look that said the unspoken words, it was the tone of voice. Jack recognised both from all those years ago in the warehouse, except here, it wasn't a handsome junior clerk, it was a shorter and less attractive gentleman of business.

'Harris gave you eight pounds for her,' he said, ignoring the insinuation. 'I'll pay the same. You won't have lost anything, but you'll know a wrong has been righted. That's what I am willing to pay, Sir.'

'Is that all?'

'It's all, Sir. It's fair, it's proper, and it ain't illegal.' The last word he added to drive the final nail in the older man's coffin of hope, and it worked.

Castor sighed and opened his briefcase, muttering, 'Today... Morning...' and finishing with an 'Ah!' of discovery.

'Yes, Sir?' Jack's hopes had risen and been dashed he didn't know how many times in recent days, but Castor had a smile on his face.

'You are in luck,' he said. 'Or she is. The animal remains in the pound until tomorrow morning.'

'Then I can buy her back?'

'It isn't usual...'

'Please, Sir. I can pay.'

Castor's eyes were halfway through their second barefaced examination of Jack's body when Jack was compelled to say, 'Pay with cash, Mr Castor,' and the inspection ground to a halt.

'Fifteen pounds,' Castor said.

'Fifteen? You paid eight.'

'I did not. Here it is in ink, Sir. Fifteen pounds.'

Harris had made twenty out of Jack and Shadow in one day, but the calculation was pointless.

'Will you take ten?'

'No. You can leave through the side gate.' Castor continued to walk.

Fifteen pounds? Jack had it, but it was all he had.

Not all. He also had the upper hand.

'Eight and the grope you're after,' he called after the man, not knowing who was on the other side of the windows, or if anyone could hear.

Castor rounded on him, and shushed him with an outraged whisper, 'What are you suggesting, Sir?'

'I'm suggesting you take my offer or find yourself accused,' Jack said, aware he was being hypocritical, but unaware of where his confidence had come from. 'Eight pounds,' he repeated, standing his ground, as Castor, now red faced and glancing at the building, scurried back.

'Impossible.'

'A dalliance, Mr Castor?' It was a word Will had laughed over when reading one of his slushy books, and Jack said it with a raised voice, adding, 'You want something 'round the back?'

'Be quiet, you idiot.'

'Oh, 'round the back in that sense.' Jack's voice echoed from the unforgiving brick walls, and he strengthened his stance in case Castor took a swing.

'Be quiet. Alright, fourteen.'

'That's an unnatural suggestion, Mr Castor. I'm not like that.'

'Silence, moron. Thirteen.'

'What was that? You want to drive a hard bargain up me...'

'Twelve, and no more of this.'

A window opened a little way behind the panicking man.

'I'll do it for nine, and not tell a soul.' Louder, 'Really, Mr Castor...?'

'Ten. Take it, or be run in for extortion and making improper advances...'

'Done.'

Jack had gone as far as he could. The head poking from the window wore a security man's cap, and a voice, called, 'Are you alright, Mr Castor?'

'Yes,' Castor yapped over his shoulder. 'Call Smithson from the pound.'

'Sir.'

The security guard vanished, and Jack pulled out two of his remaining notes.

'Where is she?'

'Smithson will take you. Then you will leave, and never return.'

Castor made a grab for the money, but Jack held it away.

'Strikes me she'll need leading,' he said. 'I'll swap you a bridle and reins for my silence.'

'Whatever. Just give me the money and get out of my sight.'

Jack only handed over the notes once he, Castor and the man called Smithson stood next to Shadow, bridled, without her mane, but saved.

'Interesting doing business with you,' Jack said, and received a grunt in reply.

The men at the gate watched in awe as he left, and one said, 'Don't know how you managed that, lad,' while the other said, 'That fine horse shouldn't have been here in the first place.'

Jack couldn't have agreed more, and, by the way she skipped when the gate thumped closed behind them, so did Shadow.

'The question now is what to do with you, old girl.' Jack clicked his tongue for her to walk on.

There was no way she would take a rider, so it was to be a walk home, but there was no place to keep her there. If he left her tethered to a lamppost, she'd be gone and back to Castor's by morning, and he knew no-one with a stable apart from Larkin Chase. That would involve a further three and a half miles of walking, and Will was waiting for him at home.

What if he passed by the house, told Will where he was going, and walked her to Dalston?

'Yeah, only to find out Larkin ain't home. Then what, eh, girl?'

Shadow wasn't interested, she was walking with her head down as if she was contemplating her brush with death.

'I could try the docks...'

It was nearly dark. The stable hands would have gone by the time he arrived, and it was unlikely they would have agreed to smuggle in a horse as a favour, let alone feed and water her. Besides, he'd have to return before the managers arrived in the morning, and he'd still be left with the problem of where to keep her.

'What to do?' he said, brushing the stubble that had once been her mane. 'Why d'they do that?'

Shadow shook her head at the touch, and he withdrew. They'd cut the hair so close to the skin, it was probably sore.

'There'll be a part of you in some chair cushion before long. You'll be propping up the arse of some toff for the next how many years. Least you won't be sticking the wooden bits together. Lucky escape, Shadow. We've both had one of them. What a day.'

A day that started in a police cell and was to end with him wandering the East End with a horse. Unless...

Jack pulled Shadow to a stop and took in his surroundings.

'I'm a bloody idiot,' he said, and faced the way he'd come.

Castor's stood by the River Lea because they used the water, and it faced what was left of the fields and pasture of Bow Creek on the other side. It was as if the slaughterhouse wanted to torture its animals by letting them live their last hours right next to the countryside they'd never seen and would never know.

'I'm sure there's a livery there who'll take you for a few days while I sort something,' he said, and turned the horse.

There was, although it took him another hour to find it, by which time night had made itself at home among the nearby gas works, puffing chimneys to the west, and the funnels and masts to the south. There should have been stars, but a breeze was blowing eastwards, bringing smoke, and taking away the scent of the paddock Jack could see in the spill from four flaming torches. They leant out from the side of a wide stable block, where men were leading horses to customers, and polishing harnesses and buckles in the gloom. More importantly, the lanterns lit the sign, 'J. Grimes Livery. Horses Stabled,' and a list of prices.

None of them were what Jack wanted to pay, and payment had to be made in advance, but there was no chance to barter, even though the yard owner was sympathetic to the horse's plight and missing mane.

'One shilling and sixpence a day including feed, water and exercise in the paddock, Sir,' he said. 'We'll take good care of her and not let her out for use.'

It sounded like a good deal, until Jack worked it out to be just over half a sovereign each week, and he didn't know how long he'd need to keep Shadow there. She had finished contemplating whatever she'd been thinking about, and was eyeing the other horses being groomed and walked as if she longed to be among them. Her large brown eyes glistened under the flames, and she looked sad and bedraggled.

'Very well. Two weeks to start with,' Jack said, and paid.

Four pounds left, two of which were for Larkin.

'She's a fine horse, Sir. Her name?'

Jack told him, and stayed with her as she was led to a stall where a lad began the grooming, and she had plenty of fresh feed and water. There, he said goodbye, satisfied the livery was professional, and she'd be well looked after.

It was only when he began the trudge home that he realised how exhausted he was. A bad night's sleep, the worry of imprisonment, the speedy way he'd been released, good food with Larkin, and the moment at the mirror, and all that before the business with Harris and Castor's. Now he faced a three-mile walk. There would be no omnibus or cab ride home because he only had two spare pounds, and he'd promised to buy something decent for supper. After that...?

There were some coins in the jar that would last a few days while he looked for another firm to rent from, if he could find one to take his private license, and borrow the initial hire charge. Yard masters were a closed group, almost a club, thriving on competition, but sticking together for survival. If Harris was true to his word, his rumours about Jack would already be spreading to Mitchel's and Dray, Simmons, Krenk, even to Collins at Stepney. Mr Wright had offered to vouch for his innocence, but even a reference from a detective wouldn't be enough to satisfy a yard manager, let alone an owner.

That was a problem to address in the morning, for now, he needed food and his bed.

Stanner's sold sausages they guaranteed weren't made from cats or horses, and when he passed, he bought a pound of them along with a few rashers of bacon for the morning. A shilling of butter, sixpence of cocoa and a few vegetables, and his arms were full.

Full, and aching as much as his legs when he passed under the railway line and emerged into the orange glow of dusk. Except dusk had happened some hours before, and it wasn't orange, it was more like red, and the air didn't smell of warehouses and docks, but of bonfires and factory smoke.

'Another one,' he muttered, peering at the weird colours above the rooftops and chimneys.

There had been a warehouse fire back in eighty-eight, and although it had been along the river towards Lower Pool, he'd stood with Will and Ida to watch from Mrs Dobson's upstairs window. Later, when Reggie came back from cabbing, they all went down to the waterside to watch the spectacle, and Reggie said someone had seen two men fall from the warehouse crane, and another two had climbed down the hoist chain to escape. It had been dramatic, and the news replaced the headlines of the East End Ripper for a day or two. As far as Jack knew, the cause had never been discovered, and the men never identified.

'Ah well,' he said, turning into his street. 'Probably for the insurance and nothing to do with...'

It was to do with him, because the fire wasn't at a warehouse, it was at the end of his street where a crowd had gathered at his tenement, and where a fire truck was pumping water.

Into his home.

Paper bags hit the pavement splattering their contents, and Jack ran. Everything was silence save for the crackle of fire and the crank of the pump, and everyone was motionless, save for a policeman trying to disperse the crowd. They were watching flames pouring from Jack's kitchen and licking to the floors above, where the window frames were already alight. Jack ploughed through, hollering, 'Will!' and throwing people out of the way, until he crashed into the bobby, and two men had to hold him back to stop him running inside.

'It's too late, Jack.' Johnny Clarke was one, and his grip was firm. 'They're trying to stop it spreading to our place.'

'Where's Will?'

A woman blocked his view, and stood as a silhouette against the inferno of all Jack owned, the only place he'd lived, his home.

'Jack?' It was Elsie Clarke, and she wasn't a silhouette, she was black with soot. 'Oh, Jack...'

'Where's Will?'

'Jack,' she said, 'I'm so sorry.'

Jack's world fell about his ears with a sickening crunch of wood and plaster, and he crumpled to his knees.

EIGHTEEN

A hand gripping his shoulder, another under his arm, someone trying to drag him to his feet, and around him, crackling flames, seething steam, and voices speaking words which made no sense.

'Where's Bob Hart?'

'Took him to Bucher Row.'

'Get out of the way, Elsie.'

'It ain't spread.'

'Thank the Lord.'

'I was upstairs, I could have died.'

'And wouldn't we have rejoiced.'

'Who saw it?'

'Jack... Jack...?'

A stinging slap on his cheek rattled his head. Somehow, he was standing, staring at Elsie Clarke's screwed up and blackened face.

'What you blubbering for, man? No-one's dead.'

'Will.'

'Will's not here.' That was Johnny Clarke.

Steam billowed from what had been the bedroom, and black water ran from the front door. Smashed in or burnt away, it was no longer there.

'What?'

'Will's not here.'

'Get back. Let the men do their work.' Elsie had taken charge and was doing a more effective job than the police.

'Where is he?'

'Jack, I'm sorry you've lost whatever you had inside, but you ain't lost your brother,' Elsie said, as she and Johnny helped Jack away from the building. 'Will got out and raised the alarm, without that, we might've all been dead in our beds.'

'He tried to go back in, but it took too quick,' Johnny said. 'He was in your kitchen, I think he were trying for your jars, but there was too much smoke. I dragged him away.'

'And Bob Hart took him straight down the doctor's.'

'Why?'

'Only 'cos he was coughing. Bob makes such a fuss of the lad.'

The relief was almost as hard to bear as thinking his brother was dead, and Jack's legs gave way. Had it not been for Johnny and another neighbour leaping to help, he would have hit the ground. As it was, they had to lower him to sit on a step, where the onlookers blocked his view.

Elsie sat beside him, and took his hand. 'You can use our kitchen floor for the night,' she said. 'Mind you, it'll stink of smoke for days. Gawd knows where her upstairs is going to go. Looks like the flames put her windows out.'

Now he knew Will was safe, and now he was sitting, drinking water someone had given him, Jack's trembling lessened, and thinking became easier.

'What happened?'

'Don't know for sure,' Elsie said. 'Marj over the way said she heard horses coming up the street, and thinking it was strange, looked out. Mind you, she's always looking out, 'cos she's got nothing better to do and she's a nosy old cow. Says two men rode past and threw things at your windows. Crash, whoosh and that was that. Will comes running out shouting fire, and the place went up like a match factory. Oh, Jack, I'm so sorry.'

'Don't keep saying sorry like it was your fault, Mother,' Johnny said. 'Oi, Jack. The police is coming over. You want to speak to them?'

'I want to see Will.'

'Bob'll fetch him home soon as,' Elsie said. 'At least, he'll bring him back to what's left of your home, and that ain't much.'

'Mother!'

'You're alright, Jack, it's Constable Wilkes.'

One of the good things about being born and brought up in Limehouse was the stability of those around him, his neighbours, the local doctor, and the beat policeman who Jack had known since he was a boy. Wilkes brought a familiar sense of security and guilt, because he assumed everyone on his beat was up to something even when they weren't, and it was that which ensured nobody was. Unlike someone of the nearby neighbourhoods, there was rarely trouble in Jack's street.

'How do, Jack,' he said, crouching at eye level. 'Ain't this a nasty business?'

Wilkes was also one for understatement.

'Marj tells me it was two men on horseback. Any idea who?'

Jack could only think of one reason anyone would arson his home, but he wasn't prepared to tell Wilkes. Not until he'd thought it through.

'No idea, Constable.'

'You've not upset anyone recently, have you?'

Yes.

'Not got on the wrong side of someone? Paid all your debts on time?'

'No. I mean, yes. I settled Reggie's debt with Harris this afternoon.'

'He's a good lad, Constable,' Eslie said. 'Always has been. Both of them.'

'I know, Mrs Clarke, but unless someone got the wrong house, it looks like he's got people after him. Jack, can you think who it might be?'

Yes.

'No. Honestly, Constable. I can't. Can I see Will now?'

'In good time, son. He's being looked after. Where were you half an hour ago?'

'Walking back from East India way.'

'Oh?'

'Bought a horse and had to put her in livery a while.'

'Bought a horse?' Elsie cooed. 'Now ain't that a good start for you and little Will? You'll soon be on your way to your own cab.'

'Thanks, Mrs Clarke, maybe you should go and see if there's been any damage to your place, eh?'

Wilkes sounded keen to be alone, and Elsie took the hint. She also took Johnny across the way where the crowd had thinned, and the firemen were winding their hose.

With them gone, and the onlookers wandering home, Wilkes sat with Jack, and they stared at the wreck.

'Bought a horse? Been saving, have you?'

'No. Got a reward.'

'Oh?'

Jack didn't want to go into detail, but he told him the story up to Flay and his accomplice being arrested, but without mentioning names. Keen to keep Will, Larkin, and Wright out of the story, he also omitted their part in the events.

'Picked up the reward his morning,' he added, hardly believing it was the same day.

'Good for you, son. Who was it you got collared?'

'Don't know their names,' Jack lied, 'None of my business. I reckon you're right, Mr Wilkes. Someone got the wrong house.'

'If you got someone arrested, and the case goes to court, you'll be called as a witness,' Wilkes persisted with mistrust. 'Are you sure you don't know who it was?'

'Yeah.'

'Doesn't matter, I can find out from the Dalston station. Least, the CID can. I expect they'll be picking up the case.'

The thought only made Jack sicker. The Flays had delivered their message twice now, and he didn't want a third, but that's exactly what would happen if detectives were involved. It was the first time he'd wished he was someone else living far away, and had never taken up cabbing.

'I'll have to write everything down, and send it up the chain,' Wilkes was saying. 'Daft of me to ask if you were insured.'

'Bloody daft,' Jack agreed. 'Can I go now?'

'Don't you want to see if there's anything left?'

'There weren't much in there to start with.'

Only their savings and everything they owned, including a photograph of Reggie and Ida, Will's books, and twenty-five years of memories. All Jack had now was his pocket watch, less than three pounds, and the clothes he stood up in when Wilkes helped him to his feet.

'I'm alright, Constable,' he said. 'We'll be alright.'

'The neighbours will look after you,' Wilkes said. 'For a while, at least.'

Jack knew it to be true because Elsie had taken in Marj when she was evicted from number twelve, and Marj had fed the Simpson family when the father was out of work. Isaac Akerman from seventeen let the Chinese sisters at number twenty make straw bonnets in his back room when there was no room at theirs after the third sister moved in with her six children. Even cantankerous old Arthur fed the horse when Joey Shovelpick was in hospital that time, so yes, finding help from the neighbours wouldn't be a problem.

The problem was, Jack didn't want to. The sooner he and Will were away from the area the better. If they stayed, there would be no end of questions which, going unanswered, would lead to gossip, which would soon become incorrect fact, and the story would never die. As far as Jack was concerned, he needed to give the Flays what they wanted; his silence. It was the only way to protect himself and Will.

Although he didn't see the point, he let Constable Wilkes take him to the house, where the policeman used his lantern to light the black and sodden remains of his life, as if by doing so, it would help him accept the disaster and start again. It didn't, it only made him more determined to turn his back. There was nothing to salvage. If their saved coins were among the debris, they could stay there, it was too painful for him to enter and search, and having seen the mess through burnt-out windows, he turned his back on the place, and walked.

Will was his first priority, and he followed the route Bob would have taken. When he rounded the corner into Butcher Row, he saw them coming towards him, and ran.

'He's alright,' Bob said, as Jack wrapped Will in his arms. 'Might cough a few days, but he'll be right.'

Jack kept the tears at bay, determined to remain strong for Will's sake. Some of his hair was singed, but not missing, his eyes were pink, but apart from that and one gloved hand, the only difference in him was that he stank of smoke.

'Why are you wearing a glove?'

'Doctor gave it to me.'

'He's got a bit of a burn,' Bob explained. 'Not bad, but the doctor wrapped it.'

'Incorrectly.'

'Will wasn't happy because the bandage weren't in a straight line, so they gave him that to cover it. Does it still hurt?'

'Stings, Uncle Bob, but the ointment appears to be working.'

'And everything else is alright?'

'Yes, Jack. I'm fine. I managed to grab some coins before Johnny Clarke pulled me away.'

'You could have died.'

'I'll buy Johnny an ale or two as a thank you,' Bob said, wittering on as they walked. 'He'll be happy with that. And we'll be happy to have you at ours until your place is put right. I expect your landlord'll be down on you, but if he gives you any trouble, you come to me. I'll see what I can get from the Cabman's Fund. I expect you'll take tomorrow off, but you'll need to get back to work.'

It didn't feel right, walking homewards, and it also felt wrong not to tell Bob about the business with Harris, but he'd find out soon enough. There was no way the Fund would assist even if he'd still been employed, because Harris was on the committee. Instead of giving his granddad's old friend more to worry about, Jack said nothing but his thanks, and listened to Will describe what had happened.

Will had been in the bedroom when the first brick came into the kitchen, and he'd just run to the curtain to see what the noise was, when the second came in behind him. Luckily, he'd turned, and had his back to the kitchen as the first flaming bottle landed, and the second exploded behind the bed, which sheltered him from the eruption. He'd tied to swamp the flames with a blanket, but soon saw there was no hope, and there was nothing he could do but flee. Heroically, he tried to save the money jars, which was how he burnt his hand.

Jack kept his wary eyes on the road, and his arm around his brother's shoulder, and when they reached the corner, kept hold of him as he drew him to a halt.

'What's up?' Bob asked. 'Not far to my house from here.'

Jack shook his head. 'Thanks, Bob,' he said, and looked Will in the eye. 'But I reckon both of us could do with being away from here a while. We've got somewhere else to stay tonight. Am I right, Will?'

Will gave a shrug, and then an 'Ah,' of recognition, and a smile appeared on his face.

'Yes,' he said. 'And on the way, we have much to discuss. Am *I* right, Jack?'

'It's ten o'clock. 'I'm turning in,' Mrs Grose announced. 'I expect there's something you want first, so what is it?'

'Nothing,' Larkin said, writing at his desk beneath the oil lamp. 'You are free to go to whatever it is you do up there.'

'Which will be none of your business. There's things in the pantry if you're hungry. I expect Emily will be home before long.'

A swish, a clunk of the doorhandle, and the sound of the housekeeper trudging upstairs told Larkin he was free of her grousing for the night, and he put down his pen to crack his knuckles. The piece he was writing about the various charities operating in the East End wasn't flowing, and he knew perfectly well why.

'Jack Merrit,' he said, pouring a sensible measure of port.

Jack and that business at the mirror.

'I don't mind... Would you do me chest?' he muttered, and

remembering fondly, took his drink to the window. 'Perhaps I would...' Stay the night, he'd meant, but he couldn't. 'Probably never will.'

Why was he obsessing over something he couldn't have? The best he could hope for was a hurried, furtive dalliance behind locked doors when Mrs Grose was out, and that wasn't what he wanted.

'What *do* you want?' he asked himself, drawing back the curtain to watch the road.

The answer was simple to find, but impossible to realise. To have a man like Jack with him permanently at his side, and not behind the closed door of a hotel room where they'd risk detection, or beneath the shrubbery in Hyde Park where he *had* been detected, but there, in his home. A home he could share with a man like...

'Not a man like Jack, but Jack himself.'

To be a couple, that would be the thing. To live as Colonel and Mrs Sharpe lived next door, except without the grandchildren calling on a Saturday to wreak havoc in the garden. A couple, like Mr and Mrs Ashmir closing up their drapery business opposite, chatting about their day, and holding hands as they walked away. Open, honest, able to share his affection freely, able to live and love like the millions in the sprawling city behind the dull brickwork of Bloom's piano shop. To be in the Crown and Castle talking openly together, or for Jack to be there while Larkin prepared lunch on a Sunday, and with it roasting in the range, to join him for a drink, a chat with friends, and maybe a game of skittles before they came home to dine together, read together, and retire to their room.

Maybe he shouldn't be writing about the bad works of good-meaning people in Whitechapel. Maybe he should be writing about the injustice of British law, or praising the author of 'Dorian Gray' for offending the moral principles of a hypocritical society.

'Now that would be daring, but would it do any good?'

It would do him no favours, that was for sure.

Neither would moping at the window watching for cabs and hoping to see Jack pull up in his hansom. There was no point in wondering what might have been had Jack agreed to stay, and he needed to drag his mind away from erotic memories of the man's form and feel, and attend to his praise of the Cheap Street Mission set against his scorn for the Working Men's Collective for the Preparation of Boys, an operation with a distinctly dubious title.

All the same, he stared at the passing traffic, watched couples with mild envy, and allowed his mind to drift to pastures unobtainable until the filigree carriage clock chimed a delicate half hour. Emily would no doubt be in the back yard with this week's catch, but he had no interest in viewing the weekly contest, and was about to drop the curtain when two shapes on the other side of the road drew his attention. They were moving slowly, one tall and broad, the other shorter and thinner, both trudging as though reaching the end of a long walk, and, now, crossing directly opposite his front door.

An exclamation of joy was immediately struck down by knowing something was wrong, and it wasn't because he wanted to reach them before they passed his house that sent him flying from the room, it was knowing they were coming to him for help. He was out on the path before Jack and Will reached the step, and he ushered them in without a word. They brought the distinct smell of bonfires, and Will wore a single glove. Both looked exhausted, had sweat on their brows, and both were dishevelled.

'What on earth has happened?' he asked as soon as they were safely inside.

The drawing room was the closest place for comfort, and he lit the gas, telling them to sit and not worry about the state of their clothes, which were as filthy as the rest of them. The devil would be as damned as himself, but he rang for Mrs Grose before pouring the men each a drink, and thrusting the glasses into their hands. Jack downed his in one, while Will sipped, turned up his nose and set the glass aside.

'Couldn't think where else to go,' Jack said. 'I hope you don't mind.'

'Heavens, no, but what...? Have you been in an accident?'

'Give me a minute,' Jack said, and Larkin refilled his glass.

When he'd taken a little more Scotch, Jack told a long story in short bursts, saying how he'd paid a debt, but been sacked from work. There was something about his horse being sold, running, bartering, and buying it back. Then came Grimes Livery Stable at Leamouth, and he was saying the place wasn't at all grimy when Mrs Grose appeared.

'What?' she demanded, from the folds of her dressing gown, but when she saw the guests, her attitude changed. 'Oh dear, Mr Chase, have we become a hospital? What do you need?'

'Not a hospital, Mrs Grose, but a refuge. As soon as Emily is home, or now if she already is, have her draw both baths. Towels, please, and the beds to be made. The men will be staying tonight, and as I will not take a refusal, prepare both the upper guest room and the one opposite mine. Then, I think, some kind of light supper?'

The housekeeper didn't even grumble as she spun from the room with the alacrity of an ice skater.

'You are staying, the both of you,' Larkin said.

'Nowhere else to go.'

Jack continued his story, and it was horrific. Will filled in some details, Larkin asked if he needed a doctor, but he said his hand no longer hurt, and the tale ended with Jack's decision to be as far from Limehouse as he could go.

'I brought you the two pounds,' he said, and offered the coins.

'That's the most ridiculous thing I've heard a man say in this room.' The gesture was as touching as it was pathetic, and Larkin wouldn't have it. There was a brief debate, but he won the day. 'What was the word you used?'

'Hobbled. It's what the detective said, or the barrister, I can't remember. Seems so long ago.'

'But, Mr Chase, it's obvious someone is following Jack,' Will said. 'If they know we are here, won't they come after us? That wouldn't be good for you.'

'If they did, I would not give a fig, but I don't understand how they knew.'

'Knew?'

'The Flay family, or one should say, mob. Yes, I understand their supporters would have seen you at the auction, Jack, and the made-up story of the assault is easy to imagine. As is the way they discovered your address; they only have to read your cab plate and examine some public records. What I don't understand is how they knew you were released this morning, and, on learning that, dispatched a besmirching messenger to your yard, and two assassins to burn down your home.'

'We were discussing this,' Will said, because Jack was having trouble keeping his head up. 'At some point in the morning's proceedings, one of the legal men suggested someone at the police station is working with the Flays.'

'Ah, yes. Sadly, very possible. Criminal activity is not exclusive to the criminal these days. The question is, what are we to do about all this?'

'Nothing,' Jack said, although it was more of a grunt. 'I've got us in enough trouble, and I ain't going to give anyone no more. They can have my silence in return for leaving us alone.'

That, for Larkin Chase, was akin to letting the rich get away with evading tax, while taxing the poor to pay for it. Under any other circumstance, he would have launched into a speech about how it was wrong to ignore a wrong, and how justice must prevail, but it was clear to see that Jack wouldn't welcome any further debate on the matter. Not at that time of night and in his state of exhaustion.

'We can think about this tomorrow,' he said. 'For now, the pair of you must take as long as you wish in the bath, and then have something to eat. Then, you are welcome to stay for as long as...'

He was interrupted by a single, echoing hammer blow of the front door knocker.

Jack sat bolt upright, threw Larkin a look of panic, and leapt to stand in front of Will.

'Who on earth...?' Larkin made to leave, but met Emily hurrying along the passage. At least the girl was home and, he assumed, still chaste. 'The maid will see to it,' he said, returning to his chair. 'I'm sure you are safe to sit, Jack.'

'I ain't trusting no-one.'

'Understandable, but you are here now, and I will do all I can to protect you. Both of you. Failing that, we could always set Mrs Grose on the villains.'

The attempt at humour fell to the carpet like a landed fish and lay twitching until Emily appeared.

'Letter for you, Sir,'

'At his time of night? Was it a messenger?'

'No, Sir. Wasn't anyone. Just that. I looked out, but...' A shrug finished the description, and Larkin dismissed her.

'Sounds like my editor,' he said, to lighten his pervading nervousness. 'Passes by on his way home. Jack, sit.'

Jack did, and Larkin examined the delivery. No seal, so it wasn't from his editor, and no return address. In fact, no address at all and no name, just a simple, blank envelope. What lay inside froze his blood, but as it did so, it also solidified his determination.

If Arthur Flay gets sent down, you is dead. Your idiot brother is dead. Chase is dead. Your horse is already dead. Disappear.

No signature, of course, and no doubt who had sent it. There was also no doubt that Jack mustn't know what the note threatened.

'Yes, just my editor.' Larkin put on a false smile. 'Now, how about you two head upstairs. I expect your baths will be ready by now. I'm sure I don't need to tell you to be careful of your hand in the hot water, Will, and I will find you some clothes and something to sleep in. They might be a little, um, alternative by way of fit, but needs must, and all that.'

His flustering continued until Mrs Grose appeared to declare the baths were drawn and soup was simmering, and processed the two men upstairs as though on her way to a royal event. The drawing room once again quiet, Larkin was able to clear his thoughts of everything apart from what needed to be done. That decided, he sat at the escritoire to compose two telegrams to be sent first thing in the morning, and with those prepared, he sat and thought for some more, until he concluded there was nothing else he could do but extinguish the lamps and make his way to bed.

The aroma of lavender and lemon perfumed the landing, suggesting Emily had scented the baths with more zeal than economy, and when he looked into the spare room, Mrs Grose had made a good job of preparing it as though it were a French boudoir. The lamps were turned low, and the bed turned down and inviting. Inappropriate though it was, he stood at the washstand, and wondered how Jack might react if he found him there, or better still, in the bed, waiting.

Jack would enter the room immodestly wrapped in only a towel, see Larkin, and close the door. With his troubles washed away, and with his lips parting in a smile, he would ask if Larkin wouldn't mind drying his back for him, and this time, his legs. Starting at the feet, Larkin would kneel before him as a supplicant worshiping the statue, and in a ritual of adoration, dry the smooth feet, the sturdy calves, the knees and...

'What are you up to?'

He was up to Jack's imagined manhood when he suffered damnation under the eyes of Hecate in her dressing gown glaring from the doorway.

'Just making sure everything is in order, Mrs Grose.'

'Obviously, it is. Mr Merrit and Mr Merrit are taking soup in the scullery, so you've missed the chance to stumble upon him half naked, and so did Emily. I made sure of that.'

Ignoring her remarks, he said, 'The scullery?'

'They wouldn't have it any other way. You think they're safe, Sir?'

'Safe?'

She pointed to the ceiling. 'I'll lock our doors.'

If anything, he would advise the men to lock *theirs*. Will, to keep him protected from the maid, and Jack, because Larkin didn't know how he was going to sleep knowing Jack was so close; he was the out-of-reach fruit tree in Hades, and Larkin was Tantalus.

'You going to bed?'

'Yes, of course.' Larkin shuffled from the room, taking a last look at where Jack would sleep, and set about preparing for the night, leaving the ever watchful and knowing Mrs Grose to settle the guests and restore order to the house.

NINETEEN

The following morning, the housekeeper woke Larkin in the usual fashion and at the usual time. What wasn't usual, though, was her talk of guests, because he rarely had any, and telling her to let them sleep as late as they wanted, and to give them breakfast when they wanted it, even if it was at lunchtime.

'In which case, I'll give them lunch,' she said. 'Are you in or out?'

'Both. I have some errands to run. Before then, I will forage in my dressing room to see if I can find anything which might fit the Merrit brothers. I imagine I am a similar size to the younger, but the older might challenge a few seams. I'll leave what I find by their doors.'

'Very organised,' Mrs Grose muttered as she tied back the curtains.

'Maybe you could have Emily launder their own clothes.'

'Already on the line.'

'Then that is that, you are free to go, and I am free to rise.'

Left alone, Larkin rose with his mind ordering a list of things to do, and as he washed, dressed, and wandered his study between tea tray and toast, he planned his morning, all the while listening for heavy footsteps on the stairs, but hearing none. Jack was still not awake when he left to send his messages, watching out for anybody near his house who appeared suspicious.

'This is the Kingsland Road,' he told himself. 'Everyone is suspicious.'

The telegrams sent, he visited Hoffman's, the clothes shop on the Balls Pond Road who sold at reasonable prices, and set the limit on his account to accommodate, 'Two gentleman who will call later in the day, or perhaps tomorrow, to be fitted with whatever they require to that limit.'

'May I put down the names, Mr Chase?'

'Certainly. Mr and Mr Merrit, brothers of my acquaintance who have run into a spot of bother, but you don't need to tell them I told you.'

'Discretion and design, Sir, as it says on the door.'

It did and always had, and Larkin had never understood why a gentlemen's outfitters needed to advertise their discretion. He could only assume it was a promise not to divulge the length of a man's inside leg to all and sundry.

'There we are, Mr Hoffman,' he said, signing the ledger to prove he had authorised their use of his account. 'Don't let them be too modest in their purchases. They have been through an ordeal, and it is my pleasure to treat them.'

'Very generous, if I may say so, Mr Chase.'

'You may, but it's not really. Good day.'

Dalston Junction was a battlefield of omnibuses, carts, and cabs fighting for a place in the queue to drop passengers at the railway station, or to slip in ahead of others as if everyone was late for the single train of the day. There was more than one train, of course, a fact seemingly unknown to the city gents and clerks, Stock Exchange runners and lawyers fighting their way to Liverpool Street for another day of drudge and drear. Steam billowed from the locomotives below, whistles shrieked at the volume of Mrs Grose discovering a mouse, and the smell of oil and heat wafted through the warm morning air, creating a not unpleasant odour of industry. Thankful he didn't need to scurry and keep to a schedule, Larkin passed by the carnage on the other side of the road, and continued to the next, more subversive item on his list.

His regular man was selling the daily news at his stand, while his boy paraded up and down hollering maxims of no interest, and Larkin picked up a copy of The Times. There would be one waiting for him at home, but this one was a prop, and reaching the police station, he paused to lean beneath the overstated portico and its lantern, and read the front page. This was to allow anyone who might be following to catch up, but there was more to his rouse, and after two minutes of staring at advertisements for all manner of balms, nerve pills and powders, he folded the paper, pretended to read the time from his pocket watch, and hurried up the step into the building. If anyone was watching, they would now also be wondering.

The entrance hall wasn't what he was expecting, but then, he'd never entered the establishment, and wasn't sure why he was doing so now, except to worry his follower, if he had one. If the building's external architecture suggested the inside would be just as grand, it had lied. The hall was divided by low railings, keeping the public from the officer who sat at a desk on a dais, protected, ironically, by a grille as though he were a gaoled criminal. Around him, the walls displayed a clock, a few bills, a noticeboard with nothing on it, a calendar, a fire hose, and a single gas lamp. All very decorative, but what Larkin found more curious, was the throng of people waiting to be served. Perhaps some great disaster had befallen the borough during the night, or maybe Monday mornings were the favoured time for reporting crime, it was hard to tell, because there was so much noise, he was unable to hear individual conversations. What did occur to him, however, was that had it not been for Mr Wright and his barrister friend, Jack would still be in this establishment, and Larkin would be heading for the magistrate's court to learn his fate.

Jack was on his mind as he sauntered near the entrance as if he was waiting for someone, watching the door in case anyone obviously unsavoury came in, and, after five minutes of seeing no-one, tucked his newspaper under his arm, and left. Standing on the step, he did his best to impersonate a man waiting for another who had failed to arrive, even shaking his head at his watch for effect, and, seeing no-one stand out from the crowd as a possible spy, made his way home.

'The gentlemen have stirred,' the housekeeper said, as she

descended the stairs like one of the four horsemen stalking down to earth. 'Scullery.'

'Mrs Grose, did I not say they were welcome to use the house as their own?'

'That's why they chose the scullery. They're from Limehouse, Mr Chase. They're not used to your... grandeur.' She sneered on the word. 'You want coffee, I suppose.'

'If it wouldn't stretch the limits of your benevolence.'

'We'll see. Message for you.'

She scowled at the hall table and continued to the basement, leaving Larkin free to collect the envelope.

Little more than an hour had passed since he'd left the post office, but already, there was a reply from the livery stable at Leamouth. Larkin had prepaid for a response of up to twenty words, so perhaps that was why the message had come so speedily, but whatever the reason, he read it with relief.

Be advised Shadow alive well and cared for. Will be vigilant. Your Servant. Grimes.

Jack didn't need to know how, acting on the anonymous note, Larkin had written to ask after the horse and explain that someone might be trying to do it harm. Neither did he need to learn that Larkin had offered to cover any extra costs in keeping it safe until such time as it could be rehomed. What Jack did need to know, however, was that Larkin had sent a second telegram, the reply to which came to his study along with his maid and his coffee tray.

Emily, being a young lady of few words, said, 'Boy's waiting.'

Larkin was equally impressed at the speed of its delivery but less apprehensive about opening this message, because it didn't concern life and death.

Will call at two. Advise. JJ Wright.

Mr Wright might also be a man of few words, and so could Larkin be when the time called for it; a fact which surprised many.

'The reply is this,' he said, and handed Emily some change. 'Will expect you.'

'To do what?'

'No, the message is, *Will expect you*. That's all you need to know. Tell the boy, he will understand.'

'If you say so.'

Emily could be as wayward with her manners as her mother, and thus, just as entertaining.

Larkin rested on the corner of his desk to sip his coffee and address his next issue. How to tell Jack and Will what he had planned. Although it seemed right for the men to be in his house, and although he and Jack had shared that moment of understanding at the mirror, he was aware he hardly knew them. Their physical aspect was as plain as the handsome nose on Jack's smooth face, and Larkin knew he had a temper, but other than that, he had no way of knowing how Jack would react when he heard what he had organised.

'Why d'you do that?' was his reaction in the drawing room later, and it was neither outrage nor anger, but something more akin to curiosity.

'There are two reasons,' Larkin replied from the opposite armchair, where he had an accidental and distracting view of Jack's lap. The man sat with his legs apart, and the trouser seams were, indeed, being challenged. 'Firstly, because I thought we should take expert advice. I am sure we don't need to guess who burnt down your home, and we don't need to ask why. With no home, the police will have trouble finding you to call you to give your testimony.'

'That don't matter. I'm not going to be there.'

Larkin understood his reticence, and said so, but added, 'However, I am not sure that you will have a choice. You were the closest witness to the crime, you identified the men at the scene, but you will have to do so in court if the villains are to be put away.'

'I gave me statement. They've got that.'

'But I am not sure if it will be enough. This is why I have asked Mr Wright to visit.'

'I think that's a good idea.' Will had taken off his shoes and was crossed-legged on the chaise, reading like a thin Buddha. 'As is your second reason for inviting the detective.'

'Oh?' Larkin said, amused. 'How do you know I have a second reason?'

'Obvious.'

'Do tell.'

Will put his book in his lap, where Larkin's trousers were a much better and less revealing fit, straightened a cushion, and explained.

'Mr Wright has an interest in gathering information about the Flay family on behalf of Scotland Yard, he said so. You have an interest in helping people, and you have a fascination for the detective. Therefore, I would say you have invited him here because, if it can be proved they destroyed our home, he will have more evidence against them to pass to his friend in the police. You also want to thank him for assisting Jack the other day, even though you gave him lunch, and that is also to do with your fascination.'

Will was quite correct in all aspects, but the word 'fascination' hung over Jack's penetrating gaze, which Larkin could easily read as mild concern, and he asked the younger brother to explain.

'When I say fascination, I mean in his job, rather than his figure. No need to look worried, Jack. I don't think Mr Chase has a fancy for anyone but you.'

'Will!'

'There are only the three of us in the room, and we all know what's what.'

'You don't know what you're talking about.'

Larkin begged to differ, but didn't. Instead, he passed a smile to Jack, who looked away, blushing, and crossed his legs.

'Will is correct,' Larkin said. 'I am interested to know the detective better because he is a detective, and his job sounds intriguing. I also thought your terrible incident of last night would be of interest to him, and of course, we could do with his advice on how to secure you against further reprisals. He's coming at two. That doesn't leave enough time for you to visit Hoffman's and have lunch, but you can go later or tomorrow.'

'I'll get back into me own clothes soon as they're dry,' Jack said. 'Don't need nothing new, thanks.'

'Don't be rude,' Will scolded.

'How's it rude? Larkin doesn't need to spend his money on us, we can look after ourselves. It's a nice offer, but we'll be alright.'

'It's rude because it is clearly what he wants to do, and he will be upset if you turn him down. In this and other matters.'

'Not at all,' Larkin offered.

Will hadn't finished. 'I can't say I know how these things work in real life, I've only read about them in books, but when a man is courting a woman, it is common for him to buy her gifts. In this situation, Jack, you are the woman…'

'Oi!'

'It's merely an illustration. Mr Chase is keen to express his affection for you, and, I suppose, for me, but that is friendship or charity rather than anything carnal. His way of doing this is to treat you to something nice, in this case, a new outfit. Previously it was two sovereigns so you could have a day off. That's all that is happening, and I for one am very happy to take Mr Chase's charity.'

'I don't see it as charity,' Larkin said, dumbfounded at Will's accuracy and honesty. 'Simply a necessary gift.'

'A gift for the man you are courting.'

There was nothing Larkin could say to that, because, having heard it said twice, he found it undeniable. It was exactly what he was trying to do, and he must have been making it obvious. At least, to Will. Jack hadn't said anything and was staring at him across the Turkish coffee table and the glasses of pre-lunch sherry.

'Let's all take that silence for what it is,' Will said, returning to his book. 'The truth settling between you, with Mr Chase wondering how Jack will react to it, and Jack not knowing what to say. What time are we eating?'

***

Lunch was at one, and before it, Larkin took the opportunity to ask Will to promise not to make any more observations for fear of upsetting the staff, to which Will said, 'Of course I won't. I am not stupid, I am precise.'

Jack said nothing about what had been discussed, and because Emily was coming and going, and Mrs Grose was fussing about the table, there was no chance to broach the subject or speak to him alone. The conversation was mainly about the weather, the finer details of Jack's trouble with his yard, horse and home, and what he intended to do about work. Convinced he would have no problem finding another company to hire from, Jack was adamant he and Will would secure new lodgings in a few days, 'Even if it's down Dorset Street,' he said, words that chilled Larkin, because that was said to be the worst street in the East End.

There was also talk of Mr Wright and what Larkin intended to ask him, and as the hour of the detective's arrival drew near, he became more concerned about two things. What Jack had made of Will's observations, and what he would agree to do about the Flay hearing. The first had to wait until they were alone, and the second, he hoped, would come clear when Mr Wright arrived.

When the knocker was struck at precisely two o'clock, it was Larkin who answered, because Mrs Grose and Emily were downstairs having their lunch, and to interrupt the housekeeper at mealtimes was more dangerous than disturbing a wild animal while it was feeding.

'Mr Wright,' Larkin greeted him on the step, and wondered why people felt it necessary to remind someone of their own name.

'Mr Chase.'

It also worked the other way around.

'Now we have assured ourselves we know who we are, come in, please.' Having closed the door, and hung Mr Wright's cap, he passed him the anonymous note, and whispered, 'My friends know nothing of this, and I would like to keep it that way for fear of worrying them. I have made enquiries, and the horse lives, but as you can see, there is a very real threat made against them.'

'And you,' Mr Wright said, handing it back. 'No prizes for guessing who sent this.'

'Quite.'

Wright nodded with a thoughtful air of professional authority, and his youthful face was set with concentration more suited to an older man. Larkin assumed this was his working persona, and it reminded him that he was the client, and Mr Wright would be charging for his time. That accepted, he made short work of the pleasantries, established that no-one wanted or needed tea, and came straight to the point.

'Last night, Jack and Will's home was set on fire,' he said. 'We believe it was another way to stop Jack from testifying at the trial, and Jack has decided he won't. I asked you here for your advice.'

The detective had a notebook out and open, and asked the brothers to tell him all they knew. Jack started by describing how he'd lost his place at the Harris Yard, how someone had told his employer about his arrest, and how Mr Harris didn't believe his side of the story. Then he described how the man, Harris, who sounded as odious as the River Fleet had once been, had said no other cab yard in the district would hire him. Will then described the incident at their home, and Mr Wright made notes throughout.

When the stories were concluded, he put the lid back on his pen, and took an envelope from his satchel.

'This came from my contact at the police station,' he said, opening a letter. 'They are keen to have Arthur and Bernard Flay in court as soon as possible. Inspector Adelaide has pulled strings and pushed buttons, and they will appear at Bow Street at ten on Wednesday morning.'

'That seems remarkably fast.'

'It is, Mr Chase, and with good reason. Everyone is keen to send this family the message that the law-abiding public will take no more of their nuisance. The police will crack down hard and fast. By putting the two eldest brothers behind bars, they will prove they mean business and are not afraid to bring them to justice. This criminal family has terrified this part of London for years, but, so far, no-one has been able to bring a case against them. You, Mr Merrit, are the first chance the police have had.'

Jack chewed his lip and said nothing.

'Jack is not prepared to be in court, Mr Wright. Does he have a choice?' Will was beside his brother on the chaise, sitting close as if to protect him.

'Not without good reason,' Wright said. 'If Creswell was here, he'd witter on about Richard the Second, the fourteenth century, writs and Chancery Court. I know, because I've had the lecture. If you are called, and you will be, and you fail to attend, you can be held in contempt of court.'

Jack groaned. 'What's a good reason?'

'Good reason to be absent when called? Er, depending on the judge, severe illness, injury or being near to death. There are no hard and fast rules, only that it would have to be bloody good for a judge to let you off in a case like this. Have they sent you a summons?'

'If they had, Mr Wright, it would either now be ash, or is currently being delivered to a pile of burnt debris,' Will said. 'We have had no letters since the arrest was made, save for the one calling Jack to claim his reward.'

'Then it's my duty, on learning this, to let someone know where you are. Shall I put this address?'

'Hang on,' Jack objected. 'You ain't come here to drop me in it.'

'No, I've come for you to help me drop them in it,' Wright said. 'It's the law, Mr Merrit, and we have to obey it.'

'What if I just disappeared?'

They'd used the word on the note; *Disappear.* It was what Jack should do for his own safety, and by the sound of it, what he intended.

'It would catch up with you in the end,' Wright said. 'No-one can disappear forever.'

'Then I'll take contempt of court.'

'It's not as easy as that.'

'Look, Mr Wright, I've been banged up, lost me job, lost me home, me brother's been injured, and all because these two persuaded me to identify a fare. I've had enough of it, and I ain't going further.'

'Jack...'

'No, Will.' Jack shifted away from him. 'It's up to me. They've got a written statement, that'll be enough, won't it?'

'Probably not in a case as important as this.'

'Well, it'll have to be. I ain't going to be there. I'm going to be looking for another yard, for another job, over west, I don't care. If I have to sleep in the bloody stall or cab, so what? I'm getting me life back to normal starting tomorrow, and it don't include aggravating these crooks. Not if they're as bad as you make out.'

Judging from their actions and the note, they were worse than Mr Wright had suggested, and Larkin could well see why Jack was frightened.

'What do you think?' The detective aimed the question at Will.

'I say it is up to Jack,' he replied. 'What I would do and what I think is right should have no bearing on his decision. If he wants us to live in a stable, then I will, and, Mr Wright, please, your tie is not straight. Would you...?'

Wright adjusted it, and was about to say something else, when Will continued.

'However,' he said, sitting forward. 'If you ask me for my appraisal of the case, it is this. Inspector Adeliade, having failed to bring the East End Ripper to justice four years ago, and having failed in a few other notable cases, is keen for a triumph. This case would be it. Therefore, he has put pressure on you, Mr Wright, to undertake some of his investigative work for him. This, you are doing because he is paying you, and you need the money. I say that because at lunch yesterday, you mentioned staffing problems and a large workload. You are keen to assist Jack because you also need a success. Now, knowing to what lengths the Flays will go to hobble my brother, you can only wield the law as your weapon of choice. What you can't do is physically force Jack to attend court. You are welcome to try, but he is bigger than you. So, you asked me what I think, and that is it. That, and this. I assume you and Mr Chase know something else that we don't, because when you entered, you did so with a furtiveness worthy of Uriah Heep. Whatever it is can only be bad news. A death threat, perhaps?'

'What?'

'I am only supposing, Jack.'

Larkin and Mr Wright exchanged a worried look, and the gesture, leading to a stilted pause, gave them away.

'Bloody hell,' Jack moaned. 'You see? I told you I didn't want to get involved in this shit. Now look where it's got us.'

It was saying the words that made Jack realise what a mess his life had become since meeting Larkin Chase, and having said them and made his point, he said nothing else. The court case was their problem. Larkin had started it, and Mr Wright had involved himself, so they could finish it together. Once the detective had gone, he'd go and look for work, perhaps at the livery stable where he'd left Shadow, maybe, as he'd said, out west somewhere. The crooks would see he wasn't in court, and leave him alone. He'd risk whatever Wright had called it by not turning up, and that would be that. Another spell in prison, a fine, whatever it led to, he'd put up with it, and Will could bunk in with the Clarke family while he was inside.

Larkin and Wright were still chatting to each other, this time about Will's observations, and how Larkin had been out looking for spies. Wright was finding it funny, and Will was scrutinising both men while offering his observations and help.

That was the other side of the penny piece. Will.

While Jack could cope with being sent down, there was the question of what would happen to his brother. If he bunked with the Clarkes, either they'd drive him mad with their ways, or he'd drive them mad with his, and there was no guarantee they'd look after him well enough. It wouldn't be fair to ask Bob and Edith to take him in, because they were old. Although Charlie Flex had the room, Jack would get back from his time inside to find Will either converted to Jesus, or run away from the endless praising of God. Whichever way he looked at it, he couldn't leave Will on his own. He needed to be among friends, and by the way he was talking with Larkin, he'd found one.

That was the impossible third side of the penny piece. Larkin bloody Chase.

This stranger who'd stepped out of the night, cheered Jack when he needed cheering, listened to him when he needed an ear, and presented him with a way out of debt at the right time. A well-dressed, clever man with his strange ways, even stranger servants, and his fine house. More, with his generosity and, even more still, his understanding of Will's ways and Jack's... Jack's what? His needs? Desires?

Anyways... This Larkin bloody Chase who'd appeared from the darkness and somehow attached himself to Jack's heart... No, be honest, it was lower down than that. To think about 'heart' suggested love, and Jack wasn't in love. Lower down, where lust lived, that's where Larkin was hanging around, doing his courting as Will embarrassingly put it, and where Jack came close to joining him yesterday.

Was it only yesterday? Yes, just over twenty-four hours ago, Larkin was close behind him at the mirror, Jack's lob was pressing painfully against the washstand, while Larkin's was pressing wonderfully against his arse. Jack had realised earlier that it was going to be possible with Larkin if he went about it the right way, and they might have gone further if it hadn't been for the housekeeper.

Anyways... None of that was helping. All he'd done, while Wright babbled on about something called Delamere, was give himself half a swelling in borrowed underwear that Larkin had only worn once, itself a thought that made matters worse. At least they had moved on from trying to persuade him to turn up in court.

'Then there's not much more I can tell you,' Wright was saying, when Jack forced his mind back to the room. 'I'll call on Creswell on my way home and tell him where Jack is, so he can arrange the summons. What you do with it is up to you, Jack, but if you don't want to be sent down for contempt...'

'I'll speak to him,' Will said, and Jack scowled.

'Creswell will want some time to prepare you before the hearing,' Wright went on as he stood to leave. 'So, please, let us know.'

There were more words, some thanks, and other chat as Larkin saw him from the room, but Jack's mind kept coming back to two things. Testify and he'd be dead, and Larkin bloody Chase behind him at the mirror.

TWENTY

The rest of the afternoon compounded Jack's confusion as Will begged him to stay at the house at least another night, and to visit the clothes shop and accept Larkin's gift. Jack gave in to please his brother and to give himself more time to think, deciding that there was no point making himself homeless straight away. That settled, Larkin told them where to find Mr Hoffman's shop, and said the shopkeeper knew the limit.

It turned out to be a generous one; two shirts, two suits, ties, collars, and all necessary under garments, plus shoes. Each. Mr Hoffman was as generous with his praise as Larkin was with his purse, and fell on the brothers with enthusiasm. Having appraised them from all angles, and taken their measurements in a process Jack found awkward, he declared, 'I know exactly what to find you for the best.'

Hoffman led a discussion about casual suits in the old Albert style, narrow silhouettes for Will, and light cloth for the summer. He asked if they would be dining formally, and when Will said that was unlikely, made them try on three-piece suits in shades of grey, suggested shirts with detachable two-inch, turn down collars, and asked if they required gloves.

After an hour of the fuss, Jack had had enough, and having chosen shirts from the shelf, and accepted two readymade suits, told Will to stop rearranging Mr Hoffman's stock by design and colour because it was time to leave.

'I shall deliver presently,' the shopkeeper said when everything was boxed, and Jack said, 'Alright,' because he assumed that was what happened in places where wealthy people bought clothes.

Back at the house, Larkin said nothing more about the court hearing, and to fill the time before dinner, invited the brothers to read from his collection of books. Will accepted the offer without a second thought, but Jack explained he had never been one for reading books, and sat with a newspaper.

It was a unique experience, and one he wasn't comfortable with. Since starting work at the docks when he was twelve, his days had consisted of eating, working and sleeping, with only the occasional day of idleness caused by illness. Since working his cab, he'd had more time to read the papers, but even then, he'd been sitting on his bench, or by the road, and not concentrating because he had to remain alert for customers. A soft seat with arm rests, a quietly ticking clock, and the distant rumble of traffic were new to him. Not the traffic, of course, but the fact that he wasn't among it, and he became aware that while he was idling in a rich man's home, work was happening beyond the net curtains and embroidered drapes, and he was not involved. It reminded him of being in the police cell with the world turning out of his control, because it was no longer his business, and he couldn't help thinking he was just as trapped in Larkin's house as he'd been in gaol.

A glance at Will, reading crossed-legged on the floor with a contented smile on his face, and he told himself not to be selfish. A longer look at Larkin in the opposite armchair, also reading but with a frown, and he reminded himself how lucky he was, and turned his attention to the newspaper.

Five minutes later, he wished he hadn't.

Her Last Confession.
The Unsolved Murder of an Informer's Girl.

It has been three months now since the body of Harriet Steele was discovered in the doorway of her home in Basing Court, Ivy Lane, not far from the main thoroughfare of Hoxton Street, and still no arrest. When discovered, it was thought by a passer-by, that Miss Steele, a seamstress, was inebriated, but it soon became apparent that she was bleeding from the throat. The passer-by, whom the police have asked not be named, raised the alarm with the keeper of an adjacent premises, at that time of night abed, and, having ensured the victim was attended, ran into Hoxton Street to alert a policeman.

Attending, Police Constable Myers blew his whistle and raised a wider alarm before dispatching the passer-by to find a doctor. The unfortunate Miss Steele, twenty-one, was dead by the time the physician arrived, and later, the Medical Examiner stated that no amount of attention could have saved the poor woman. Her throat had been severed to a depth that was just enough to ensure death came slowly, and when the corpse was examined, her clothes were found to be saturated with blood, although there had been very little of it about the scene.

'It was as if the murderer wanted to inflict a painfully slow death, as if, in some macabre way, to allow the victim time to contemplate her end,' Mr French, the Medical Examiner stated.

It was thanks to the nature of the injury, and the gradual loss of life, that the victim was able to describe to PC Myers what had taken place. 'Her last confession,' the policeman called it at the inquiry.

It transpired that the father of Miss Steele, being of a very low income, had been watching the goings-on in Basing Court on behalf of the constabulary in return for a small stipend, a not uncommon practise in extreme cases where the police need public assistance by way of an informer. When questioned, PC Myers was at first reluctant to give the name of those Miss Steele's father was paid to observe, but when pressed, admitted she had mentioned a man by the name of Dodge as her attacker. This was not a Christian nor surname, but a street name given to the man, as each member of his gang went by a word derived from the first letter of their first name. Basing Court, Myers said, was where this particular gang met and stored contraband, the family leaders of the organisation being the owners of the dilapidated buildings and cellars of the area. (Readers may remember our recent article, 'The Colombia Road Disappearance', and how, in that case, the missing person was found in the cellars at Ivy Road, sadly, too late. It is assumed the same criminal gang were responsible.)

PC Myers could expound no further, he said, for fear of retribution from the gang, and asked that his evidence be kept undisclosed. This, the magistrate denied.

Due to the fact that Miss Steele was an innocent party, and not the informer, the magistrate concluded that the man, 'Dodge' had 'Sent a message to the informer.' He said, 'The father would spend the rest of his life regretting his part in assisting the police, and that is a far greater punishment than death.'

Also disclosed was the rest of Miss Steele's 'last confession', in which she stated her father had been watching members of the gang for some time, that they were engaged in many a criminal activity, and their operations centred around the Basing Court area of Hoxton. That was all she knew.

'What she knew was common knowledge,' PC Myers said. 'Miss Steele's only crime was to be the daughter of a reliable police informant, and a man who felt it his duty to assist the law.'

The father was not at the inquest, and has moved away from the city for fear of further acts of vengeance.

The police have yet to bring anyone under arrest for the murder, and it seems to The Times as though they are afeared to do so. A little investigation of our own revealed the name of the gang, indeed, the real name of 'Dodge,' so it would be a simple matter to present a court of law with Miss Steele's last confession, and have justice brought against her killer. Perhaps the police fear further acts of vengeance if they bring the Flay family to justice; we at the Times, do not.

There was no escaping his predicament, not even when reading in a soft chair, with his brother content and safe, and a man opposite who looked up now and then to offer the sweetest smile Jack had known.

Jack threw aside the paper and sighed.

'Nothing of interest?' Larkin said.

'No.'

'I fear you are bored.'

It would be rude to say yes, but dishonest to say no, and Jack was just about to lie when there were two heavy knocks at the front door.

'Emily will go,' Larkin said, putting down his book. 'Do you play chess?'

'No.'

'Ah. Cards, perhaps? I could ask the colonel next door if he and his wife would like to make a four for bridge.'

Some of the men at the docks had played cards during their brief breaks, but they'd played for money, and Jack wasn't a gambler. Also, he had no idea what bridge was, so he declined the offer.

Larkin was running off a list of other card games Jack hadn't heard of when the maid appeared in the doorway, and announced, 'Delivery. Lots.'

She wasn't wrong. It took her and the men to carry the boxes to the appropriate upstairs rooms, where she left them to go and work on dinner.

Jack stood in the guest room, hands on hips, head shaking, and said, 'I will be paying you back for all this. One day, you'll see.'

'If that's what you want, Jack,' Larkin said. 'Did you try them on in the shop?'

'No, only the jackets. Your man said he knew what he was doing.'

'That sounds like Mr Hoffman. I get most of my clothes from there, but it's disappointing he doesn't do hats. Maybe, if you tried these on now, it would relieve some of your boredom.'

'I ain't bored.'

'And I am not blind, Jack. What do you say, Will?'

Will was straightening the boxes so their edges matched. 'I'd say it was obvious you were not blind, Mr Chase.'

'About trying on the clothes? If there's a misfit, we can have it replaced tomorrow.'

'Very well,' Will said, and having satisfied himself the boxes were as they should be, swung his head between Jack and Larkin. 'I'll leave you alone and try on mine downstairs. I know how to collar a shirt and measure an arm length, because I have read about it in books. Jack, on the other hand, has less experience, and may need instruction. Mr Chase, once I am in my new nether-garments, I shall launder those you have lent me, and will see you at dinner. I will, of course, be wearing more than my underwear throughout.'

Once Will had left them, Larkin said, 'I'm sure you don't need me to help you change.'

He said no more, but gave a laugh, and the smile remained, as if he was expecting Jack to disagree. Jack wasn't sure what to say, because he wasn't sure what the man meant by the statement, and a pause grew between them, increasing in awkwardness the longer he dithered.

'I'll call back in a few minutes to see how you're getting on,' Larkin said to break the deadlock. 'I'd like to be assured Mrs Grose and her girl will be kitchen-bound for some time.'

With that strange remark, he left Jack to explore the collection of boxes, and begin unpacking as though he was moving into a new home.

Was that what Larkin intended? Was it his way of dropping a broad hint that, should Jack want to, they could both live with him? If so, it seemed a strange thing for a relative stranger to do, but then Larkin was like that. Jack had seen it in his eyes, and Larkin had told him he had a desire to assist, and to make someone's life better. That was, after all, what he did with his writing.

'Yeah, he's a nice man,' he admitted, laying a suit on the bed.

Trousers, waistcoats, jackets, all put on hangers and hung in the otherwise bare wardrobe, the shirts came next. They would need pressing where they had been folded in their boxes, but he hung them in the hope the creases would fade.

'You'll look like a right gent. Them on the rank won't recognise you.'

They would, because Jack, like his grandfather, always dressed smartly for work, but thinking of the rank caused him to wonder what his colleagues were doing at that moment. Sweating beneath bowlers, their arses sore from a day on the bench, dust in their eyes and in their throats, a few coins jangling in their purse, and the constant smell of horse manure about their nostrils.

'I'll get back to it one day,' he sighed as he laid out socks, garters and undershirts.

The drawers were white and made of a fine, light material like the borrowed pair he was wearing, much more comfortable against the skin than the woollen ones he was used to, and soft to the touch. They would also be a better fit, because Larkin's were tight all over, particularly at the ankles and waist. Will said he was going to launder his, and thinking he might as well join him at the tub, Jack began to undress.

There was water in the bowl, a towel and soap beside it, and it seemed appropriate to wash before climbing into new clothes.

'The same bowl,' he said, unbuttoning his shirt before the full-length mirror, and remembering the time before. 'Still only yesterday.'

Maybe that was why the moment was so easy to recall, and the feel of Larkin behind him so easy to enjoy again as he'd enjoyed several times since.

'Nothing to do with time,' he told his reflection. 'All to do with...' Hardly believing he needed to tell himself, he said, 'Desire,' and with his shirt off, unbuttoned his trousers.

Larkin's trousers, he remembered, and his fingers were popping the same buttons as Larkin did the last time he wore them. If the man was in them, and Jack was doing the exact same thing, he would discover the same white underwear, but what would be beneath that? What had filled the cotton when Larkin last wore them? What had pressed where Jack's lob now strained?

Socks off, vest removed, only his legs remained covered, and even though the waist was tight, he was reluctant to remove the drawers. The tightness was part of the pleasure, but there was more pleasure to be had in his imagination.

There he was, watching himself in the mirror from his half-combed hair to his bare feet, but he pictured Larkin. His open face with its intelligent eyes and perfectly manicured moustache, a sign of both manliness and manners. His high forehead, free of blemish or wrinkle, and his tidy hair, lightly oiled and slick, dark and trimmed to show his ears. The look of fascination, the twitch of the smile, and the round, smooth chin.

Where Jack's naked shoulders were broad, how would Larkin's be without his suit? Where Jack's chest had only a smattering of fine, blond hair, would Larkin's be forested and dark? Would his muscles be as obvious as Jack's, and his stomach as flat? Jack had worked physical jobs all his life, had Larkin? Or, did the body of a man who sat and wrote turn to flab through lack of exercise? Maybe he played sports; he'd never said. Maybe he knew how to moderate his fine dining, and what if he didn't?

Did it matter?

Just thinking of the man caused a greater swelling in the front of the drawers. The tight press of the material added to the pleasure as he stared at his reflection, but he needed to change, and putting his thumbs beneath the waistband and lowering it, he revealed himself. Where he stood half-proud, thick and long from a tangle of light brown, and hung heavy beneath, how would Larkin look? Darker, smaller?

Did it matter?

Washed, and with the new drawers on, he continued to examine his reflection, and imagine. Still half-proud, the thought of Larkin naked, compounded by the feel of the new underwear, perfectly fitting and cool against his skin, brought him to full erection. It was pressed against his thigh, and refused to diminish, even when he tried to force it downwards. Touching it only made things worse, and he was unable to let it go, yet knew, if he continued to grip it and picture the man downstairs, the first thing he would do in his new clothes was create a stain.

Did it...?

A knock at the door.

Jack grabbed the nearest thing to hand, the towel, and held it against the swelling. With his back to the door, he called, 'Who is it?'

'Larkin. Are you decent?'

No, was the answer, but that would send him away. Yes, would be a lie.

'Come in,' was what he wanted to say, and it was only when he saw the door open did he realise he'd said it aloud.

'Oh.' Larkin was surprised and turned his head. 'I can come back.'

'No, I don't mind, not if you don't.'

A glance behind, and Larkin slipped into the room and closed the door.

'I don't,' he said. 'They are a better fit. At least from this angle.'

'Are they?'

Jack twisted to see his arse in the mirror, and even though it was vain to do so, had to agree. When he looked up, Larkin was smiling, and he turned to see what was funny.

'Good Lord,' Larkin said. 'I should avert my eyes.'

He didn't. Instead, he stared at the towel. Only, Jack hadn't grabbed the towel but a flannel, and it hid only part of what he'd meant to cover.

Unable to refuse himself, he dropped it, and said, 'How do they look now?'

Larkin's Adam's apple rose and fell as his face lifted, and the two men locked eyes.

'Michelangelo could not have done better,' he said. 'Though his sense of proportion was clearly too modest.'

Jack didn't understand the comment, but he understood why his heart was racing and his flesh was tingling. There was no question about what he wanted to happen next, as he made no attempt to cover the obvious, and said, 'What material is this?'

'I would have to feel it to tell you.' Larkin took a step closer.

'I don't mind.'

Another step, and he was there. A few inches away, and still holding Jack's stare, he reached to touch the leggings at the hip, but Jack caught his hand, and glanced at the door.

'I took the liberty of turning the key,' Larkin said. 'Your brother is causing havoc in the scullery with the washtub and staff. They will be kept busy a long while. We are safe.'

Still holding Larkin by the wrist, Jack moved his hand the last few inches, and placed it over his erection. Larkin gasped, and in return, took Jack by the back of the neck and pulled him down until their lips met.

What came next was passionate and quick, but natural. As Jack tore Larkin's clothes from his body, their mouths still clamped, he could only wonder why he hadn't allowed himself to know the sensations before. The feel of another man's firm buttocks in his hands, another man's rigid length battling with his, and soon, in his grip.

Standing pressed against the wardrobe, one led and the other followed, and one experimented and the other learnt. One lay the other down to press and slide, to grasp hands and hold them behind the head while tongues clashed, and hips writhed. Time melted away. It was of no consequence, all that mattered was the other man, the freedom to explore him, to test and taste, to give pleasure and receive it equally in return. Kisses travelled over chests, smooth and light, dark and hairy alike. Lips trailed lower, gripping and gliding, while calloused fingers messed oiled hair, and smooth palms cupped cheeks. Gasps became more frantic, movements more urgent, until, when it was undeniable, they lay with lips pressed together, shuddered, whimpered stifled moans of release, and shared disbelief at the pleasures finally known.

TWENTY-ONE

The images returned to him throughout the evening; a naked man in his arms, beneath, on top, sliding, sweating, and later, washing and dressing, as Jack languished on damp and crumpled sheets, unbothered by his nakedness. It was impossible to resist the secret smiles and shared looks across the dining table, even though Will would have noticed, and it was hard to make conversation. Every sentence took on a new meaning.

'Pass the salt.' Larkin's skin tasted of salt. 'This steak is a little firm.' His buttocks were firm in Jack's grip. Every action, too. The way he held the long-neck decanter; the same way he'd held Jack's erection. The way he ran a finger around the rim to catch the drips; the same way he had run the same finger over Jack's blissfully sore lips, before saying, 'We must dress. We will be missed.'

Jack missed the sensations as soon they were over, and although he tried to think of other things, they stayed with him, and once in bed, intensified. There was a man across the passage, willing and available, and with everyone abed, he only needed to sneak from one room and enter another. What else would he experience with a whole night and less fear of discovery?

Although he dozed in and out of semi-alertness, it took him a long time to fall asleep that night. Twice he relived the entire scene while bringing himself to the same conclusion, and washed with the same flannel, yet still sleep evaded him. It was only when he heard a clock strike two did it approach. Fragments of unrelated moments interrupted his thoughts, weird faces danced across his eyes, and voices spoke meaningless words. The house creaked, and he woke again, thinking Larkin was coming to him. An unlikely smell hung in the room, as if someone else had come in, but it wasn't Larkin's scent, and there was only him and the silence. The faces returned, advancing through a dark tunnel that darkened further as they led him deeper beneath the earth until, with his body aching, there was nothing more to see and nothing left to know.

Morning came with shocking suddenness, and he sat up in bed wondering what he'd just heard. The mild hubbub of traffic, a newsboy calling, a crow, it hadn't been any of those things. It had been a voice, and it came again. The housekeeper beyond his door barking an order. 'Tea.'

The clock read eight, the room was light, and his belly was rumbling. There were things to do. To look for a new yard, to visit Shadow, to consider his role as a witness. That last thought brought with it the same misgivings, and drained the joy he had woken with as he plunged his face into last night's water, rinsed the flannel, and dried with a clean towel. Mr Wright had talked about a summons and a punishment, and Jack still had a decision to make. Deciding he would think about it later in the day when he was away from the house and far from Kingsland Road, he dressed, and went in search of breakfast.

Larkin was in the dining room, and Jack greeted him with a good morning in the way he would greet anyone. He felt no embarrassment when sitting down with the only man who had touched his body so intimately, and he felt no shame about what they had done. There was no sudden leap of the heart, or stirring in his loins as there had been the day before, and that was probably a good thing for propriety. Yet, where he'd expected to feel different, he felt exactly as he would have done on any other morning.

Apparently, Larkin was the same, or else he was pretending to be because the maid was about, and the day began as anyone would expect.

'Mrs Grose has conjured up some mighty fine bacon,' Larkin said. 'I also recommend the sausage. More tea, please, Emily.'

The atmosphere changed as soon as the maid left, and Larkin leant forward to whisper.

'I dreamt of our union,' he said. 'I am so happy we have crossed that bridge.'

'Oh,' was Jack's reply, because he wasn't sure what the man was saying.

'I hope you have suffered no regret.'

A shrug.

'Perhaps, if chance allows, we can attend a repeat performance.'

If only the man would speak plain.

'Maybe,' Jack said. 'Where's Will?'

'Still asleep, I imagine.'

'He don't sleep this late. I'll go and knock.'

'Are you avoiding me?' Larkin asked, as Jack rose. 'Please, suffer no embarrassment.'

'Eh? No. I ain't suffering nor avoiding, just want to get Will up. Just because we're in your nice house, don't mean he can lounge around like a lord. Won't be long.'

'Mrs Grose will go,' Larkin said, and before Jack could stop him, had rung for the housekeeper. 'Your breakfast will go cold.'

Jack gave in, sat, and pushed things around his plate while Larkin sent the housekeeper to wake Will, and prattled on about what was in the news. Jack only half listened, and was wondering if he could borrow the paper to look for cab firm advertisements in the west of the city, when Mrs Grose reappeared.

'I don't know how you live in your home, Mr Merrit, but we don't expect that kind of slovenliness in this household.'

There was an accusation in there somewhere, and Larkin picked up on it first.

'What are you saying, Mrs Grose?'

'The boy's room's a disgrace. Don't expect me to clear it up.'

Will, make a mess? 'You sure you got the right room, Miss?'

The housekeeper's glare would have been enough to scare a carthorse, and Jack shuddered.

'Where's Will then?'

'How would I know?'

'Perhaps he is downstairs.'

'No, Sir, and why would he be?'

'I don't know, Mrs Grose... Maybe he took a walk.'

'If he did, he's gone in his unmentionables. Anyway, it's your problem.' She threw that at Jack, and left the room mumbling, 'Clothes all over the place, bed upturned, this isn't Limehouse.'

Jack was pounding up the stairs before the housekeeper had gone below them, and threw open Will's door to be met by a mess his brother would never have made. His clothes lay scattered, half the bedsheets had been pulled off, and the pillows were nowhere near the bed. A check of the wardrobe revealed his other suit, both pairs of shoes were there, and his notebook was on the table. Will never went anywhere without that.

'Good heavens.'

'This is bad,' Jack said, pushing past Larkin in his hurry to check the study, and to climb the stairs and look in his own room.

No Will. Not in Larkin's room, and not in either bathroom.

'Perhaps the back yard?'

They leant from the landing window to find Emily below emptying a bucket.

'Is Mr Merrit with you?' Larkin called.

'No.'

'He's not here,' Jack said. 'That's not how he'd leave a room. Someone's taken him.'

'Taken...? Come now, Jack. I understand your concern, but...'

'I'm telling you. Someone's been in and taken him.'

'How? The house is always locked.'

'If they can break into a pawnbroker, they can get into a house.' Jack was on his way down with Larkin at his heels.

'And do what? There is no indication he has been taken, Jack. Maybe he had a... I don't know. Something went wrong in his mind.'

Jack rounded on him.

235

'There ain't nothing wrong with his mind,' he spat. 'They've come and nabbed him.'

'Where are you going?'

Jack reached the hall, and charged into the drawing room. No Will, just the morning light and expensive furniture.

'The window...'

Examining it, he found it closed, but the catch was unlocked.

'I expect Mrs Grose threw it wide to welcome the day,' Larkin said at his shoulder.

Jack lifted the casement with ease and peered into the front garden. The house stood ten feet from the road, and the garden was surrounded by a low brick wall. The path led to the front door, and the rest of the area consisted of shrubs, none of which were trampled.

'You think someone came in through here, up the stairs, took your brother and exited without leaving a trace, and without waking anyone?'

Larkin had backed away from the window and was standing in the middle of the room, confusion written large on his face.

'What else?' Jack said. 'I can see you don't believe me.'

'It's not that. In fact, I would agree it is possible if not probable, but there's another thing.'

Larkin sniffed, and Jack noticed it too. The smell of... something unusual.

'It was in my room last night,' he said. 'I thought I was dreaming, or that you'd come in.'

'Would that I had,' Larkin said. 'I may have disturbed whoever has been in the house. One thing's for sure, I would not have worn this as a scent. It is far too sweet and lingering.'

'What is it?'

'I have no idea. The question, Jack, is what to do? If you are this concerned, I suggest the police.'

'What, them what's working with the Flays?'

'We don't know it's them.'

Jack's jaw dropped. How could a man so intelligent be so dim?

'They got me bunged inside thanks to their bent coppers. They torched our home. They've made threats against us. Oh, God.'

Had the armchair not been there, Jack would have hit the floor. Death threats. Will gone. The article in the newspaper. The lengths the Flays would go to. They had taken his liberty, his livelihood, possessions and home, all that remained was life. Not his, but Will's, because if they killed his brother, Jack would live the rest of his days knowing he was to blame.

'Mr Wright.'

It was obvious who had him and what they would do, but would they let him go when Jack failed to appear in court? Was Will already dead?

'Mr Wright.'

'What?'

'Gosh, Jack, you are very pale.'

'Wright?'

'Yes.' Larkin crouched beside him. 'I will telegram and ask his advice.'

'You've got his card, right?'

'Yes.'

'I'll go there. Now.'

'He may not be home.'

'Bloody hell, Chase, will you stop thinking with sense and try a little heart?' Jack was out of his chair and halfway across the room. 'What's the address? I'll take a cab.'

'No, wait.'

Larkin took him by the shoulder. Instinctively, Jack spun, balled his fist, and raised his arm, but it hung there, blocked by Will's voice and Larkin's expression. It wasn't fear, nor was it anger. It was sadness, and Jack relented.

'We shall send a message and ask him to come immediately,' Larkin said, as if Jack hadn't just threatened him. 'I'll ring for Emily; you sit and collect yourself. There is nothing to be gained from panic. We will proceed with calm and common sense, because that is the only way we can help your brother.'

Hearing a sensible course of action spoken in such a calm voice was like hearing Will recite the simple route from Limehouse to Tower

Hill, and Jack felt his feet on carpet for the first time since he'd left the dining table.

*　*　*

With Emily dispatched to send the telegram, the only thing to do was wait, and Larkin sat beside Jack on the chaise in the way they had sat on the park bench the night they met. The poor man was wretched with worry, staring into nowhere, but twitching at every sound within the house, and now and then crossing to the window to peer out, clicking his fingers when he paced, or fiddling with his empty pipe. When Larkin asked if he wanted to smoke it, Jack threw it into an armchair, and twisted his handkerchief instead.

Larkin understood his torment, and thanks to the events of the previous evening being so sharp in his memory, likened Jack's not knowing to the sight of him in and out of clothing. To see a man dressed in ill-fitting and revealing underclothes led the mind to imagine what lay beneath. That was erotic because it engaged the imagination. Later, the sight of his nakedness negated imagination, and what had been erotic became carnal. Larkin wasn't complaining about either. However, to be uninformed about something beyond one's control also engaged the brain, but not in an enjoyable way. Jack was imagining the worst, inventing dreadful scenarios and disasters, and he was letting his imagination torment him. Release would only come when he knew what was happening, when the currently hidden facts were laid bare, and he knew what lay beneath. Even if tragic, at least he would no longer need to imagine.

At one point during the wait, Larkin persuaded him to sit, and Jack listened while he comforted him, being careful not to use expressions such as, 'I am sure he will be fine,' because both knew that was unlikely. The more Larkin spoke, the more Jack's expression crumpled, until he broke down and sobbed on Larkin's chest.

They were in that position when Mrs Grose wandered in, said, 'Bloody hell,' and wandered out again, a moment later shouting, 'Tea. Upstairs.'

'Her and her bloody tea. Shall we?'

'I can't,' Jack moaned.

Larkin insisted, Jack gave in, and the housekeeper's intervention drew him back a little from the edge.

They were in the study, Jack's cup rattling in his saucer, and Larkin at the window, when a hansom drew up outside, and Larkin very nearly thanked God.

'Mr Wright is here,' he said, and dived out of the way as Jack lumbered to see for himself. 'Be calm. We will be in the best possible hands.'

A short while later, they were. The moment the detective brought his professional, assured self into the room, Jack calmed, and Mr Wright came straight to the point.

'Your message left no doubt something terrible has occurred,' he said. 'What?'

'They've taken Will.'

'Jack believes the Flay gang have his brother,' Larkin clarified. 'Will is not here, and we can think of no reason for his absence.'

'Why do you think this? Tell me everything.' Mr Wright helped himself to a seat, and had his pen at the ready.

Jack told him how he'd found Will's room and how unlike him it was, how his clothes were still there, old and new, and how, like Mr Wright, he never went anywhere without his notebook.

'What does he keep in it?'

'How far he's walked, the number of steps, how many of what kind of birds he's seen, how many pages he's read. It's like a diary of numbers and facts.'

'I see. Go on.'

Jack told him about the unlocked window, which, Larkin added, hadn't been opened by the servants as he'd first thought. He also mentioned the strange smell, and Larkin agreed it was one he didn't recognise.

'It's gone now,' he said when Mr Wright asked.

'Was it a sweet smell?'

'Yes, I would say so.'

'And where did you notice it?'

'In my room first,' Jack said. 'I was having trouble getting to sleep, and there were sounds...'

'Sounds?' The detective leapt on the word.

'Yeah, you know, how the gas ticks when you've turned it right down, the house settling.'

'Someone walking about?'

'Well... I heard a board creak, and I thought someone had come in me room. That's when I noticed the smell.'

'What time? Can you say?'

'I can. It was around two. There weren't much traffic, if any, and I heard the clock.'

'Anything else from that time?'

Jack shrugged. 'Like I said, I was half asleep and dozing off. There might have been other sounds or voices, but I can't tell you if they was real or dreaming.'

The story told, Mr Wright asked to see the house, and Larkin led him up to Will's room. There, the detective told them to touch nothing while he picked his way to the window, examined it, surveyed the room, and made notes. That done, he used his pen to open Will's notebook and read the last entry. A frown and a shake of his head suggested there was nothing of use there, and once he had seen enough, asked to visit the drawing room.

At the top of the stairs, the detective made a strange request.

'I'd like you to go first, Mr Merrit, then you, Mr Chase, and I'll come last, but Mr Chase, could you go sideways, with one hand on his shoulder and one on mine. Keep that position until we reach the ground floor.'

Larkin didn't ask why.

'Don't let go, and you and me, Mr Merrit, we have to keep contact with him, understood?'

Jack said he did, and in a slow and ungainly way, they continued down the main stairs to the hall. Larkin walked sideways, placing one foot first, then the other beside it, and repeated the process on every step. It was laborious and ached his legs, but he managed the journey without tripping.

'Interesting,' Mr Wright said, and having swept his fringe from his forehead with his pen, entered the drawing room.

'The smell was also apparent in here,' Larkin said. 'Faint, but out of place. I'd certainly not noticed it before.'

'Flowers?'

'My housekeeper won't have them. They make her sneeze.'

'Polish?'

'Beeswax with copal and rectified spirit of wine. She makes her own.'

'Was it the copal? Sweet with lemons and pine?'

'No. I well know the scent of Mrs Grose's weapons of work, and it was not as hideous.'

Mr Wright was at the window, holding back the nets to examine the frame. Fascinated, Larkin watched as he lifted the bottom casement and sat half in, half out for a closer look of the garden. Once back inside, he continued to ask about the smell.

'A bit like being at the doctor's,' was all Jack could add, but it was worthy of a note in Mr Wright's book.

Larkin took the detective to speak to the servants, who could add nothing, except to confirm the doors had still been locked when they came to them at six, both front and back, and nothing else in the house had been disturbed. With the questions over, Mr Wright asked everyone to the study, and there, wrote two messages which he gave to Emily to dispatch immediately.

It was only after the maid had left, and Mrs Grose had been asked to provide coffee, that he announced his conclusion.

'You are right, Mr Merrit,' he said. 'Your brother has been taken. It is safe to say, by the Flays, and we know why.'

'Will they kill him?'

The look Mr Wright gave Larkin said everything. They would kill him whether Jack testified or not. Will was to be used as an example for anyone else who might try and stand in the way of the family Flay. It had happened before.

'No,' the detective said. 'Not yet.'

The *not yet* had an instant impact on Jack, and it took Larkin some time to assuage his anxiety.

'Look,' Mr Wright said, and put aside his notes. 'This is what's happened. Sometime around four-thirty this morning, two men slipped a knife into your front casement window and slid the lock. From there, they came up first to Mr Merrit's room, and then, down to Will's. They'd been watching the house, and they knew which room was your front bedroom, Mr Chase, so they had no need to look in there. Having found Will, they knocked him out and carried him off. Our strange descent proved there is room for two men to carry another on your stairs without too much trouble, but it's not so easy to avoid the creaking boards, which is what you heard. You weren't dreaming, Mr Merrit, but it wasn't two o'clock.'

'How can you be sure?' Larkin was now more than intrigued with the detection, and more than impressed with the detective.

'Because what you smelt was chloroform, and although it cloys and lingers, it doesn't hang around for more than four hours. You smelt it in the drawing room just after eight, you said, so it had to be in the house no earlier than four, probably on a cloth covering Will's face. He put up a struggle by the looks of his room, but he would have been asleep in seconds. Now…'

Mrs Grose made one of her timely appearances with a tray. She served Mr Wright and Jack, and left Larkin to fend for himself, warning him, 'Biscuits are for the guests,' as she left.

'That was what took place during the night,' Mr Wright continued. 'Here's what will happen now. The hearing is tomorrow at ten. We need to have Will safe by then. You, Mr Merrit, must go to court. Here is your summons.' He dropped a document on the coffee table.

'I ain't going.'

'Hear me out. Sir Easterby Creswell is the prosecuting barrister, and you are his witness. You stand in the witness box and do exactly as he tells you. If we have Will safe, you give your evidence. If we don't have your brother, Creswell will cite an ancient law that's never been repealed, and the case will be adjourned while his objection is considered. That will give us more time. Meanwhile, I must go and make enquires.'

'Is that it?' Jack was on his feet, the same as Mr Wright. 'You just going to tell us Will's been taken, I'm in court, and now you're buggering off?'

Where Larkin expected the detective to be insulted, he laughed, and slapped a hand on Jack's shoulder.

'That's exactly what I'm doing, Jack. But don't worry. I will be back later, and in the meantime, you can expect a friend of mine to call. You're under the protection of the Clearwater Detective Agency now, gentlemen, and more importantly, so is your brother.'

TWENTY-TWO

More waiting, and more pacing from Jack. The clock ticking away the hours, the daylight fading as the roll of traffic increased, thrived, faded and died in waves of time passing. The housekeeper came and went bringing trays Jack ignored, and later, lighting lamps, and drawing curtains. Jack said little more than, 'Where is he? What's he doing?' and Larkin could only offer vague reassurance. Much as he wanted to engage in a discussion of what had happened between them, it was not appropriate, and although his concern for Will grew with every lost hour, he kept a calm head for Jack's sake. Having finally persuaded him to sit and eat, and hopping it would ease his distress, he dispatched the maid to buy Jack some new pipe tobacco.

Emily left the house by the front door, and having fixed her hat, fixed her mind on Jepson's on the corner of Downham Road. She would venture no further on the Kingsland Road, and she only used that tobacconist because Mr Jepson's son was her age and, by her standards, fair of face. Reaching the shop, she crimped her cheeks, put on her coyest smile, and stepped inside.

The bell jangled as her eyes scanned the shop with its shelves of boxes and tins, but she wasn't looking for products, she was looking for

Billy Jepson. There was no sign of him that evening, but there was another man at the counter, and although badly dressed, she deemed him worthy of closer inspection.

He was tall enough for her taste, although young, and smelling worse than gone-off meat, it only took her a glance to know he lived on the street. Had he been clean, his features might have been suitable, but there was too much working-day grime to tell. Apart from that, the creature was buying a twenty-four tin of Player's Navy Cut, and she couldn't abide that brand. She stood away from the tramp, and was pleased to see him leave.

The tramp stepped from the shop with a sense of having been scrutinised, and had he been himself, he might have said something to the rude girl in the straw hat. There was work to be done, though, and no time to lose, because his colleague was waiting. Having turned the corner, he approached a man in a bespoke suit standing by a modern two-horse trap.

'These be the ones you suggested?' he asked, offering the tin.

'That's them, Mr Pascoe, Sir, perfect match for the garb,' his colleague said in his chirpy, London accent. 'You puts five or six in your pocket, and I'll take the rest. Don't want to look like you can afford the whole tin. You got the poney and matches?'

'Poney?'

'Money.'

'Ah. Aye.'

'Then you be all set. I'll wish you good luck, though I knows you don't need it. Me and Joe'll be going on to the Crown. Will we see you after?'

'That be hard to say, Mr O'Hara. Depends if I learn what Mr Wright needs to know. There be much to do afore he be happy, but I'll find you there if I don't get set upon and end up in Barts. See you later, God willing.'

'You'll be fine, Mr Pascoe, Sir. You done it before, and you look the part right down to the stink of oakum. Be seeing you.'

The suited man, whose rough accent was the antithesis of his appearance, climbed into the trap. The tramp made signs at the driver, who, in turn, offered a thumb, made the shape of the letter L, and passed it across his face. Good luck wished, he snapped the reins, and the trap was on its way, giving Mr O'Hara a comfortable ride back to his fashion house in the West End.

There was to be no comfort for the tramp, however, a man more used to kid gloves and pressed shirts than festering costume, but he watched his colleagues leave with no concern. Mr O'Hara was right, Pascoe had done this before. Since starting work at Delamere House, Maxwell had proved himself equal to Silas Hawkins in his ability to mimic and become someone else, and although he'd never admitted it to Mr Wright, he enjoyed the breaks from silver and service, and aspired to one day tread the boards at the Lyceum.

For now, though, thoughts of etiquette and politeness had to be put away like the saltshakers in the plate safe, and the doors closed on his daytime work. A cigarette lit and hanging from his lips, he shuffled to the junction, hung against a lamppost, and counted pennies while slipping into character.

'Be just enough fur an old sea dog a buy a man a toothful a gin,' he snivelled at the coins.

His Cornish accent would serve him well, as would Mr O'Hara's disguise, and having assured himself he was not being watched, continued to shamble south towards the Dog and Duck.

A limp, head down, coat open to reveal his threadbare jumper and oversized trousers tied with string, he pushed his way through the creaking doors into a melee of bad piano playing and raised voices. His cigarette smoke mingled with the fog as naturally as he mingled with the vagabonds and crooks who huddled in corners, and swore over card games, illegally gambling stolen money. Listening for plots and gossip, the tramp fell upon the bar as though he'd just crossed a desert, and slammed down coppers.

'Gilbey's,' he croaked. 'Whatever me made money'll get me.'

'Get you a fair tub full, will that, sailor,' the diminutive lad behind the bar told him. 'All in one mug, Sir? Will you be staying long?'

'None of your fucking business, boy. Gilbey's.'

'Alright, you loathsome old tar. Keep your monk on, and you'll get to suck the monkey good as any other.'

'Just off the ships, mate?'

An old crone struck up an instant acquaintance, no doubt having heard and seen the *made money*, a street expression for stolen, but Pascoe was wise to the tricks of the underclass.

'What be my makings to you?'

'Just being matey, mate. You're a long way from the docks.'

'Aye. I been looking fur work this past month, and you know what I found? Naught but the landlubbin' workus. Bain't nothing else fur an unwanted man a the sea, but I got me wiles learnt me over time on the barques from Bombay a Boston. Under the cat, over the swell, and ne'er a penny grog fur a tar 'til Tilbury. Ach, the sea's me blood, me blood's the sea, and there be more salt in me than Neptune's piss. I'll stand ye a pint if ye'll listen a how I'm reduced to thievery, and another if you'll hear how I came by this coin. It's been a lonely voyage from the Indies to where I be aday.'

By the time the gin arrived, Pascoe had a friend, and by the time he'd bought the crone a second beer with his allegedly stolen coins, he was learning information. It was past eight o'clock when the crone became his best friend, and nearly nine when he was trusted enough to be introduced to Lucker and Snout. From then on, the tramp had to do nothing more arduous than he did for his household; listen, remember, and stay sober.

'What's he playing at?'

'Patience, Jack. I am sure Mr Wright knows what he is doing.'

They were at the drawing room window, which Larkin had opened to release the pipe smoke, the clock had struck ten, and Jack had twice excused himself to run to the upstairs bathroom, wiping his mouth on his return, and with a sour look on his pale face.

Although Larkin had said he was sure of Mr Wright, he was about to doubt his own judgement when Mrs Grose appeared, bringing more than her usual disapproval.

'So now we've become a charity, have we?' she demanded, rather than asked. 'There's a man... I'd rather say, a *creature* at the kitchen door. I think he's young. Hard to tell. Says he was told to come here by your detective.'

'Yes, yes!' Larkin threw Jack a look of relief, and stopped his pacing. 'Send him up.'

'I don't think so. He smells like the back end of a horse.'

How Mrs Grose would know that smell was a question for later. Meanwhile, Larkin insisted.

'Seen better clothes on a long-dead clapperdudgeon,' she scowled. 'You sure? He's foreign.'

'For pity's sake, woman, send the man up. Ask him if he needs feeding while you're about it.'

The housekeeper mumbled, 'I don't think so,' and vanished.

'You think he's got news?' They were the first words Jack had said in a tense and silent while.

'He's come for a reason,' Larkin said, trying to reassure him. 'We shall shortly know what that reason is.'

Jack refilled his pipe as Larkin wafted some of the smoke towards the window, and peering out, saw Mr Wright leap from a cab.

'He's here,' he said, and his pulse pumped with expectation.

The first to enter was Mrs Grose, and on hearing the knocker, she left, thumbing over her shoulder and saying, 'Here it is.'

She was succeeded by a tall man in a floor-length overcoat of the naval variety, who was preceded by a waft of tar. The state of his features and hands suggested he had come directly from the oakum shed of a nearby workhouse, and he limped to a standstill clutching a weathered cap, all the while staring at his laceless boots.

His appearance and arrival were so strange, Larkin could only think to ask, 'Yes?' and he wasn't sure if he dared risk inviting the stranger to sit. Mrs Grose would hang them all out to dry if the visitor marked the upholstery.

'Evening, Sirs,' the arrival said. 'Been told a come 'ere and wait.'

'Who are you?'

'That, Sir, be a question fur Mr Wright a be answering.'

'And you shan't have to wait long to hear it.' The detective was in the room, bringing a carpet bag and hope.

'Well?' Jack was on him in a second. 'Where is he?'

'Be calm, Jack. We have much to do and a long night ahead. Have you only just arrived, Pascoe?'

'That I have, Sir, and with things a be telling ye.'

'Excellent. Here...' Mr Wright gave him the bag. 'Perhaps Mr Chase would let you wash and change first.'

'Perhaps you would like to tell me who this man is before I let him loose in my house.'

'Oh, yes, sorry. Maxwell Pascoe, my butler.'

'Your...?'

'He works for the agency in a few capacities,' the detective said, and Larkin caught a hint of pride in his expression. 'Right now, he's in disguise.'

'I should hope so.'

'I'm sure he would appreciate a change of clothes, and while he's doing that, I can tell you what I've learnt.'

'Yes, yes. Mrs Grose?' The housekeeper was shadowing the doorway with displeasure. 'Would you like to show Mr Pascoe to my bathroom?'

'You mean I have a choice?'

'To the bathroom, Mrs Grose. Tout de suite.' To the stranger, he said, 'You will be quite safe, Sir. Bark worse than bite. Please, use whatever you want from my shelves.'

'Can I burn his clothes after?' The housekeeper had retreated into the hall with a handkerchief pressed to her nose.

'Yes,' Mr Wright said. 'Please do.'

The smell of oakum lessened once Mr Pascoe had left, and Mr Wright suggested they sit to listen to what he had to say.

'I'm hoping to get more information from Pascoe shortly,' he began. 'Meanwhile, I've spoken to Sergeant Culver at the Dalston Lane station. This afternoon, he put out a few enquiries to see if any of his informers had heard of a kidnapping.'

'Hang on...' Jack interrupted. 'You trust this man, yeah? Only, I don't trust no-one at that place.'

'Understandable, Jack, but yes. I trust Culver completely. He has helped me with cases in the past, and he's an honest policeman. His brother, as I might have said, is in business with my great friend Lord Clearwater. The earl and the Culvers go back a long way.'

'That means nothing to me, Sir. You say he's a good copper, yet he works with bent ones, and he ain't done nothing about them, am I right?'

'Not entirely. This is all part of a wider and ongoing case, Jack. For some time now, Inspector Adeliade, Sergeant Culver, myself and others have been working backstage to bring the Flay family to justice. You just happened to fall into the middle of it.'

'But what of Will?' Larkin suspected Jack and Wright could debate the detective's credentials for hours, and he was aware they had less than twelve before the hearing.

'I'll come to the point,' Wright said. 'Culver's whiddler said there was word going around Hoxton of an insurance, and people's got to stow their tattle.'

'So no-one's saying nothing?'

Jack had no trouble understanding what Larkin assumed was street talk, but he couldn't fathom it, and asked Wright to translate.

'Culver's informant is a cousin-by-marriage of Violet Flay, the woman at the head of the food chain. He's keen to get her and her eldest boys sent down, because that would break up the gang, and, I suspect, leave the cousin free to take over. The whiddler, the informant, Mr Chase, learnt that the gang currently have insurance, by which they mean...'

'They have Will, so Jack won't talk.'

'Quite. Therefore, we are now certain who took him. What we need to establish, is where, and because there's an instruction to stow, in other words, to not speak, we had to get someone to infiltrate. Hence, Pascoe.'

'And we need to establish where they are keeping Will with haste, Mr Wright.'

'With alacrity, not haste, Mr Chase. If we are too hasty, we will make mistakes, but I agree. Time is not on our side.'

'Did your copper hear anything about where they got him?'

'Sadly not, Jack. That's why I'm relying on my butler.'

'Yes, now there's a thing...' Larkin pointed at the door, and lowered his voice. 'Your butler?'

'A long story made brief... The son of a Cornish farmer on the Larkspur estate, footman to Earl Clearwater at the Hall, and then at his house in London. Now, butler at Delamere, which is my home and office. Max turned out to be a fine actor. We are an unusual household.'

'I dare say. So, what do we do now?'

'We wait for Pascoe. Meanwhile, I will ask you and Jack to tell me again what you heard last night and saw this morning, in case I've missed anything.'

Where a homeless sailor had left the room, twenty minutes later, an entirely different man returned, and Larkin was so confused by the transformation, he nearly spilt his port. Where there had been hair matted with grey grime, there was now the silkiest cut of black. The face had been weathered and creased, but was now smooth and youthful, and instead of the tattered clothes of a failed man, Pascoe wore a dark, tailored suit that highlighted his trim figure. There was no limp as he entered in shoes that could double as mirrors, and he held himself upright in the practised manner of a professional servant.

Larkin expected Jack to share his amazement, but he held a worrying look of admiration, attraction even.

'Excellent.' Mr Wright, having made himself at home as soon as he'd arrived, invited Pascoe to join them. 'It's getting late, so we best be quick. What have you got to tell us?'

'Well, Mr Wright, I have everything and nothing. First off, it took me a while a get in with them as knows what's afoot, but I got there in the end. There's much whispering about the insurance, but nothing clear about where he is. The talk was more about tomorrow and the case. It be the first time two of the top dogs have been up afore the bench, and seems like there'll be a crowd. All I could hear was everyone's going early to get seats, except for one who'll be standing by the insurance, waiting for word, if that means anything to you?'

If Larkin had translated correctly, it meant someone would be guarding Will until Jack had given his evidence. Mr Wright confirmed this, and asked Pascoe to continue.

'Like I says, it were all the tattle in the pub, but only in whispers and backtalk, you know, code. Later, when two men came in, the place went silent. Not only did they stop the chatter, they also cleared the space wherever they stood. It were like when you drop bleach on dirt water and the dirt draws back in a ring. These two men were to be afeared, I could see that. Once they'd sat, the others talked about the horses, and the dogfight they'll be having come Sunday, pigeon racing, gambling, anything but the court hearing. My new mate, keen to impress more drink out of me while showing off, got me to meet the new arrivals. I had money enough for a tongue loosening, and a little deference, ignorance and gin go a long way if you're paying your respects to legends like the Flay family, or least, pretending to.'

'Try and stay on point, Max,' Mr Wright said.

Larkin wasn't sure if that was Pascoe's first name or his secret agent's name. The evening was becoming more clandestine by the minute, and were it not for Will's life being in danger, and Jack being so tormented, he might have found it thrilling.

'Right. I got meself in with two of the Flay gang, one calling himself Snout, the other calling himself Lucker. Snout handles made money, Lucker does the physical dirty work. I entertained them to a few measures, and, they thought, took enough to send meself a sleep by their table. Like everyone else, their talk turned to tomorrow, except with a lot more contempt for Mr Merrit and the police, and they talked about the insurance. Because of their local cant, all I could take from me eavesdropping was something which means nothing to me, Mr Wright, but might mean something to you. Will Merrit is being held, and I quote, "Between James Hemsworth's Aldgate house under the hums." That, Sir, be all.'

Mr Wright wrote the strange words, repeating them as he did so to check he had them correct. When he'd finished, he looked up. 'Does that mean anything to anyone?'

Larkin couldn't recall knowing anyone called James Hemsworth, either in the past or present, or anyone who might have had a house in Aldgate, and having told the detective this, turned to Jack. As he'd been doing during Pascoe's story, he was staring at the wall as a man might look at the horizon to prevent seasickness.

'Hums?' Mr Wright queried. 'Are you sure?'

'That I am,' Pascoe said.

'Did you hear anything else?'

'Not much, Sir. That was all about the hearing. They finished their gin, said they all had a busy day a morrow, and talked about who was going to the court. Mother will be there.'

'Violet Flay is going to Bow Street?'

'So they said.'

'She is the gang leader, correct?' Larkin asked, not wanting to be left out in case there was anything he could contribute.

'Yes, and for her to step into a court room among police and lawmakers shows how confident she is her sons will be let off. Her presence will be a slap in the face for justice.'

'I can well believe it,' Larkin said. 'Mr Wright, I have a collection of directories upstairs, would it be of use if I trawled the indexes for references to James Hemsworth?'

'More useful to look for bathhouses,' the detective said. 'Is that right, Jack?'

Jack made no reply. Paler than before, his fingers were jittering on his knees, his bottom lip was clamped by his teeth, and it was hard to tell if he was thinking or fighting back anger. Larkin assumed both, and his heart bled more for the man.

'Hums are bathhouses in street talk,' Mr Wright explained. 'From the old cant word hummum, which is from hammam, Arabic for bath.'

'Meaning the insurance is under a bathhouse in Aldgate?' Pascoe said. 'I can't think of one.'

'There ain't one,' Jack said, and all heads turned to him. 'Nothing at Aldgate but the pump, a church and the start of Whitechapel High Street. You want a Turkish bath? Nearest is in the City, or over in Jermyn Street.'

'Perhaps it has another meaning.'

'No, Larkin, it don't,' Jack said. 'All it means is we have no clue where Will is, and whether I give me evidence or not, he's done for.'

'No, Jack.' Mr Wright crouched by his chair, and took his wrist, but Jack continued to stare at the wall. 'We have a clue, and we are going to work on it. We have over ten hours, and I have solved more complicated riddles than those left by gossiping thugs. Have hope, Jack. We're all on your side.'

Jack pulled his arm free, and his fingers continued drumming, leaving Mr Wright to frown.

'Right. Jack, you will be safer at Delamare,' he said, and beckoned Pascoe to his feet. 'Max, find us two cabs who can be persuaded to lose the tail we're bound to have when we leave. You take one, we'll take the other, and we'll go by different routes.'

Larkin's heart sank. He'd envisioned a night comforting Jack, holding him, and keeping him safe. There would be no repeat of last night's adventure, just compassion and care, because that was what Jack needed. The things he'd longed to give a man for many years were in his grasp, yet not to be.

'I also have directories, Mr Chase,' the detective said as he packed his bag. 'I'll scour them and put my mind to work through the night. You can do the same if you like, and if you think of anything, here is my private telegraph number. Whether we discover anything or not, Jack and I will be at court at nine tomorrow morning, be there if you want, otherwise, the best thing you can do to help is stay here, look after your servants, and remain vigilant.'

'I will,' Larkin nodded. 'And I will be at court. May I have a word with Jack before you leave?'

'Of course. We'll wait outside.'

Alone, Larkin stood face to face with Jack and forced down the urge to kiss him. Jack's eyes were dull, his face displayed no emotion, and his hands hung by his sides, as if he had given up all hope.

'Stay strong, Jack. They will find him safe and well.'

There was no reply because it was an empty platitude.

'I will be there for you tomorrow,' Larkin said. 'I would love to be with you tonight, but Mr Wright is correct. You will be better guarded with him, and you may be able to help locate your brother, but will you promise me something?'

Still no reply, but at least his eyes moved to meet Larkin's.

'That when this is over, when Will is safe, and you have done your duty, you will both come and stay. You and I can be together as we were before, for what we shared was a few minutes of frenetic joy, and we deserve more time together. I know you feel it too, this bond which is growing between us, and were these easier times, it would flourish. They will be easier again when Will is safe, and you can return to your work and your horse, and you can do it from here where we can be with each other. I mean, properly with each other. A couple in all but outward appearance.'

No words, no emotion, but no objection.

'Your guards are waiting. I shall not stop thinking of you until I see you again. You will be in my dreams, Jack, and they will be made more special if I may have a parting kiss.'

Jack swallowed, drew in a breath through his nose, and said, 'Words, Mr Chase. You use too many of them.'

TWENTY-THREE

In the way he was a passenger in the cab and not its driver, Jack's life was no longer his own to command. Someone else was directing his life away from Kingsland Road, and he was filled with an overwhelming sense of leaving Will behind. Somewhere among the city's vast, sprawling mismatch of streets and roads, alleys and courts, tunnels and bridges, his brother was trapped.

It was a terrible picture to imagine; Will terrified and helpless, at the mercy of cutthroats, not knowing or understanding what was happening, and worst of all, alone. Jack could do nothing but put his trust in the man he rode with, and hope he came up with an answer before morning, because Jack couldn't. He was a cabman, not a detective; a working man, not a man of means; a barely educated grafter from Limehouse, not a clever investigator from North Riverside. Jack was helpless, and, as far as he was concerned, the Flays had already won.

'Bucks Avenue,' Mr Wright told the cabbie. 'And make sure we're not followed. Extra for your vigilance and speed.'

The driver wasn't one Jack recognised, but he was good at his job. For a start, he took off north and east, where Bucks Avenue was south and west, and doubled back on himself through Ridley Road, deserted apart from nighttime scatter-pickers searching for the last remnants of the market unsolds. Across towards Highbury, through the narrower lanes of Canonbury, and only turning south after Pentonville, the cabman knew his routes, and made it a complicated journey as if he was used to avoiding detection.

Jack rested his head against the trim, and listened to the turn of the wheels as they shuddered over cobbles and brick, and became smoother over the asphalt of newer roads. Kings Cross to Bloomsbury, the maze of Seven Dials and Soho brought the ever-changing rhythm of the streets, the cool of the night air, the regular clop of hooves, all familiar yet happening almost without him, certainly without Will.

'Are we alone?' Mr Wright was talking up through the hatch.

'That we are, Sir.' A disembodied voice from above. 'There's been no-one behind since Barnsbury.'

'I reckon we're safe,' the detective said, closing the trap. 'Not long now. You can have a decent sleep.'

Jack wouldn't be able to sleep, but he grunted, 'Thanks,' and stared at the passing buildings.

Behind curtained windows, men and women slept soundly and warm in the grand houses of Mayfair. Servants on the upper floor, children in the nursery with Nanny next door, the family dog asleep in the kitchen, the cat hunting for mice. Into Park Lane, where the open space was a mass of shadow behind streetlamps dripping condensation, trees hiding who knew what or who, each blackened patch a hiding place for villainy and vice, for men like Larkin Chase and his soldier. Men like Jack.

Hyde Park Corner, briefly, before Knightsbridge, westwards, dropping down to Rafael Street for a few yards, and finally into Bucks Avenue. More massive buildings, more streetlights, but these with their flames shimmering through clean glass. Not a speck of litter on the wide pavements, the trees cultured, like the rich who admired them from their drawing rooms and safety.

A lane, a mews, a gate and a darkened yard, the horse slowed, and the cabbie drew her to a halt.

'There you go, Sir.'

The familiar creak of the apron, the rock as Mr Wright stepped out, and Jack followed into the unfamiliar smell of damp foliage and fresh air.

'Very kind of you, Sir. You're a gent.'

The well-tipped cabbie turned his hansom, the wheels grated over gravel, and the night fell silent.

'Where are we?'

'Delamere House,' Mr Wright said, and in the gloom, Jack heard the jangle of keys.

'No need.' Mr Pascoe's voice from behind a dim lantern in a porch. 'You took your time.'

'Our driver did, and I'm glad of it. He lost the tail miles back.'

Jack was aware he was beneath a looming building with windows a lighter shade of dark grey than the bricks that rose for storeys above. There was a smell of hay and horses, a snort and a shuffle, and footsteps in the grit as he followed the detective's dark outline.

Pascoe stood aside. 'I've not lit lamps,' he said. 'But if you are sure you weren't followed, I can do so.'

'I'll take a recce from upstairs while you show Jack to a room,' Mr Wright said, and vanished into a void.

'Follow me, Mr Merrit. Are you hungry?'

'No.'

'The ground floor would be best. I have my quarters down here, and you can be next to me. The rooms connect, and you will be quite safe. Mr Wright keeps the house like a bank vault. This way.'

A passage, the lantern throwing odd shards of light on tiles, whitewashed walls made yellow, unlit sconces and closed doors. An arch, a long table beyond; a kitchen. Another room with a table, chairs around it, dressers with crockery; a rich man's servants' hall. Opposite, 'My room,' Mr Pascoe said. 'Yours. Wait here.'

Jack stood with nothing ahead but the dancing lantern shards as Pascoe entered, crossed the room, and closed a pair of shutters at the window.

'That will make you undetectable,' he said, and lit the gas.

The room glowed into being with a subtle sigh. A made bed as if the house had been expecting guests. Beside it, a table, a wardrobe, furniture Jack could never have afforded, and this was for the servants. Two more doors.

'This is to my room,' Pascoe said, opening one and swinging his lantern inside. 'Knock if you need anything. This...'

The second led to a bathroom in the same fashion as Larkin's house. A tub with a water heater and brass taps, a sink with the same, pipes running along the walls, a mirror, table, and an inside toilet, clean, and for Jack alone to use.

'If you are sure you don't need anything right now, I'll be away to see to Mr Wright. I expect he'll be down in a short while.'

Pascoe... What was he? A butler, an investigator? Whatever he was, he left Jack alone to wait and worry. It was little different to being on the rank where he'd spent hours waiting for a fare and fretting about money.

'No matter where you're at, the trick is to make yourself as comfortable as you can,' Grandad Reggie used to say. 'It might be raining cats and dogs, and you might be stuck out at Ilford, but wait, and a fare will come. While you're idling, keep dry and warm, as there's no point being miserable as well as wet and cold.'

Jack wasn't either, and he wasn't quite miserable; he was helpless, and having thrown off his jacket, he fell backwards onto the bed, covered his face with his arm, and held back a yell of frustration.

It was still bubbling inside when Mr Wright appeared, the passage behind him now lit.

'Got everything you need?'

'Apart from me brother.'

The detective came further in, and sat by the bed. 'I'm going upstairs to work on it,' he said. 'You should try to sleep. If I come up with anything I'll let you know.'

'What was it? The message?'

'The location?' Mr Wright tore a page from his book and scribbled. 'I'll leave it with you, in case you want to think on it. First thing in the morning, I'm going to send a message to Cheap Street, to see if anyone there can help.'

'Cheap Street? Why?'

'The Clearwater Mission,' Mr Wright said as if it explained anything. 'The lads there know the streets, they know the underworld, and they're all keen to get away from both. Someone's bound to know the Hoxton gangs, and Doc Markland and Toviyah will know who to ask.'

The names meant nothing. 'Yeah, alright, but the hearing is at ten.'

'It is, but Creswell can delay it if we need more time. Now, you try and get some kip, mate.'

Mate? When did they become mates?

'I'll not sleep.'

'I know, but try. If you're hungry, the kitchen's along there. It's an informal house, so don't worry about what you might take. Max is next door if you need him.'

'Your butler?'

'It's Max when we're working a case, Pascoe when we have guests, and you're more than a guest, Jack, you're a...' He stopped talking, and changed his mind. 'Now's not the time for that. Sleep if you can, and we'll talk more in the morning.'

Mr Wright slipped from the room leaving his piece of paper and a mystery. Jack was more than a guest, he was a... what?

Whatever he was, he was alone, and with nothing else to do, he read the message.

Between James Hemsworth's Aldgate house under the hums.

There was nothing in it he recognised as street slang, apart from *hums*, the Turkish baths men retired to when they wanted to discuss their private business, either legal or criminal. Jack had never used one, but he'd taken fares to a few. There was one at Bishopsgate in the City, all red and grey bricks with pointed arches for windows, another at Bell Street near Marble Arch, and the one he'd first thought of over in Jermy Street. None of them seemed likely places to for a gang to keep their 'insurance.'

'Pointless,' he said, and threw the paper to the floor.

Nothing stirred within the house. If Mr Pascoe was washing or changing for bed, he did so in silence. If Mr Wright was upstairs, he made no sound overhead. There wasn't even the settling of the house, only the endless sigh of the gas, and the faint ticking of a clock as it counted away the seconds before Jack appeared in court, and Will breathed his last.

* * *

There was a man he'd met once but now didn't know, and he was in the wrong body. The voice came from a face distorted by memory, and the words made no sense. That was because they were walking on the ridge of a hill so close to the night sky, Jack pulled down a star and lit his pipe. When the smoke rose, it cleared the distortion, and for a moment, he was aware of being in the arms of Larkin Chase, naked, with the man's passion pressed hard against him, but his own already spent. It was a comforting moment, but he'd forgotten about the boy in the cellar.

A cellar, he saw when he stepped down from the ridge to the stone floor of an arched room, that was as hot as the Turkish bath Larkin Chase had mentioned in the cab just a second before. Time wasn't relevant, because there was no time in dreams, but he wasn't dreaming. Or, if he was, he'd just woken from one to find himself inside another.

Wheels turned, and the sound changed. Charlie was teaching him the knowledge, standing beside him at the bench, directing him through the maze.

'Listen to the streets, Jack. They each have their own voice. Close your eyes. It's alright, Blister knows what she's about. Go on, and you'll know when you're in Ivy Lane.'

The ribbons slack in his hands, the horse leading through the night. A jolt and the cab dipped twice, and then the only sound came from Blister's horseshoes.

'Double drain beside the bathhouse. A good marker on a dark and foggy night.'

Then, it wasn't Charlie beside him, but a dashing man with a trimmed moustache, ruddy of complexion and more blond than Jack, broader than Will, well spoken with the edge of a London accent, and he had lately been abroad. James was his name, and he was now on the same ridge, walking beneath the brick arches through steam, until the path ahead became a map. No ordinary map either, but Bacon's

Ordnance Atlas of London, only four years old. Jack walked over the paper with him, turning left into Pearson Street, ducking beneath a cardboard railway line, and crossing Kingsland into Harman. From there, across Hoxton to...?

'Lane or Street, Jack?'

'What?'

'Lane or Street?'

A double drain.

Charlie Flex put his arm around Jack's back, and it was enough to wake a deep longing, but that was afterwards. After...?

'Lane or Street, Jack?'

'I don't understand, Mr Wright.'

'James, or Jimmy, if you will. Maybe the Aldgate pump? You said there was one there.'

Aldgate was miles from Hoxton, and his cab took a twisting journey where the streets crept and tangled like a vine grown over hundreds of years with no thought or plan.

Will was his passenger, leaning out now and then to shift a house into alignment, or to remove one dead leaf from a green tree, and sit back to read an upside-down book.

'You want Aldgate?'

Where had the stars gone? It was still nighttime, but there was no light save for a pinprick ahead, somewhere off Hoxton Street.

'I don't want Aldgate, Jack. *You* do. Now, cabbie, Lane or Street?'

James, lanes, streets twisting like ivy to the Aldgate pump, the double dip...

Jack woke with his heart beating hard, and his skin coated with sweat. There was nothing but the tick of the clock and the hiss of the gas, and holding one beneath the other, showed him it was six in the morning.

'Street or...?'

Rolling from the bed, he fell on the piece of paper and stared at the words.

Between James Hemsworth's Aldgate house under the hums.

No longer dreaming, he knew where they were holding Will. In Hoxton, between James Street and Hemsworth Street were two roads; Ivy Lane being narrower than Ivy Street. Between them was Baring Court, where the woman had been murdered, and on the other side, the double drain outside the Turkish baths.

'Aldgate house?'

He was putting on his jacket when it came to him.

'The Aldgate pump of death.'

Grandad Reggie had once talked about cholera caused by the water supply coming through a cemetery. Jack had been ten at the time.

'Turkish baths have pump houses.'

It was a leap over potential failure, but he'd risk falling if there was a chance of saving Will. He'd even risk drinking from the Aldgate pump if he had to.

The clock. 'Just gone six.'

The decision? To wake Mr Wright and Mr Pascoe and tell them, or to go alone? There had been a horse in the stable. Take a carriage, or hope for a cab?

'I ain't stealing their carriage.'

From the south side of Hyde Park to Hoxton.

'Four and a half miles, a two-and-six fare, at least an hour and a half on foot.'

At that time of day, half an hour in a cab.

'No money.'

Not true. He had the two sovereigns Larkin had refused.

Cold water on his face. The eyes looking back at him were narrow but awake. Stubble. 'Who cares?'

No clean clothes. 'Who cares?'

The decision.

Alone, or with Mr Wright?

'You got Will into this, Jack Merrit, you get him out.'

TWENTY-FOUR

Mrs Grose presented more than her usual rush of aggression, entering Larkin's bedroom at seven thirty with the complaint, 'No callers for months, then you can't keep them off the step.' The curtain rings screeched on their pole. 'Don't know what he wants, but that man is here again.'

'Mr Merrit?'

'The other one.'

'The other Mr Merrit?'

'Moustache. Looks like a pugilist.'

Mrs Grose was an expert at raising and crushing Larkin's hopes in a few short sentences.

'What does he want?'

'Why anyone should get out of bed so early to come looking for you...'

She was gone, leaving Larkin to dress, and fly downstairs where he found Mr Wright studying his pocket watch.

'Is he here?'

'Good morning, Mr Wright.'

'Is Jack with you?'

'No. Isn't he with you?'

'He was. Now he's not.'

'Well, he's not here.'

'Damn it!'

It didn't take a sleuth to see the detective was agitated, and as the news sank in, Larkin experienced the first tremors of panic.

'Perhaps he took a walk?' It was a lame suggestion, and Mr Wright ignored it with the contempt it deserved.

'Max went to wake him at six thirty. The bed had been slept on, not in, he wasn't in the house, and had gone out by the back door. No note. Vanished.'

'Which means he won't attend court?'

'Who knows?'

'That would be a shame.'

'Our most important witness. Fled.'

'Or taken?'

'No sign of a struggle, and Max would have heard.'

'They took Will without being detected.'

'No smell of chloroform, no windows tampered with, no locks forced. In fact, he locked the back door after himself, and left the key in the post box.'

'Or someone did.'

'I've considered every option, Mr Chase, and the only conclusion is, Jack Merrit doesn't have the courage to face those who have done him and his brother harm. He's probably on a train to Scotland.'

It was so random, Larkin couldn't picture it. Jack wouldn't leave his brother.

'Your clue,' he said, taking the detective by surprise by clicking his fingers at him. 'The words of the clue your butler overhead. Could Jack have deciphered it and found the location?'

'If that's the case, I wish him luck, because he'll need it if he thinks he can take on the Flays by himself.'

'Tea. Study.' Mrs Grose yelled amid the clattering of a tray and footsteps on the stairs.

'You have time for tea, Mr Wright? Or breakfast? We could ponder some more.'

Mr Wright was still swinging his watch, and having looked at it a second time, agreed.

'I need to be at Bow Street by nine to meet Creswell. We can only hope Jack is there by ten. If not, and if Creswell can't stall proceedings, months of work comes to nothing, and Mr Merrit the younger...'

There was no need for him to finish the sentence, and Larkin was glad he didn't. Will's fate was the primary consideration, but along with it was the thought he might not see Jack again. Both were too hideous to contemplate, and, like the detective, all he could do was hope Jack appeared at the courthouse.

* * *

One and a half miles away, Jack had also been swinging his watch and checking the time, not in a town house, but on the step of a disused shop on Ivy Street, smoking his pipe with his bowler hat pulled low. Smoke, carts and awnings shielded him from the cracked windows of the opposite buildings, and he blended with the market shoppers like a man taking a break from haggling for oranges. Where he was just another nameless nobody in a sea of others, the building he watched stood out from those around it, made different by its ornate brickwork.

Red and grey, like the Turkish bath at Bishopsgate, but nowhere near as grand, it stood on the corner of a nameless passage that connected Ivy Street on his side to Ivy Lane on the other. Too narrow for anything but handcarts, it was a thoroughfare for costermongers and stallholders, and held the entrance to Basing Court. There was no other exit from the court, nor from the hammam; he knew, because he'd already scoured the area playing the part of a down and out searching for scraps while the traders set up their stalls.

It might have been Wright or his man—too much had happened for him to remember—but someone had said the Flays were planning to be at the courthouse at nine to ensure they made it into the public gallery, and at twenty-to, a group of men and women appeared in the alley. A large, older woman decked in furs, laughed as she waddled to the far street and clambered into a waiting carriage with three men, while others sauntered towards Hoxton Road and the omnibus.

With the family left for court, and with no idea what he would find inside, Jack entered the hammam at ten minutes past nine to find an inner porch and a noticeboard. As another man was reading a poster, so Jack thought he should do the same, and doing his best to blend in, examined the list of options, hoping to learn the layout of the building. A Turkish bath including a vapour rub and shampoo for three shillings, something called a vibratory massage for the same price, and alcohol rubbing for one and six. What was of more interest was the promise of a steam room and 'Suites—Bachelor Chambers', because it conjured images of naked men in private, and he'd heard talk on the ranks of the kind of things that went on in such 'suites.' That was an aside, what he focused on was the steam room, because steam needed heat, baths needed water, and both needed a pump room.

The stranger said something about invigoration, and passed through to the inner hall. Following, Jack did his best to ignore the colourful columns, ornate mouldings and marble, and listened to the stranger buy his requirements. Three shillings later, he'd done the same, and was directed to a changing room. It was nothing special, but then, Hoxton was lucky to have running water, let alone a hammam, and it reminded him of the sweat-scented changing room at the boy's boxing club of his youth. Like the club in Limehouse, benches and hooks were all the residents of Hoxton were allowed for comfort and security, but judging from the many piles of clothes, it was a popular place. It was also the place where the criminals held their prisoners, and as it backed onto Basing Court, he wouldn't have been surprised to learn of underground passages linking their cellars to those beneath his feet.

Jack averted his eyes as the other man undressed, and pretended to wrestle with a knot in his bootlace while he planned his next move.

Clothes were a problem he'd not thought about. How would he examine the building and look for the entrance to a pump room while being fully dressed when everyone else was naked? That would arouse suspicion, but to rescue Will wearing only a towel...? Assuming he found him, there wouldn't be time to change afterwards, and he wasn't going to run through the streets with no clothes on. Perhaps he should have involved Mr Wright after all. With his skills, Pascoe, could have acted his way in and out, but Jack had only his wits.

'Excuse me,' he said, when the other man was wrapped in a towel and about to leave. 'First time here. Is there a plan of the place?'

'A plan?'

'Yeah. How d'you know where to go?' Jack made the pretence of undoing his shirt buttons.

'Ah, I see. Yes, I believe there is,' the stranger said, and left.

'Well, you're no bloody help, are you?' Jack muttered, and scanned the walls.

Like him, they had no plan.

The entrance was the best place to look, and back in the main hall, he took the trouble to admire the walls and pillars until he found one with a board displaying a diagram of the building. It was hardly complicated. Various rooms led from the central, circular hall, and none of them looked large. They were labelled and all were connected, except for a space between the steam room and something called a douche. In the gap, and set back, a row of straight lines might have represented stairs, and having orientated himself, and having checked the man behind the counter was busy with a customer, he sidled behind a column and began a cautious tour of the outer wall. Stopping to read other posters advertising painful-sounding treatments and therapies, he counted off the rooms until he came to the empty space, and sure enough, a narrow flight of stairs leading down to a door marked 'Private.'

What or who was on the other side? More to the point, what did he have for protection?

And what if Will wasn't there?

It was too horrible to contemplate, and not knowing what to expect, he put his hand to the door, and pushed.

* * *

'For God's sake, Wright, I have never lost a case. Are you a complete maniac?'

'I did all I could, Sir Easterby.'

'You could have locked him in.'

'Don't be ridiculous.'

'What do I tell His Honour?'

'He may yet be here,' was Larkin's contribution to the frantic discussion.

'Who is this?'

'Larkin Chase at your service, Sir Easterby.'

'At my service? This isn't a church, man, it's the central court at Bow Street, with Judge Brownhill presiding in forty-five minutes, and me with no witness.'

'You have the owner of Clarington's.'

The barrister stopped flapping into his silks, and gave Mr Wright a glare that shivered Larkin's skin.

'Who can say what? Yes, I was burgled. Those are the things that were taken, and now, I have them back. That won't get the Flays six years, but it will get me laughed out of court.'

'Mr Chase is convinced he will be here.'

'Your evidence, Sir?'

'He is a decent man,' Larkin said, but there was more than that. 'I believe in him.'

'What is he, a deity?'

Larkin took no notice of the remark. The barrister had invited them into his robing room, and he didn't want to upset the man, but his attitude was beginning to grate, and despite his admirable moustache being more cultured even than Larkin's, Sir Easterby was turning out to be something of an annoyance.

'He is a deity to his brother, Sir,' Larkin said. 'And I am certain he is with his brother now.'

'This is the brother you believe has been taken by the Flays and is being held against his will?'

'Yes,' Mr Wright said, tapping his fingers on his watch as if it would slow down time.

'Get *him* on the witness stand and you might be onto something,' the barrister said, lifting his wig from its box. 'But as you can't even get your main man to appear...'

'He will,' Larkin insisted.

'You don't know that. What we do know is that he is not here, I cannot brief him, I will not be able to call him, and the case will be thrown out.'

'But you can have it postponed.'

'On what grounds, Wright? The Summons and Disappear legislation of fifteen-sixty-three, otherwise known as the 'We've lost our bloody witness Act?'

It sounded hopeless, but Larkin had meant what he said; he believed in Jack, and although he couldn't prove it, he was convinced Jack knew what he was doing.

* * *

Jack had no clue. All he had was his hope and his rising anger. There was no counting down from ten, because there was no Will to temper him. They had stolen his brother, these men who'd helped themselves to his money, had him arrested, and burnt everything he owned. The more he thought about it as he slipped into the bathhouse basement, the more the count increased.

'One, two, three...'

Ahead was a passage, and at the end of it, a man seated directly in front of a door. There was one other room, it's entrance unguarded, and from behind the iron door, came the grind and thump of an engine telling him he was in the right place.

The guard was but a vague shape through the clammy heat and clouds of steam escaping from joints in the pipework, and had his head down on his wide chest, dozing. As yet, he'd not heard Jack's tentative approach. The churning of the engine masked the sound of his entrance, and the steam disguised him, but it wouldn't last long.

Four.

Who were they to harm Will? Who were they to make people fear for their lives?

Five.

Water ran on the walls and into gutters either side of the cobbled passage, and although he was doing his best to keep his balance, he slipped. An echoing squeal of leather on stone, and the slap of his hand on the wall alerted the dozing guard, who shot to his feet.

'Who's that?' he demanded, his voice booming above the clank of iron.

'Come for the boy,' Jack replied, hoping the steam and racket would be enough of a disguise.

'Who are you?'

Thinking fast, he said, 'Chancer sent me,' but quick thinking wasn't always good thinking.

The man was on his feet and advancing. 'I'm Chancer,' he said. 'Who are you?'

Closer, Jack made out his features down to the scars on his face, and the hair on his knuckles that gripped the handle of a knife.

Six.

'Put that away.'

'Last chance, son. Chancer only gives one.'

Seven.

'You got the boy in there?' His pretence wouldn't hold for much longer.

'What's it to you if I have?'

That was enough evidence.

Eight.

'I come to get him. Out of the way, or you'll go down like a skittle.'

Chancer laughed. 'Leave, son. Better fled than dead.'

Nine.

'Not without my brother.'

'Brother?'

The thug's face froze, and Jack used his shock to seize the advantage. Aware he was setting his anger free, he reached ten. One fist crashed into the thug's hand, clattering the knife to the floor, while a right hook to the face sent him following. Jack made the end of the passage, but the door was locked, and the thug was on his hands and knees, reaching for his blade. A foot on his arm put a stop to that, and Jack felt it crack. So what if he got sent down this time?

A key. There had to be a key somewhere, and Jack fell to his knees on the man's stomach, ending his screamed protests. Nothing in the jacket.

'Where is it?'

A muffled grunt as a hand stretched for the knife.

'No you don't.'

A fist in the face, followed by a demand.

'Key.'

Fingers touching the blade. The thug wasn't giving up, but neither was Jack. Lifting the man from the floor, he slammed his back against the wall, took him by the throat, and kicked away the knife.

'Where's the fucking key?'

Painful confusion. A head slammed his nose. His teeth rattled. Elbow to the chest, fist beneath the chin, hair clasped, skull to stone. Grunting, more than a scuffle, a release of everything with no care for damage he might cause, or what he might suffer. A horse without a mane. A brother without hope. Knuckles on his temples, his knee to the bastard's groin. A girl killed as a warning. A right to the ribcage, and a left to the cheek. Repeat. Harder. Again. Harder.

'Here... Take it...' The thug pleaded in submission, and dug into his trouser pocket.

A click, a swish, and a glimpse of steel. Jack hurled the man aside, but not before the flick knife cut through the steam, his sleeve and his flesh. If there was pain, it didn't register, and it didn't matter. His hatred for Harris and the Flays, his failure to protect Will, the mess he'd made of their lives, and his frustration combined in a visceral yell, as he flew at the thug, now rushing at him, blade out, face distorted. Yells echoed among the clangs and shunts, as Jack raised his leg, and booted the thug in the gut. The man flew back, fell, cracked his head on the floor, and didn't get up.

'Fuck you,' Jack spat blood from his mouth.

How did that get there?

It didn't matter. Where was the key?

In a trouser pocket, and only once he'd found it did he check the man was still breathing, and to his relief, found he was.

Taking both knives, and having checked for any others but finding none, he kept one of the blades in his hand as he unlocked the door.

Beyond was a chamber, but no other guards. At first, he thought there was no-one at all, but his reason took over, and he told himself there had to be something, else, why have a guard?

Arches supported a stone ceiling lit by a jaundiced gas lamp. A filthy, high-up and barred window let in enough light from the pavement to show shackles and chains hanging from the walls. The floor was strewn with straw. A dead brazier, a bowl and a bucket.

'Will?'

A movement in a gloomy corner. A quick check behind; the thug was still out cold.

'Will?'

'Jack?'

Thank God. Jack was at his side, but Will's arm was bound to an iron bedstead by a rope. The thug's own knife saw to that, and Will was in his arms, while Jack was fighting back tears of relief.

Will was shaking and speaking fast about an uneven arrangement of arches, and the annoyance of irregular brickwork. The torture of a bent strut in the headboard he could do nothing about, and having to keep his eyes closed.

'Calm it, Will, calm it.'

'The straw lies crooked. A sweep is all it needs. No-one listened.'

'Shush, Will.'

'Distressing. Very distressing.'

'Shush. Ten, nine, eight...'

They had to be moving, but Will wouldn't let him go.

'Softly, Will. It's alright now, it's alright.'

'Jack?'

'Of course.' Jack held him at arm's length. 'Will, I'm so sorry.'

'It's Jack,' Will said. 'I'm alright. It's Jack.'

'We have to go.'

'Go?' Will's eyes snapped open, he scanned the room, and gasped. 'Yes, we must. Hello, Jack.'

'Are you hurt?'

'No. I heard things.'

'Come on.'

'Yes, yes, but listen. I have heard things about the Flays and what they have planned.'

'Did they hurt you?'

'No, actually. They gave me clothes and have been rather good to me. Apart from keeping me tied to a bed, and only giving me a bucket... Don't open the lid. It is very unsatisfactory. What time is it?'

Will was back.

'I don't know. Half nine?'

Jack helped him to the door, but Will no longer needed his assistance.

'Then we must get to the court.'

'No. We're leaving the city for good.'

'Don't be silly. Oh, you're bleeding.'

Blood was trickling over Jack's hand, and for the first time, he felt the sting of cuts and the ache of bruises.

'Nothing deep,' he said, with no way of knowing. 'Listen. We got to run. The way out's straight ahead at the top of the stairs. Don't say nothing, don't look at no-one, just walk fast.'

'What did you do to this man?'

They were in the passage, and the man called Chancer hadn't moved.

'He'll come round sometime. Did you hear me, Will? Walk out fast, straight to a cab, then...'

Despite whatever he might have been through, Will was now calm as he stopped Jack at the steps and put a hand on his chest.

'Listen to me, brother. I have something to ask of you...'

'Not now, mate.'

This was no time for one of his brother's long rambles, but Will had other ideas.

'You will listen to me and not interrupt,' he said. 'Else we will not be free of this place before that horrible man becomes conscious, and I assume you don't want us to be here when that happens.'

'Be quick.'

'I am going to ask you to do something for me, and you are not going to like it. I only ask because I love you, and you will agree to do it because I am your brother. After that, you can flee to wherever you want us to run away to.'

'We got to move.'

'Now then... Ah.' Will had seen something over Jack's shoulder. 'Say yes, Jack, and quickly.'

'Yes to what?'

'To what I am about to ask of you, and don't delay, because he's waking up. We can discuss details once we are outside, where we will also patch up your face. Well?'

A groan from behind prompted Jack to say, 'Yes, alright,' and he hurried Will to the top of the stairs.

Through the door, out into the marble hall and across, heads down, through the main doors and out into the street without a challenge.

'Gosh, it's very bright out here,' Will said.

The daylight gave Jack a chance to examine his brother, and apart from being filthy, he appeared in good health and good spirits. Surprising? Not for Will Merrit who accepted disasters as if they were expected, and carried on regardless.

'You have just agreed that we must talk,' he said, as Jack led him across the street and down the cut-through, heading for the more anonymous main road. 'Tell me, what are your plans?'

'I've got eleven shillings. Enough to get us to Leamouth.'

'Why on earth would anybody want to go there?'

'To collect Shadow. Then, we're walking.'

'Where?'

'Backs to London, out towards Essex. I'll find farm work. Shadow can pull carts. We'll find something. Are you sure you're not hurt?'

'I am sure, yes. My burn is sore from the rub of the rope, but... Jack, stop a minute.'

They were dodging traffic, crossing to Mary Street towards Kingsland Road, and reaching the other side, Will caught Jack's arm and pulled him into the recess of a shop doorway. They were far enough from the Flay manor to be safe. For now.

'Listen to me,' his younger brother said, employing his large, round eyes to good effect.

Jack didn't need them; he'd have done anything for Will right then, he was so happy to see him in the fresh air, unscathed and unchanged, but most of all, alive.

'Go on, what?'

'You want us to head east to Essex?'

'Yeah, it's one idea.'

'And it is a very bad one. Remember when you promised me we would better ourselves and move further west...'

'Yeah, but...'

'Don't interrupt. I have never asked you to do anything you didn't want to do, but now, that must change.'

'What d'you mean?' They may have been off the Flays' streets, but Jack was still wary and only half listening.

'Larkin Chase.'

The name claimed his full attention.

'What about him?'

'He has much to offer you, and I don't mean money and resources. The man is falling in love with you, and you him. What does that tell you?'

'Tells me you're barmy. Can we go?'

'No. The way you are with him, the way you change when you are around him, the way he fusses and panics around you... I know things have happened, and I know you want them to happen more.'

'Leave it out, Will. There's people about.'

Will raised his voice. 'I know what it is you want, Jack, and he doesn't live in Essex.'

'Be quiet.'

Will took his hands, and looked deeply into his eyes. 'Jack Merrit will not be settled until he accepts his heart and does what he knows he must do.' He sighed. 'I love you because you are my brother. I only have one, but I need no other, even though you fret and fuss, blunder about doing what you think is right and get it wrong. Even though you think I need protection as though I were a child, and even though you buy the worst sausages in Limehouse. I'll stick with you whatever you decide, but, in my opinion, the answer to everything we want lies to the west where you once promised me a better life. You must decide if we run away from the opportunity and go east to Essex with Shadow, or if we go west to Bow Street, Larkin Chase and all the risk that goes with them. That's the long and short of all this, but know I am by your side, and for always. That said, this decision is yours alone to make.'

Will helped himself to Jack's watch, tutted, and replaced it in his pocket.

'So, Jack, is it east or west?'

TWENTY-FIVE

Larkin berated himself for persuading a cabman he didn't know to do what he believed to be the right thing, only for that man's world to be ruined, and all because he'd taken a fancy to Jack's face. To more than that. To his physique and his personality, and to a man he wanted to be at his side by the fireplace in winter, by the Serpentine in summer, in his house and in his bed.

Look where such hopes had brought him.

Pacing the corridor outside the Central Criminal Court, watching the clock, and listening to the muffled drone of the judge instructing the jury to convict only on the evidence, and to barristers introducing their cases.

The fact was, Larkin's problems and pain didn't matter as much as those of Jack Merrit, currently who knew where, doing who knew what. Mourning the death of his beloved brother, more than likely, and all because Larkin Chase...

'Any sign, Sir?'

The same usher as a short while ago, asking the same question, carrying the same ledger with no change in his level of boredom.

'No,' Larkin replied, and indicated the waiting room. 'Only Mr Clarington.'

'Then I will wait,' the usher said, and retreated with a yawn.

Ten twenty. No Jack.

Resigned, Larkin let himself back into the courtroom, and slid in beside Mr Wright with a shake of his head.

'If it pleases the court, I shall call my first witness,' Creswell was saying. 'The prosecution calls Mr Archibald Clarington.'

Some fuss followed as an usher shouted the name at the door, quite unnecessarily, Larkin thought, as the man was only a few feet away. The public gallery took the opportunity to shuffle and cough, the newsmen turned to fresh pages in their notebooks, and the jury sat upright, their faces grave. The Flays were opposite them at the front of the public gallery, glaring menacingly at the twelve men who would decide the fate of their family members, and possibly, their entire criminal operation. Mr Wright had identified them as they took their seats. Violet, the mother and mastermind, bedecked like a dowager, but with paste, not taste. Three of her sons, each a monster to a man, with hooded eyebrows, and tattoos on their knuckles which Larkin wouldn't have been surprised to see scrape the ground when they walked. With them was an assortment of flouncy women, each with her own variation of a scowl, and all directed at the prosecution and jury, their men seated like gargoyles beside them. Had Hogarth been there, he would have etched them in the style of his 'Gin Lane and Beer Street,' with breasts falling loose in revolting abandon, and babies being force fed rotgut before being dropped in the gutter. Although they whispered, Larkin imagined their cackles and bawdy laughs, their foul mouths and fouler smells of cheap perfume and rum. No doubt, they wore the rum and drank the scent.

The court hushed as Mr Clarington made a stately entrance, and confidently swore his oath.

'I might leave,' Mr Wright whispered.

'Why?'

'To avoid Creswell's wrath, the press, and the embarrassment of failure.'

Larkin understood.

Over their brief breakfast, Mr Wright had confessed his agency was in trouble. Not financially, because he had the support of the fifth richest nobleman in the country, but because he was working alone. Since starting his business, there had been mysteries to solve and adventures to be had, but mostly, these had been on behalf of friends. Apart from those cases, he had been called upon to investigate little more than what he called in-house thievery, where a servant had run off with a trinket or money. Other cases were limited to finding evidence for divorces, and minor misdemeanours, and he longed for something more noteworthy. The Flay case, as the newspapers were calling it, was his 'make or break.'

However, at that moment, with Creswell asking Mr Clarington his details as though they were old friends, Mr Wright's business was not Larkin's, and although he sympathised, all he could do was hold to his belief in Jack, and pray he and Will were safe.

The witness confirmed his name, address and business, and described what had been stolen. Creswell played up his loss and the damage to his reputation, assured the court of the man's worthiness and reliability, and dragged out his questioning at such a slow pace, the judge had to ask him to hurry along. With his evidence concluded, the stolen items identified, and the defence having nothing to ask him because the provenance of the items was not in question, Clarington was told to stand down.

'Your next witness?' the judge said, setting aside a piece of paper, and peering down on the barrister from his position beneath the royal coat of arms.

'Your Honour...' Creswell cast a glance at Mr Wright who shrugged. 'Apropos the next witness, M'lud. I have his statement.'

'We can all make statements, Sir Easterby, and my next one is this. Where is your witness?'

'There may be a delay, M'lud.'

'Oh?'

'Indeed, Your Honour. However, the prosecution has something of an unusual but related excuse.'

'Excuse, Sir Easterby? That is not a word we are used to hearing from your learned self.'

'Kind of you to say so, M'lud, but this is an unusual case.'

'In what way?'

'In the way of hobbling.'

The word created a ripple of interest in the public gallery, and a look of concern from the defence barrister. The two men being tried together in the dock, however, carried contemptuous smirks, and one winked at the fur-covered Violet Flay, then picking at her nose with a pointed fingernail.

'Please clarify, Sir Easterby. Has someone been injured?'

'Possibly, M'lud, but in this case, we must take hobbling as street vernacular. From the original meaning of the verb to hobble—to strap together the legs of a horse to prevent it from straying—comes the modern expression, to hobble a witness. To metaphorically tether it by use of foul means. This, I suggest, is what has happened to my witness, and because of it, he may not be able to appear.'

The judge frowned. 'I am confused. Your witness is a horse?'

Derisive laughter waterfalled from the Flay tribe, and was brought to an abrupt end by a crack of the gavel.

'No, M'Lud. A man.'

'Ah. Thus, your point is...?'

'My point is my aim, M'lud. To include the hobbling within the content of the evidence, and allow the jury to hear what and who lie behind this case. The prosecution seeks to achieve a conviction by making the jury aware of the wider context.'

'I see.'

Larkin wasn't sure that he did, and concentrated harder.

'However, M'lud, this will mean introducing indirect evidence. My learned friend...' Creswell gave a cursory nod to the defence '... is aware of this move, but had nothing to say on the matter when previously discussed. No doubt, he is biding his time for the moment he can leap to his feet and shower objections on my head. I am prepared to rebuff with my metaphorical umbrella.'

'Your grandstanding aside, Sir, this sounds interesting,' Judge Brownhill said, and sat back in his chair with a wave. 'Please continue...'

'I am obliged, Your Honour.' Cresswell gave another pointed glare which took in both Mr Wright and Larkin, and cleared his throat. 'We have it on good authority...'

'Objection.'

'I haven't started yet.'

'The defence objects.'

'To what, Mr Sparrow?' the judge said with a smile. 'Patience, Sir. A virtue. Continue, Sir Easterby.'

'Obliged.'

It was all very formal, and yet akin to listening to a friendly debate among university fellows, and Larkin formed the impression Creswell, the judge and the defence would later take lunch together and praise one another for their performances.

'I have it on good authority that my witness has been hobbled, Your Honour. I will present a clear case of what the newspapers refer to as witness tampering.'

'Objection. Where is my learned friend's evidence?'

'If you'd give me a chance...' Creswell rolled his eyes.

'Again, patience, Mr Sparrow. You will have time to peck later.'

Creswell continued. 'The Crown intended to call Mr John Anthony Merrit to the stand, M'lud, but it is quite possible he is currently engaged in a rescue. Thus...'

'A rescue?'

'Indeed, M'lud, from the clutches of the gang of miscreants led by the defendants.'

'Miscreants?' Sparrow objected. 'Really, Your Honour.'

'Is my use of the English language now on trial, M'lud?' Creswell shot back, and ignored his opposition. 'The following, I state without prejudice. Since Mr Merrit did what any decent citizen of our great metropolis should do, and informed the constabulary that the defendants were in the act of selling Mr Carrington's stolen goods, he has suffered at the hands of their colleagues.'

'Objection. Conjecture.'

'Still not finished, Sparrow. To wit, Mr Merrit has been subjected to a false arrest, and I have Sergeant Culver here to attest to that if Your Honour would like and allow. Not only this, but his name has been besmirched to the extent he has lost his position as a reliable and hard-working driver of a London taxicab. A profession on which we all rely to transport us from A to B through all weathers and at all times of the day and night. A cabbie, you see...'

'Get on with it, Sir Easterby.'

'M'lud, I intend to call Mr Merrit, but...' The barrister eyed the door where a hovering usher glanced out, looked back, and shook his head. Creswell frowned. 'Yes, er... As if the scam of the false imprisonment and the resulting slander were not enough, we believe the Flay family have also committed arson against him in the burning down of his home, thus robbing him of all he owns.'

The defence objected, and the public gallery erupted into jeers and boos, with the Flays on their feet, shaking fists, and yelling threats. It took the judge some time to quieten proceedings, and warn that any more of that behaviour, and the gallery would be cleared.

'Does the prosecution have a witness to call on this matter or not?' The judge was losing his patience.

'We live in hope, Your Honour, and we would have called him more easily had not the defendants allegedly broken into another man's home and stolen Mr Merrit's brother. We believe they are currently holding him as a hostage against Mr Merrit's testimony, and that is why my witness is not in court.'

More outrage, but warier, and ended by three short blows of the gavel.

'I think it is you who needs rescuing, Sir Easterby,' the judge said. 'Or myself, for I feel as though I am a character in a sensational novel. You were correct. This is indirect evidence at best, conjecture at worst, and has no direct bearing on the selling of stolen goods. Were you able to prove it with a witness, the court might be more sympathetic.'

'But it does have bearing on the characters of the defendants, M'lud.'

'It *might* if there were evidence. Otherwise, these are separate and individual allegations which would need to be heard another time and following an arrest.'

'Indeed, Your Honour, but the point is, the two defendants are only part of a wider organisation that has prevented Mr Merrit from giving evidence in your court. This is why my witness is unable to attend today, and thus, I would ask for the behaviour of the organisation to be considered as evidence. In a related...'

'Enough of your fudging, Sir. This is an excellent example of no witness, no case.' The judge raised his gavel. 'Without the necessary testimony, I have no choice but to...'

'Hold on, mate. I'm here.'

All heads turned to the door.

Jack, his face bruised, and his perfect upper lip swollen, entered the courtroom looking like a man who had just been knocked down by a tram. His clothes were as dishevelled as his sweat-matted hair, but his expression was firm.

'Where do I go?'

Creswell grinned, and raising his voice above the outrage and panic from the public gallery, said, 'If it pleases the court, I call Mr John Merrit.'

'Certainly,' the judge said. 'I am rather looking forward to an explanation of his condition, if nothing else.'

'I assume my witness appears thus because he has been engaged in his rescue,' Creswell said. 'I am sure all will become clear.'

The Flays were in a flap. Some were poking others accusingly, while others threw up their hands, appealing to the courtroom as if they had suffered a wrong. Silent and unmoved, Violent Flay hunched forward like a vulture waiting to fall on a lame horse, and squinted at Jack as he took the stand.

Mr Wright said, 'Thank fuck,' but Larkin was only half aware of his presence. Not only had Jack appeared, but so had Will, following him into the courtroom in a similar state of dishevelment, before being pulled aside by the yawning usher.

'Mr Merrit, are you well enough to give evidence?' the judge enquired after Jack had sworn the oath. 'Do you require a physician?'

'I'll be alright, for now, Sir,' Jack replied. 'I've had worse.'

'My client apologises for his appearance, M'lud. If you would rather we postpone while he seeks medical attention...?'

'No, Sir Easterby, he has stated he is capable. The court is more interested in his evidence than his appearance.' To the jury, he said, 'You will disregard the witness' physical condition. It has no bearing.'

Larkin hissed across the aisle, and beckoned Will to sit with him, and he squashed in beside Mr Wright.

'Are you harmed?' he whispered, because Creswell had begun speaking.

'Not as much as my brother.'

'Is he alright?'

'He has a cut on his arm exactly two inches long but not very deep. I bound it with his handkerchief to the necessary torque. It took me much persuasion to get him here, and he is not here only for me.'

'I don't understand.'

'He didn't want to let you down. Despite it all, I believe there are still feelings there. Now, silence.'

There was no chance of silence, neither inside Larkin's head nor without. As Creswell questioned, and Jack told his story, the public gallery made its opinion known, and as the evidence became more damning, so their protests became more those of fear than outrage. Several times the judge had to order silence, and at one point, the bailiffs removed three men because of their remonstrations. Jack, however, remained unaffected, and spoke clearly as he described recent events.

Mr Wright and Will fell to whispering, and by the looks, were having an in-depth discussion, probably about the chances of success, or Will's recent ordeal. Mr Wright was taking down notes.

Larkin only had ears, eyes and admiration for Jack, but while trying to concentrate on what was happening in the pit, he kept coming back to Will's words. Jack still had feelings. They could only be speculation, though, and Larkin needed proof before he gave in to daydreams of what the future might bring.

'And can you describe any of the goods?' Creswell was asking when Larkin paid attention.

The allegedly stolen items were still piled on a central table, but covered with a sheet.

'I can,' Jack said, standing tall and assured. 'Particularly a great big silver cup with jewels that looked like it come from a church. It had two red stones and a green one in the middle. Then, there was some silver cutlery, candlesticks and the like, and all wrapped up in a rug with a great big bird on it.'

'Can you describe this bird?'

'Big, wide tail, all colourful, long neck... a peacock.'

'If it pleases the court, I shall display what Mr Merrit has described.' Creswell spoke to the jury. 'Remember, Mr Carrington has previously identified these items as being from his shop, but they have been in the custody of the police since the night of the arrest. Mr Merrit has not had an opportunity to see them since the auction.'

When he revealed the stolen goods, they were exactly as Jack had described. The press scribbled their notes, while the people at the back of the gallery grinned, and the family at the front glowered and grimaced.

Mr Wright left his seat and approached Creswell's bench, where a furtive exchange of words took place. The detective gave the barrister a page torn from his notebook, and Creswell glanced to Will, who nodded.

'Your Honour,' Creswell said, once the court was quiet. 'I have no further questions for this witness, but before I hand over to my learned friend, I would like you to entertain more from a second witness currently unlisted.'

'Objection.'

'Of course, Mr Sparrow,' the judge said. 'Allow me to investigate on your behalf.'

'Obliged,' an unhappy Mr Sparrow grumbled.

'An unlisted witness, Sir Easterby?'

'Indeed, M'lud, and this relates to our previous discussion. In light of very recent events, to wit, the hobbling to which I referred, I feel it would be judicious to hear his evidence, so the jury may make a more informed decision.'

'That does rather seem to be the point of a witness, Sir Easterby,' the judge said with a hint of sarcasm.

'Indeed, M'lud, but I meant on the wider implications of this case.'

'Unfortunately, the witness has not been previously listed. Furthermore, as I have no idea to whom you refer, I cannot use my authority to call him or her on your behalf. So, no, Sir, you may not call a witness out of nowhere. It would not be fair on the learned defence nor Messrs Flay.'

Creswell hoisted his silks at his shoulders, and ignoring the judge, addressed the press bench. 'It is unusual is it not?' His smile was as wide as the Thames and just as treacherous. 'Interesting to hear the words *fair* and *Flay* in such close proximity. Fair-Flay could be considered the antithesis of fair play.' The pressmen gave huffed laughs, and continued their writing. 'Is it fair they should have Mr Merrit incarcerated? His brother kidnapped...'

'Objection, objection...'

'And objection, creeps in this petty pace from day to day,' Creswell interrupted his opposition by shouting a bastardisation of Shakespeare, and Larkin was mightily impressed. The outburst brought stillness to the court and Larkin to full attention.

'Mr Sparrow is right to object. If you have finished with this witness, Sir Easterby, we will continue.'

'Lennox versus Seyton,' Creswell said, and, his anger a mere act, beamed like a benevolent uncle.

'I'm sorry?'

'No need to apologise, M'lud, it's not often cited. Lennox versus Seyton allows for just this irregularity.'

'I am unaware of the case, Sir. Is it contemporary?'

Sparrow was thumbing through one of his thickest books, as the judge looked on perplexed, but Creswell continued to smile with confidence.

'Hardly recent, thus I am not surprised it might have slipped Your Honour's learned mind. It does, however, remain on the statute books as precedent. The year was sixteen-hundred and six, when, at the Court of Requests, a Mr Lennox brought a case against a Mr Seyton for the false imprisonment of his brother. Under remarkably similar circumstances, the prosecution called a last-minute, unlisted witness, and the judge allowed his testimony. The witness, a one William Shakespeare, brought with him not only evidence of the crime in question, but evidence of further crimes by the same criminal party with whom the defendant, Mr Seyton, operated. The judge determined such a character appraisal was pertinent to the case, and the crime was serious enough to warrant the witness' late entry. In other words, indirect evidence that has a bearing on a case may be presented by an unlisted attestor.'

'Sparrow?'

The judge peered at the defence, who turned to his clients with a long face, and, back to the judge said, 'Agreed, M'lud.'

'Jolly good,' Creswell chirped. 'By the way, thanks to that indirect evidence from the Bard of Stratford, the rest of the criminal gang were arrested, tried, and hanged. Something of a bonus, I'd say. Sergeant Culver is on hand should he deem an arrest of others appropriate.'

The policeman composed himself, his chin high, meaning business, and with even the Flays stunned into static silence, his movement created the only sound until the defence barrister spoke.

'But in sixteen-o-six, Your Honour?'

'Indeed, and never repealed.' Creswell pointed to the book on Sparrow's bench. 'Page nine-hundred and sixty-three, second paragraph.' To the judge, he said, 'It's interesting to note that both Lennox and Seyton appear in the tragedy of Macbeth, which, it is believed, was written that same year. Inspiration comes in many forms. May I call now, Your Honour?'

Larkin was not uneducated, but he'd had trouble keeping up with all the details. Mr Wright, however, had not, and whispered, 'The man's a genius. They're all done for now.'

How they were to be 'done for' and exactly who was to be 'done', Larkin wasn't sure, the events were unfolding at a pace around him, and he wasn't listening to the legal argument, but watching Jack as he was stood down from the witness box. Without returning Larkin's gaze, he approached an usher. A few words were exchanged, the usher shook his head and showed him the door. Before Larkin could say anything, Will was also escorted from the court, and Larkin rose to follow.

'Leave them,' Mr Wright said. 'They'll be back.'

'How can you be sure?'

'The prosecution calls William Reginald Merrit.'

There was his answer. No sooner had Will left than he was brought back in, shown to the witness stand, and sworn in.

'Would you give the court your name?' Creswell began.

'William Reginald Merrit. I was named after my grandfathers...'

'Simple and honest answers, please, Mr Merrit,' the judge ordered.

'And your address, Mr Merrit?'

'I don't have one.'

'Don't have one?'

'Well, Jack pays our rent on a tenement in Limehouse, but it is currently uninhabitable.'

'Uninhabitable. Why?'

'Because it was burnt down.'

'Burnt down?' Creswell was incredulous.

'Yes, Sir. Two men threw flaming bottles at it while I was inside. Had it not been for a neighbour, I might have died.'

'Might have died?'

Will turned to the judge. 'Excuse me, but is it necessary for the Crown Prosecution to repeat everything I say?'

A chuckle scurried around the courtroom, and Larkin's admiration for the precise young man increased.

'Just answer the questions, Mr Merrit.'

'I would if there were any.' Turning to Creswell, he said. 'Try again.'

None too pleased, Creswell continued. 'I am informed you were taken against your will,' he said. 'Can you tell us more about that?'

'Only that I was asleep one minute, and the next, a man had a cloth over my face. The next thing I knew, I was tied to a bed in a cellar.'

More questions followed, Will answered succinctly, the judge waved away the defence's objections, and listened to Will's story with interest.

'You heard their names?' Creswell asked.

'I did, Sir, and a lot more. They chatted quite openly around me, assuming, I suspect, that I am in some way touched, when in fact, I am merely precise.'

'Just answer the question,' Creswell said with his hand pressed to his forehead.

'Yes, Sir. One called himself Chancer, the other, Snout. They spent much time in my accommodation discussing the theft, the auction, and the trouble my brother had caused the family. They discussed many other things too, including the work of Hoxton Arty and Badger, who to my mind, sound like characters from a children's novel. There was one *job* where they made off with several hundred pounds worth of fur coats and jewellery as a gift for their mother. I remember this, because their story ended with much laughter. Apparently, what they had stolen was later valued by a fence at only a few pounds because it was cat fur, and the gems were paste.'

Every head in the court turned to the front of the public gallery where there was great consternation, and Violent Flay slapped the man beside her.

'Oh,' Will said, pointing. 'Hello, Mr Snout. I am sorry I didn't have time to empty the bucket.' To the judge, he said, 'He was rather kind, actually, and scraped the mould from the bread before he made me eat it.'

The judge's gavel fought against laughter, and eventually won.

'Sir Easterby,' he said, pinching the bridge of his nose. 'Your intent in dragging up a precedent much in need of amendment is as fascinating as always. However, I think you have made your point in regard to the character of the defendants and their associates. You have given Sergeant Culver food for thought, I am sure, but may we now give Mr Sparrow a chance, do you think?'

'I believe the jury has heard enough, M'lud,' Creswell said.

'Then you may stand down, Mr Merrit.'

'I am obliged, M'lud,' Will said, causing more laughter. Tapping his chest and pointing to the judge, he added, 'By the way, your jabot is crooked.'

Judge Brownhill fussed with his ruffle as Will left the court, and when order was restored, the trial continued.

It didn't take long to conclude. The defence put up a good fight against all three witnesses, but thanks to the work of James Wright and his agency, Creswell was able to pull apart every false alibi, and thanks to Jack's testimony, and Will's innocent character assassination, Hoxton Arty and his brother, Badger, stood no chance. It took the jury less than an hour to return a verdict of guilty, and the men were sent down for sentencing at a later date.

Larkin found the whole thing fascinating to the point he

considered becoming a court reporter, but only while he was waiting to hear the verdict. When it came, he could only think of Jack, potential reprisals from the crooks, and what the brothers would do next. Everything that had come about had happened because of Larkin, and all because he had fallen for the charms of a cabman. Whether his affections could be reciprocated after what he had caused was doubtful, and the Old Bailey was not the place to find out, except, he had to see Jack, if only to apologise for causing him so much trouble.

Mr Wright left the courtroom first, but Larkin was delayed by the crush, finally making it to the cooler air of the outer rooms a few minutes later. Jack should have stood out a few inches taller than the heads of most, but there were too many hats and bonnets to see clearly. With so many people milling towards the exits, he was unable to hurry ahead, and arrived in the afternoon sunlight with the last of the spectators.

There was no sign of Jack there, so he returned, hoping to find him at a briefing with the barrister or the detective, and was ready to offer his sincerest apologies, and invite him and Will to Kingsland Road. They could stay as long as they wished, or as long as they could stand Mrs Grose, and not only because of Larkin's sense of guilt, but also, because he wanted Jack to be nearby. The need to see him grew with every empty passage and room, until he reached the inevitable conclusion that Jack was not interested, could not forgive him, and had done as he had wanted to do; gone away, taken a train to Scotland or some other unlikely place, and turned his back on Larkin once and for all.

His lonely footsteps resounding in the empty corridors were as hollow as his heart as he made his way to the exit to find a cab, realising with bitterness cabs were now vehicles that would for ever remind him of losing Jack Merrit.

'Lost, Sir?'

The usher who had guarded Mr Clarington was coming the other way, and it took Larkin a moment to recognise him without his robes.

'Ah, hello again. I was looking for Mr Merrit.'

'The witness? Yes, Sir. He and the other left with Mr Wright some time ago. I'll walk you out.'

As Larkin was shown from the building, so he told himself Jack had shown himself out of his life. The memory would always be there along with the possibilities, but by leaving without a goodbye, Jack had made a statement, and despite what Will said about him having feelings, the last person on Jack's mind was Larkin Chase.

TWENTY-SIX

Two years previously, while Jack was learning the cabman's knowledge by night and working at the docks by day, he returned home to find Uncle Bob, Edith and Charlie gathered at Grandad Reggie's bedside. Ida was crying in the kitchen room, and Will was pacing the few steps from the sink to the window, and counting.

Something was wrong.

'What is it?' Jack said, throwing down his lunch pail.

'Saying goodbye.'

'The doctor just left,' Ida sniffed. 'You best go in.'

Reggie was dying, Uncle Bob said, and seeing Jack's consternation, held his shoulder and told him his grandfather had not got long.

'But you're nearly there, Jack,' Bob said. 'You'll get your licence in a week or so and can take over the cab. Believe me.'

'Believe in yourself,' Charlie said as he also prepared to leave. 'I'll miss our time on the bench, Jack, but if you ever want to ride out, just to be alone, you can call on me.'

It was a troubled moment. Jack's eyes were fixed on Reggie's white and withered face, but he thought of being alone with Charlie Flex.

'Just to talk,' Charlie said, and left him deflated.

Alone with his grandfather, Jack sat on the bed and took his limp hand.

'You going, Reggie?' he whispered.

Reggie's reply was a mumble and a gasp, but the head made a tiny nodding movement, and his face screwed up as he fought for words.

'You... Will...' His voice was faltering, but Jack listened with patience. 'Take care of my Ida... and your brother...' A sucking-in of saliva, a faint gasp. 'They'll need you.'

'I'll look after your Ida, Granddad, don't you worry.' Determined to be the man, Jack held back tears. 'I've nearly learnt the knowledge. Your old hansom will be back on the streets right soon, and with Shadow pulling.'

'Promise me, Jack... Will... he's... special.'

'I know. He's special to everyone.'

'Not stupid. Special.'

'Shush, Granddad. Rest.'

'No point resting, son. Remember...' His voice was fainter, and his eyes were losing their love of life. The cold touch of death transferred from his wasted hand to Jack's youthful skin as if he was passing on what remained of his life to give Jack a few more seconds at the other end of his. 'Be good, Jack... Be true... Love is rare.'

Ida and Will joined him, standing by the deathbed with their sadness wrapped in acceptance, and with Will mouthing the time passing since the doctor's final diagnosis, Reggie Merrit drew his last breath.

'Two hours, sixteen minutes, twenty-two seconds,' Will said, as Ida closed her husband's eyelids, and lay her head on his chest.

Jack stared at the scene, hollow, and frightened for what he now had to take on, but trepidation vanished when Will took him in his arms, and hugged him tighter than he'd ever done.

'We'll manage,' Will said. 'I got my brother, you got yours. I love you, Jack.'

Jack filled his lungs, and held tight.

'Love you too, mate.'

'He's with God now.' Ida stood, and straightened her apron as if they'd just finished a meal and the table had to be cleared. 'I'll call the neighbours in. Will, put water to boil for washing the body, and fetch the towels from the drawer. He picked out his cabbing suit and tie. Bob will tell the others at the rank, Jack, so you find the vicar. We'll bury him proper at Tower Hamlets. The men'll want to follow in their cabs, so be sure to tell the vicar, and say we only need a short service by the grave. It's in a decent spot and there's a place for me alongside.'

'Grandma...'

'No time to grieve, son. We've work to do.'

***

Jack could still hear her words as the trap left Bow Street and headed south towards the Strand.

'How are you feeling?' Mr Wright asked.

'Alright.'

Will was beside him, holding his hand, and at first, he couldn't recall how he came to be there. It came back to him in pieces of memory; from walking into the intimidating courtroom thinking, 'Things can't get any bloody worse,' returning to it later to answer questions from a man named after a bird, being shouted at, spoken down to and derided, to being protected by a buffoon in a black gown, until Mr Wright told him they had won the case.

Now, he was trundling through the afternoon sunshine in an open carriage as if on a Sunday jaunt. Will was free and safe, and Wright had promised rest and comfort. Jack needed both, and didn't mind admitting it, but all the same, he couldn't help but feel he'd left something behind.

An old life, Limehouse, the rank, his livelihood; he'd left many things, but all of them could be salvaged. Reggie and Ida's grave would always be there in Tower Hamlets, he could visit any time. There were other yards where he could rent a hansom, and he'd collect Shadow as soon as he could afford a stable. He must be as his grandma had been after her Reggie died, practical, just as everyone was in Limehouse. One thing was done, now he must move onto the next, organise, think logically and simply get on with life. Whatever that life was to be.

Yet, there was still the nagging feeling that he'd left something.

Twisting in his seat to look back, all he saw was traffic and pedestrians, a few carts on their way to Covent Garden, and, when the driver pulled into the Strand, the front of the Lyceum.

The theatre reminded him of his father, although he'd never progressed further than the music hall, and the cabs and carts reminded him of Reggie. All gone, as was whatever he'd forgotten, and he patted his pockets, just in case. There was nothing in them apart from the change from two sovereigns.

As Ida would have said, there was no time to grieve, there was work to do. The question was how?

Distracted by the behaviour of cabmen going about their business, it was only after Will poked him in the side did Jack realise Mr Wright was talking to him.

'Will has been asking what happens to the criminals next,' he said. 'Thought you might like to know.'

Jack shrugged. If he'd left anything behind it was the bloody Flays, and good riddance to them.

'Creswell thinks they will get the maximum. Culver says he will take a statement from Will about the other matters, and if he can, he'll make arrests. He's reasonably confident.'

'Mr Wright, I assume I will have to appear in court,' Will said 'I don't mind one bit, if it's the right thing to do, and I found the process fascinating, but I would like to ask...'

Will chatted on as they passed the Savoy, Charing Cross and Trafalgar Square with Jack looking vacantly at the traffic until they came to the Mall. It was while watching St James' Park trundle by that he realised what he'd left at Bow Street.

It lay among disjointed memories; a clerk in a warehouse, Charlie Flex putting an arm around his shoulder, and the double-dip of the drain. With them, his grandad's last words, 'Love is rare,' caused him to recall someone else's first words, 'I hope I find you available and willing.'

It wasn't what he'd left at the courthouse, but who.

'Mr Chase?'

Jack paid attention.

'Yes. I am sure he wouldn't mind,' Mr Wright said. 'I can send him a message, thank him for his assistance, and ask him to send them on.'

'Did you hear that, Jack?' Will was happy about something. 'I'm for it, as long as Mr Wright means what he says.'

'I do.'

'Ah. I see Jack wasn't listening, and I am not surprised.'

'It's a lot to take in,' Wright said. 'Let's get home, get you two cleaned up and settled, and we'll talk about it over dinner. You can meet the others, and see what you think.'

'You said Mr Chase?'

'Yes, Jack. It seems a terrible imposition, but he is such a kind man, I am sure he wouldn't object.'

'To what?'

'Sending over the clothes he bought us.'

'Oh.'

Jack had had enough and rested his head on the back of the seat with his eyes closed, letting the sun warm his face, and the carriage vibrate his exhaustion until he was numb.

The Mall, smooth under the wheels until the tarmacadam of Constitution Hill, the clatter and commotion of Hyde Park Corner, the gentle slope of Knightsbridge, and the quietening of traffic, leading to the turning into Buck's Avenue. From east to west, from one world to another, and from there... To where?

For now, Jack didn't care.

The rest of the afternoon passed by as though he was an onlooker in someone else's life. He was a neighbour who stood unmoving in the midst of the commotion as a fire raged, and men brought buckets and threw water. As bells rang, and people scurried around him. An island in a river of traffic that always threatened to swamp him, but always missed. Once again, his life was not his to control, but this time, it was Will who was taking the lead, making the decisions, ensuring Jack knew what to do, where to change, how to use the bathroom contraptions that delivered the unusual feel of hot water, and when to be where.

Jack wasn't ungrateful for Mr Wright's hospitality, he was simply unable to take it in, and did as his brother told him, hardly speaking, because all the time the words spun around him, he was thinking. His thoughts meandered through a street map looking for a way out of a maze, but he always arrived at the same dead end. The road ahead was blocked by one thing; money. He had none, and that meant no place to stable Shadow when his payment at Grimes ran out, nowhere for him and Will to live, no cash to hire a cab even if he could find a yard, and no way to even go looking for one except on foot.

It wasn't until the sun was setting that the world finally began to slow, and he was able to put his feet on it for the first time since Will had disappeared. As if waking from a long, clinging sleep, he found himself standing at a window overlooking a tended garden, beyond which stood a line of plane trees. The lower casement was open, and a warm breeze rose to bring him the scent of flowers and recently cut grass. From beyond the treeline came the sound of children's laughter, and the casual clomp of horses' hooves, while now and then he caught sight of private carriages through the branches, and heard the soft coo of pigeons. All sights and sounds Limehouse could never offer.

No time to grieve, son. We've work to do.

With a deep breath, he turned to face the room.

Someone was reading by the second window, the evening sunlight pink on his face, and sensing movement, the person looked up, closed the book, and put it to one side. The hair was combed and perfectly trimmed, the clothes looked expensive, and a good fit. His legs were crossed in the manner of a man contented with life and happy to let the days pass as he enjoyed the spoils of good fortune, but above all, he was happy.

'Mr Wright's borrowed clothes fit you very well,' Will said, and came to be with his brother at the window. 'Have you decided to join us?'

'Eh?'

They stood side by side looking at the view, and Will laid his head on Jack's shoulder.

'You have not been with us since leaving Bow Street,' he said.

'I have.'

'Yes, in body, but in nothing else, and I know why.'

'Yeah?'

'The clues, as Mr Wright would say, are all there. I have been thinking about them. Do you want to know my deduction?'

'What time is it?'

'Nearly time for dinner. Don't worry, I was listening to instructions and know what we are to do. But my deduction?'

'What's that?'

'What I have deduced.'

'Speak plain, Will.'

'Very well. It's Larkin Chase.'

'Eh?' The name brought the view into sharper focus. 'Why do you say that?'

'Truth, brother. You don't know what to do about him. Having tasted what he has to offer... Oh, that sounds very rude. Let me try again. Having explored what you have longed to explore since you were eighteen... No, still not right.'

Will gave a sigh of frustration, and having scraped a blemish from the windowpane with a fingernail, started again.

'Starting out from Curiosity Street, and having encountered several no-through roads, you finally found your way to a destination. Let's call it Experience Road. However, now you have gained the cabman's knowledge, you find yourself embarking on another journey, but in this case, the terminus is unknown. The problem is, you are both the driver and the fare, but neither of you know where you are heading. This afternoon, you hardly noticed the scenery, the way Mr Pascoe applied ice to your bruises, and bandaged your arm before bringing us to this room. I watched as you changed as if you were one of Pollock's mechanical puppets, and someone else was pulling your strings.'

'What you talking about?'

'I am talking about you and how you are currently lost on a map of unfamiliar streets. I would say you are at a junction. One way leads to Mr Chase and all he has offered, and the other, to Mr Wright, and everything we talked about in the carriage.'

'Talked about?'

'Yes, I know. You weren't there either, but it will become clear later. Mr Wright understands you have had some difficult days.'

That was an understatement.

'Therefore, I can only offer this, and it is to repeat, whatever you decide to do, I will be with you. Whether that is for you to return to Mr Chase, accept his kindness, housing and companionship, or to take Mr Wright's offer, or to wander blithely to the wilds of Essex with a horse in the hope of finding labouring work, Will Merrit will stand by his brother.' Will chuckled, but Jack could find nothing to laugh about. 'I was just remembering how Grandma Ida used to say, *When others won't, Will will*. Do you remember?'

Jack didn't reply. His brother's loyalty was too overwhelming.

'Anyway, we must go downstairs. Just to say, Jack, if you want to return to Mr Chase in the hope of finding love, then I...'

'Love?'

'Or, if you want to go looking for lodgings, a dock to labour in, a farm or a cab yard, then that's what we shall do. First, though, I think you should listen to what Mr Wright has to say. Also, you must rebutton your shirt, because you have missed one, and it is very worrying.'

Jack put his arm around Will's shoulder, and his hand on his head.

'Do not ruffle my hair, please. It is one of your more annoying habits.'

'Wasn't going to,' Jack said. 'Was going to do this.' Kissing the top of Will's head, he said, 'You, Sir, would make a good detective.'

'Ah,' Will said. 'On which note, let us go to dinner.'

Jack had existed in the house and its room, but hadn't noticed any of it until then. With his mind clearer, he followed his brother from an elegant bedroom he could never have imagined into a corridor he could never have dreamt up. His feet sank into carpet as he walked at a distance from tables on which stood valuable-looking ornaments, not wanting to get too close in case he broke something. The walls held paintings of rich people in jewels, and not the paste of Violet Flay. The staircase was wide, and met another one when it turned, leading them to a vast hallway with a marble floor like the hammam, coloured glass in the windows, a stand for umbrellas on which was hanging Mr Wright's newsboy cap. There were more tables to the side, and even a fireplace. His self-consciousness increased as his shoes squealed on the stone, and the noise did nothing for his awkwardness as he moved from his afternoon state of dreaming and indecision into one of bewilderment and uncertainty. The house was grander than Larkin's, but colder, and even more estranged from Limehouse life.

Will knew where he was going, and Jack wondered how, but before he could fathom the answer, they passed through a door onto another staircase. This one was narrower, had nothing on the walls but whitewash, and took them down to a basement.

'Where we going?'

'To dinner,' Will replied. 'It's informal.'

A corridor that smelt of polish took them past a door Jack recognised.

'That's the butler's room,' he said, hearing himself speak as someone else. Jack Merrit didn't use words like butler.

'It is. I had the tour while you were in the bath. Here, we are.'

They'd arrived at the room with a long table. It was set with matching crockery, unknown in Jack's tenement, and around it hung the smell of cooking that set his stomach rumbling.

'Six places?'

'Yes, six, Mr Merrit.' Mr Pascoe appeared through a cloud of steam carrying a large dish. 'Sit where you like, we're not fussy.'

Before Jack could ask any of the many questions lining up like the cabs at the station rank, two other men appeared behind the butler, also carrying dishes, and by the time they were set, Mr Wright had arrived, and ushered Will into a seat.

'Sit, Jack,' the detective said. 'Good to see you looking more with us. How's the injuries?'

'Yeah, alright, thanks...'

A tall man with a small mouth and a centre parting thrust a hand. 'Alright, mate?' he beamed, and Jack recognised an East End accent. 'Dalston Blaze. This is me man, Joe.'

A second man of equally young age but with a more serious face, glided to the table, placed his dish, and took no notice.

Assuming he was a servant, Jack was surprised when he sat, and even more surprised when Mr Blaze, tapped him on the shoulder and pointed. The servant jumped to his feet, and offered Jack a wide grin.

'E-oh,' he said, also offering a hand, which Jack took by instinct.

The situation became even stranger when the man threw his hands around, pointing and making signals, which, to Jack's amazement, made Mr Blaze laugh. When Blaze returned the gestures, the servant bit his bottom lip, nodded, and laid a hand on Jack's shoulder.

'Orry,' he said, and resumed his seat.

Will and Mr Wright were already chatting, and the detective was doling out soup. Pascoe was circling the table pouring wine, and it took Jack a moment to realise he was still standing.

'You should grab it before Joe does,' Blaze said, kicking out a chair. 'Sit here, mate. Tuck in. We're impressed with your battle scars, but sorry to hear you've had problems. Sit, will you?'

In danger of returning to his earlier state of utter confusion, Jack did as he was told, and after a few prompts from the others, served himself and began to eat.

The meal began quietly, as if each man needed sustenance before conversation, but when Mr Pascoe and Mr Blaze took away the empty soup bowls, and chops and vegetables arrived, so did a discussion.

Having told the others about the courtroom and outcome, Mr Wright mopped his gravy with bread, and, addressing Jack, said, 'Do you remember what I said to you last night?'

Everyone was watching, Will with more interest than the others.

'Last night was a long time ago,' Jack said.

'I was leaving your room, and said you were more than a guest, you were a... Then I thought better of it because it was the wrong time.'

'Yeah, I remember. I think.'

'Well, the time is now right to explain. I was going to say, you were more than a guest, you were a possibility, and that's something I want to talk about.'

Jack's head was aching, and the detective wasn't helping. Befuddled, all he could say was, 'Eh?'

'I mentioned that my agency hasn't been doing so well of late,' the detective said. 'The same could be said of my private life, but that's another matter. Until recently, we had a researcher working with us, a cheery Scottish chap who had a way of discovering information from the records offices and other sources. He has now left to take up a job at Somerset House, and we all wish him well. Also, since last

December, my business partner has been more sleeping than active due to his other work, and that has left me...'

'Sorry, hold on,' Jack interrupted. 'To be honest, Mr Wright, I ain't really up to following all this.'

'Mr Wright is short of staff,' Will said.

'Exactly. Silas, my business partner, has other work with Lord Clearwater in Cornwall and, sometimes, in London, and now I have Maxwell, who has equal abilities, Silas is happier to be a sleeping partner and take a back row seat. Of course, we still have others to call on when we need to. Joe drives, but he's often away digging and studying, and Dalston has his own business in the breakfast room, but he's handy in a fight. And...'

'No, got to stop you.' Jack fell back in his chair and clutched his head. 'I don't know who any of you are, what your breakfast room in Dalston has to do with anything, and I've never heard of Lord Clearwater.'

'I'm sorry. I am just excited by my proposition,' Mr Wright said.

'Yeah, well, if you told me what it was...'

'Gosh, you can be dim sometimes, Jack,' Will tutted across the table. 'Will you give us the details, Mr Wright?'

'Jimmy.'

'No. Mr Wright. It is only proper if you are to offer us employment.'

'Hold on, what?'

'And that is one of the reasons I can't let you go,' Mr Wright said, pointing at Will with admiration. 'You are different.'

'I am not different, Sir. I am exact.'

'Whatever you are, you have the ability to... well, it's almost premonitions. You observe, listen and remember. You can cope with being held prisoner, and then stand up in court and give Creswell as good as he gives. You are special, Will, and I have no idea how you do it.'

'I was brought up in Limehouse, Mr Wright. You have to be special to survive.'

'Fair enough. You, Jack...'

'I ain't special.'

'Of course you are. Determination, bravery, honesty. You can clearly look after yourself.'

'Ha. I nearly got meself stabbed.'

'But you were willing to take a risk.'

'For Will.'

'And he drives. Mr Wright, if your man here is away digging, I assume you are thinking...'

'I am, Will.'

'Thinking what?'

'That you must come and work for me,' Mr Wright enthused. 'We have the room. Dalston and Joe share one suite, and I have another, but that still leaves two. Max has the downstairs, and there are rooms on the top floor if you'd rather...'

'No, no, no... Stop.' Jack's head was a rage, and the pain compounded his frustration. It didn't help that Blaze and his man were flapping their hands at each other. 'I'm a cabbie, Mr Wright. I know the London streets, how to grease an axle, and how to look after me horse. That's it. That's what I do.'

'How about eighty pounds a year?'

'I beg your pardon?'

'Eighty, and of course, there's no rent, and the agency pays most of the bills, though we chip in for food and take it in turns to cook. Nice chops, by the way, Dalston.'

'Ta.'

Jack wanted it all to stop, and to be on his bench with Shadow at the end of the ribbons, the wheels rolling, and nothing to think about except the traffic ahead and the passengers below. As Mr Wright blabbered on about what Will might do, how Jack could manage the stables while helping with cases, and how they would fit in well, all he could think about was life returning to normal. The jars on the mantlepiece, the shared room, cold water in the bowl, Will's books, and the one china cup used only for the most important visitors.

All gone because he told a stranger his story and did what he thought was right.

A stranger? A man who stirred in him feelings and desires he never though he would be able to release, and one who offered everything he'd wanted.

Which was?

A home, an income, and for Will to be happy.

Exactly what Mr Wright was offering.

'Of course, you'll want time to think about all of this, and for us to discuss the finer details,' the detective was saying. 'We can start by Joe showing you the stable.'

'Why?'

'So you can drive when you're not solving clues. What was it? James Hemsworth, the Aldgate pump and hums? I'd never have got that without your knowledge. Then there's Will, and his unique ability to observe and remember.'

'Ability?' Will scoffed. 'Sometimes it is a burden.'

The conversation raced on with Will enthusing, Mr Wright praising, and Blaze and his friend throwing fingers around. His friend? They shared a suite.

Mr Wright's words came back to him. *Men of a similar heart*, of the same inclination. Not only was he being offered a job and a home, but also safety among men who accepted each other as Larkin had accepted him.

Larkin bloody Chase.

'Is there room for Shadow?'

The words were out of Jack's mouth before he knew he was saying them.

'Shadow?'

'Jack's horse,' Will explained, as unbothered by the interruption as everyone else. 'He bought her back from the knacker's yard.'

'Yes, plenty of room,' Mr Wright said. 'Take a look after dinner.'

Will regarded Jack with a mixture of hope and understanding. 'So, brother. Are we staying?'

They were for the time being, for Will if nothing else. What other choice did Jack have?

'If you want. For now,' he said. 'I'll pay you back, Mr Wright.'

'It's Jimmy, and you won't. Nor will you regret it.'

Before Jack knew it, Joe was shaking his hand across the table.

Sitting, he proceeded to gesticulate and point while mumbling half words.

'Not now, Joe. Let the man take it in,' Blaze said, as a bell rattled somewhere, and Pascoe left the table. To Jack, he said, 'Joe can read your lips, so talk normal.'

'Then that's that,' Mr Wright said. 'I expect it will take you both a while to find your way around, but treat the house as your own. We do our own housekeeping under Max's watchful eye, but agency maids come and go as well. You'll get used to life at Delamere, Jack, and when you do, I reckon you're going to be a great asset to the team.'

'The team?' The only team Jack had known was a team of horses.

'The Clearwater Detective Agency,' Mr Wright clarified. 'Eat up. There's strawberry cake for afters.'

Pascoe returned under the weight of several bundles wrapped in brown paper.

'Delivery,' he said, dumping some on a chair, before offering a package and an envelope. 'For Mr Merrit.'

'Which one?'

'Both. From Mr Chase. Looks like your clothes.'

Not Jack's clothes, Larkin's, and returned as his way of saying farewell.

A devastating wave of sadness washed over him, accompanied by fear that he had lost something dear and would never find such friendship again. Larkin had walked into his life, turned it on its head, and was now walking out? It wasn't right, but Jack was helpless to do anything about it.

'It's my notebook,' Will said, unwrapping one of the parcels. 'How kind of him. You have a letter, Jack.'

Jack took it, and while the dinner conversation continued without him, opened it to read.

Dear Jack,

I missed you after the hearing, when I wanted to offer you and your brother respite at my home. You are welcome here always and for any length of time. I fear our chance meeting has led to a great deal of upheaval, and if I have played an incorrect part in that, I apologise. Whatever I need to do to put things right for you, you only have to say. I will be here.

The room opposite mine is terribly empty tonight, but it is at your disposal should you ever feel able to return. If not, I wish you every happiness in whatever you decide to do next.

I remain, I hope, your friend,
Larkin Chase.

Ps. The Grimes Livery Stable report that Shadow is in good health, and is being well cared for. I hope you are too. LC.

Happiness in whatever he decided to do next. Could he find fulfilment doing what Wright had in store for him instead of driving strangers across the city? Could he find happiness without the annoying, attractive, talkative, caring and longed-for Larkin Chase?

Jack had the cabman's knowledge of the London streets, and could travel from east to west with his eyes closed, but although he now had the opportunity to journey towards love, he didn't know the route.

Love?

There, he'd admitted it. The love of another man was waiting for him, it was available, and he was ready to give his own in return. All he had to do was find the way.

TWENTY-SEVEN

One lit cigar, one person seated, one glass of gin. The slow, deliberate knock of a gold ring against a scored wooden table was out of rhythm with the anniversary clock, and louder than the men's breathing. Anticipation hung beneath the ceiling with the fug of tobacco. The cloud was undisturbed by movement, as the remaining sons watched the mother, and the in-laws watched the sons, not daring to speak, but willing to take instruction, no matter how drastic. To be protected by Violet Flay was to be guaranteed safety for as long as a man remained in favour, and at that moment, no-one was in Mother Flay's favour.

Her tapping ceased, and her hands dropped beneath the table as her powdered face turned to an injured son-in-law.

'You did your best, Chancer,' she said, and the hairy top lip quivered in what passed for a sympathetic gesture. 'Come here, son. I want to give you something.'

Heads turned to Chancer, and someone drew a sharp breath.

'Ah, no, you're alright, Mother. No need for that.' Chancer gave a nervous laugh.

'Come here,' Mrs Flay repeated, and pulled the ring from her finger. 'A present for trying.'

'Honestly, Mother...'

'Ha! Nothing honest about you,' the old woman cackled, and still laughing, tapped the table beside her. 'Here, son. It's a gift.'

Chancer shuffled forward cradling a broken arm, as Mrs Flay examined the ring against the quivering gaslight.

'Finest karat,' she said. 'Belgravia, weren't it, Dodge?'

'That is was, Mother. A fine job, that one.'

Chancer stood beside her, his face pale in the yellow light, and paling further when she took his hand.

'This'll fit you nice,' she said, taking him by the wrist and placing his palm on the tabletop. 'Something for you to keep. You're not to hock it, mind,' she added as a humorous warning. 'One of these bastards might nick it.'

Amid the laughter, she slipped the ring onto his index finger, and although Chancer winced at the painful tug in his arm, he sighed with relief at being forgiven.

'Yes. Suits you real nice,' she said, nodding thoughtfully. 'So does this.'

Her grip tightened, and before Chancer could pull away, she'd whipped a meat cleaver from beneath the table, and brought it down with a sickening thump of metal on wood. Three fingertips shot away amid spurting blood. Chancer screamed and fell to his knees.

'Ah, scream as much as you want, you useless kinchin,' the old woman scorned. 'Dodge? Get him out me sight.'

Dodge dragged the screaming man away and threw him into the passage while the table dripped in silence, and returning, he handed his mother the ring.

'Same for the lot of you,' Violet Flay spat. 'I didn't bring you up to be a herd a hopeless scraps. Crank? You're me third. What d'you say?'

'Torch them.'

'Won't get Arty freed.'

'Go after the judge so he don't sentence.'

'Nah, not that one. Tried before, and the Flays don't fail twice.'

'That's right, Mother,' the second youngest said. 'We could top the beak.'

'Too obvious. Anyhow, they'd only get another in to do it.'

'Maybe we have to face it.' Dodge, dabbed blood from his trousers, and when no-one said anything, looked up. 'Face it, Ma. Art and Badge are going down, and we know who's to blame.'

'Fucking Chancer, is who.'

'But he's not alone.'

Violet Flay stopped fiddling with her jewellery, and tipped her head, as a signal her son could speak.

'There's someone working with the Dalston nick. He's not on our side, and we still don't know who. Someone in this room, most likely, or close by.'

'Scum.'

'Right, Ma, scum, and clever scum at that to grass under our noses. Leave it with me, while you think about the other thing.'

'What, that smug bastard what put Chancer down? The driver? His idiot brother? What's to think about?' Turning to the husband of one of her girls, she said, 'We know where they are. Want to do another torch?'

'Say the word, Mother.'

'No,' Dodge countered. 'They've got taken in by Wright, and what good would it do to torch his place? He'd move somewhere else and carry on, 'cos he's got some rich toff behind him. Besides, Wright ain't the full picture, not now.'

'And it'd also be too obvious,' her youngest son said.

Etch rarely spoke, but when he did, he made sense, and Mrs Flay was inclined to listen to him more than the others.

'Go on, son. You're the only one in this pit a shit what's got sense.'

Etch slid out a chair, and to prove he was different to the rest of the family, sat. Although his brothers looked to their mother for her reaction, she gave none, except another tip of her head.

'Time,' Etch said. 'Take your time, Mother. Let it settle. Arty and Badge are going away. End of. Nothing needs to change for now. Keep your revenge 'til they ain't expecting it.' He picked up Chancer's thumb and studied it as an example. 'Hit where it hurts, when it hurts hardest. When they think they're safe. When they've forgotten.' With the thumb back on the table, he held his mother's thoughtful gaze. 'Time, Ma. Like Arty and Badge'll be doing. Bide your time.'

Blood splattered as he flicked the thumb to her, and she trapped it with one slap of her flabby, jewelled hand.

'After what the idiot boy said in court, we can expect a visit from the rozz.' She spat on the floor. 'No telling what that'll bring, so we need to be ready. While you good for nothings is doing that, we'll do as Etch says. Watch them, bide our time, and think, ready for later. Dodge?'

'Yes, Ma?'

'We'll need Chancer, so get him stitched, and while you're out, buy him some fingerless gloves.'

A smile cracked her rough-rouged mouth, and the bubbling in her throat became laughter. It shattered the gloom, rebounded from the peeling wallpaper, and settled somewhere near the desolate fireplace.

'Time,' she said, wiping drool from her lip. 'Like us, Arty and Badge have plenty of it, so we'll wait and watch, but make no mistake, boys. We'll bring 'em down, them as what's hurt us. Leave it with me for now, but one day, I'll find a way.'

Continued in Book Two.
'A Fall from Grace.'

AUTHOR NOTES

As with my previous series, The Larkspur Mysteries, I have fallen into the habit of providing some notes and explanations at the end of my mysteries. In the case of 'Finding a Way', there are few.

The idea for the story came from a piece published in 1883 by James Greenwood. Greenwood was what we would now call an investigative journalist, and 'The Night Cabman' was published as part of his book, 'Odd People in Odd Places.' The article begins: *The spectacle of a cabman in tears is so uncommon that, under ordinary conditions, it would attract one's attention but, in the case that came under my observation, the circumstances were so peculiar, that to have passed him without a word of inquiry as to the cause of his tribulation, would have been little short of inhuman.*

Talking to the cabman as he is driven home, Greenwood learnt various tales of woe, which I amalgamated to make my story. The location of the robbery was actually Fulham, but the use and finding of the handbill, the twenty-pound reward, the cabman finding the pub and the auction, are all in the original cabbie's tale. The rest I have invented.

Larkin Chase bears no resemblance to James Greenwood (as far as

AUTHOR NOTES

I know), but Greenwood's brother was editor of the Pall Mall Gazette, as is Larkin's brother. There, the similarities end.

I also used James Greenwood's research for a scene in the Clearwater Mysteries' prequel, 'Banyak & Fecks' where Silas spends a night in the casual ward of a workhouse. If you want to read the originals, then victorianlondon.org is a good place to start your research. It is from there, Greenwood and many others, that I take my inspiration for the sights, sounds and smells of Victorian London, and in this case, of Limehouse in particular.

It's also from that site, books, and a dictionary of street cant (slang) that I take words used by some of the characters. In this story, you may have thought 'poney' was a spelling mistake, and was meant to read 'money', but it's street slang from the eighteenth century in use in East London in the nineteenth. Ditto, 'lobcock', shortened to lob (or cock). 'Lob' is also cant for a till, and to 'frisk a lob' was to steal from a tradesman's till. 'Going on the lob' was to enter a shop for change, and a prison was also a 'lob.' The definition for lobcock, according to Dictionary of the Vulgar Tongue (Francis Grose, 1811) is: *A large, relaxed penis: also a dull inanimate fellow.*

The new Delamere Files series exists in the Clearwater world, and thus, if you have read my previous two series (Clearwater and Larkspur), and if you can remember back to the end of book one, 'Deviant Desire', you may recognise references to previous events.

Chapter 17 of 'Finding a Way', for example:

There had been a warehouse fire back in eighty-eight, and although it had been along the river towards Lower Pool, he'd stood with Will and Ida to watch from Mrs Dobson's upstairs window. Later, when Reggie came back from cabbing, they all went down to the waterside to watch the spectacle, and Reggie said someone had seen two men fall from the warehouse crane, and another two had climbed down the hoist chain to escape. It had been dramatic, and the news replaced the headlines of the East End Ripper for a day or two. As far as Jack knew, the cause had never been discovered, and the men never identified.

If you have read 'Deviant Desire', you'll know who they were. You will also recognise characters from the past, including James Wright,

AUTHOR NOTES

Dalston and Joe, and Sir Easterby Creswell. I expect more will make appearances throughout the series.

I ought to explain that the law business in chapter twenty-five is made up. Very little is known about Shakespeare's life, and there is nothing to suggest he gave evidence at a court case in 1606, from which he took the names Lennox and Seyton to use in his 'Macbeth,' allegedly first performed in that year. Had it happened, however, it would be just the kind of obscure get-out Creswell would pull out of his wig.

Finally, the routes, street names and costs of fares. It's virtually impossible to find out exactly how much cab fares would have cost in June 1892, not without happily falling on the information at random. One of the reasons for this is because the cost of hansom hire charges increased and decreased through the year, there were various regulations about costs and charges too, and the closest I could come was by reading 'The History of the London Cab' (Trevor May, 1995), where vehicle hire and fares are discussed, but from a few years earlier.

The routes, however, and the street names, come from a set of maps published in 1888, and although some London streets might have changed between then and 1892 thanks to slum clearances and other works, a London Street atlas from 1888 is more accurate for the period than today's Google maps and the A to Z. Having said that, although Ivy Street and Ivy Lane did exist between James Street and Hemsworth Street in Hoxton, there is no Turkish bath marked on the map. What was there, was a ragged school.

You can find all of my books on my [Amazon Author page](#).

Please leave a review if you can. Thanks again for reading. If you keep reading, I'll keep writing.

Jackson

Printed in Great Britain
by Amazon